Religion in Science Fiction

Scientific Studies of Religion: Inquiry and Explanation

Series Editors: Luther H. Martin, William W. McCorkle, and Donald Wiebe

Scientific Studies of Religion: Inquiry and Explanation publishes cutting-edge research in the new and growing field of scientific studies in religion. Its aim is to publish empirical, experimental, historical, and ethnographic research on religious thought, behavior, and institutional structures.

The series works with a broad notion of "scientific" that includes innovative work on understanding religion(s), both past and present. With an emphasis on the cognitive science of religion, the series includes complementary approaches to the study of religion, such as psychology and computer modeling of religious data. Titles seek to provide explanatory accounts for the religious behaviors under review, both past and present.

Religion in Science Fiction

The Evolution of an Idea and the Extinction of a Genre

Steven Hrotic

Bloomsbury Academic
An imprint of Bloomsbury Publishing Plc

B L O O M S B U R Y

LONDON · OXFORD · NEW YORK · NEW DELHI · SYDNEY

Bloomsbury Academic
An imprint of Bloomsbury Publishing Plc

50 Bedford Square	1385 Broadway
London	New York
WC1B 3DP	NY 10018
UK	USA

www.bloomsbury.com

BLOOMSBURY and the Diana logo are trademarks of Bloomsbury Publishing Plc

First published 2014
Paperback edition first published 2016

British Library Cataloguing-in-Publication Data
A catalogue record for this book is available from the British Library.

ISBN: HB: 978-1-47253-355-5
PB: 978-1-47427-317-6
ePDF: 978-1-47252-745-5
ePub: 978-1-47253-427-9

Library of Congress Cataloging-in-Publication Data
Hrotic, Steven.
Religion in science fiction : the evolution of an idea & the extinction of
a genre / Steven Hrotic.
pages cm
Includes bibliographical references and index.
ISBN 978-1-4725-3355-5 (hardback)
1. Science fiction, American–History and criticism. 2. Religion in literature.
3. Religion and literature. I. Title.
PS374.S35H84 2014
813'.0876209–dc23
2014003678

Series: Scientific Studies of Religion: Inquiry and Explanation

Typeset by Newgen Knowledge Works (P) Ltd., Chennai, India

To Paula Jean West-Eddy, David and John Wilcox, and
the New Brighton Public Library, for your liberal lending policies;

To Huck Gutman, advisor on an early stage of this project,
and everyone else who doesn't read stories set in space;

To Luther Martin, for making many things possible,
and to Christine Hrotic, for making all things worthwhile;

This book is gratefully dedicated.

Contents

Introduction

There are two kinds of people in the world—
sf fans and those who think everything's fine the way it is.

The Author

In 1958, James Blish published *A Case of Conscience*. A Hispanic, Jesuit priest and biologist with a talent for languages is a member of a small "mission" to make contact with the first sentient aliens humans have discovered. The people they discover are pleasant; some even feel like friends to the priest, despite being shaped like overly tall kangaroos. In fact, they seem ideal, almost as a Christian might imagine humans would have been like had we never left the Garden. But what the priest later discovers radically changes his interpretation: rather than confirming his belief in God, this previously idyllic planet creates a deep crisis of faith. The majority of the novel is concerned with how the protagonist comes to terms with this crisis, supported in part by a woman who reminds him of the relationships he gave up in order to become a priest.

In 1996, Mary Doria Russell published *The Sparrow*. In it, a Hispanic, Jesuit linguist is a member of a small mission to investigate the first sentient aliens we have discovered—aliens who seem perfect, but later create a deep crisis of faith in the protagonist, which he faces with the support of a woman. There are slight differences—Blish's kangaroo-shaped aliens are reptilian, while Russell's are mammals; Blish's "Liu" feels to the priest almost like a daughter, Russell's "Anne" feels almost like a wife—but in every important way, *The Sparrow* virtually recapitulates the conflicts of *A Case of Conscience*.

The juxtaposition of these two books evokes a number of curious implications. First, Russell and Blish are by no means the only science fiction authors who have incorporated strong elements of religion in their works. In fact, there is a long tradition of addressing these topics. The existence of this tradition may be a little surprising—after all, why would a body of fiction dedicated to exploring technological and scientific possibilities keep coming back to religion?—but there is a clear tendency for science fiction to ask questions like, what will religion be like in the future? Would aliens believe in gods, and if so, would their gods look and act like ours? If we could travel back in time to investigate the historical realities of Buddha and Jesus, how would Buddhism and Christianity be affected?

Second, parallels between *A Case of Conscience* and *The Sparrow* are neither accidental nor plagiarism. Russell has maintained that she had not read Blish's novel when she wrote her own, and I believe her.[1] On one hand, the nature of the SF narrative is such that it constrains some of the possibilities: for example, if we are imagining a future where space travel via space ships is possible but still difficult, it is easier to accept a small group making the journey, so this similarity between *Case* and *The Sparrow* isn't surprising. On the other hand, SF itself has a number of tropes that transcend a particular text. A protagonist who is also a priest will tend to be a Jesuit. Why? Perhaps it is because such a protagonist is most effective if s/he is: (1) from a Western tradition familiar to the readers (i.e., Christian); (2) from a traditional, strongly doctrinal religion to highlight the contrast between religion and modern secularism (i.e., Catholic); but (3) from a sect believed to be drawn to scientific problems and with an established history of exploration (i.e., Jesuit). In short, Russell (and, for that matter, Blish) were not writing in isolation, but participating in a collective effort—members of a group of authors, readers, publishers, editors, etc., all sharing and building ideas.

Third, if the crises of faith experienced by Blish and Russell's heroes have strong similarities, the *resolutions* of these crises in 1958 and 1996 are strikingly different. This difference reflects more than simply two authors finding different solutions to similar problems, but rather reflect a number of intermediary steps science fiction's conceptions of what religion "is," and what it should and could be.

I argue that these representations literally evolved over time, and the sequence of representations can be approached as a *metanarrative*. Science fiction authors use and adapt existing tropes taken from earlier texts; some new variations are then selected and used by later authors. In writing their own stories each author participates in a collective, creative act—not just creating their own narrative, but contributing to a metanarrative over decades. A single science fiction story may be read, understood, and enjoyed in isolation, but their place in this sequence adds another level of understanding, another way to understand the significance of a particular story.

By extracting science fiction's metanarrative of religion, I can show how religion has been understood within the genre, and how understanding has changed over the past century. One could of course focus on any number of metanarratives: how do science fiction's attitudes toward gender evolve; how does the relative importance of each scientific discipline change; how does the intimacy of individuals' relationships with technology develop, etc. But in focusing on religion, I believe I am focusing on perhaps the central metanarrative of science fiction. The recurrence of religion in science fiction reflects the pervasive Western belief that religion and science are inevitably in conflict; that they represent opposite poles in a epistemological spectrum. If so, then in a body of literature strongly identified with science the tension between science and religion would be the most important tension in need of resolution. Science fiction's metanarrative for religion is its—and, in a sense, all of our—attempt to reconcile two different ways of understanding the world. As this tension plays out, we discover that perhaps religion and science are not as inevitably opposed as we once supposed.

To do this, I have identified the most relevant and most influential science fiction stories and books from the twentieth century that clearly represent "religion." As a necessary first step, Part One outlines the basic methodological choices made for this project—the rules I will follow—and the ancestors of the modern science fiction genre. The most important choices are to operationally define both religion and science fiction. Some may be surprised at how problematic these choices can be. Imagine a volume of stories, imagining the use of computers and other technologies to remove the consciousness of individuals from the body, perhaps giving them practical immortality in a database. Would this describe "religion"? It does, after all, describe an afterlife—a commonsense definition of religion for many people. What if the technique was not electronic but medical, and immortality was achieved in the body? Would that be "science fiction," or is medicine the wrong science? (Incidentally, one needn't *imagine* this volume: see Dann and Dozois's *Beyond Flesh* [2002].)

Having defined our terms, Parts Two and Three take us through these texts in chronological order, analyzing each for what they have to say about religion and comparing each representation to its contemporaries and predecessors. Taken together, they show a sequence of steps in the evolution of science fiction's understanding of religion from the "Gernsback" period of 1926 to 1937 (Chapter 4), through the 1990s (Chapter 10)—a "story" about religion told by many authors, with the full cooperation of a community of readers, over generations. It is my hope that anyone with at least a casual interest in either science fiction or religion will find a few titles worth exploring further; when possible, I'll try not to ruin the endings.

Part Four puts this "metanarrative" in broader contexts. Chapter 11 asks if the metanarrative for religion has concluded, and if so, has the science fiction genre similarly ended. Then (in Chapter 12), what are the theoretical implications of the existence of this coherently evolved metanarrative and the method described in Chapter 1? I employ a cognitive anthropological perspective: what does science fiction as a case study suggest for our cognitive and behavioral flexibilities in light of historically novel ecological conditions? Specifically, does science fiction give us a clue about how social groups may form in a dispersed, globalized world?

Despite generations of philosophers predicting religion's imminent demise (Karl Marx, Max Weber, Marcel Gauchet, etc.), it has inexplicably failed to disappear. Richard Rorty and Gianni Vattimo, for example, predict that we are (or perhaps already have) moving from the Age of Reason into the Age of Interpretation, in which religion becomes merely personal and ethical, as the "man of postmodernity" learns to accept his finitude (Rorty and Vattimo 2005: 12). My own field, cognitive anthropology, takes a different view. Given that beliefs in supernatural agency seem to have been part of our history for longer than that history has been recorded, and that a growing amount of research in the cognitive science of religion demonstrates that this trait is intimately associated with our most basic and universal mental processes, it seems unlikely to the extreme that *Homo religiosis* will abandon religion *en mass* any time soon.

However, religion has *changed* significantly before: compare the small-scale imagistic rituals of prehistory (and their modern hunter–gatherer analogs) to the strongly centralized Catholicism of the High Middle Ages to individualistic New Age philosophies. Perhaps religion is not dissipating, but transforming, as it has before. But transforming into what? Given the importance religion has played in human culture up to this point, this is a possibility we should play close attention to. Science fiction authors have been asking the right questions for over a century; their speculations are worthy of consideration.

Part One

1

The Rules

The reader capable of deciphering the hidden meaning of a book from the order of the entries has long since vanished from the face of the earth, for today's reading audience believes that the matter of imagination lies exclusively within the realm of the writer and does not concern them in the least.

Dictionary of the Khazars, *Milorad Pavić*

This is a book on religion in science fiction. The natural place to start, I think, is to describe my particular goals, why my book took *this* form rather than another, and, frankly, why anyone should care! I would humbly suggest there are three main reasons: social, academic, and practical.

The social reason concerns the perceptions of religion in Western, and especially American, culture. One long-running characteristic has been an assumed conflict between religious ways of understanding the world and our place in it, and scientific explanations for similar (but never identical!) questions. For example, the question of human origins has been legislated and adjudicated into a dichotomy between Creationism and evolution: *State of Tennessee v. John T. Scopes* in 1925, through *Kitzmiller et al. v. Dover Area School District* in 2004, with no definitive end in sight. Science fiction offers unique insights into this conflict and (perhaps surprisingly) evidence that the conflict is by no means inevitable: if *science fiction* can accept religion, perhaps those science-minded can, too ... and perhaps religiously minded readers will question the inevitability that they must be suspicious of scientific perspectives.

In addition, the science fiction genre is an excellent test case for cognitive anthropology in at least two ways: as a long-running and distinct example of the evolution of cultural schema, analogous to the genesis of a modern myth (*sensu* Saler, Ziegler and Moore 1997) and as inferring a process of collective identity unusual in human history in that shared identity and common cultural values are produced and maintained through exposure to a body of texts, and conspicuously *not* reinforced by geographical proximity or other shared, independent experiences (cf. Whitehouse 2004). The academic significance of the texts described here is the subject of Part Four.

I suspect that perhaps not every science fiction fan who picks up this book will initially be fascinated by cognitive anthropology, but I would challenge such readers to give Part Four a try: what does it mean to be a science fiction "fan" rather than just someone who has read a few books that might qualify? Why is the distinction between "mainstream" and "genre" science fiction so important? On a personal level, one of my goals was to try to understand why I seem to enjoy even *bad* science fiction—even unoriginal, derivative works feel like "mine" in a way I couldn't initially explain.

The practical reason is simply that there is an embarrassment of riches when one begins assembling science fiction stories that attempt to "deal with" religion. In fact, Parts Two and Three of this book are essentially a survey of my favorites within the genre, ranging from Barclay's "The Troglodytes" (1930), to Arthur C. Clarke's *Childhood's End* (1953), to Ray Bradbury's "The Messiah" (1973), to Octavia Butler's *Parable of the Sower* (1993). Each generation seems to have something to say about religion—and something *different* to say. I will try to avoid ruining the endings for people who haven't read them; one of my intentions is to encourage readers to try less well-known but excellent books like Leigh Brackett's *The Long Tomorrow* (1955) and George Stewart's *Earth Abides* (1949).

It may surprise some that there *are* so many examples. Why science fiction has anything to say about religion in the first place may not be immediately obvious—the label *science* fiction, after all, would seem to be exclusionary of anything to do with the supernatural, mysticism, magic, and so on. As James Morrow (see Chapter 9) wrote:

> Like cabbages and kings, theology and science fiction are not normally mentioned in the same breath. It could scarcely be otherwise. Within the Roman Church and the Protestant denominations, doctrines emerge through a kind of sacralized dialectic informed by exegesis, prayer, and presumably inspired disputation. Science fiction, meanwhile, is keyed to what we know—and might eventually learn—about the physical universe through induction and experiment. A resolutely materialist-romantic literature, it either ignores supernatural explanations of reality or confines them to the psyches of pious secondary characters.
>
> Braving the risk of narrative incoherence, a handful of writers during the previous century managed to give us novels that participate simultaneously in the medieval and the post-Enlightenment worldviews. (Morrow, n.d.)

Laying aside Morrow's assertion that a religious worldview is necessarily "medieval," I would protest that authors incorporating ideas about religion into science fiction are by no means rare. From the mid-1920s, science fiction has evolved specifically to engaging not "science" but scientific ways of viewing the world and the societal impacts of technologies. Naturally, given Western assumptions about the supposed oppositional stances of science and religion, genre authors considered the contrasting end of the hermeneutic spectrum. For example, members of the Science Fiction and Fantasy Writers of America—the organization that produces the annual Nebula Awards for the best science fiction—chose the best science fiction short stories from 1929 to 1964 (i.e., the stories from the early days that might have won the Nebula had it started before 1966). Even the *titles* of the stories show a recurrence of religious imagery: "Microcosmic God" (Theodore Sturgeon), "Born of Man and Woman" (Richard Matheson), "Mars is Heaven!" (Ray Bradbury), "The Nine Billion Names of God" (Arthur C. Clarke), "A Rose for Ecclesiastes" (Roger Zelazny), and "The Quest for Saint Aquin" (Anthony Boucher) (Silverberg 1970/1998). Since then, there have been entire collections devoted to science fiction stories in which religion figures prominently (e.g., Mohs 1974, Ryan 1982, Warrick and Greenberg 1975).

It is one of the ironies of the science fiction genre that science and religion seem to have evolved a rather symbiotic relationship since the 1920s, in sharp contrast to the outside world which insists on seeing them as dichotomous. Note that science fiction was not a literature "for scientists," per se: Brian Aldiss quipped that saying science fiction was for scientists made as much sense as saying ghost stories were written for ghosts (quoted in Ashley and Lowndes 2004: 45). Rather, science fiction was initially intended to *promote* scientific perspectives on the full scope of human culture (see Chapter 4). So, I would argue that representations of religion in science fiction are an object lesson that should be taken seriously and that the *evolution* of these representations constitutes a fascinating "*meta*-narrative" in its own right.

So, Part Four of this book describes the cognitive anthropological significance of the metanarrative described, step by step, in Parts Two and Three. The goals of Part One are to describe the raw materials out of which science fiction was created (Chapters 2 and 3), and to define my terms, outline my strategies behind which texts were selected and how they were approached (this chapter). The first major methodological decision was to employ a qualitative strategy. Rather than quantify elements within a large number of works that more or less fit my goals, I have identified a smaller number of more tightly defined key works representative of each period (roughly four per decade from 1930 to 2000), which allows me to dig a little deeper into each one.

The other two most important decisions were to *define* science fiction and religion—a variety of definitions have been suggested, and different definitions would yield very different books. Since my goal is to *compare* examples of religion in science fiction, it behooves me to define both as precisely as possible, to avoid comparing apples to oranges. Note that I do not argue mine are the "best" definitions, but rather that they are the best suited to my goals.

Consider the following hypothetical (though with precedent) texts. Which of these are science fiction? For that matter, which are *fiction*?

- An author has particular religious beliefs or theological ideas that s/he wishes to promote. S/he decides to write a novel presenting these beliefs and ideas, in hopes of convincing others of their value, perhaps as a reaction to other novels they find theologically distasteful. This novel takes places in a science fiction setting. (See, e.g., C. S. Lewis's "Space Trilogy," beginning with 1938's *Out of the Silent Planet* [Lewis 2011].)
- An author may be critical of specific religious institutions in their community and write satirical fiction with the intent of undermining the popularity of those beliefs and ideas, or simply to make light of them. Such writings have a long history, and may be set in a strange, distant land (e.g., Holberg 1741/1812), or in the future:

for example, Mark Twain's cynical portrayal of a Christian Science future in "The Secret History of Eddypus, the World Empire" (Twain 2003: 176–225).

- An individual may take a novel they know and acknowledge to be fiction, but feel the ideas within are significant enough to warrant basing their lives on them, and ultimately construct a religious institution using the novel as (i.e., not just in lieu of) a religious text (see, e.g., Cusack 2010: 53–82).
- An author considers the historical tendencies of religion and projects these patterns forward, in essence speculating about the future of religious institutions as a kind of pseudo-scientific thought experiment. From this, the reader may draw conclusions as to the appropriate role of religion in the present.

Similarly, consider the range of possibilities for academic analyses:

- An academic could select texts created as mythic narratives within religious traditions and read them as examples of proto-science fiction (e.g., Gunn 2002; cf. Weber 1812: xviii).
- On the other hand, an academic could argue that science fiction is "really" a religion because it includes narratives with supernatural abilities, organized group functions, and individuals who base their lives on these narratives and groups (e.g., Kreuziger 1986; cf. Disch 1998: 136–62).
- One could argue that religion and science fiction have similar functions. For example, humans seem to have a need for transcendence; religion and science fiction both fill that need—they are parallel solutions (one sacred, one secular) to a basic problem (e.g., Cowan 2010).
- Or one might argue that the contents religion and science fiction have similar structures, and are therefore attractive for similar reasons. For example, both can be described as communal mythopoeic enterprises (e.g., Blish 1970/1987, esp. p. 33; cf. Robertson 2011).
- An academic could identify recurring themes in various religions—healing, for example—and then describe any characters associated with these themes—a mental health counselor, for example—as "religious specialists" (e.g., Kraemer et al. 2001: 93–127).
- A social scientist could argue that the production of texts is a behavior, and therefore stories (including science fiction) could be used as examples of various behaviors for classes in Sociology (e.g., Milstead et al. 1974), Psychology (e.g., Katz et al. 1977), . . . or for Religion Studies (e.g., Warrick and Greenberg 1975).

All of these options have been explored, and while I must admit I found one or two difficult to take seriously, most have been quite impressive. But note how different they all are from each other.

There is another, rather obvious avenue that has *not* been explored in depth: rather than consider how religion and science fiction are structurally related, I ask how they are *perceptually* related, not as academic categories but as popular schema; not as philosophical, theological, or psychological categories of behavior but concrete *institutions*. Simply, what do (these) people *think* religion is? Is it beneficial? Misguided? Inevitable? And crucially, how does it compete or complement science?

As a result, the book before you is very different from others described as focusing on religion and about science fiction. I must hasten to add that I would not argue that my book is necessarily better—though I do believe the historical analysis I'm attempting here has advantages over looser, descriptive studies. Rather, I would say I'm asking different questions, and therefore require different assumptions.

As an example, Kraemer et al. published a book called *The Religions of Star Trek* (2001). The authors begin by acknowledging how important it is to define "religion."

> Although we are well aware of the methodological difficulties in using terms like "religion" and "religious," we have written this book with a specific audience in mind and intentionally use ordinary language to make our points. In this regard, our approach is similar to that of the Star Trek writers, who crafted TV scripts and screenplays that are sophisticated yet use common language and imagery to depict religion. (Kraemer et al. 2001: 6)

Ironically, their book described much that I would not have thought of as "religion." The authors' examples of religious specialists, for example, include the characters T'Pau and Deanna Troi (ibid. pp. 93–127). T'Pau is an acknowledged expert in Vulcan tradition, the possessor of rare and esoteric knowledge, including the practical uses of rituals. According to Kraemer et al., T'Pau "affirms and upholds Vulcan traditions—in fact, she embodies them—thus *deserving recognition as a priestess*" (p. 104, emphasis added). However, even if we stipulate that religions have traditions and rituals, it does not follow that all traditions and rituals are religious. As a member of the logic-idealizing Vulcan race, T'Pau herself would likely object to the supernatural implications of the label and argue that her rituals were no more "religious" in the human sense than mind-melds and nerve-pinches. Deanna Troi is described as a "spiritual healer" (ibid. p. 103), but how likely is it that someone from our own society would include their therapist in a list of religious specialists? In short, title aside, Kraemer et al. tell us little about religious institutions as they are commonly understood, and it is precisely the broadly shared, cultural understanding that interests me.

With this in mind, I have devised a few guidelines for this research, specifically: what exactly do I mean by "religion," what is genre science fiction (and how does it differ from mainstream literature), and how can cognitive anthropology help us understand how science fiction changes over time.

Defining religion

- For the purposes of this book, religion is defined as a social system, like any other within a given domain, which is legitimated by the claim of supernatural authority.

"Religion" is a complicated academic category. One could argue the study of religion demonstrates just how convoluted and ironic our research can be. Even the word is problematic. "Religion" is a textbook example of polysemy: the same word means different things at different times, and to different people. For much of the nineteenth century, "religion" was perilously close to being defined as something only "we" in the West have: much of the rest of the world was full of "superstitions" and "fetishists," or at best "pagans." Twentieth-century academics struggled with the problem that some cultures lack an equivalent term. For example, the "religions" of classical China (Buddhism, Daoism, and Confucianism) were referred to as the *san jiao* or "three teachings"—the character for "teaching" portraying an old man supervising a child, lacking any trace of the supernatural. Yet we see rituals, prayers, myths, apparent beliefs in supernatural entities, and afterlives. It is impossible for us to argue that they *have* no religion; rather, they must not categorize the world in the same way as we.

Academics, incidentally, are not immune from the problems of defining religion. All too often (in my opinion), even my colleagues assume that "religion" is necessarily associated with "morality." However, counter-examples are easy to find. Many divine figures (e.g., Zeus) are described as fairly reprehensible characters (e.g., as a philanderer); the US legal system is based on the assumption that one can act morally with or without a religious identity; for a great many religions in our history, abstract questions like morality are insignificant compared to a successful hunt, avoiding sickness, and military prowess.

So, defining religion is a nontrivial problem: I chose the working definition above simply because it seems to describe with some clarity those phenomena I wish to include. This definition is taken from Prof. Luther Martin from the Department of Religion at the University of Vermont (see Martin 2014), the first (or possibly second, depending on one's take on Western Michigan University) independent academic department in the United States devoted to the secular study of religion. Martin argued that, first and foremost, religion is a *social* phenomenon, not a supernatural one. One may perhaps have an experience one believes to be connected with some externalized divinity, what Otto called "the numinous" (1950/1958). But even if we stipulate that such experiences involve an actual supernatural entity, *they do not constitute "religion."* This is simply because the majority of individuals in a religion typically do not share in these experiences; the question, then, becomes why an individual will accept, without objective evidence, another person's *claims* to contact with the supernatural. Even more interestingly, why and how do some individuals internalize the patterns of religion within their culture with sufficient strength to influence perceptions of their own less-than-mundane experiences? I suspect, given a strong Christian upbringing, that an individual with a "near death experience" is unlikely to see Vishnu or Amida Buddha at the end of the tunnel.

Even given my relatively strict definition, religion is then more than just a group with an organized structure, leaders, and doctrine, nor even a more small-scale system of individual influence due to a supernatural claim. It is also the system of beliefs itself, learned within a community, that distinguishes that community from others. Note that there are *many* systems that can distinguish one group from another: not just religion, but also ways of dressing, traditional foods, collective symbols, language, laws, etc. In any society there are multiple coexisting social systems: one can be Catholic, *and* an American, *and* a soldier, each role having its own relationships and obligations. By virtue of being a social system, religions share some similarities with the rest: various forms of leadership, patterns of how one joins a group, costs of defection, and so on.

But religion is unique in the kind of authority the system rests on. If one is a soldier, deserting may result in imprisonment or execution; if one fails to pay one's taxes as a citizen, the result is fines and possibly imprisonment. Religious obligations, however, may be under threat of supernatural costs such as an uncomfortable afterlife. *This does not mean that religions do not* also *have mundane, observable authority*—but religions have other avenues to power and authority unique to them.

I must hasten to add that Martin's is not the only legitimate academic definition of religion; it is simply the one that is most useful, considering my goals. If one prefers a more "holistic" definition of religion, my goal is simply to understand one specific facet; again, Martin helps me isolate the data of most relevance. In fact, this could be the litmus test for *any* definition of this kind: are the generalizations they imply useful? Do they help one meet one's stated goals? For example, people may commonly assume the definition of a "species" to be self-evident, but to biologists the category is fraught with complications. Darwin himself wrote "It is really laughable to see what different ideas are prominent in various naturalists' minds, when they speak of 'species' . . . It all comes, I believe, from trying to define the indefinable" (quoted in Zimmer 2008: 74). Different biologists with different questions would do well to categorize the natural world differently. Those who want to know how organisms exploit particular niches would do well to focus on *morphology*; those who want to understand adaptations *to* niches might categorize according to genetic similarities, by ancestral *descent*. Even widely accepted definitions, such as defining a species as a population of individuals who reproduce together, have unexpected subtleties and contradictions (see, e.g., de Queiroz 2005).

If a "species" is so difficult to describe, how much harder is it to define definitively "religion"—an even less natural category, and a word that in some languages has no equivalent? And how much more varied are the possible goals involved? For a Christian missionary, for example, the only reasonable definition of religion *is Christianity*. As an anthropologist, my goals are different, and hence I need a different definition. Mine is not more "accurate"—accuracy, after all, is impossible to judge given such an artificial category as religion—but simply does what I want it to. It conforms to my assumptions and includes those behaviors I want to include while excluding the rest. I want to include specifically social behaviors—the claim to supernatural authority, the collective acceptance of that claim, and the changes to ones perceptions that result from accepting certain cultural-specific beliefs about the supernatural.

This definition of religion will be used here to determine which of a large body of literature will be considered. It is in some ways broadly inclusive, as it would admit narrative descriptions of religious systems ranging from the shamanism of a hunter–gatherer group to medieval Christianity to urban Wicca. But in other ways, it rules out many of the examples previous studies of religion in science fiction, with looser definitions, would include. Deanna Troi is not discussed elsewhere in this book: her authority is not reliant upon any claim to the supernatural (valid or otherwise). Within the fictional cultures of the Star Trek universe, her role as an emotional healer would not be understood as being that of a religious specialist, any more than Neelix (the some-time cook of another Star Trek show) would be a religious specialist simply because some religions have communal meals.

So, our definition of religion selects certain items from a body of literature. But how is that body defined? To put it another way, we have our definition of religion; how will we define science fiction? Much of the next two chapters is devoted to this question, so I will limit myself here to outlining the strategy employed.

A cognitive anthropology of narratives

- Culture can be defined as shared, mental schemas: an epidemiology of representations commonly shared by members of a community, interpersonally transmitted and/or generated by shared experiences (Sperber 1996).
- These representations cumulatively and culturally evolve. Taken in chronological sequence, narrative representations constitute a meta-narrative—a "story" told collectively by successive generations. By "ratcheting" multiple individuals' efforts (*sensu* Tomasello 1999), the products of cultural evolution may be more complex than those produced by any single individual.
- Like biological evolution, the selection of cultural schema is dependent on (cultural) environments. Unlike biological evolution, cultural evolution sometimes proceeds via goal-directed "intelligent design."
- The representativeness of any individual schema or collective meta-narrative is dependent on pervasiveness and durability; consumption, not production— popularity trumps quality.

"Everyone knows" that creativity is the purview of an individual, not a group. The best a group can produce is an uneasy compromise between creative individuals, its only advantage that it appeals to the lowest—and therefore most common—denominators. There can be no art by committee.

However, counter to this is the idea that no artist creates out of whole cloth; creativity is meaningless without the cultural context in which it is situated, even (especially?) if the product is intended to contrast and/or criticize it. As Ludwig Fleck argued in the 1930s:

> The individual within the collective is never, or hardly ever, conscious of the prevailing thought style which almost always exerts an absolutely compulsive force upon his thinking, and with which it is not possible to be at variance. (Fleck, quoted in Douglas 1986: 13)

Artists, like anyone, are part of a culture-specific "thought world" (*das Denkkollektiv*). It is not simply that the cultural environment constrains creativity; culture *creates* creativity—it gives the artist, and the author, the raw materials with which to express her or himself. Mary Douglas objected to such functional, Durkheimian concepts of the group not on principle, but simply on the practical consideration that such interactions with the group would require some sort of mechanism, noting, "No general theory equivalent to biological evolution applies to human behavior" (1986: 33).

Cognitive anthropology is, essentially, the study of the mechanism to which Douglas referred: a biological account of individual and collective behavior, and an evolutionary account of themes and variations of the minds which *direct* behavior. Chapter 12 describes this in a broader academic perspective, but a primer of the concepts most important to *this* book will be useful.

The most fundamental idea is to view culture as *particulate*. A specific culture (America, science fiction fandom, anthropology, etc.) can be seen as a collection of characteristic information: ideas as well as facts, shared experiences, common references, stereotypes, etc. Membership in such groups is probabilistic, based on the proportion of shared information. More accurately, membership is based on the *perception* of the proportion of shared information. Individuals within a group may focus on different information as key markers of membership. Recall the old World War II trope of a sentry challenging a stranger approaching camp: "If you're American, who won the World Series?" By most formal criteria, *I'm* American, but I'd fail that particular test of citizenship. (Baseball, right?) Note that these are the kinds of tests one would apply in real-time, interpersonal interactions, not objective legal definitions.

Now let us look a little closer at these pieces of culturally characteristic information. They include a much broader category than simply "facts." Dan Sperber (1996) calls them "schema"; Strauss and Quinn note how compatible Sperber's model is to other models of culture-specific thoughts and behaviors, such as Bourdieu's concept of "habitus" (1997: 44–7). The key insight is that whatever is shared by members of a group is transmitted via the mechanism of shared experience—participating in the same culture produces similar (never identical) mental representations in most (never all) members. Like Dawkins' old idea of the most fit (i.e., memorable) "memes" spreading, gene-like, throughout a population (1976), one can track schemas' distribution through transmission, but unlike Dawkins, Sperber proposed that a better metaphor for this transmission would be a disease. The spread of particles of culture can be seen as an "epidemiology of representations," resulting in both the endemic traditions of long-term stable culture, or relatively transient epidemic fashions (Sperber 1996: 56–61). To apply this to our current topic, if I were to encounter a stranger who describes herself as a science fiction fan, but who hadn't heard of H. G. Wells or Jules Verne (e.g., the endemic culture of science fiction), I would suspect she wasn't *really* a science fiction fan. Reciprocally, if I hadn't read the newest science fiction best-seller, she might suspect *my* claim. Knowledge of no single schema would be proof either way; rather, membership is based on the preponderance of evidence of familiarity (determined subjectively) with group-specific schema.

There are two important implications of this. The first is that familiarity with cultural schema shapes and constrains the production of *new* schemas. "In other words, schemas . . . are well-learned but flexibly adaptive rather than rigidly repetitive. They can adapt to new or ambiguous situations with 'regulated improvisation', to use Bourdieu's term" (Strauss and Quinn 1997: 53). This applies not only to negotiation of social situations but also to producing new art. A science fiction author writes within the world of science fiction, which necessarily constraints her/his options (e.g., rules one must follow, as described in the next subsection). The second is that, as schemas spread, they *change*. No schema is transmitted intact, hence Sperber's description of them as "mental representations." We do not learn "the schema"; we construct our internalized version of it. Through this process, cultural schemas *evolve*. I do not mean metaphorically; I mean that any given schema exists simultaneously with multiple variants, the least fit of which will die out (i.e., fail to transmit), and thus the most fit will come to dominate.

> [A]ny author of genre sf is conscious of working within a genre with certain habits of thought, certain 'conventions'—some might even say 'rules'—of storytelling. These conventions are embedded primarily in a set of texts which are generally agreed to contain them. This may seem to be a circular definition . . . it is in fact a spiral. A text published in 1930 may describe something . . . so well that in 1935 the description has become recognized as a model or a convention; and in 1940 a second text may be published which shows its agreement with the convention by repeating it, with variations which themselves enrich it. (Clute and Nicholls 1995: 483)

This selection is, of course, dependent on the environmental context. When it comes to science fiction, schema, tastes change. At the beginning of modern science fiction in the 1920s and '30s, for example, science-driven, technological progress (as popularized in the US World's Fairs of 1933 and 1939) was viewed as an unalloyed positive. After 1945, this changes: one feature in the intellectual landscape of post-WWII US is an attempt to come to terms with the horrifying destructive potential of nuclear weapons. This encourages authors to produce, and influences audiences to buy, stories set in a post-nuclear apocalypse (e.g., Brackett's 1955 *The Long Tomorrow*). Parallel to this, the comfortable assumption that scientific progress is positive dissipates: stories that assume technology yields pleasant social impacts largely become, if not entirely extinct, then endangered.

Two qualifications of this "cultural evolution" (*sensu* Mesoudi 2011) concern to what extent these changes are conscious. It does not necessarily follow that even coherent change over time implies a goal-driven "intelligent designer." In biological evolution, startlingly complex, impressively "clever" solutions to problems of survival and reproduction occur through random processes that we researchers, *post hoc*, must work very hard to understand. As evolutionary biologist Leslie Orgel famously quipped, "evolution is cleverer than you are." Correspondingly, some of the long-term (which is to say, multi-generational) shifts in science fiction schema reflect changes in the public's disorganized taste. *Unlike* biological evolution, however, some variations are produced intentionally; some selection *is* goal directed. For example, the hugely influential science fiction editors Hugo Gernsback in the late 1920s and '30s, and John W. Campbell in the 1940s into the '50s both used their influence strategically in an effort to direct its development in specific directions, both to appeal to *and* to affect the *Zeitgeist* (see Chapters 4 and 5). In short, *cultural* evolution is, in part, via intelligent design.

Taken as a whole, the evolution of a specific schema across many stories over several generations creates a story in its own right; thus, this book is not about a specific narrative, but a *meta*narrative. In this book, we are primarily concerned with religion, specifically, how religion (as defined above) is represented in science fiction, and how that representation evolved in response to both hyper-influential individuals and more general changes in the *Zeitgeist*, from, as we'll see, a largely antagonistic view toward religion seen as in conflict with science, to science and religion as alternative, not contradictory, ways of understanding the world and ourselves.

Two implications of this may not be immediately obvious. With one notable exception (Orson Scott Card in Chapter 9), I am relatively unconcerned with individual authors' religious views. Larry Niven is quoted as saying, "There is a technical, literary term for those who mistake the opinions and beliefs of characters in a novel for those of the author. The term is 'idiot'."[1] Though I would phrase it more gently, this seems curiously apropos for science fiction, where our *raison d'être* is to speculate on *possible* worlds, not to describe the world as we see it, and in choosing what to buy, to read, and to recommend, consumers of science fiction primarily access the texts themselves, along with advertising, book blurbs, reviews, and so on. So, for our purposes, what the author actually believes is less important than what readers actually find in the text—or, at least, what they *believe* they find.[2]

The other implication is that I am ironically unconcerned with questions of *quality*. In short, I am not looking for the best, but for the most *representative* science fiction from each period. I am less interested in remarkable individuals' artistic achievements than patterns in what choices the common group member makes: which stories did they choose to buy? Which ones did later authors choose to imitate? Which stories resonated enough to have an impact on the group's cultural output, as opposed to those which vanished without a trace? Robert Heinlein was one of the most seminal of science fiction authors, and his 1938 novel *For Us, the Living* gives us remarkable insight into the personality and methods of one of the genre's heroes. However, that novel is uninteresting here: since it was not published until 2003, it literally had no direct impact. With regard to quality, A. E. van Vogt wrote the most purile, formulaic of space opera, yet had legions of fans and many imitators; his impact is more important than (lack of) quality. (On a personal note, one of the reasons I'm so drawn to this topic is to understand why I enjoy van Vogt so much, when I *know* it's simply awful.) My rationale is, then, by focusing on only the most *influential* authors (e.g., Asimov, Herbert, Moorcock; Hugo and Nebula Award winners, etc.), and avoiding the interesting but idiosyncratic, I will focus on the most representative texts, giving me the best chance of identifying the evolution of science fiction's schema of religion.

Defining genre science fiction

- One may distinguish between mainstream science fiction (abbreviated here as "mSF") that includes a diverse set of thematic and structural elements, and genre science fiction ("gSF").
- Defining science fiction by a finite set of themes and plot elements fails to distinguish genre from mainstream.
- Genre science fiction is made distinct from mainstream through three co-centric mechanisms: as the product of a partially bounded society (English-speaking Western world, predominantly American), as contained within an isolated niche

(e.g., fandom, specialty publishing, etc.), and through the influence of 'intelligent designers' (e.g., Gernsback, Campbell).

The problem

As with "religion," defining "science fiction" is a nontrivial task. Even in 1952 (when SF was still relatively homogeneous), this was problematic:

> Science-fiction seems difficult to define with precision. For some it consists of fiction dealing solely with speculation about the future; for others it is the fiction of prophesy; for yet others it is fiction concerned only with interplanetary adventure. (Derleth 1952: 187)

Even to science fiction insiders, the problem is frustrating. Editor and author Damon Knight ultimately defined science fiction as simply "what we point to when we say it" (quoted in Clute and Nicholls 1995: 314). I argue that Knight was not dodging the question, but suggesting the proper strategy: science fiction is what *we* say it is. Who's this "we"?

The first *sine qua non* characteristic of a definition we can use here is that it must distinguish between science fiction and, well, everything else—to take into account the fact that most people (in and out of the genre) label some texts, and some authors, as "science fiction," more regularly than others. Unfortunately, we run into problems like Franklin (1978), who wrote, "There was no major nineteenth-century American writer of fiction, and indeed few in the second rank, who did not write some science fiction or at least one utopian romance" (ibid. p. ix) and then proceeded to describe "science fiction" written by Washington Irving, James Fenimore Cooper, Herman Melville, Oliver Wendell Holmes, and Nathaniel Hawthorne—great authors, but rarely considered great *science fiction* authors. I wouldn't include Mark Twain, either, but apparently Twain wrote enough to fill an anthology (Twain 2003). HiLo Books is currently producing a series of science fiction books written between c. 1890 and c. 1920, so far including Jack London (1912/2012), Rudyard Kipling (1905/2012), and Arthur Conan Doyle (1913/2012). Contrast this to the common tendency within science fiction to refer to Jules Verne and H. G. Wells as the "fathers of science fiction" (explored in Chapter 3)—clearly, our definition must be more exclusive.

Another important characteristic of a useful definition, especially from a cognitive *anthropological* perspective, is that, ideally, I will use the same processes, the same criteria to decide what is and what is not science fiction as a science fiction insider (e.g., fans, authors, and editors). That is, *why* a certain author "counts" as science fiction is as important as who is included. From this perspective, a common academic strategy—to define science fiction according to its structure and functions (see examples in Kreuziger 1986: 85–6)—appears flawed. As mentioned above, one could argue that science fiction is mythopoeic (e.g., Blish 1970/1987; cf. Robertson 2011); though this seems logical enough, it cannot distinguish science fiction from other mythopoeia (but see Philmus [1970: 1–36], who distinguishes between public and private myth) and runs the risk of conflating science fiction and religion (e.g., Kreuziger 1986), though occasionally examples from one category are transformed into the other—that is, someone might read *Revelations* as science fiction (ibid. p. 47), or make a religion out of a science fiction book (e.g., Cowan 2010). More importantly, this seems to have little to do with how science fiction readers choose what to read: I've never dismissed a book as insufficiently mythopoeic. Similarly (to choose another more or less at random), Scholes (1976) defines science fiction as a modern form of narrative fabulation influenced by Darwinian conceptions of time. Even if Scholes is correct, I doubt many science fiction fans would recognize his definition. Like defining religion as anything to do with philosophy, theology, ethics, healing, etc., such strategies do little to describe a distinct category, and do not reflect the emic experience.

A more logical—but still flawed—approach is to determine the thematic elements that distinguish science fiction: space travel, alien life, speculations of utopic and dystopic societies, predictions for the future, etc. Unfortunately, given the common understanding of science fiction as a modern phenomenon (certainly not pre-dating formal "science"), these elements have *very* long histories. Catholic saints' *vitas* were linked with journeys to the center of the earth two centuries ago (Weber 1812: xviii; cf. Scholes 1976: 47); if "science fiction" equals technological speculation, then da Vinci's notebooks qualify; Lucian of Samosata was writing about space travel and aliens in the second century. "If myths and legends are to be credited as SF, then half of world literature before the novel must be accounted ancestral to SF" (Disch1998: 32). Such strategies would produce an exceedingly broad and heterogeneous set of narratives, with no reason to expect distinct patterns in representations of religion.[3]

One further complication is quite important: within the science fiction community, it is routine to distinguish between *genre* science fiction (hereafter "gSF") and *mainstream* science fiction ("mSF").[4] The former is "real" science fiction; "ours." Mainstream may share superficial characteristics, but lack some ineffable quality. The definition of science fiction used here must take into account intuitive recognitions that some texts may *look* like science fiction superficially, but don't *feel* like real science fiction. Both Greg Bear's *Darwin's Radio* (1999) and Michael Crichton's *Andromeda Strain* (1969) describe plagues caused by a microorganism in the present day. Despite the extraterrestrial origin of *his* microorganism, Crichton's book is understood to be a techno-thriller (and shelved in bookstores accordingly), while Greg Bear's is clearly genre science fiction and has the awards to prove it (it was nominated for the Hugo and Campbell Awards, and won the Nebula). I am fascinated by the regularity of this distinction and the frequent (but never universal) similarities in judgments, despite individuals' difficulty to articulate precisely where the difference lays, and despite that fact that "trying to get two enthusiasts to agree on a definition of it leads only to bloody knuckles" (Damon Knight, quoted in Westfahl 1999).

The solution

I believe the solution is to view gSF not as a set of texts distinguished by similar structural or thematic elements, but as the cultural products of a bounded group, working in collaboration with each other. Note that I do not mean to limit the group to authors, but also readers, editors, publishers, cover artists, etc.: the whole community whose cumulative actions affect how a bounded set of science fiction changed over time.

A cultural perspective simplifies the problem enormously. "Real" science fiction is what science fiction readers have read; following (author and critic) Norman Spinrad, gSF is "anything published as science fiction" (Clute and Nicholls 1993: 314). This argument is not circular—genre science fiction is the literature of choice for a community, and any common themes result from this in-group feedback. "This whole living matrix, not just the fictional texts that had initially occasioned it, came to be called 'science fiction'" (Clute and Nicholls 1993: 312). This community has distinctive normative views, hero figures, and traditional *raisons d'être* (cf. Knight 1974: 7)—including cultural schema that evolve within the gSF niche into something distinct from the mainstream. Note that the distinctiveness of gSF schema does not merely *reflect* the isolation of its niche: it reinforces it.

> Fans . . . read a *lot* of science fiction. A concept that is new and different and far out to the general public can be old-hat to the fans; and fan pressure can push an author towards ever-new, ever farther-out ideas . . . adding to our isolation. (Pournelle 1982: 159)

So, is *Darwin's Radio* really science fiction? Yes, we know it must be *because it won the Nebula*. A sufficient number of insiders chose it to be representative, so to argue it is not would privilege a reductionist, analytical approach that does not reflect how individuals within the community actually behave. Whether or not we can make explicit the criteria applied by these individuals may be a different matter. If we accept that each may be judging whether or not something is gSF according to the schema of the genre, *and that no single individual possesses all of these schema*, it is even possible that different individuals may arrive at similar judgments for different reasons. Note that these schemas would be as impossible to list as all possible thematic elements: there are too many, most are quite subtle, and deliberate violations are not just standard practice; they are part of the fun.

Defining science fiction as the narrative culture of a particular group, united through sharing similar experiences (chiefly, reading the same books), opens up more possibilities than shared schema and implicit categorization judgments (see Vint [2014: 55–72] on the "megatext"): it allows for the emergence of complex explicit patterns (e.g., through Tomasello's [1999] "ratchet effect"), implicit assessments of individual texts, as well as a framework of themes and variations for innovation—a framework for the construction of new textual variants (see, e.g., del Rey 1979: 327–41). One schema which will be encountered several times in this book is that religious specialist protagonists are disproportionately Jesuits (cf. Blish's *A Case of Conscience* [1958/2000], Russell's *The Sparrow* [1996]). A new story with a Dominican hero might seem like a purposeful act on the part of the author. Violating this single convention would not be enough to suggest the book wasn't "really" gSF—but the accumulation of similar violations would. Incidentally, the existence of common cultural schema also makes the construction of "inside jokes" possible (Flamson and Barrett 2008; Chapter 12, this volume). We know, for example, what FTL, BEM, and TANSTAAFL mean.[5] I will quote (in full) "The Shortest Science Fiction Love Story Ever Written":

> Boy meets girl.
>
> Boy loses girl.
>
> Boy builds girl. (Renner 1964)

Even the label of "science fiction" implies certain expectations which influence our interpretations; identical words could have different meanings in and out of the science fiction community (Samuel Delaney, quoted in McCaffery and Gregory 1987: 90–2).

So, what happens when a genre outsider writes a story that is superficially science fiction (e.g., contains gSF themes like time travel, speculations of future technologies, etc.)? The resulting mSF may be indistinguishable from gSF by those *outside* the community, but insiders will recognize the difference. Expected elements are missing, as are the subtle influences of previous authors, and unexpected elements may appear. More significantly (for the purposes of the current discussion), a mainstream author will be not only unfamiliar with specific schemas, they will be unaware of the current stage of evolution of those schema as well (cf. Blish 1987: 30). As their work will not fit into gSF's metanarratives, the result can look rather silly.

> If you're going to write science fiction, within even a moderately narrow definition of the term, you must have read it. If you haven't, you're wasting your time and everybody else's. There are several mainstream writers who have happily launched themselves into the sea of science fiction because they see what a glorious field it is; and since they haven't read any science fiction, they do things that were done forty years ago, and have been done a hundred times since. A situation embarrassing for everybody. (Ursula K. LeGuin, quoted in McCaffery and Gregory 1987: 184)
>
> The thing that strikes you about literary [i.e., mainstream] writers is that each one was working more or less by himself . . . whereas the commercial writers [in the 1930s and '40s] were building up a set of shared assumptions (the widespread use of space travel, the galactic empire) and even a set of shorthand terms, a kind of jargon (hyperdrive, space warp, and so on) which helped them get on with their stories but repelled and irritated the literary writers, and readers even more. (Damon Knight, in "Grand Masters")

As a concrete example of the hazards of mSF, Fritz Lang's movie *Metropolis* (1927) was a hugely influential example of German expressionist film. The setting and plot seem obviously science fiction: in a future world, the process of industrialization has exaggerated class differences into an elite class—for whom the world is a utopia of leisure and fulfillment—and a worker class living a dystopic existence in service to (and consumed by) the machines. The leader of the elites attempts to undermine a revolt among the workers through the use of a robot. I personally love the movie and believe it to be one of the high points of the silent era. But is it good science fiction? H. G. Wells thought not.

> [Metropolis] gives in one eddying concentration almost every possible foolishness, cliché, platitude and muddlement about mechanical progress and progress in general, served up in a sauce of sentimentality. Čapek's Robots have been lifted without apology, and that soulless mechanical monster of Mary Shelley . . . breeds once more in this confusion. Originality, there is none, independent thought, none [. . .] Now, far away in dear old 1897, it may have been excusable to symbolize social relations in this way, but that was thirty years ago, and a lot of thinking and some experience intervene. (Wells 1927)

I would note in passing that science fiction is not the only genre of literature with characteristic schemas, producing normative assumptions. Many inside the mystery genre, for example, have put a great deal of thought into the genre's rules (House 2002). Mystery fan W. H. Auden (1962) described the essential elements of a detective novel—"the milieu, the victim, the murderer, the suspects, the detective" (p. 149)— and the appeal resting on the expectation of the restoration of innocence following an anomalous guilt. The Detection Club (which counted among its members Dorothy L. Sayers, Agatha Christie, and G. K. Chesterton) described in c. 1930 the characteristics of a true mystery novel, including that the author plays fair with the audience by not withholding key evidence, and that s/he does not rely on "Divine Revelation, Feminine Intuition, Mumbo-Jumbo, Jiggery-Pokery, Coincidence or Act of God" to solve the mystery (Brunsdale 2010: 88). Note that the Detection Club did not *invent* the rules so much as recognize and formalize conventions already in place, and that the rules were not taken too seriously: one member, Agatha Christie, is rather (in)famous for *breaking* the rules (e.g., in *The Murder of Roger Ackroyd* [1926/2001]). Fans, too, enjoy displaying and debating the rules (see, e.g., http://www.seattlemystery.com/rules-fair-play).

Nor is the idea of a genre a particularly new one. Gilgamesh is not a Babylonian epic poem, but a *tradition* of epic poems about a well-known hero dating back centuries to the Sumerians (George 1999). The existence of this tradition both facilitates the creation of new stories—it gives the author a framework on which to build—but also constrains the options: it seems unlikely that a Babylonian author would attempt to portray Gilgamesh as a bookish fellow afraid of conflict. Constraints like these affect more than "fictional" stories: Chalupa (2014) described how difficult it is for modern historians to discern what the oracular Pythia at Delphi was really like, as contemporary accounts are "problematic sources which rather than rendering a neutral and disinterested description of Delphic divinatory practices follow conventions typical for the particular literary genre."

Genre SF, then, is not a particular kind of story, but rather a product of the collective, creative acts of a community of individuals who, by virtue of shared experiences, share similar schemas which evolve within the bounded group. These experiences shape choices of what next to consume: the point of purchase is a selection event, in which less fit variants (stories, authors, *and* editors) are culled. I would like to emphasize the experience of the reader, here. Acquiring and *using* these schemas—not just when deciding what to buy but while reading—is not epiphenomenal: it is a strong part of the attraction to a gSF reader. (I suggest some reasons *why* this should be enjoyable in Chapter 12.) One could privilege the intellectual puzzle aspects of gSF, for example, by relating its narrative speculations to Mills' definition of the social sciences as investigating "all the social worlds in which men have lived, are living *and might live*" (quoted in Milstead et al. [1974: xii], emphasis added). More immediately, however, it is as if authors and readers are playing a game. Pavić wrote *Dictionary of the Khazars* (1989; p. 11 quoted at the start of this chapter) as an experimental, nonlinear novel. His book is structured as three dictionaries, each related to the same event from three distinct perspectives. The reader *could* start on page 1 and proceed, or read just one dictionary out of order, or read on *entry* in all three dictionaries, or read an entry at random and develop an individualized thread from there. Genre science fiction is the same kind of game, writ large—a game in which the matter of imagination does *not* lie exclusively within the realm of the writer.

In the next four chapters, we will explore sacred ancestors. The first two cover pre-genre ancestors in ancestral "genres" (Chapter 2) and authors with the strongest claims to the title of "Father of Science Fiction" (Chapter 3) for their representations of religion as examples of genre's most primitive (i.e., not "crude" but lacking derived characteristics) schemas for religion. The next two chapters will look at the choices of the most important of the "intelligent designers" in the early days of the genre: the seminal editors Hugo Gernsback (c. 1930s, Chapter 4) and John W. Campbell (c. 1940s, Chapter 5), both to understand their influence on the emerging genre and to explore representative stories for contemporary views of religion. Remember throughout, though, that such a top-down focus on the leaders of the genre is incomplete. The creation of a genre is not individually creative, but collective and organic; the reader does not passively receive, but is an active participant—and, insofar as the choice of what to purchase is a selection event, is the mechanism by which less fit variants (stories, authors, *and* editors) are culled. To recall the quotation that began this chapter, in science fiction more than any other kind of literature, the matter of imagination does *not* lie exclusively within the realm of the writer.

The Raw Materials of Science Fiction

This and the next chapter essentially describe science fiction before the genre; the raw materials from which genre science fiction (gSF) was constructed. What are the origins of gSF? The plural ("origins") is necessary: there is no single author, or even literary category, that can lay claim to being the first science fiction novel—the stimulus from which all else followed. However, some disproportionately influential candidates can be identified.

Part Two begins our discussion of science fiction proper: in the 1920s, Hugo Gernsback virtually assembled the science fiction genre out of a mix of re-prints and imitative new stories (this chapter); and the "Golden Age" of the 1930s, when editor John W. Campbell pushed the evolution of gSF with his strong vision of the genre, and no reticence about advising even the most successful authors on proper material and technique (Chapter 3). To a significant degree, gSF was the creation of these two men; they should be rightly acknowledged as the Mothers of Science Fiction.

No, I'm not confusing gender: these two men were not primarily authors (though both did write and publish fiction), but were magazine editors who nurtured science fiction, often with a heavy hand; their periodicals became the metaphorical womb in which gSF developed. In filling the pages of the first magazine dedicated to science fiction, Gernsback was not sifting through the utopias and earlier adventure fiction. He was picking from more contemporary authors, who were influenced by these traditions, and who published shorter works that could be included or serialized in magazine issues—and ideally which did not require the magazine pay royalties. In Gernsback's own words:

> Edgar Allan Poe may well be called the father of "scientifiction."[1] It was he who really originated the romance, cleverly weaving into and around the story, a scientific thread. Jules Verne, with his amazing romances, also cleverly interwoven with a scientific thread, came next. A little later came H. G. Wells, whose scientifiction stories, like those of his forerunners, have become famous and immortal. (Gernsback 1926)

If Gernsback and Campbell are the maternal ancestors, the *paternal* ones are those earlier authors who contributed the seminal ideas of the nascent genre—not just thematic ideas, but styles of writing, ideals of structure, and even some normative opinions which were to come to define gSF.

In these two chapters, I will run through some of the most likely suspects. There are some caveats. My initial intention was to present the prototypes for gSF's representations of religion—the first generation of schemas from which gSFs evolved. What I found was that the *kinds* of ancestors were much broader than I expected, and within any single kind, multiple opinions about religion were evident. Thus, of my first three candidates (described in *this* chapter), one (Edgar Allen Poe) is *maternal* in the style of Gernsback and Campbell, while the other two are not individuals but *categories* of literature (adventure fiction and late-nineteenth-century utopias), each with heterogeneous views of religion. The next three (in Chapter 3) are more clearly autonomous influences through key works of fiction—but again, I must deviate from expectations. It is traditional within the genre to consider the Fathers of Science Fiction to be "Wells, Verne, and _____." That is, a typical rhetoric is to acknowledge the normative view of Wells and Verne as primary sources (to draw a connection, I believe, with the readers' schema of the genre's ancestry), balanced with a more surprising or obscure third (to make a case for original scholarship *and* a deeper awareness of the genre) (see, e.g., Chatelain and Slusser's introduction to Rosny [2012: ix]). This strategy, too, failed: Verne had little to say about religion. So, I will rely on the almost-as-traditional claim of Mary Shelley as Wells' co-paternal ancestor (again at the risk of gender confusion), juxtaposed by my idiosyncratic favorite: Olaf Stapledon as the "last Victorian."

Poe: Another mother?

Gernsback's candidates for paternity were (in chronological order) Poe, Verne, and Wells. According to Aldiss, Poe's candidacy was first proposed remarkably early—in 1905, the year Verne died, and a mere ten years after the publication of Wells' first novel—though Aldiss comments that the claim seems to be "based more on a thorough ignorance of literature than a thorough knowledge of Poe" (1973: 45).

One problem with Poe is that his attitudes toward science contrast that of early gSF. Stableford (2010: 20–3) includes him as one of the "creators of science fiction," but then focuses on Poe's adolescent "Sonnet—To Science," which Stableford describes as "solidly anchored in the Romantic Movement, likening science's keen-eyed inquiry to a vulture whose wings cast a shadow of 'dull reality' upon the landscape of the imagination" (ibid. p. 20)—hardly a sentiment familiar to fans of the early genre. I personally think of the mature Poe's darkly comic "Some Words with a Mummy" (Poe 1904: v. 5, 103–28) in which a revived Egyptian is utterly unimpressed by modern advancements in architecture, astronomy government, science, etc. (ibid. pp. 122–6). "I then mentioned our steel; but the foreigner elevated his nose, and asked me if our steel could have executed the sharp, carved work seen on the obelisks, and which was wrought altogether by edgetools of copper" (ibid. p. 125). Even the closest parallel among Poe's more famous material—a narrative about a trans-Atlantic balloon voyage (Poe 1904: v. 3, 81–100)—was published as a hoax, though it is of course possible that later authors (e.g., Verne) took rather more earnest inspiration from Poe's little joke.

The 1905 date of the earliest claim of Poe as father of science fiction is problematic as well. This would be a full two decades before Gernsback's *Amazing Stories* began branding science fiction under the original label of "scientifiction," and thus the claim itself is too early to refer to *genre* SF. However, Poe is too *late* to be father of mainstream science fiction (mSF). One of his earliest stories, "The Unparalleled Adventure of One Hans Pfaall," easily qualifies as mSF—it is an earlier balloon hoax, describing travel to the moon rather than across the Atlantic—but was published in 1835, by which year Hartwell (1984: 118) states the "scientific novel" had already begun to emerge as a distinct category of literature.

Further, Poe's claim to being *our* father is undermined by his promiscuity: he was a better father to at least two *other* genres, including mystery and horror fiction. "In the beginning—as far as the received history of the short detective story is concerned—there was Edgar Allen Poe" (Cox 1992: x). My copy of Poe's *Works* (1904) includes volumes on "Tales—The Detection of Crime" (v. 4), "Tales—Mystery and Occultism" (v. 5), "Tales—Fantasy and Extravaganza" (v. 7), as well as adventure stories, humor, and poems; a volume of science fiction is conspicuously missing.

Nevertheless, it is "received wisdom" among fans of gSF that Poe is an ancestor. From a cognitive anthropological perspective, the fact that there *is* such "wisdom" is interesting, and a schema as misleading as this one is arguably *more* culturally significant than one which endures simply by virtue of being accurate (e.g., Hrotic 2012). However shaky Poe's role as Father of gSF, I believe Poe did make a strong contribution—but a *maternal*, not paternal one. Rather than indulge in a revisionist interpretation of his legacy by ignoring that most of his writing was not concerned with science—and the fiction that was had rather cynical views of it—I would suggest we acknowledge our debt to him through acknowledging the success during his lifetime as a literary critic (but see Aldiss 1973: 43), his ability to develop multiple, distinct styles of stories characterized by implicit rules, and his recognition of the possible abuses of such rules (see, e.g., "How to Write a Blackwood Article" [v. 10, pp. 115–30]). That is, perhaps Poe should be remembered not as a father of the science fiction genre, but as the mother of the modern publishing concept of the "genre."

Science fiction on a desert island

Poe may have contributed to categories of fiction having such well-developed rules, but of course more loose genera are ubiquitous to literature. Many of these generated ideas embraced by early gSF authors. For example, Bleiler introduced his exhaustive study of early science fiction (i.e., pre-gSF) with a discussion of relevant "story clusters."

> Writing about the early history of science-fiction could be considered an exercise in oxymoron, for until the late nineteenth century such history does not exist, if by history we mean a chain of development within a reasonable set of bounds.

There do exist, however, a few rather peripheral early literary genres or subgenres that can be considered ancestral or cousinly to science-fiction in displaying motifs or ideas that later were adapted to the wider genre . . . [T]hese include the utopia, the imaginary voyage, and the lunar voyage . . . By the end of the eighteenth century two other story types ancestral to science fiction emerged: the story of the future and the invention story. (Bleiler 1991: xix–xx)

Within any *one* of these ancestral bodies of literature can be found a heterogeneous mix of representations of religion. There is no reason to expect otherwise—it is the homogeneity of twentieth-century gSF which is anomalous. To demonstrate the varieties of religion (and since lunar voyages have already been mentioned as a red herring [Lucian of Samosata, 'Hans Pfaall']), I will limit myself to brief examples from two categories: eighteenth- to early-nineteenth-century adventure stories and (in the next section) late-nineteenth-century to early-twentieth-century utopias.

As exemplar for the former, I would like to present Johann David Wyss. Himself influenced by Daniel Defoe's 1719 *The Life and Strange Surprizing Adventures of Robinson Crusoe*, in 1812 Wyss published *The Swiss Family Robinson*: a tale of rugged self-reliance, depicting the creation of a new way of life in an initially hospitable environment that the protagonists come to love. Though lacking in any clearly science fiction elements (except perhaps the unnaturally diverse biosphere the Robinsons find themselves in), the influences of Wyss's book are far-ranging. Jules Verne was a great fan of Wyss and his many imitators (e.g., the now-forgotten "The Twelve-Year-Old Robinson" and "The Robinson of the Desert") and wrote that he "felt that the story did not really end with the arrival of the *Unicorn*. The surface of the island had not been fully explored" (Verne 1924: iii–iv). Verne went on to write his own sequels: *The Castaways of the Flag* (1923) and *Their Island Home* (1924).

One can see echoes of the Robinsons in many later science fiction heroes (e.g., "Bill Lermer" in Heinlein's [1953b] *Farmer in the Sky*), including post-apocalypse stories in which the protagonists' survival initially depends on the remnants of an absent civilization, but gradually shifts to materials they can produce for themselves (e.g., George Stewart's 1949 *Earth Abides*, see Chapter 6). A facet of Wyss that was not echoed in gSF was his views of religion: the novel is a virtual homily to the Protestant work ethic, as the characters trust in Providence as they tame and exploit the remarkable bounty of His creation, reproducing the culture (including religious) of the European lowlands without critique, speculation, or even a close exploration.

In particular, there is no hint in *The Swiss Family Robinson* of what Baines (1995: 1) described as characteristic of previous, seventeenth-century narratives about adventures to distant lands, in which "the telescope is actually a mirror." For example, in Ludwig Holberg's *Niels Klim's Underground Travels* (1741/1812), the protagonist travels to a utopia-like land inside our hollow Earth, and tries to explain Christianity to their king.

I then explained to him, in a concise manner, the several articles of our faith; at the recital of which he somewhat softened his countenance, attesting that he could readily subscribe to them . . . But when he heard that the Christians were divided into sects without number, and that, upon some differences in matters of faith, people of the same blood and family would cruelly persecute one another, he answered thus: Among us also there are a large variety of different sentiments considering things pertaining to divine worship; But one man does not persecute another for that; all persecution for speculative matters, or errors arising from the sole variety of our perceptions, can spring from nothing but pride, thinking oneself wiser and more penetrating . . . [we tolerate] any one who shall happen to dissent from the received opinions in points of speculation, provided he does so sincerely, and also conforms in practical matters to the public worship of the Deity. (Ibid. p. 129)

Holberg's intent, it seems, was not to explore the possible patterns of religious institutions, but to hold a utopian religion up to contrast the practices of the institutions of his own society. As such, religion as he has encountered it is the result of "errors" and "pride, thinking oneself wiser." Spirituality is acceptable, but not claiming the authority to interpret, let alone mediate. More succinctly: "It is prohibited here, under pain of banishment to the firmament [i.e., above ground], to comment upon the sacred books; and if any presume to dispute about the essence and attributes of God . . . [he is] then confined in the public Bedlam; for they think it is the height of folly to offer to describe or define those things, to which the human mind is as blind as the eyes of an owl to the light of the sun" (ibid. p. 133).

Nor does Wyss display any hint of curiosity about other cultures, albeit fictional ones. In contrast, Robert Paltock in *The Life and Adventures of Peter Wilkins* (1751/1812) displays an almost anthropological enthusiasm for describing the daily lives and customs of the people who inhabit his distant world (in this case, isolated by sea). Paltock even includes a glossary of names and terms, in case one has forgotten that a "Mouch" is a church, "Ragan" means "priest," and a "Hoximo" is a place to bury the dead (Paltock 1751/1812: 347–8).

The traveler is respected there and becomes an important member of their society. Note, he *is* a member: he even marries local and describes how his children are raised. The startlingly modern—and sometimes censored—16th chapter describes the "author's disappointment at first going to bed with his new wife" (cf. Paltock 1751/1844, 1751/1884). Because of his unique origins, he is granted considerable deference, and though he values his Christianity, but he does not place himself *categorically* above "ignorant natives." This extends to his description of "The Religion of the Author's Family" (Paltock 1751/1812: 259–61). He learns that his new wife is conversant with her people's religion, which includes belief in a Supreme Deity, which sometimes inhabits clay idols, and "there are a great number of glumms on purpose to serve him, pray for us to him, and receive his answers" (ibid. p. 261). In short, there was a basic belief system in place on which to build: "I should soon have the satisfaction of bringing her to a more rational knowledge of [the Supreme Being]" (ibid. p. 260), and he soon "had a little Christian church in my own house, and in a flourishing way too, without a schismatic or heretic among us" (ibid. p. 261). Note that Wilkins' missionizing is more a matter of convenience than zeal—he is already married with children when he embarks on perfecting his wife's beliefs and practices, and, even if he *does* hold Christianity to be superior, he does not see local customs as savage nor unholy.

In short, we have here three examples of mid-seventeenth- to early-eighteenth-century adventure fiction, with three very different attitudes relationships with religion: Holberg uses his fictional world to satirize religion, Wyss uses it to *promote* it, and Paltock, within the boundaries of his own society, views it with tolerance and curiosity. Insofar as adventure fiction is one of those "early literary genres or subgenres that can be considered ancestral or cousinly to science-fiction in displaying motifs or ideas that later were adapted to the wider genre" (Bleiler 1991: xi), while the basic structure of an exploration-based narrative is present, as well as a plethora of representations of religion, schemas characteristic of gSF are not. The closest we see to gSF's identity is Paltock's curiously anthropological perspective, which *is* characteristic of the early genre (Barnard 2006), but in our search for the primitive representations of religion in gSF, we need to identify a later ancestor.

Such an ancestor may well be H. Rider Haggard, an extremely popular adventure fiction writer in the late nineteenth century. The worlds Haggard were concerned with were not "lost" (i.e., desert islands, hollow Earths) but colonized, as he famously, and imaginatively, explored "deepest, darkest" Africa in books like *King Solomon's Mines* (1885/1928) and *She* (1886/1928). In tone and technique, Haggard often resembles contemporaries in other "genres": for example, *She* is not told from the dashing hero's point of view, but his rather more educated and unattractive mentor/sidekick "Horace Holly," just as chronicler "Watson" insulates us from detective fiction's "Holmes" (Doyle 1892/1975), and "Dr. Hesselius" occult investigations are related by an editor after his death (Le Fanu 1872/1993)—a technique largely absent from gSF (in which case we are meant to identify directly with the hero), but present in Verne's pre-genre SF novel *Around the World in Eighty Days* (1873/1984).

Haggard's representations of religion, however, are all too familiar to readers of early gSF. One has already been mentioned: the inability of the "natives" in *King Solomon's Mines* to distinguish between magic and science, and the heroes' willingness to use this confusion to their advantage. In *She* (sometimes subtitled "A History of Adventure"), this small-scale pattern is most fully developed in another voyage to unknown regions of Africa.[2] It contains elements of upper-class arrogance, of course: when their boat threatens to capsize, their party responds with "with a sort of howl to Allah from the Arab, a pious ejaculation from myself, and something that was not pious from [their servant] Job" (Haggard 1886/1928: 198).

The British explorers' sense of superiority is most marked in their relationship with "Ayesha"—the queen/goddess of an isolated system of tribes who refer to her only as "She-who-must-be-obeyed." Ayesha has strange powers, including the ability to see from afar, to kill at will, and is apparently immortal; the people live in awe of her, though (served by deaf mutes she was seen only every few years [see, e.g., ibid. p. 215, 219]). After asking Horace Holly about events in the outside world ("The Hebrews, are they yet at Jerusalem? . . . is their Messiah come . . . ?" [ibid. p. 253]), she explains that she *is* immortal, but this and her other powers are not supernatural. Of her apparent clairvoyance, "it is no magic; that is a fiction of ignorance. There is no such thing as magic, though there is such a thing as knowledge of the secrets of Nature" (ibid.

p. 256); her method of immorality was discovered "half by chance and half by learning" (ibid. p. 255).

Despite her lofty status, she views Holly as, if not an equal, then a peer to be treated with some respect—unlike the tribes which serve her, who either do not deserve or would not understand her explanations. When asked about the customs of her people, Ayesha answers, "My people! speak [sic] not to me of my people . . . these slaves are no people of mine, they are but dogs to do my bidding . . . call me not queen—I am sick of flattery and titles—call me Ayesha, the name hath a sweet sound in mine ears" (ibid. p. 257). In due time, she declares her love for one of the explorers and offers to share the secret to immortality.

Religion in *She* is an institutionalized form of Clarke's Law: the ignorant cannot understand, so view her as divine. For her part, it is convenient for Ayesha to accept their worship—it is an effective method of controlling the population and of imposing a kind of social order. But "we" are capable of understanding the reality behind the illusion, and are, thus, *almost* her equal.

Haggard does seem to include schemas, including representations of religious social systems, that prefigure the schemas of gSF. However, "adventure fiction" is far more varied than gSF, and it would seem (especially given the contrast between gSF and earlier adventure stories, such as those mentioned above) that it would not be profitable to look much earlier than Haggard's day for the raw materials from which the genre was constructed—which would be reasonable, given that the late Victorian era is precisely the generation of available (and copyright-free) texts for periodical editors who (like Gernsback) had limited budgets and pages to fill, while being rich sources of ideas for later authors. Of this rich source of raw materials, Haggard's schemas echo most strongly.

U- and dys-topias

Utopia fiction was very popular in the late nineteenth century, following the popular success of Edward Bellamy's *Looking Backward: 2000–1887* (1888). Inspired by Bellamy—whom John Dewey called "a great American prophet" (quoted in Westbrook 1991: 454)—utopias became something of a fad, with dozens written specifically in response to *Looking Backward* (Bellamy 1888/1986: 24). Bellamy's works were, by some, not seen merely as *commentary* on contemporary society,[3] but as serious suggestions: 162 clubs were created intending to put his "lessons" into practice, as was a prosthelytizing journal (*The Nationalist*) (ibid. pp. 19–20). "The moral crusade of education proceeded . . . in dedication to principles enunciated in *Looking Backward*" (Bellamy 1887/1986: 19–20). Bellamy himself participated regularly in the journal (e.g., 1889b, 1890), explaining that his initial goal was to set a "literary fantasy" in the year *3,000*, but decided instead to write "a romance of the ideal nation" instead of one of "an ideal world" (1889a). From an anthropological perspective, it is noteworthy that Bellamy's fiction was incorporated into readers' individual identity, as well as the construction of loose corporate identities in ways one tends to associate with gSF two generations later. From a critical perspective, the connection between utopias and later pulp science fiction is clear, but under-recognized (Milner and Savage 2008).

At this point, an authorial confession may be in order. I found it extremely difficult to decide what to do with the late-nineteenth-century utopia novel tradition. As polemics and sermons on the societal effects of technological and other progresses—Disch called *Looking Backward* "the first sustained fictional presentation of the modern welfare state" (1998: 104)—they are compelling to anyone interested in gSF schema. Plus, it is simply a rich body of literature. There is a body of impressive, feminist utopias, including Charlotte Perkins Gilman's *Herland* (1915/1998) and Mary Bradley Lane's *Mizora* (1880–1881 [serialized]/1975). (See Teitler [1975] for examples of contemporary literary responses; Donawerth and Kolmerten [1994] for critical analyses.) There is a fascinating community of readers which grew around Bellamy's *Looking Backward* (1889). As critical as some of these are of religion, others were written as deliberate religious expression (e.g., Benson's *Lord of the World* [1908]) . . . frankly, it is difficult to know where to stop. It would be tempting to ignore them altogether—but that would be impossible, given a variety of representations of religion even more varied than we see in the adventure novel, compressed in a brief span of time, contemporary with the popularity of Wells, Verne, and Haggard. As compromise, I have simply chosen some of my favorites, but understand these are just the tip of an iceberg.

Bleiler (1991, discussed above) includes utopias as one of the "story clusters" ancestral to gSF. For the early gSF author, these utopias could have been a rich source of ideas that could be "borrowed" as appropriate, including speculations as to what religion was, could, and should be. Indeed, utopias were still common as the first dedicated science fiction periodical was published in 1926. It would be surprising if there *wasn't* some degree of imitation.

But for all its similarities (the imaginative construction of a distant, social world with different technologies and cultures), the differences between utopias and gSF are telling. In distinguishing between gSF and classic utopias (Plato, Thomas More, Jonathan Swift, etc.) as well as contemporary "mainstream" dystopias (e.g., Aldous Huxley, George Orwell), Asimov (1983: 340–5) argued that nongenre examples lacked the "intent" of modern science fiction. Unlike gSF, these authors' goals were to critique and sometimes satirize contemporary societies: to hold up a funhouse mirror that encouraged the reader to see their world differently—to draw attention to failures, inequities, even unexamined bizarreness of the reader's own society. gSF, on the other hand, was dedicated to exploring the possible directions of change and thus is focused primarily on the fictitious society itself, and preferred worlds in which the nature or extent of technology differs from our own (ibid. p. 345). Also, it must be said that the target audience for the first magazines was rather more interested in adolescent adventure over serious social commentary. "What does a youngster make of *Gulliver's Travels*? He considers it an English *Sinbad*" (ibid. p. 347).

One such element which failed to find fertile ground in the gSF periodicals was discussion of gender roles, despite a well-developed presence in the utopias as well as significant attention in other literatures (cf. the confessional memoir, beginning with Mary MacLane [1902/2013]). Consider Annie Denton Cridge's wonderfully titled

Man's Rights; or, How Would You Like It? (no date, but Bleiler [1991] places it c. 1870) in which the author lampoons gender roles by reversing stereotypes:

> I looked into the churches, which were principally filled with elegantly-dressed gentlemen. "Ah!" I said to myself, "in religion these down-trodden men find some consolation;" but, in an instant, I was shocked by realizing that more than half went from custom, or to show their dress and see the fashions. (Cridge n.d.: 18)

Dentith (1995) argues that this "inversion" of contemporary society typifies the utopia above creating new societies out of whole cloth. Quoting George Eliot, he compares the ease in which one can represent a fully fantastical beast like a griffin with the more difficult but also more satisfying task of representing a real-life lion.

> Certainly utopian writing can be of little interest if it seeks only to draw griffins, that is, if its visions are unconstrained by "susceptibility to the veriest minutiae of experience": but if it seeks to construct "fresh and fresh wholes," with a creative energy that is indeed susceptible to the "veriest minutiae of experience," then perhaps we are nearer to an imaginative transformation. (Ibid. p. 137)

He then proceeds to speculate as to what inversions are present in the texts he describes, noting, "At a fundamental level none of these texts are even comprehensible without the constant reference that they make to the society to which the utopian place offers a contrast" (ibid. p. 138).

Two caveats must be made. First, utopias are necessarily situated in the place and time of their creation—a twenty-first-century reader of a nineteenth-century-utopia might not recognize contemporary social references. It does not follow that the later reader cannot *enjoy* the novel. Rather, there are layers to a utopia novel that will not be recognized; indeed, the utopia might be read *as if* it were imaginative science fiction. Second, the griffin/lion relationship is not a dichotomy but a continuum: how *direct* is the connection between the text and real life? It is meant to consciously target a specific element of known society—that is, is it a utopia in Dentith's sense? Or does it address more abstract issues such as the flexibility of human identity (i.e., more generally relevant and closer to Asimov's view of science fiction)? For our purposes, the latter form of utopia is more ancestral to gSF, and (thus) the representations of religion in the more "imaginative" utopias are more relevant than situation-specific commentaries.

For example, Mark Twain's story "The Secret History of Eddypus, the World-Empire" (Twain 2003: 176–225 [written in 1901–1902]) projected the Christian Science of his own time into a satirical future, complete with an absolute theocracy, a shaky knowledge of history (George "Wishington had a younger brother by the name of Napoolyun Bonyprat, but of him we know nothing" [ibid. p. 185]), the "prodigious" destruction of books (ibid. p. 181), and an inability to distinguish fact from fiction (due to Twain's novels he is remembered as the "Father of History" [ibid. p. 190]). Even the narrative structure has later echoes (e.g., Jacomb's *And a New Earth* [1926], discussed below). However, our interest is in opinions of religion in general, not any specific example. Given Twain's extended writings expressing his dislike of founder of Christian

Science Mary Eddy (Twain 1899/n.d.), and "the movement's tendencies towards institutionalization and commercialization" (Gillian 1998: 457), we cannot extract from "Secret History" any normative views of what religion will and should be.

One normative view which *would* seem to be relevant to gSF was the intellectual trend in nineteenth-century academia to dismiss religion as a relic of a barbarous past. To use nineteenth-century philosopher and historian of religion Ernest Renan as a representative voice:

> The worst social state . . . is the theocratic state, like Islamism or the ancient Pontifical state, in which dogma reigns supreme. Nations with an exclusive state religion, like Spain, are not much better off. Nations in which a religion of the majority is recognized are also exposed to serious drawbacks . . . As long as the masses were believers, that is to say, as long as the same sentiments were almost universally professed by a people, freedom of research and discussion was impossible. A colossal weight of stupidity pressed down upon the human mind.
>
> [. . .] This is a state of things which is coming to an end in our time, and we cannot be surprised if some disturbance ensues. There are no longer masses which believe; a great number of the people decline to recognise the supernatural, and the day is not far distant, when beliefs of this kind will die out altogether in the masses, just as the belief in familiar spirits and ghosts have disappeared. (Renan 1883: xvi–xvii)

However, he continues:

> Now beliefs are only dangerous when they represent something like unanimity, or an unquestionable majority. When they are merely individual, there is not a word to be said against them, and it is our duty to treat them with the respect which they do not always exhibit for their adversaries. (Ibid. p. xvii)

And elsewhere:

> The brain, parched by reasoning, thirsts for simplicity, like the desert for spring water. When reflection has brought us up to the last limit of doubt, the spontaneous affirmation of the good and of the beautiful which is to be found in the female conscience delights us and settles the question for us. This is why religion is preserved to the world by woman alone. A beautiful and a virtuous woman is the mirage which peoples with lakes and green avenues our great moral desert . . . Woman restores us to communication with the eternal spring in which God reflects Himself. (Ibid. p. xii)

Religion, among some of the nineteenth century's intelligentsia at least, is acceptable so long as it is an individual expression, not a social institution—that is, so long as "religion" is not defined the way I define it in this book. Compare this to how Jesus Christ is represented in Harben's "In the Year 10,000" (1892/1978): "He was a spiritual genius . . . he himself was killed by men who were too barbarous to understand him. But long after his death his words were remembered. People were not civilized enough to put his teachings into practice . . . And when he had been dead for several centuries, people began to say he was the Son of God." He then elaborates on why exactly this is a problem: "The numerous beliefs about the personality and laws of the creator caused more bloodshed in the gloomy days of the past than anything else. Religion was the foundation of many of the most horrible wars" (1892/1978: 400–01).

Also, "religion" as Renan approaches it is dichotomous to the rational, the complex . . . and to the male. Perhaps here we see one of the trends that lend to a perceived conflict between religion and that most rational, complex, and non-spontaneous of institutions: science.

It might be interesting, then, to see how the feminist utopias envisioned the future of religion. The two greatest of these are Mary Bradley Lane's *Mizora* (1880–1881/1975)—a very early Victorian utopia, predating Bellamy's by some years—and the fairly late *Herland* (1915/1998) by Charlotte Perkins Gilman (more famous now as the author of "The Yellow Wallpaper"). Both women envision a society in a remote region (Lane's is a hollow Earth story) without men, arguing in effect that the dominant assumptions about women's roles and abilities are just that: societal assumptions, not laws of nature. Visitors from outside (a lone woman for Lane, three men for Gilman) are surprised at the competence and independence of the people they find. Also, all are surprised and/or shocked at the apparent absence of formalized religion.

> "Where do you perform your religious rites and ceremonies?"
>
> She looked at me with surprise.
>
> "You ask me such strange questions that I am tempted to believe you a relic of ancient mythology . . . or slept for ages in unchanged possession of ancient superstition [. . .] If you want me to answer your superstitious notions of religion, I will, in one sentence, explain, that the only religious idea in Mizora is: Nature is God, and God is Nature" . . .
>
> "But how," I asked in bewildered astonishment, "how can you think of living without creeds, and confessionals? How can you prosper without prayer? How can you be upright, and honest, and true to yourselves and your friends without praying for divine grace and strength to sustain you? How can you be noble, and keep from envying your neighbors, without a prayer for divine grace to assist you to resist such temptation?"
>
> "Oh, daughter of the dark ages," said Wauna, sadly, "turn to the benevolent and ever-willing Science." (Lane 1880–1881/1975: 119–21)

The male visitors in Gilman's story are also confused by a near lack of religion, beyond a deification of maternity.

> What Terry meant by saying they had no "modesty" was that this great life-view had no shady places; they had a high sense of personal decorum, but no shame—and no knowledge of anything to be ashamed of.
>
> Even their shortcomings and misdeeds in childhood never were presented to them as sins; merely as errors and misplays—as in a game. Some of them, who were palpably less agreeable than others or who had a real weakness or fault, were

treated with cheerful allowance, as a friendly group at whist would treat a poor player.

Their religion, you see, was maternal; and their ethics, based on the full perception of evolution, showed the principle of growth and the beauty of wise culture. They had no theory of the essential opposition of good and evil. (Gilman 1915/1998: 87)

"Our" beliefs were equally incomprehensible to them. When one of the men was talked to one of them about outside religion, he chances to mention the Catholic principle of infant damnation. She became very still, went pale, and quickly runs to the nearest "temple" in a terror. She quickly returns, relieved, as the woman she finds there (not a priestess, and they did not understand the word "worship") explains:

> "[Y]ou've got the wrong idea altogether. You do not have to think that there ever was such a God—for there wasn't. Or such a happening—for there wasn't. Nor even that this hideous false idea was believed by anybody. But only this—that people who are utterly ignorant will believe anything—which you certainly knew before." (Ibid. p. 94)

So much for Renan's supposition that women are the link to simplicity and spirituality.

Not all utopias envisioned a world without religion. Jacomb's *And a New Earth* (1926), in fact, seems to see religion as inevitable and—flawed as it may currently be—perfectable. It begins with a framing story, describing newly discovered documents that record the origins of the future society before the Second Flood in year 1 of the new era (a.k.a. AD 1958). The primary narrative is not entirely pleasant, given its heavy-handed rhetoric and simplistic characters, and the recurrence of prejudiced descriptions of the character of the poor, women, Jews, and anyone with dark skin (e.g., pp. 85, 119, 115, 123–4, respectively). While I resist conflating the personal opinions of any author with fictional descriptions (especially given the speculative nature of utopia and gSF texts), in this case the Author's Note explains that the "mentality, opinions, and beliefs" portrayed in the book are ones he personally holds, before explaining carefully that the name Jacomb is Italian in origin, "and possesses no Hebraic origin whatever" (ibid. p. 5).

Nevertheless, the treatments of religion and of science are interesting. First, science is assumed to be socially beneficial and progressive. In a cyclical description of great civilizations' rise and fall, the protagonists' choice of heroes is telling: the king of Babel, traditionally accused of hubris against God, but interpreted here as held back by men of conservative vision; Daedalus, inventor of a flying machine; the rebellious Prometheus—"*I* think of Prometheus as a learned scientist, and picture him in his laboratory in some great city, experimenting to wrest the power from the atom" (ibid. p. 80).

Second, religion in the sense of beliefs and perhaps theology is distinguished from religious hierarchies: while religious ideas are promoted, traditional religious leaders are alternatively pitied and ridiculed. The protagonist of the main story—who is not overburdened by modesty—sets about to find a project in order to benefit humanity with his considerable wealth. After dismissing more mundane avenues (e.g., endow hospitals, employ thousands in building projects, etc.), he decides to hit at the root of human suffering. He initially finds it inexplicable that, despite technological achievements and the "inherent goodness of humanity," war, poverty, and disease continue to exist. He concludes that luxuries will always be in short supply, and as a result "strong or cunning individuals were ready to requisition the services of weak or less clever individuals," and that leaders (including "Hierarchies of priests") tend to work to maintain their disproportionate share (ibid. pp. 74–8).

Religion in *And a New Earth* does not necessarily have negative societal impacts: it is the leaders and their self-interested interpretations that have been the problem. Indeed, Jesuits are described as educators and (as a result?) as members of "a great religious order" (ibid. p. 81). In principle, religion here seems to be a tool used by people to solidify their power, as a goad to action, and a means of maintaining identity; as such, religion should perhaps be judged purely on its effects. Indeed, he himself decides that in creating his new order he cannot dismiss religion, based on the recognition that the recurrence of religion in human history suggests that "men and women have felt the necessity of believing in something or someone outside their immediate surroundings," and "the vastness of the Universe must possess in addition to order and design, some purpose in which the human race might expect to play a part" (ibid. p. 131).

The description of the history of the Jewish people is a case in point. "This race was small, extremely individual, and greatly skilled in the arts of war: moreover, its rulers were extraordinarily ambitious. By reasons of promises contained in their holy books that they had been chosen by God as the ruling nation . . . these ambitions were believed in and shared by the whole race." The protagonist implies a degree of respect for their ability to maintain an identity despite captivities and diasporas—until they rejected their looked-for Messiah, who, being accepted by everyone *else*, put them at a disadvantage and pitted them inevitably against the Christians. In a disturbingly anti-Semitic passage, he describes a "secret Jewish hierarchy" engaged in a centuries-long struggle to overthrow established governments, sparking the Bolshevik Revolution and hating others as they have been hated (ibid. pp. 84–90).

In contrast, the protagonist not only acknowledges Jesus, but is (alone) able to recognize his true significance. Jesus reflected the source of the human mind and thus the only part of nature irreducible to electrons. By means of his miracles, he demonstrated "complete mastery over matter"; by dedicating his life to improving the lot of others, he proved his divinity. The echoes of Daedalus and Prometheus are clear, as is the connection to the king of Babel, whose legacy was similarly misinterpreted. "Christianity was certainly not taught in any of the churches labelling themselves Christian," with even the Bible fragmented, with clear signs "of sub-editing, if not actual forgery on the part of the church hierarchs" (ibid. pp. 137–8). He summarizes his "higher Christianity" in one ironic word: "Tolerance." There is to be "no elaborate church to give an excuse for the formation of a Priesthood which could do its contemporaries no good, but could do them considerable harm," and basing his new belief system on Christianity is justified by "its promise of a Kingdom of Heaven *on earth*" (ibid. pp. 139–41, emphasis in original). In sum, the only restriction on human behavior was that anyone harming another was harmed in turn; otherwise, moral rules were abandoned as they merely created opportunities to sin. For example, sexual activity was no longer to be regulated by monogamy. "Being free, woman need no longer await man's sanction for her actions, but could obey the dictates of Nature as taught by her own heart . . . by the removal of manufactured sin, it lifted love from the slough of subservience, distrust, and fear" (ibid. p. 148).

Having set up his perfect society on an isolated island, conflict with the outside world was sparked by the accidental arrival of an Anglican priest, who (naturally) ignores his host's direction not to explore the island. "I was foolish in overestimating his sense of decorum, and in underestimating his ecclesiastical curiosity" (ibid. p. 155). Suffice it to say that the sexual awareness of the young men and women on the island sparked "a torrent of perfervid oratory . . . [in which] he scourged his surprised and astonished audience with the direst threats contained in his religion" (ibid. p. 157).

> I cannot find it in my heart to blame the poor man. His life had been spent in half-blind civilisation, he was imbued to the marrow with the worst sort of its obsolete traditions, and he was soaked to the soul in superstitions whose outward manifestations involved the strictest principles of puritanical negation. (Ibid. p. 157)

The priest's report causes the English church to force a military confrontation which, due to their technological and moral superiority, the islanders easily win.

The book ends with a global natural disaster. I leave it to my readers to guess how well the islanders fare, relative to lesser civilizations.

In *And a New Earth*, religion and science are not opposed. Both are tools, and if the author has greater confidence in the beneficial impacts of science over religion, it remains that religion is described as a necessary part of human life. Unfortunately, this particular social tool has been misused for the benefit of a few at the expense of the many—but, as human nature can be improved, the perfection of religion is possible.

Other utopias are suspicious of such blithe claims that religion is merely a relic of the past or a challenge to overcome. Like *And a New Earth*, Victor Rousseau's *The Messiah of the Cylinder* (1917, originally published in *Everybody's Magazine*) argues that mankind's essentially religious nature is acknowledged. In this case, however, religion has a civilizing, rather than manipulating effect, and if blind belief represents a problem, such behaviors are not the purvey of religion alone. In *Messiah*, eugenics proponent Lazaroff is presented as fanatical as any religionist, placing too much faith in the perfectibility of human nature, in this exchange between his employer and prospective father-in-law.

> "You [eugenists] think that human nature has changed; that the fury of the Crusades will never be renewed in fantastic social wars, and the madness of religious fratricide in the madness of Science become Faith. All the old evils are lying low, lurking in the minds of men, ready to spring forth in all their ancient

fury . . . I sometimes think that Holy Russia has man's future in her charge. For without Christianity the moral nature of man will be where it has been in ages past. Social and economic readjustments leave it unchanged."

"A religion of slaves, of the weak and incompetent," said Lazaroff loudly.

"You think, then, that human passions have become emulsified by education? What a delusion!" (Rousseau 1917: 13)

Elsewhere in *Messiah*, what finally "flung half the civilized world back into paganism" was Protestantism's collapse, brought on by compromise on divorce and other changes which undermined "the old ideal of the family as the unit of society" (ibid. p. 179).

As a later example of sympathetic views of religion, consider M. Jaeger's fairly late *The Question Mark* (1926). She (Bleiler [1991: 388–9] identifies the author as *Muriel* Jaeger) begins with an introduction expressing her appreciation of previous utopias, noting "They become more and more numerous and more and more insistent" (Jaeger 1926: 9). She attributes this popularity to the growing belief that change is inevitable, and the growing body of ethnographic, theoretic, and even experimental evidence ("the small half-playful model communities of the past" [ibid. p. 9]) that human society can be more perfect. However possible she finds Utopias, Utopians appear less plausible.

> I accept the Bellamy-Morris-Wells world in all essentials—with one exception; I do not and cannot accept its inhabitants. At this point my effort to realize Utopia fails. With the best will in the world, I have found myself quite unable to believe in these wise, virtuous, gentle, artistic people. They do not seem to have any relation to humanity as I know it. (Ibid. pp. 11–12)

Our visitor from the twentieth century finds in the twenty-second an ideal world society in which basic needs and most wants are met with little effort. As "Guy" gains familiarity, however, not all aspects of the society are as easily accepted: assisted suicide, capital punishment, and euthanasia for the "hopelessly diseased or insane or unsocial" (ibid. p. 167). More fundamentally disturbing to Martin, our species seems to have diverged into "intellectual" and "normal" subspecies, the later dependent on the former. The latter are almost childlike in their susceptibility to emotions (e.g., ibid. pp. 157–8), and more prone to suicide due to an "emotional *impasse*"—intellectuals, by contrast, are emotionally detached and generally find the world too interesting to voluntarily leave it (ibid. p. 168).

Centralized religion remains, but reflects the "intellectuals" mode of thinking, and appears unable to meet all of the needs (e.g., emotional) of the "normals." A charismatic leader is becoming popular: a New Franciscan friar named Emmanuel.

Guy's closest friend among the intellectuals, John, laughingly shows him a newspaper article about him, noting "He believes what he says, and a man who does that always makes an effect of some sort" (ibid. p. 197) and later criticizing a journalist as a "sham intellectual" for wondering if Emmanuel's prophesies and apparent miracles could have some significance (ibid. p. 199). Guy and the "normals" do not dismiss Emmanuel so lightly, including a dysfunctionally eccentric man Guy had befriended, who seems to have taken great strides toward mental health after hearing Emmanuel speak.

Then one day came the great startling headlines:

> "Emmanuel claims to be the Messiah. Can it be true? End of the World prophesied for next Sunday. Half London goes into the Fields."

> The paper described scenes of "indescribable" enthusiasm—the flocking of huge multitudes of people out of town and from the surrounding country; there were more miracles and spiritual voices heard; an aura of light had been seen to play about the self-styled Messiah. It was added that the Pope was dispatching a special legate to inquire into the new religious movement. (Ibid. p. 204)

The intellectual John is cynically grateful that Emmanuel's prophesized end of the world was believed to take place quite soon, so—once proven wrong—life could return to normal as quickly as possible. He then suggests they attend after all, as a lark, perhaps adding "a new play with a religious motif" to the party (ibid. pp. 207–8). When the moment approaches, huge crowds are singing, praying, bowing; at the precise moment, Emmanuel falls over. Nothing else happens. "'Fainted or dead, it is the end of this Messiah' . . . John laughed and said: 'Most of [Emmanuel's followers] will be back to-morrow—all who are not drunk. Even a normal's religion won't stand up against such a cold shower-bath as this'" (ibid. p. 214).

After, Guy and John argue about John's derision of Emmanuel and the "normals." John retorts that, in his day, the normals would have been considered morbid and hysterical. "There isn't one of them that wouldn't have been called a crank in the old times" (ibid. p. 217)—but the "intellectuals" are worse: they understand the injustices of the world, could do something about them, but do not because *they* are happy . . . as so many times before, the elite are happy at the expense of normals. "I would rather a thousand times be one of them than one of you!" (ibid. p. 219).

What are we to make of this? Given Jaeger's introduction, it would seem that those who suggest that disposing of religion would heal class-based ills are naïve; that doing so would not change human nature; part of human nature is moderation—neither reflexive religious obeisance nor cynical atheism is really *normal*.

Conclusion

The take-home message of genres ancestral to gSF (e.g., adventure novels *and* utopias) is, I think, that it would be misleading to approach them as diluted examples of "proto-SF," as if they represented a more primitive form of science fiction in which various imperfections had yet to be sifted out. Rather, they should be considered genres in their own rights.

Much of the variation in these utopias was not present in the early gSF periodicals. They lack imitators not through lack of quality, but because they did not match the goals of the creators of gSF in the early twentieth century. They spread the wrong ideas, unwanted schema: for example, the preceding surge of utopia novels (Teitler

1975: ix), such as Gilman's (1915/1998) and Lane's ([serialized] 1880–1881/1975). The absence of feminism in early gSF only emphasizes its masculine character; Bleiler's (1998) list of motifs does not list gender, feminism, or anything of the sort—though "women stressed" does appear (p. xx). Similarly, generally positive representations of religion (in particular religiously motivated works) and more negative portraits of technology were certainly common in nineteenth-century utopias, but did not make the cut.

3

Uncertain Paternity

For reasons outlined in the previous chapter, the origins of genre science fiction (gSF) are multiple *and* varied. Not only are there many sources, but many *kinds* of sources. The previous chapter looked at ancestral genres, and both mentioned that Jules Verne and H. G. Wells are broadly assumed to be the Fathers of gSF, and pointed out the recurring rhetoric of describing the Fathers of gSF as "Wells, Verne, and _____," the writer choosing a third to emphasize those aspects of gSF they deem most important. Thus, I have chosen the three that best illustrate the problem of tracing the origins of gSF's schema of religion: Shelley, Wells, and Stapledon.

The fatherhood of Mary Shelley

Especially as promoted by gSF author, editor, and historian Brian Aldiss (1973: 7–39), Mary Wollstonecraft Shelley's 1818 *Frankenstein* has become known as a strong candidate for the first modern science fiction novel. Appropriately, Aldiss titles his chapter on Shelley "The Origins of the Species." The relevance is obvious: Shelley specifically explores not simply possible technologies or possible applications, but the *impacts* of such efforts. Aldiss argued, "Frankenstein was the archetype of the scientist whose research, pursued in the sacred name of increasing knowledge, takes on a life of its own and causes untold misery before being brought under control" (quoted in Bainbridge 1986: 107).

In considering Shelley's legacy, Disch focuses on a particular statement from Aldiss: "For a thousand people familiar with the story . . . not one will have read the original novel" (Aldiss, quoted in Disch 1998: 33). (Similarly, Stableford notes that people forget "Frankenstein" refers to the scientist, not the creature [Stableford 1995: 47].) Disch then argues that *Frankenstein* cannot be (as Aldiss claims) "the first great myth of the industrial age" (Aldiss, quoted in Disch 1998: 33). "An unread author is no one's intellectual ancestor" (Disch 1998: 33). Indeed, it is impossible to consider *Frankenstein* as *genre* SF, as it predates any colleagues by half a century, and, though "it began the exploration of imaginative territory into which no previous author has penetrated,"

Stableford notes that speculation "was not its initial purpose" (1995: 48). Insofar as Shelley may be seen to explore the possible negative effects of irresponsible scientific advancement, this attitude did not typify gSF until the 1940s (see Chapter 5).

Ironically, these observations actually cement Shelley's position as one of the important Fathers of science fiction. In his work on religious myth, Paden notes that myths are not like regular stories, but are instead the stories that really *matter*; that define us and form part of our mental world (Paden 1994: 69–73), that can be simultaneously "profoundly true" *and* "merely imaginary" (ibid. p. 70). "Stories that simply spin imaginative accounts of supernatural beings but that have no sacred status and force for defining human behavior are just folktales" (ibid. p. 73). This particular narrative displays a life independent of the 1818 text: consider the frequency with which we continue to revisit, reenact, and reinvent the Frankenstein myth almost two centuries from its creation; the varieties of critical interpretations that have been applied, for example, "The monster . . . is in a sense a *tabula rasa*, and the evil that he does, he is shaped to do by the revulsion and persecution of others . . . Alternatively, he can be thought of as an embodiment of the evil latent in mankind" (Clute and Nicholls 1995: 1099). This shows that Shelley's creation remains an important foundational myth of gSF and has indeed become one of the root metaphors of Western culture. I would strongly disagree with Stableford's opinion that "*Frankenstein*-the-novel is a book well worth having even if *Frankenstein*-the-myth is a nest of viperish ideas we could well do without" (2010: 18). Shelley's work has not been diluted; it has been expanded enormously.

What was Shelley's contribution to the later genre conceptions of religion vis à vis science? There would seem to be a strongly implied warning to scientists' encroachment of God's domain; Frankenstein's foray into the role of life creator proved disastrous and ultimately futile. However, Frankenstein's transgressions were not necessarily into the domain of *God* as creator; one could as easily argue that Frankenstein as scientist may have been successful, but that Frankenstein as *mother* exemplified the fatality of his pride. (I cannot resist noting that this perspective was endorsed by Mel Brooks— the director of that most sublime of Frankenstein satires, *Young Frankenstein* ["Mel Brooks" 2013].)

However, the dangers of transgressions (be it against God or woman) are not the only interpretation. One of the self-imposed rules of this book is to privilege the common interpretations of a work above an author's intent, especially when these diverge—*Frankenstein* is complicated by the fact that no single interpretation has dominated, and there is ample evidence to see *Frankenstein* as *pro*-science. For example, though she apparently did not challenge such interpretations later in life, Shelley apparently did not initially intend to promote pro-religious and anti-scientific sentiment (Stableford 2010: 17). Stableford also emphasizes the subtitle of *Frankenstein*, which sympathetically identifies Frankenstein as a modern Prometheus, suggesting he should be viewed more as heroic, misunderstood victim rather than mad fool (ibid. p. 12). For oblique implications, one might note that in Shelley's husband's play *Prometheus Unbound* (published soon after *Frankenstein*) the eponymous hero can be free only after the king of the gods is dethroned. My personal reaction was that *Frankenstein* should be read as a cautionary tale not against scientific exploration so much as failing to assume responsibility for the results of one's actions. Perhaps it is precisely the ambiguity that makes *Frankenstein* such a potent myth—there are no clear statements about the religious *nor the social* significance of Frankenstein's actions, allowing each generation to re-invent it.

In short, whether or not *Frankenstein* is the first authentic science fiction novel (stipulating for the moment that such a claim would be possible, given the varieties of definitions), the general acceptance of Shelley's role and the ubiquity of the Frankenstein narrative confirm her position not just as an ancestor of women in gSF (Donawerth 1997), but as a Father of science fiction. However, its comment on religion is at the very least ambiguous. In fact, the clearest representation of the societal nature of religion is in her *second best*-remembered book, *The Last Man* (1826), which begins with an unambiguous passage, spoken without irony by an admirable protagonist: "So true it is, that man's mind alone was the creator of all that was good or great to man, and that Nature herself was only his first minister" (ibid. pp. 1–2).

H. G. Wells' social speculations

Finally, we come to the most famous of the Fathers of science fiction: the Victorians Jules Verne and H. G. Wells. First, why Victorians? Part of the reason is practical— the late-nineteenth- and early-twentieth-century texts were the most freely (in both senses of the word) available to early gSF periodical editors. Also, I would suggest the association with a more democratic technological advancement is attractive for reasons of its own: Gernsback's original audience was full of electronics hobbyists, after all, and given the rugged individualism of the typical gSF hero, the generation of heroes like Tesla and Edison suits the *Zeitgeist* Gernsback was trying to construct (see also Aldiss [1973: 81–112] on "The Gas Enlightened Race"). As a result, when late *twentieth*-century fans feel nostalgic, this is the generation to which they return (Hrotic 2013). (Unfortunately, one can only imagine the result of modern gSF authors feeling nostalgic about *other* ages of dramatic technological advancement and change, such as the Elizabethan rather than Victorian Age [cf. Harkness 2007].)

In any case, the fact that Verne and Wells are the most significant of the Victorians is another piece of received wisdom. It does not follow, however, that Verne and Wells intended to create a new genre, nor that they were operating in concert—and neither claimed to be a Father of science fiction, nor claimed the *other* was (Clute and Nicholls 1995: 1275). It fact, they arguably had little in common.

> [T]here was a disposition on the part of literary journals at one time to call me the English Jules Verne. As a matter of fact there is no literary resemblance whatever between the anticipatory inventions of the great Frenchman and [my] fantasies. His work dealt almost always with actual possibilities of invention and discovery, and he made some remarkable forecasts. The interest he invoked was a practical one; he wrote and believed and told that this or that thing could be done, which was not at that time done . . . But these stories of mine collected here do not pretend to deal with possible things; they are exercises of the imagination in a

quite different field . . . they do not aim to project a serious possibility; they aim indeed only at the same amount of conviction as one gets in a good gripping dream (Wells 1934/1978: iii).

Verne agreed: "No, there is no *rapport* between his work and mine. I make use of physics. He invents" (quoted in Philmus 1970: 31).

As a simplistic rule of thumb, one could say that Wells was concerned with speculating on the development of social issues—how current trajectories would extend, social reactions to invasions—in which technological developments are merely one facet. For the strongest example, see Wells' *The Shape of Things to Come* (1933/2006). Verne, on the other hand, focused more on speculations about technology, especially *applications* of existing technology: he did not invent the balloon or the submarine, but imagined what remarkable things one could *do* with them. A commonsense characteristic of gSF is to speculate on the social impacts of future technologies: Verne rarely did either. "One expects such a futurist to have been a progressive. One discovers an idiosyncratic conservative. Surely one expects to meet an apostle of progress. But Verne ended his life issuing jeremiads about the dangers of another Dark Age" (McDougall 2001).

Ironically, I have little else to say about Verne, simply because, in his fiction, he had little to say about religion as an institution. For example, "The Master of the World" (Verne 1928) shows the dangers of a lack of humility in the face of human mortality, but does not suggest a religious institution would fill the gap; his last story, "The Eternal Adam" (Verne 1957), echoes a religious myth (it describes a Noah-like survivor of a *man*-made disastrous flood), but does not focus on religion. "Clergymen and the Church are strikingly absent in his novels. Only two priests of any importance appear in the sixty-four volumes, and they function as the partisan leaders of oppressed nations rather than spokesmen for theology. God, on the other hand, is omnipresent both as the Divine Architect and the Providential force behind events . . . Verne refers to the mysterious purposes of God, The Creator, or Providence [or elsewhere] as Nature, Fate, Destiny, Chance, or just The Unknown" (McDougall 2001). We might speculate that Verne's relatively devout Catholicism may have restricted his willingness to speculate in such areas, but our interest here is the schema present in an author's works, not privately held views.

Wells is fortunately more forthcoming. His works elicit much of the religious: the theological implications of his works were discussed early in the twentieth century in light of spiritual "wants of this perplexed and inquiring age" (Craufurd 1909: viii). For specific depictions of religious systems, I will mention the two most interesting.

The first is *When the Sleeper Wakes*, serialized between 1898 and 1899 in *The Graphic*. The setup is simple: "Graham," a man from Wells' time, falls into a catatonic-like sleep, and does not wake up. A side effect of his condition is that his body does not age; doctors are able to keep him alive (though continually unconscious) until the year 2100, when he abruptly awakes.

Wells' rather brilliant (and often imitated) twist is that, after 200 years of compounding interest, Graham's savings are the foundation of society's economy. The world has become a plutocracy ruled by a Council who controls Graham's fortune.

Understandably, they are not pleased by the possibility of Graham arranging his own affairs, imprison him (politely), and seem about to kill him. The action of the novel consists of our hero escaping, helping "Ostrog" to overthrow the system in order to benefit the common man, exploring this new society, and—realizing the new leader Ostrog is no better than the Council—fomenting a second rebellion.

Religion in Wells' future appears two ways. First, Graham's exploration of his city includes a trip to the "religious quarter." Organized religion, having been separated from local communities, has been corporatized to what seems to Graham to be a blasphemous degree, including lurid advertising slogans like: "'Salvation on the Third Floor and Turn to the Right.' 'The Sharpest Conversion in London, Expert Operators! Look slippy!' 'Be a Christian—without hindrance to your present Occupation.'" His guide is initially surprised at Graham's revulsion, but then understands. "'Nowadays the competition for attention is so keen, and people simply haven't the leisure to attend to their souls, you know, as they used to do.' He smiled. 'In the old days you had quiet Sabbaths and the countryside'" (Wells 1898–1899/1978: 445). The future, it seems, is too busy, too business and work oriented for either leisure or spiritual exploration.

A second form of religion is more pervasive. Graham's guide notes, "popular religion follows popular politics" (ibid.). The politics and religion of the elite are similarly entwined. His guide explains that the upper classes have different kinds of churches (quiet, personal attention, incense), but more significant to them is a series of ritualistic observances devoted to the most important feature of society: Graham himself or rather the power Graham represents. For example, the room in which Graham wakens seems part temple, part museum. He finds himself naked, on an air mattress inside something like a glass case, in a richly furnished room not unlike an exhibit or perhaps shrine, with "polished pillars of some white-veined substance of deep ultramarine" and "a roof [that was] broken in one place by a circular shaft full of light" (ibid. pp. 369–71).

It is a very Durkheimian view, society worshiping itself, but with one exception: the rulers *use* these rituals as tools to manipulate the masses, whom they believe to be foolish and in need of being tamed (ibid. p. 443); they do not "believe" in them. Graham slept at a kind of pilgrimage site, while the council, clad in white robes, emphasized their power with similarly magnificent surroundings and a huge statue of Atlas (ibid. pp. 382–4). Those in the upper class pay lip service to Graham, but place their faith in the secular powers, and urge Graham to do the same: "'The Revolution accomplishes itself all over the world. Friction is inevitable here and there, of course; but your rule is assured. You may rest secure with things in Ostrog's hands'" (ibid. p. 434).

However, the powerless common people place their faith in Graham as one who will someday save them—perhaps we should say religion in the future has only a Durkheimian façade over a Marxist core. Some disbelieve: "'this Ostrog—has suddenly revolutionized the world by waking the Sleeper—whom no one but the superstitious, common people had ever dreamt would wake again—raising the Sleeper to claim his property from the Council, after all these years'" (ibid. p. 406). Even so, he is greeted by the mob: "'The Sleeper is with us! The Master—the Owner!'" (ibid. p. 394). It is only later that someone finally makes Graham understand how he was perceived as the Sleeper.

> "For at least half the years of your sleep—in every generation—multitudes of people, in every generation multitudes of people, have prayed that you might awake—*prayed* . . . do you know that you have been to myriads—King Arthur, Barbarossa—the King who would come in his own good time and put the world right for them? . . . Have you not heard the proverb, 'When the Sleeper wakes' . . . Every first of the month you lay in state with a white robe upon you and the people filed by you . . . When I was a little girl, I used to look at your face . . . it seemed to me fixed and waiting, like the patience of God." (Ibid. p. 438)

Here is one of the prime schemas of religion for gSF, repeated and developed (cf. the section on Heinlein in Chapter 5): religion is a social tool, used by unbelieving leaders to manipulate the ignorant.

The next example is Wells' story "In the Abyss" (Wells 1896/1978), which begins with the protagonist, a Mr Elstead, descending five miles into the ocean by means of a free-falling bathysphere. On the ocean's floor, he sees the expected variety of flora and fauna, as well as an unexpected bipedal creature, intelligent enough for speech and tool use. Several such creatures disable the clock-work mechanism meant to disengage the bathysphere's ballast, preventing Elstead from returning to the surface on schedule, and instead tow him to their underwater city. The inhabitants proceed to worship Elstead for several hours, led by one "dressed as it seemed in a robe of placoid scales, and crowned with a luminous diadem, who stood with his reptilian mouth opening and shutting as though he led the chanting of the worshippers" (ibid. p. 348).

Note that to the modern reader, there is nothing at all unusual about this representation. Likely contemporary readers would not have been particularly startled by the Wells' originality here, either; in fact, Wells' underwater dwellers seem parodies of Haggard-style "natives." What makes Wells' story intriguing is that, upon returning to the surface and sharing his fantastic story, the academic community is utterly unimpressed.

> Startling as is his story, it is yet more startling that scientific men find nothing incredible in it. They tell me they see no reason why intelligent water-breathing vertebrated creatures . . . might not live upon the bottom of the deep sea, and quite unsuspected by us . . . We should be known to them, however, as strange meteoric creatures wont to fall catastrophically dead out of the mysterious blackness of their watery sky . . . Sometimes sinking things would smite down and crush them, as if it were the judgment of some unseen power above . . . One can understand, perhaps, something of their behavior at the descent of a living man, if one thinks what a barbaric people might do, to whom an enhaloed shining creature came suddenly out of the sky. (Ibid. pp. 348–9)

What makes this another important prototype for gSF is the portrayal of religion as a problem "scientific men" *have already solved*. In religion there remains no mystery, nothing worthy of awe; it is just a simple effect of insufficient information for understanding.

It may well be that Wells meant to imply a subtle criticism of the hubris of these "scientific men," or at least of their inability to experience wonder. It even seems likely that Wells meant the ending of "Into the Abyss" to be ironic and amusing. If so, this subtlety seems to have been largely lost on his gSF heirs. After writing these stories, Wells died only after witnessing two world wars. A friend recorded that an elderly Wells said his epitaph should be "God damn you all—I told you so" (quoted in Stapledon 1997: ix).

Olaf Stapledon: The last Victorian

Stapledon should, in my mind, be recognized as one of the greats of proto-science fiction. Aldiss described Stapledon as "the greatest of Wells' followers, who said of Wells' influence, 'A man does not record his debt to the air he breathes'" (1973: 201). This statement is problematic. First, stylistically it is difficult for me to identify any similarities between the two men beyond superficial (and possibly accidental) echoes. Stapledon's greatest book, *Last and First Men* (1930/1999), is not even a novel in the usual sense: individual characters and interpersonal conflicts are merely occasional and quickly forgotten minutia in a historiographical depiction of millennia of human evolution. Second, professional courtesy aside, Stapledon seems to have been largely unaware of Wells' work. In a letter written to Wells after *Last and First Men* was published (the same letter Aldiss quotes, incidentally), he begins by acknowledging the connection between his and Wells' work noted *by reviewers*, not himself, and while Stapledon expresses admiration, "curiously enough I have only read two of your scientific romances, *The War of the Worlds* and [the short story] *The Star*. If I seem to have plagiarized from any others, it was in ignorance." Robert Crossley (editor of the volume collecting Stapledon's letters) noted that Stapledon "took some trouble to emphasize the ways in which he was not a Wellsian." Any influence of Wells would seem to have been oblique, and primarily through Wells' influence on society generally, not through Wells' fiction. "Your later works I greatly admire . . . They have helped very many of us see things more clearly" (Stapledon 1997: 279).

Stapledon's subject matter was not entirely unprecedented: Fawcett's story "Solarion: A Romance" (1889) portrays the position of a dog with scientifically enhanced intelligence, not unlike Stapledon's *Sirius* (1944/2010); Bleiler (1991: 389) described Jacomb's *And a New Earth: A Romance* (1926) as an "obvious source for Olaf Stapledon's *Odd John*" (1935/2011), even as "odd" John foreshadows Superman and all his imitators. However, his extended treatment of these ideas is impressively original, even if Stapledon *had* encountered the rather obscure Jacomb. The scope of Stapledon's "cosmological" novels, *Last and First Men* (1930/1999) and the even more ambitious *Star Maker* (1937/1999) (in which Stapledon narratizes life itself), was not only unprecedented, but has rarely been attempted since.

I think of Stapledon as an unnaturally late Victorian. Working outside the genre (even though the genre had begun its formal existence), Stapledon was the last science fiction writer working in relative isolation to have a significant impact on the genre, while presenting potential the genre never really fulfilled. I will focus on Olaf Stapledon's *Last and First Men* (1930/1999), as it represents an impressive comment on religion, a strong influence on some of *genre* SF's founders, and a sharp contrast to the shallow, dismissive view of religion so common in SF's "Golden Age" of the 1930s.

The Last and First Men is a masterpiece of world construction in terms of complexity, coherent texture, and the sheer epic scale of the narrative. Stapledon was not the first to project humanity's evolutionary future using extraordinarily long time scales and positing *Homo sapiens'* replacement species (cf. Belgium's Rosny "the elder," and in particular his 1910 novella *The Death of Earth* [2012]), but he had the greater popularity and impact on American science fiction. Clute and Nichols (1995) describe his impact on the themes of gSF as "probably second only to that of H. G. Wells" and the release of his first novel as "something of a sensation. Contemporary writers and critics acclaimed it, though later it would be nearly forgotten" (ibid. p. 1151). This is due in part to the fact that Stapledon did not publish in the pulps and that his long works could not be adapted to the anthologies which serve as common access points for the modern reader interested in the roots of the genre (ibid. pp. 1151–3).

Stapledon's view of humanity is structuralist: our evolution shapes and is shaped by our culture and our personalities as much as physical environment or specific events. This view is arguably dated (or pre-sentient, given current work in the cognitive science of religion), and indeed his first chapters, predicting Stapledon's immediate future and our immediate past, are startlingly wrong.[1] But when the story takes on its broadest, pan-hominin scope, any awkwardness disappears: "one start[s] to soar on the wings of inspiration—'myth,' Stapledon calls it. Politics then give way to an inquiry into life processes" (Aldiss 1973: 202). Religion recurs repeatedly, but never in the same form twice. Each species of humans is viewed as an expression of the interaction between environment, infrastructure, leadership systems, historical and evolutionary antecedents, and the "typical" psychological makeup; thus, religion is one piece in this hierarchical structure, reflecting and unifying individual selection pressures.

Last and First Men is a *long* book, detailing 18 distinct species of hominin, of which we are the most primitive. The most detailed depiction of a particular religion occurs during the decline of the "First Men," prefaced by a typically succinct description of all that had happened since a long "dark age":

> The Patagonians passed through all the spiritual phases that earlier races had experienced, but in a distinctive pattern. They had their primitive tribal religion, derived from the dark past, and based on the fear of natural forces. They had their monotheistic impersonation of Power as a vindictive Creator. Their most adored racial hero was a god-man who abolished the old religion of fear. They had their phases, also, of devout ritual and their phases of rationalism, and again their phases of empirical curiosity. (Stapledon 1930/1999: 87)

It is tempting to detail Stapledon's specific representations of religion, as each is an impressive thought experiment, but it is not really necessary. All are variations on a theme. Wells' "Into the Abyss" presented religion as something perfectly understandable given a culture's developmental stage. Stapledon *starts* there, but expands it enormously: yes, the specific form religion takes is perfectly understandable, provided one has taken into account the relevant variables. A "typical" development pattern is, for Stapledon, merely the *starting* point. He considers many more variables than merely social complexity; he considers the entire system, including environmental, cognitive, and idealist constraints on individuals' behavior. If he is overly quick (from today's perspective) to allude to characteristic mental states—cultural personalities, if you will, in the style of Benedict's Apollonian vs. Dionysian dichotomies—he balances this with what is, to my mind, still an appropriate perspective by considering universal patterns as merely the foundational strategies before individual cultures apply them as environmentally fit tactics. Whether these mental states typify individuals, we are not told: *species*, not individuals, are the actors here.

As a single example, the Second Men were in most ways our superiors, in terms of intellectual and social growth (but *not* technological). Unfortunately, tragedies still overcame them on occasion, including a rare interaction between sentient species, a civil war, and a "malaise" because their (for lack of a better word) spiritual growth had not kept pace. Stapledon described that conflict as if he, too, found it difficult to choose the right words.

Altruism, for the Second Men, was a much more normal and widespread pattern than for the First Men; however, their perception of *society* as something to be altruistic/loyal to was considerably diminished. "War was not quite unknown amongst them. But even in primitive times a man's most serious loyalty was directed towards the race as a whole; and wars were so hampered by impulses of kindliness toward the enemy that they were apt to degenerate . . . They were never prone to exalt the abstraction called the state . . . [but rather were] more intensely and accurately conscious of each other" (ibid. p. 115).

Within my own field of cognitive approaches to culture, it is typical to consider religious beliefs as hyper-social behaviors used to generate group cohesion, but in such a way as to allow between-group competition. Second Men, it appears, were different. Also in my field, specific religious beliefs are seen as counter-intuitive beliefs that are so memorable that they survive, even when inaccurate. Again, there is a contrast. "This superb clarity of mind enabled the second species to avoid most of those age-long confusions and superstitions which had crippled its predecessor" (ibid. p. 117). Stapledon goes so far as to call them "Natural Christians," as they are so reflexively "loving one's neighbor as oneself," and repeatedly in their "career" rediscovered a "religion of love" (ibid. pp. 117–18). By extension, *we* must be unnatural Christians, in that we require a religious system to encourage what they did by nature and habit.

However, by an accident of disease and the environment, two halves of the species become separated for so long that, once contact is re-established between the two "second civilizations" of the Second Men, they were "so alien" to each other, and "subconscious differences" accumulated to such an extent that their loyalty to their species no longer recognized the other as kin. *Then* they could war as we do, and (apparently) could have *religion* as we do. "Religion finally severed the unity which all willed but none could trust. An heroic nation of monotheist [sic] sought to impose its faith on a vaguely pantheistic world. For the first and last time the Second Men stumbled into a world-wide civil war; and just because the war was religious, it developed a brutality hitherto unknown" (ibid. p. 126).

But the greatest challenge faced by the Second Men—one which they could not overcome, but instead sank into another dark age—was spiritual, and of a nature not familiar to First Men, thus difficult for Stapledon to explain. "To say that they were suffering from an inferiority complex, would not be wholly false, but it would be a misleading vulgarization of the truth. To say they had lost faith, both in themselves and in the universe, would be almost as inadequate. Crudely stated, their trouble was that, as a species, they had attempted a certain spiritual feat beyond the scope of their still-primitive nature" (ibid. pp. 160–1). To simplify what Stapledon already describes as an oversimplification, they had achieved an intellectual understanding of the universe as wonderful and perfect, but lacked the ability to embody that knowledge (not belief); they could not overcome the gap between perception and experience.

It is sometimes difficult, then, to decide if *Last and First Men* should be read as a novel, a textbook, or a tone poem—I certainly fall prey to seeing groups like the Second Men as case studies. (It was with some delight, after I had chosen an excerpt for a literature class, that I received an e-mail from a student convinced I had accidentally assigned something from an anthropology class.) Religion, here, is defined much as I define it at the beginning of this book, but Stapledon also considered spirituality as a separate, sometimes overlapping system. Religion is natural, not because it is intrinsically good (or bad), any more than a particular cognitive ability, environment, or social structure can be: it is nothing more or less than one part of the whole (cf. Wilson 1999: 23–9).

Stapledon's work is impressive, intellectually and artistically. It certainly impressed many of the Golden Age authors, including Arthur C. Clarke, and continues to inspire. Given its scope, however, it has few imitators, and none as successful.

I will close with an excerpt of a letter written the day before Stapledon died, in which his final views on organized religion are made bare, emphasizing both the recurrence of religion and the instability of any one system.

> But granted that some people do greatly need an organized religion, and that we should all be much better if there was an adequate one that we could sincerely join, it still remains a fact that real live religion is much more fundamental than any organized system of doctrines and institutions. And the most genuinely religious people at any time are very apt to be either simply not members of any contemporary Church, or members with their tongues perpetually in their cheeks, or interpreting the doctrines poetically instead of literally. These are the people who may become founders of new religious orders or sects or Churches. But very soon after the new organization has found its feet it loses its soul. (Stapledon 1997: 294)

Conclusion

In this and the previous chapter, we explored a sample of the great many schemas for religion in literature predating gSF. This included a few examples from each of two of the kinds of stories Bleiler called "ancestral" to gSF: adventure novels and utopias. These few were chosen not to reveal the characteristic schemas, but to suggest that there *are* no characteristic schemas—rather, that neither category is homogeneous when it comes to portrayals of religion.

We also explored three candidates for Fathers of gSF, including H. G. Wells, Olaf Stapledon, and the seminal myth of Mary Shelley's *Frankenstein*. There is certainly no shortage for other candidates. Stableford (2010: 24–46) includes Camille Flammarion alongside more traditional candidates like Jules Verne; Clute and Nicholls mention an 1820 "hollow earth" novel by Capt. Adam Seaborn (1995: 568), among many others. An even more *outré* gSF father could be Savinien-Hercule Cyrano de Bergerac: his 1657 novel *A Voyage to the Moon* would certainly seem to fit, offering as it does technologically enabled space travel, complete with descriptions of alien cultures, including their religious behaviors (see the description of death and burial rituals in 1657/1899: 197–201)—this seems to have been enough for Miller to describe this book as "arguably the first science fiction novel" (2010: 170). But even the three discussed here show disparate schemas for religion.

Thus, these two chapters describe the origins of gSF as a mass of raw materials from which the genre was constructed. Some of these representations resemble those of the first dedicated science fiction magazines of the 1920s described below; others do not. The search for consistency within the genre, then, must begin with the individuals *choosing* from these myriad options which to perpetuate, which is to say, which exemplars later authors would embrace. The evolution of gSF, then, begins with the Intelligent Designers and the selections they made.

Part Two

4

Gernsback and the Pulps

If Verne and Wells were among the Fathers of genre science fiction (gSF), the maternal ancestors were Hugo Gernsback and John Campbell, and the womb was the American magazine—logically enough, given the role periodicals played in the popularization of science (see Whalen and Tobin 1980; Lightman 2007: 295–351). Though SF inherited themes from the Victorian novel, its *style* came from the cheap and deliciously lurid "pulp" magazines. Earlier SF delved into the sensational[1] but the tone was more "anthropological" curiosity than sensationalism to sell copies (see Barnard [2006], figure 2). These low-brow origins may continue to prejudice some against gSF (cf. Howell 2009).

Gernsback published the first magazine about electronics, 1908's *Modern Electrics*, and then *Electrical Experimenter*, which added content like Nikola Tesla's autobiography and fiction stories in which new technologies figured prominently. The target audience was initially scientific hobbyists; fiction was merely a bonus (Ashley and Lowndes 2004). In contrast with Verne and Wells, narratives were underdeveloped and merely facilitated descriptions of the technology. Several historically significant stories (such as Gernsback's own "Ralph 124C 41+") are virtually unreadable today.

Quality of fiction improved with 1926's *Amazing Stories* periodical. Significantly, *Amazing* leaned heavily in its first year on reprints by Wells, Verne, and Edgar Allan Poe despite Gernsback's description of "a new sort of magazine." Aside from occasional standouts like Murray Leinster and the first appearance of "Buck Rogers" in 1928, the quality of original stories remained uneven, most being "ill-written and poorly thought-out, and much of it was downright puerile—indeed, a good deal of it was written by teenagers" (Pringle 2000). Gernsback routinely justified the magazine on science-education grounds (e.g., recurring "science questionnaires" referencing stories in that issue).

Given that my focus here is the schemas contained in gSF texts themselves, I will not discuss Gernsback overmuch, except to make a few generalizations about his impact. First, Gernsback clearly saw himself as committed to science education and felt he was making a positive social impact by promoting scientific understandings of the world. Second, and most obviously, he was instrumental in creating a discrete genre out of an amorphous mass of mainstream science fiction (mSF). But third, this achievement is not always remembered fondly, as he simultaneously consigned gSF into the most lurid of popular mediums, the pulp magazine. As such, he created a virtual ghetto out of which some in the community feel they still struggle to avoid (Barnett 2009, Flood 2009). "In simple parlance, it became the in thing to 'knock' Gernsback," as authors and editors like Brian Aldiss, James Blish, and Damon Knight sometimes argue that Gernsback did more harm than good for the genre. From my perspective, the isolation of gSF from mSF facilitated the development of something *different* from the mainstream, so is uniquely valuable. However, even I cannot claim that the inhabitants of the ghetto's first decades were on par with mainstream writing. Regarding one of his early purchases, c. 1915:

> The story, rather like Gernsback's [own writing], was written in a juvenile, boys'-adventure style, and lacked literary skill. But that was neither here nor there. The import was that Stratton [the author] had selected a few basic scientific principles, and woven them into a stirring topical story. The intent of the story was obvious. In his introductory blurb, Gernsback asked, if a foreign power declared war on America, "Would American genius prevail? Would our inventors rise to the occasion?" (Ashley and Lowndes 2004: 47)

In defending Gernsback, I would not do so by arguing that, among the trash, there are a few really excellent stories (even if they *do* target juvenile audiences—see Barclay's "The Troglodytes" below).[2] Rather, I would try to explain why I even *enjoy* the trash, and understand why so many *bought Amazing* and why some of them were inspired to write for Campbell when they got a little older. It does not follow that I and they share reasons; rather, I would argue that those who love the genre *now* will be curious about where it came from. Hartwell[3] argued that "the Golden Age of Science Fiction is Twelve"—that is, the Golden Age not a particular calendar year, but whatever one was reading when one was 12 years old (presumably the age at which many of us discovered gSF) (Hartwell 1984: 3–24). Perhaps those who grew up with gSF feel a sense of ownership of its origins.

In any case, it seems wise to simply provide a few examples of Gernsback-era science fiction in which religion appears and move on, not just as a matter of not trying my readers' patience, but in acknowledgment that descriptions of religion here are limited and rather narrow. *Non*-scientific ways of viewing life and the world were not valued by Gernsback overmuch. When science fiction became located primarily in periodicals, "religious" motivations, moral lessons—and, indeed, any discussion of a religion with which readers might be familiar—became rare. Some similar themes appear fairly regularly, such as "von Dänikin" stories (after Erich von Dänikin's *Chariots of the Gods* [1969/1999]) in which various mythic figures and gods are re-invented as tales of "super-science" (Burtt's "Lemurian Documents" stories [1932a–f] are good examples), but social systems based on religious claims are more rare. "If you didn't find very much religion in science fiction, you didn't come across very much sin either, so there was little cause for complaint" (Moskowitz 1976: 4).

As an example of the general lack of depth of representations of religion, Gernsback published Edgar Rice Burroughs' *The Master Minds of Mars* in the 1927 issue of *Amazing Stories Annual*. Burroughs had previously embraced a Haggard-like schema of religion. In *Gods of Mars*, for instance, religion is exotic temples, bizarre rituals, and a dizzying series of claims and counterclaims of divinity used as justification for attacking one another (1918/2004). But with *Master Minds*, Burroughs attempted the kind of topical statement Gernsback appreciated, as it describes the sad state of the citizens of "Phundal" in the grip of a fundamentalist religion.

> If we consider the middle 1920s . . . we may well believe that it was this satirical element that frightened away the pulp editors, who did not criticize the story as a story, but declared it not suitable for their publications. Many of their readers lived in the Bible Belt. In the murky aftermath of the Scopes Trial (July 1925), what with the increasing power of the Fundamentalists, religious satire and contention would have been a topic to be avoided in a pulp magazine. Burroughs probably did not help matters by directly indicating Fundamentalism as his target in the name of the land itself—Phundal. (Bleiler 1998: 560)

Before Gernsback bought it, *Master Minds* was rejected by several publishers, including Street and Smith, even though Burroughs offered to waive his fee if sales did not increase with that issue. "In later years Gernsback took a pussyfooting position with regards to organized religion, but his sympathies seem obvious" (ibid.).

Walter Kateley, "The Fourteenth Earth" (1928)

The *Amazing Stories* short story "The Fourteenth Earth" (Kateley 1928) is a stereotypical example of pulp science fiction: entertaining, if a bit shallow; a re-working of old adventure/proto-SF template, in this case the discovery of a "lost race"; and a slightly pretentious insistence that, though fictional, the story is built on accurate scientific knowledge, in this case by quoting a 1923 issue of *Scientific American*.

The protagonist shrinks himself to subatomic size. The earth orbiting the sun turns out to be more than a metaphor for protons circling a nucleus: he finds an entire world and civilization of people. After learning their language, he describes their culture as somewhat more advanced than our own. They possessed technology we do not, but not so advanced as to be incomprehensible—smaller, more efficient motors, for example. Socially, they seem civilized and stable, respecting the sciences and loving of liberty. Even physically they seemed slightly more "evolved": greater dexterity from a small change in the placement of the thumb, no tonsils, etc. Only their religion caught the narrator aback.

> Of their religion, I was able to learn but little. Their word for the divinity is Thegel. They build no churches and hold no public services; but when any progress is made in science or invention, the tangible evidence of this achievement is placed in a small chapel or shrine [. . .] I asked Akon about this peculiar custom, but his

answers were a little vague. "That is for Thegel," he said. "Is it for him to see?" I asked, and after some hesitation he explained. "We do not know if Thegel sees or hears, or ever has need of any of our earthly senses; but we hope that there is some kind of a realization that we are making earnest effort, in fact some progress, meager though it may he, to avail ourselves of the divine gifts; that we are struggling up to a higher plane of existence" (Kateley 1928: 1096)

The protagonist is curious how, despite their advances in all other areas, this aspect of their culture could be so under-developed. Upon reflection, however, he notes in the history of religion in his own culture there is a strong shift toward simplicity: from polytheism to monotheism, from huge temples to more modest buildings, paralleled by a lessening of the phenomena understood as having supernatural explanations. He concludes:

So it may be in the course of a few thousand years, our conception of the Deity may become less personal, and many of our present religious beliefs may be relegated to the realm of superstition, and our quest of the divine Will may take the form of delving into nature's secrets. (Ibid. p. 1096)

Note that his perception of future man is not atheistic, but the organized social structures related to "the Deity" are as vestigial as his hosts' toes. There is no conviction that the deity is even aware of us, let alone that he/she/it requires anything of us, but simply a vague belief in the value of "struggling up to a higher plane of existence." Also note that this view of religion is specifically described as conducive to scientific progress, not a hindrance.

Even given the short story format, religion is not the focus, but is rather just one of the interesting things one might encounter in an alien culture. This is fairly typical of Gernsback era stories. They are not "about" religion per se, but religion appears as a routine feature: as evidence of the barbarism of some societies or as models to which we should aspire. "The Fourteenth Earth" falls into the latter category, implying that, as they are ahead of us in Kateley's progressive view of history, we should embrace aspects of religion that inspire us—including encouraging scientific innovations—and jettison the rest.

Fred Barclay, "The Troglodytes" (1930)

Barclay's "The Troglodytes" (1930) falls into the latter category: religion, here, is where the irrational and brutal parts of an otherwise admirable society are kept. Here, the journey itself is more mundane: the described culture is subterranean, rather than subatomic. Three men are traveling together, demonstrating many of the ideals of the Gernsback-era hero: they are reasonable, intelligent engineers with a taste for adventure. The key feature of the protagonist, Joe, is that he operates at the midpoint between his two companions: the older, more cautious and thoughtful John, and the joking, hot-headed Jim. Much of the tension involves Joe observing arguments between the two extreme perspectives, including disagreements about how religion should be treated.

During an impromptu spelunking expedition, the trio are captured by the Ampu and taken far underground. Despite the aggressiveness of their capture, the Ampu prove to be a peaceful, technologically advanced people, though curiously passive. We learn of two tensions within Ampu society. First, there has been a long-running argument between those who believe themselves to be descended from surface creatures and those who believe that the Ampu were created by their god (Barclay 1930: 495–6). Second, the elders are concerned, perhaps as a result of having everything necessary and desirable provided with little effort, that each generation is apathetic and less competent than the last. General technological ability seems to be fading as well, especially among the common people.

The only mysterious aspect of their existence is a conspicuous reverence to a symbol comprised of eight spheres moving in two linked circles, which refers to "the gods of the center." John learns the reality behind the Ampu's image of divinity: rather than molten lava, the center of the Earth is filled with huge spheres, moving as if by mechanical design, providing the power on which the Ampu rely. "'Then I understood the significance of the sign . . . and I knew that these were the gods of the Ampu.'" John later relates: "'Such a feeling of reverential awe came upon me that I must have felt as a pagan feels in the presence of the mystery of his gods. It was with an effort that I shook from myself that feeling of dreadful worship and persuaded myself that these were nothing but natural phenomena'" (ibid. p. 503). The priests are primarily responsible for maintaining this power source (ibid. p. 504), mirroring an earlier description of their society: "There were certain machines to be watched, but those duties were delegated to the priesthood" (ibid. p. 498).

The stresses of living underground exacerbate Jim's instability, often portrayed in contrast to John. For example, when they notice the difficulty with which their guests negotiate the dim surroundings, the Ampu provide bright light sources, provided they use them cautiously. Jim immediately suggests they use them to blind some Ampu in order to steal transportation. John refuses: "'I have already given my parole in regard to these things'" (ibid. p. 493). In recounting the history of *H. sapiens* to the Ampu, John emphasizes positive aspects of our technological and social development; Jim adds, against John's wishes, a strategic (and antagonistic) account of our military capacity, so "'they won't want to start any monkey business with our people up top'" (ibid. p. 498).

Predictably, John and Jim have different reactions to the tensions inherent in the Ampu civilization. John suggests they avoid all questions of the Ampu's origins. "'Look here fellows, we're stuck with these Ampu, for a time anyway, and it looks to me as if that difference of opinion about their origin may lead to trouble'" (ibid. p. 496). When asked by the Ampu for their reactions to the apathy problem, John (through words) and Joe (through deeds) present two different solutions, two different ways to get people active again. Both react to the Ampu's origin beliefs, and both introduce competition, but their solutions are very different.

John (with appropriate humility) explains the processes of evolution in light of his people's fight to control the elements, and perhaps eventually time and space. "'I mention these things because the continued struggle to overcome them is what has developed our race physically and mentally.'" His suggestion, then, is to implement a form of capitalism based on luxury goods, "'so that all will find happiness in labor and its rewards and joys in possessing those things in which his fellows have no part'" (ibid. p. 502). In short, John carefully dodges origins, and suggests intra-group competition, but of a "civilized" and very much American kind.

Jim, on the other hand, consistently goads the most staunch of the Ampu creationists and eventually becomes the symbolic head of the opposite faction. His motives are little more than entertainment—his goal is not to promote one view or another, but to create dissent (ibid. p. 502). He does not offer an opinion as to the apathy problem, but note that his actions provide an alternative solution: competition in a more direct, divisive fashion, which would certainly bring the Ampu out of their too-comfortable positions. Unfortunately, we do not learn if John's capitalist solution would have worked; Jim's actions too quickly produce results. After Jim is executed by the priesthood—the first in a line of "sacrifices," some willing, others not—violence erupts. John is also killed, trying to save one of the Ampu. Only Joe escapes to the surface.

Note that both the emotional response to "power" and the institutional expression of that power are present, but separate. The priesthood's authority rests in part on their monopoly on the mechanical power on which the Ampu are reliant *and* on theological doctrines such as their origin myth. Note that the emotional reactions to superhuman power are shared by the religious Ampu *and* those who do not consider that power to be super-*natural*. Even the idealized John experiences something like awe, but he quickly overcomes it and does not allow it to dictate his actions. Meanwhile, some of the priesthood's actions (e.g., executing Jim) appear motivated primarily by self-interest. Both the emotions—which are presented as valid—and hierarchical power structures exist, but combining them is dangerous: the priesthood represents the only brutal facet of Ampu civilization.

"The Troglodytes" is, in my opinion, a perfect example of Gernsback-era fiction: a good story, not too fancy, with strong ties to the genre's roots (cf. Verne's *A Journey to the Center of the Earth*). It also assumes a tension between scientific and religious understanding of phenomena, and offers an atypically "reasonable" solution in the character John: "we" should not pick at religion, but calmly offer more rational alternatives: evolution, not creation; capitalism, not violence. (Note the secondary assumptions that Creation and violence are necessarily linked to religion.)

Arthur Jones, "The Inquisition of 6061" (1933)

Like "The Troglodytes," in "The Inquisition of 6061" (Jones 1933) mechanical power and social power are held by the same people, who use a religious institution to maintain their authority.

Unlike Barclay, Arthur Jones is not a good writer: "The Inquisition" is awkward and internally incoherent. Ironically, that does not exclude Jones from consideration: in determining what is representative of the Gernsback era, one cannot ignore the fact that flawed stories were common. More, as I described in Chapter 1, the quality of a story is relatively unimportant, as the focus here is on what fans actually read, not what one thinks they *should* have read. Neither Barclay nor Jones published in the pulps again (according to ISFDB.com, though one cannot rule out pseudonyms), and both have been largely forgotten, but nevertheless they were two of the relatively small number of authors to appear in the magazine at the center of gSF during a crucial period.

The story begins promisingly enough. A man, "J" (one cannot help but wonder if "Mr Jones" is soapboxing), flings a popular history book out his 75th floor window.

In J's view, the steady march of progress had been beneficial for much of history, but no longer. Progress had largely stopped, and the world would have been better off without some of the recent achievements. The eighth world war had ended the year before. The first five do not concern him overmuch, as the weapons used were not that terrible: merely guns and bombs. The last three were the bad ones, fought with electricity, able to destroy a city from above, or sink a ship in the middle of the ocean from shore. "It was a world that was mechanically correct and soullessly inhuman" (ibid. p. 441). (The foreshadowing of the genre's reaction to the atomic bomb was one of the motivations to choose to include this particular story.)

Now, J (like the Ampu above) worries, "There is nothing left for the world to do but rot in its own idleness" (ibid.), and that the world had become too homogeneous: the last wars had been fought to unite the world under a common language and culture. This bothers J not because he values diversity, but because of the implications for individual liberty, including freedom of religion.

> J knew there was now only one thing left that was individual. It was the only thing the world now held in deference [sic, "difference"?]. Half believed in a Creator. Must he soon part with his last ideal? There were hints that it was to go. And that was to go for the God of Electricity. The other half believed in it. (Ibid. p. 442)

J is one of these "last worshippers of God" (ibid.). It is interesting that Jones presents religion as the most durable of cultural differences, but J's commitment to his religion is not out of a sense of personal devotion, but simply because this is the last facet of his life in which J feels he can be an individual: his responses are not on behalf of his community, but for himself. If other languages had outlived religion, I suspect J would fight for his, even if no one else still spoke it. Similarly, the leader of the world ("X") is not a zealot, but a man devoted to consolidating his power.

By the second page, the heretics (including J) are rounded up. J refuses to utter the words that would free him ("Electricity is my God") and is tortured, but saves one of the guards who had walked too close to the torture devices. When the guard asks why J saved him, J says that the guard is not at fault: it is the "master mind" who had manipulated people into not thinking for themselves, into not recognizing the self-serving motivations behind the leader's actions (ibid. p. 445).

The guard immediately helps J start a revolt, and within minutes a riotous mob has appeared to hear J give an impassioned speech, saying that electricity is quite useful, but "Should we bow down to something just because it can kill? Should we bow down to something just because someone says we should? Should we not think as we wish? [. . .] Do not our hearts beat with the blood of thought?" (ibid. p. 446). The wording is crude, but the sentiment is clear: freedom of individual thought over all. Religion was J's last reason to fight, but not the motivation: if "X" had been a religious leader first, most of J's speech would still apply. In any case, the people buy it, and kill "X."

I am certain that Jones is not suggesting that, if people like electricity *too* much, society will fall under the yoke of a tyrant. Rather, tyrants will use whatever tools they have, including religion and especially if that religion stays under their control. Here, what is worshipped is literally power. Slightly more subtle is the implication that religion as a social system does not necessarily have anything to do with morality, philosophy, etc. Presumably, if, in Jones' world, religion can make do without divinity or spirituality in the usual sense, then the reverse is possible. Thus, to be religious is a choice each individual must be allowed to make for himself, but in this story the claim that religion is necessary for us to be moral, and/or explore our spirituality, is irrelevant.

Conclusion

These three stories are not "about" religion per se, but they illustrate the features most common to representations of religion in the early years of science fiction as a genre distinct from mainstream literature (gSF).

First, religion was typically only a supportive thread to the main plot and was not yet a major theme in gSF. Having said this, religion is a remarkably *frequent* thread. Bleiler (1998) cataloged all stories printed in science fiction magazines from 1926 to 1936. I identified 67 stories in which religion features prominently, from which I chose representative samples. In comparison, Bleiler (1998: xviii–xxi) listed the most "important story motifs" in the same magazine issues. Several routine motifs seem to appear less frequently than religion: mad scientists appear prominently in only 66 stories; there are 56 stories about the Moon, and 28 about relativity. This comparison is not direct (my criteria and Bleiler's likely differ), but is sufficient to demonstrate that the appearance of religion in an early genre science fiction story is not at all unusual in the Gernsback era; religion appeared even more frequently in the Campbell era (i.e., from 1938).

Second, religion is presented in distinctly normative tones. Through typically negative associations made by the authors, it is clear how religion should be viewed and that we should strive for a future in which religions' influence is severely curtailed. Most religious societies we see in early gSF are not enlightened, but savage (e.g., the genetically inferior cannibals in John Wyndham Harris's "The Venus Adventure" [1932]). Religious leaders of other races are usually manipulative and dishonest (e.g., Clifford D. Simak's "The Voice in the Void" [1932]). Our own leaders appear to escape notice, but religious myths are given scientific "explanations" (e.g., J. Lewis Burtt's "The Never-Dying Light" [1935]). Note that, given the variety of representations of religion in pre-1926 mSF, gSF authors *could* have chosen more pro-religion writers to imitate: see, for example, Benson (1908), who describes a future without religion as depressed and dystopic, or Harris (1905), who views space travel through a clearly religious lens (see Moskowitz 1976: 3–21).

Third, representations of religion in science fiction are homogeneous. Outliers are startlingly rare, and are not remembered fondly, in particular those written from a religious perspective. Ray Cummings's "The Great Transformation" (1931) is described by Bleiler (1998: 87): "All through the story the narrator makes foolish religious comments about souls and divine will . . . pretty bad"; and in reference to Bauer's "The Forgotten World" (1931): "A religious element enters when the Noenians wax enthusiastic about the Bible that [the protagonist] always carries in his pocket . . . a boring, amateurish work" (Bleiler 1998: 15). Whether such representations of religion make for a bad story or whether better authors avoided similar representations could be debated is difficult to answer with such a small sample. I am inclined toward the latter explanation: those particular stories *are* inferior, and Bleiler is no less critical of similarly bad stories in which religion does not appear.

Fourth, religion and science are presented as contrasting ways of knowing about the universe: in the idealized "Thegel" religion described above, religion is something safely subsumed under science, though we are usually warned against allowing religious trappings to support technology (e.g., Francis Flagg's "The Cities of Ardathia" [1932]). This particular theme proved (as we will see) to be extremely popular in the pulps, pitting, for example, scientifically minded, individualist heroes against evil priestly castes. The proper response to that tension varies, but we are clearly meant to root for the scientists.

Campbell's "Social Science Fiction"

By the summer of 1938, genre science fiction (gSF) had been published in dedicated magazines for over a decade, and *Amazing Stories* had accumulated four rivals: *Weird Tales*, *Thrilling Wonder Stories* (formerly *Wonder Stories*), the new *Marvel Science Stories*, and most notably *Astounding Science Fiction* (formerly *Astounding Stories of Super-Science*). The market had grown: the 1930s' World's Fairs popularized a progressive view of science, Orson Wells' 1938 radio presentation of Wells' *The War of the Worlds* was a popular phenomenon (see also the contemporary *Life Magazine* article ["Speaking of . . ." 1938]), and those who had read the first issues of *Amazing* as children were now having children of their own. Though editors (e.g., Harry Bates as first editor of *Astounding*, Mort Weisinger at *Wonder*, and even Ray Palmer at *Amazing*) continued to overtly display commitments to science education, and often improved scientific accuracy, they no longer allowed education to trump a story's effectiveness (Westfahl 1999). gSF was moving into its "Golden Age."

This was predominantly the era of *Astounding* editor John W. Campbell. *Astounding's* second editor, F. Orlin Tremaine, had managed to make *Astounding* a financial success, but by 1937 had begun scaling back his involvement in order to run several other magazines; the May 1938 issue was the first produced entirely by Campbell (del Rey 1979: 91–102). Campbell acquired the best stories by established writers like Henry Kuttner and C. L. Moore (in part because he was willing to pay more), and discovered authors who were to lead the field for the next decade: he published Lester del Rey's first story in 1938, Robert Heinlein's first story and Theodore Sturgeon's and A. E. van Vogt's first *genre* stories in 1939. Technically, Isaac Asimov's appearance in 1939 ("Trends") was his *third* published story, but Asimov was later to write "The first two, however, did not appear in *Astounding* and so I rarely count them" (Asimov and Greenberg 1979: 229).

Campbell's influence was more pervasive than simply identifying talent; his strong opinions and hands-on approach led some contemporaries to worry that he was imposing his own ideas instead of allowing gSF to develop "naturally" (Ashley 1975: 61). His distinct vision for the genre included normative views of religion.

Some Gernsback-era representations remained, such as an assumption that religious beliefs were essentially primitive, but Campbell insisted on unprecedented realism in many areas. This realism extended to include religion; it is telling that the unusual representations of religion in Gernsback's magazines, described as outliers at the end of the previous chapter, are missing under Campbell.

Mars, for example, had to be portrayed as it was currently understood to be, which excluded early writers like Edgar Rice Burroughs as well as contemporaries like Ray Bradbury (perhaps the best of the twentieth-century *mainstream* science fiction (mSF) authors, see Chapter 8) (Asimov and Greenberg 1981: 11). Social sciences, just as the physical sciences, had to be up to date; religious beliefs acquired broader interpretations. For example, see P. Schuyler Miller's "The Cave," which alludes to different interpretations of the same signals. "To some of the more barbaric tribes of the north, it was more than just a beast—it was His emissary" (Miller 1943/1981: 17). Note the implied continuity: the beast is the same, but the interpretation is different . . . and the shift in interpretation is itself a natural process. Arthur C. Clarke (whose first story appeared in *Astounding* in 1946) formalized what came to be known as "Clarke's Third Law": one cannot distinguish magic from sufficiently advanced science (Clarke 1962/1999). By implying that *we* are as vulnerable as so-called primitives, the law similarly means primitives (and primitive representations) cannot be dismissed as inferior.

Characters' *motivations* had to be similarly comprehensible: even heroes were gainfully employed, and adventure could no longer be their sole reward (Asimov 1983). Caricatures of human sacrifices and evil priests had become passé: compare the images of religion described in this chapter to the insane ritual in the contemporary "The Words of Guru" (Kornbluth 1941/1980b), which appeared in the relatively peripheral *Stirring Science Stories*. In Golden Age gSF, priests were not necessarily *positive*—they were often manipulative and destructive—but their motivations had to be rational (e.g., self-interest; see Heinlein below). The older images of "bug-eyed monsters" never completely went away; E. E. "Doc" Smith remained popular, for example, but never stopped describing the bad guys as from "some alien and horribly different other" (Smith 1948: 12)—but for new authors at the core of the genre, the psychologies of both good and bad guys were relatively mundane.

Religion may not have been assumed to be entirely negative, but it *was* held at arm's length. Protagonists could tolerate religious belief in others, so long as beliefs did not determine behavior, did not contradict scientific facts . . . and as long as people did not insist on talking about them (see de Camp below). In this chapter, we consider representative works of two of the most important gSF writers from any period in their heyday—Isaac Asimov, who looked at the epistemological tensions between religion and science; and Robert Heinlein, who presented religion as social tool for good or (usually) ill—and two other strong voices: L. Sprague de Camp's "Ultrasonic God," in which true belief is more distasteful than cynical manipulations, and Lester del Rey's "Into Thy Hands," which foreshadows the next stage in gSF's metanarrative of religion.

Isaac Asimov, "Trends" (1939)

The Golden Age of science fiction has retroactively been declared to have begun in either 1938 or 1939. The two most symbolic events were the May 1938 issue of *Astounding Science Fiction* (the first issue Campbell published under his own authority) and the July 1939 issue, with its conspicuously talented authors, including Catherine L. Moore, Nelson S. Bond, and Amelia R. Long, and more than a little religious imagery.[1] Moore's story "Greater Than Gods" is more about the long-term effects of a single decision than social institutions (cf. Moore 1935). Bond's story in the May issue is not important here, but his "Meg the Priestess" stories started in *Amazing* in October (Bond 1935): set in a culture with little technology, a girl in training to be the priestess/leader discovers the gods of her people are simply the leaders of a technologically superior past, and *we* discover Meg is our future—a recurring motif, popularized in the movie *Planet of the Apes*. Long presents even stronger recurring images. In "When the Half Gods Go—," a Martian undermines the religion of a group of Venusians. "'[The God Lalu] has kept me and my people fed when the crops of our neighbors failed.' 'That . . . was the result of your own cleverness and industry, and not a gift of Lalu'" (Long 1939: 112–13). Unfortunately for the Venusians, "believing in the adage that a religious people is the easiest to govern" (ibid. p. 112), the Martian is only doing this to enable him to take the gods' place.

These would have been enough to make this a solid issue, with several representations of religion that were to typify the Golden Age: religion is a misunderstood past, misunderstood science; individuals can manipulate religion to give themselves power, and religious people are easily controlled. But this issue *also* contained the first story by A. E. van Vogt, who was to become a major author within the genre, and an early story by a teenager named Isaac Asimov.

"Trends" (1939/1979) describes the first manned rocket, and the historical tendency of cultures to swing between the extremes of "religious and conventional" and "scientific and free." (Note the assumed correlation.) The rocket flight, unfortunately, is planned during a "religious" phase, and the religious leaders are trying to stop it. To Asimov's credit, he does not present the religious perspective as wrong:

> "After the First World War, you know, the world as a whole swung away from religion and toward freedom from convention. People were disgusted and disillusioned, cynical and sophisticated . . . It was [also] a time of political chaos and international anarchy . . . culminated in the Second World War . . . People were disgusted with the 'Mad Decades'. They had had enough of it, and feared, beyond else, a return to it. To remove the possibility, they put the ways of those decades behind them. Their motives, you see, were understandable and laudable." (Ibid. p. 234)

Their motives may perhaps be wrong, but not necessarily their methods.

> "We have prohibition; smoking for women is outlawed; cosmetics are forbidden; low dresses and short skirts are unheard of; divorce is frowned upon. But science has not been confined—*as yet*." (Ibid.)

As spokespeople for each extreme, "Trends" gives us descriptions of a preacher and a scientist. The preacher is described as a genius "with a golden tongue and a sulphurous vocabulary," able to "hypnotize" his audience (ibid. p. 233). He has been using that tongue to try to stop the rocket flight, which he says would be "profaning the heavens. Tomorrow, in defiance of world opinion and world conscience, this man will defy God. It is not given to man to go wheresoever ambition and desire lead him. There are things forever denied him, and aspiring to the stars is one of these" (ibid. p. 230). Interestingly, in Asimov's story (in contrast to many of his colleagues, including Heinlein below), while the focus is on religious *leaders*, the leaders themselves do not have direct secular authority. This preacher's power is through swaying public opinion, who vote accordingly. Restrictions on science eventually follow his actions, but through the legislative branch of government (ibid. pp. 240, 244) and the judicial, where, after a close vote upholding an anti-atomic energy law, "*Science* [was] *strangled by the vote of one man*" (ibid. p. 244, emphasis in original). That is, the religiously motivated actions against science are not just top-down from a few leaders, but bottom-up from a zealous population. The first rocket is blown up by a member of the preacher's congregation; the scientist is blamed (ibid. p. 241).

But the hero of the story is the scientist. Despite significant social and increasing legal opposition, he launches his second rocket in secret, unsubtly christened *New Prometheus*. He justifies his position against the public by pointing out that "intelligent men are on the side of science, aren't they?," by referring to science's tradition of "glorious rebels: Galileo, Darwin, Einstein and their kind," and declaring his "inalienable right to pursue knowledge. Science has an unalienable right to progress and develop without interference. The world, in interfering with me, is wrong; I am right" (ibid. pp. 235–6). Note the implication: intellectual progress trumps societal opinion or even societal *impact*. The scientist is so confident that technological progress is beneficial in the long term that any short-term chaos is justified.

His successful launch, spectacular crash next to the Potomac, and defiant speech ("Go ahead, hang me, fools. But I've reached the Moon, and you can't hang *that*" [ibid. p. 246]) sway the fickle public. By the time he is released from hospital, he is a hero and the fickle world has swung the pendulum back again. Defiant science triumphs over conservative religion.

Two years later, Asimov's more mature story "Nightfall" is published.[2] On a planet with multiple suns, an exceedingly rare simultaneous eclipse is about to plunge the planet into darkness for the first time in centuries. Scientists, knowing all about phobias and intelligently self-aware, prepare to face it boldly. It is a clever story; Asimov shows the scientists speculating on the possibility, unlikely as it may seem, that life could exist on a planet with only *one* sun. They also hypothesize about what will be seen in the planet-wide dark.

The public (read: mob), however, is preparing to panic, led by a religious group.

"You mean this myth of the 'Stars' that the Cultists have in their 'Book of Revelations.'"

"Exactly," rejoined Sheerin with satisfaction. "The Cultists said that every two thousand and fifty years [our planet] enters a huge cave, so that all the suns disappeared, and there came *total darkness all over the world!* and then, they say, things called Stars appeared, which robbed men of their souls, and left them unreasoning brutes, so that they destroyed the civilization they themselves had built up. Of course, they mix all this up with a lot of religio-mystic notions, but that's the central idea." (Asimov 1941/1998: 119)

The scientists are dismissive of the public's superstitions, and, as in "Trends," disregard any anger or unrest. The twist is, the scientists *are* aware of a cycle of destruction and rebirth in their history, which seems to follow a similar period as the eclipse. The scientists are altogether more reasonable than "the public," and factually correct, but are unable to avoid the worldwide panic when the sky goes dark and the Stars appear. Note that the ability of science to sway public opinion in *this* story is negligible, and that *the Cultists had accurate information.* They remembered the cycle of destruction, *only* they recorded the Stars . . . and their prediction of the public's reaction is more accurate. Of course, the Cultists do not "understand" the information, nor is the social result they contributed to at all positive—but science would be wrong to dismiss *everything* religion says, based solely on the source.

Robert Heinlein, "If This Goes On—" (1940)

The very next issue of *Astounding* included among its talent Lester del Rey (I will discuss his 1945 story "Into Thy Hands" below), L. Ron Hubbard (who was later in his career to blur the lines between religion and science fiction), and the first story by Robert Heinlein.

Heinlein had an immeasurable influence on the development of gSF. To cite a single formal recognition, he was awarded the very first "Grand Master" award by the Science Fiction and Fantasy Writers of America (the same organization that presents the Nebula Awards); informally, his peers' imitations of his straightforward prose, of his pioneering habit of setting multiple unconnected stories within the same universe (Heinlein's "future history"), and frankly of some of his attitudes are also evidence of his impact. More subtly, he was (initially) a favorite of Campbell, and as somewhat older than his fellow *Astounding* authors (a military career was already behind him), there was certainly an element of personal charisma affecting his contemporaries. Asimov later remarked, "It was a one-man phenomenon that will probably never be repeated" (Asimov and Greenberg 1979: 412).

Even his fans, however, admit that his work is sometimes polarizing (e.g., Robinson 1980), and not all interpretations of his impact have been positive. "[T]he man stands head and shoulders above the field when he is good and represents a major catastrophe when he is horrid. For others, Heinlein is a card-carrying fascist and racist whose philosophy is evil, whose prose is leaden, and whose dialogue has always been twenty years out of date" (Spinrad 1981: *vi*). Predictions of his impending irrelevance often proved premature. In the 1950s, Campbell felt Heinlein had gone off the rails, both in his ideas and mode of presenting them (see, e.g., Campbell 1959, discussed in Chapter 6). Panshin (1968) was sure his best days were behind him, just as *Stranger in a Strange Land* (Heinlein 1961) was becoming a major cultural phenomenon, in and out of the genre.

For my purposes, his work must figure prominently. As unambiguously opinionated as they were, his depictions of religion constitute the prototype for the Golden Age schema, and his long career (his last novel was published in 1987, the year before he died) demonstrates that, no matter his stubborn refusal to bow to others' suggestions (even his editor's), his work certainly changed with the times. In fact, he is the only author significantly considered in two chapters of this book: here, as exemplar of the Golden Age, and below as a mark of how far gSF had evolved by the 1960s.

However, he *could* have appeared much more frequently. Inversely, due to the cultural and political depth of each of Heinlein's worlds, one could critique the few stories I have included in a number of ways. I find it curious that *Stranger in a Strange Land*, which I use in Chapter 7 to explore religion (facilitated by a break from mainstream norms) as a way to form tight, kin-like bonds, is, for Planck (1978: 101–103), a novel full of vicarious sexual activity. Sarti (1978: 115) sees his story, "If This Goes On—," as clearly evidence for a feminist critique. I will use the same story here to explore the use of religion as a manipulative, hegemonic social tool.

The protagonist of "If This Goes On—" (Heinlein 1940) is an earnest young soldier, guarding the palace of "The Prophet." While on watch one night he meets (and dares speak to) one of "the virgins ministering the Prophet."

> "Do you attend the Holy One this night, Elder Sister?" I asked, to make an opening.
>
> She nodded, and some vague fear seemed to haunt her eyes. "Yes, I serve tonight, my Brother, but I have as yet some ten minutes before I must be at the portal. I came out to feel the peace of the stars."
>
> "It must be a memorable privilege to serve him directly."
>
> Again that veil of trouble and fear. "No doubt. I cannot say, for tonight is the first time my lot has been drawn" (Heinlein 1940: Feb. 11)

We discover in the next pages that the story takes place in a near-future America, under the control of a theocracy. Society is frighteningly restrictive, and Inquisition is a very real threat for anyone suspected of heretical disloyalty. Our hero, John, is falling in love with the young Virgin, Judith; we learn that the Prophet is in the habit of taking sexual advantage of his Virgins, whether or not they are willing. Judith is not.

We also learn that not everyone accepts the rule of the Prophet. John's friend, Zebadiah, tells him about the rebellious "Cabal," and they witness the public stoning a follower of a religion other than the Prophet's.

> "Why," I said defensively, "do these pariahs persist in their heresy? They seem such harmless fellows, otherwise."
>
> Zebadiah cocked a brow at me. "Perhaps it is not heresy to them. Didn't you see that fellow resign himself to his God?"
>
> "But that is not the true God."
>
> "He must have thought otherwise" (ibid. p. 13)

Motivated more out of a desire to save/be with Judith than any moral objections, John helps Judith escape, is tortured, then escapes himself to join the Cabal. Two interesting details are: the Cabal appears to be built on the Freemasons and Zeb, John's cynical friend, was considered for the priesthood, because "*he stood first in his class in mob psychology*" (ibid. p. 32, emphasis added).

After an adventure during his journey to Cabal headquarters (to give the end of the first installment a cliff-hanging ending), John arrives and shows us a different scene than we, the readers, would have expected in a *Gernsback*-era story: "I had expected subconsciously to be treated as some sort of conquering hero on my arrival . . . I was vastly mistaken. An impersonal machinelike routine took me in charge on arrival, and whisked me through the necessary details to make me a cog in the machine" (Heinlein 1940: Mar. 127–8). The Cabal, it seems, is not resisting the Prophet only militarily; while John works in support of *that* branch, Zeb has been assigned to the Propaganda Bureau.

> Just at present I'm engaged in writing a series of intimate articles on life in the palace of the Prophet. Very respectful and respectable articles they are, too . . . how many servants they have, how much it costs to run the place, about the complicated ceremonies and rituals—all of it perfectly true and told with unctuous approval. But I lay it on too thick. (Ibid. pp. 128–9)

(The Prophet's system has a corresponding Department of Applied Miracles [ibid. p. 130].)

After adjusting public opinion as much as possible, the military attack begins. The good guys win, of course, and the palace taken. Again in non-Gernsback fashion, John plays an important but unrecognized supporting role. They do not manage to arrest the Prophet, however: "The Virgins had gotten there first: they left barely something to identify at an inquest" (ibid. p. 150).

This may be the end of the action, but not of the narrative. A postscript gives Heinlein the opportunity to wax topical.

> There isn't anything wrong with the minds of the American people; they just suffer from a tendency to sell their birthright for a mess of pottage [. . .] What we have to do now is to restore all the old civil liberties, plus a steel-clad, air-tight new civil liberty, one which will prevent dogmatic notions of every sort from being made into law. Especially we must avoid teaching dogma to children [. . .] There need not be any conflict between science and religion. Science is concerned with natural phenomena, like the physical universe, whereas religion is apersonal matter between each manand his God. Men seek God by many paths, and under many names. The best that government can do is to insure his right to seek his own path. (Ibid. pp. 150–1)

Note Heinlein's implication that the current Constitutional guarantees (i.e., the Free Exercise, Establishment clauses) are insufficient and that science and religion are not necessarily oppositional. However, what he advocates is not an agreement between the two, but a separation akin to Stephen Jay Gould's "non-overlapping magisterial" (1997). This could be seen as an apology for representing religion as a self-serving, freedom-inhibiting institution perpetuated by hypocritical leaders.

But note too his depiction of religion as something *not* opposed to science is qualified by a definition of religion as something purely a matter for individual adults. There is no place for religion as defined in this book: as collective enterprise associated with communities. When the story was republished in book form a decade later, the careful postscript has been removed. Instead, the volume contains an *essay* by Heinlein (thus removing even the semblance of fiction from his opinions) in which he states, "it is a truism that almost any sect, cult, or religion will legislate its creed into law if it acquires the political power to do so, and will follow it by suppressing opposition, subverting all education to seize early the minds of the young, and by killing, locking up, or driving underground all heretics" (Heinlein 1954/1986: 212). He also notes that he had considered writing a story about the Prophet's rise to power, but decided against it. "I dislike him too thoroughly" (ibid. p. 213).

Religion recurs in Heinlein's fiction throughout his career, in many forms, but always with skepticism. For example, in the 1941 stories published as *Sixth Column* (1949/1988, elsewhere published under the title *The Day After Tomorrow*), America has been invaded; rebels organize under the cover of a fake religion, with which— aided by technology-assisted halos and miracles—they organize a resistance (see pp. 100–13). Sometimes even the public-manipulating, social system version of religion is deemed acceptable, but only provided the motivations of the leaders are reasonable, *and* that they do not fall for their own rhetoric, and are willing to surrender power once the mission is accomplished: contrast *Sixth Column* to Leiber's "Gather Darkness" (1943) and a generations-later echo in Weber's *Armageddon Reef* (2007).

Also, recall Asimov's "Nightfall." Heinlein, too, wrote a story in which religion retains important information, scientific and otherwise, but, failing to understand it, interprets it as scripture. *Orphans of the Sky* (1941/1987, collecting the *Astounding* stories "Universe"[3] and "Common Sense") describes life on a huge, multi-generational ship. Following a rebellion long ago, the survivors have become primitive and forgotten a great deal. For example, they have forgotten that the ship *is* a ship traveling through space; for them, the Ship is the Universe. Mostly forgotten knowledge about the ship's hierarchy, fragmented details such as the Captain's name (Jordan), all have become a religious framework (controlled by "Officers" and "Scientists") used to interpret the world, often with ludicrous results. "Hugh" (naturally, for a Campbell-era hero) asks too many questions about "the culmination of Jordan's Plan, the end of the Trip to our heavenly home, Far Centaurus":

> "Many of these ancient writings speak of the Trip as if it were an actual *moving*, a going somewhere—as if the Ship itself were no more than a pushcart. How can that be?"

> ". . . The answer, of course, is plain. You have again mistaken allegorical language for the ordinary usage of everyday speech. Of course, the Ship is solid, immovable, in a physical sense. How can the whole Universe move? Yet it *does* move, in a

spiritual sense. With every righteous act we move closer to the sublime destination of Jordan's Plan." (Ibid. p. 17)

When Hugh discovers the Control Room, he understands the Ship *is* a ship and returns to tell the Captain, who cannot accept Hugh's evidence. "'When an apparent fact runs contrary to logic and common sense, it's obvious that you have failed to interpret the fact correctly'"; he also admits that he did not check to see if Hugh was correct: "'I don't have to cut myself to know that knives are sharp'" (ibid. p. 136).

Whether the Captain is psychologically unable to challenge his own assumptions, or merely unmotivated to undermine a system in which he is leader, is unclear. What is more apparent is that, in Heinlein's fiction, conscious hypocrisy in a religious leader is harder to justify than ignorance: the Prophet is Virgin-raping dictator; the Captain may just be an idiot.

L. Sprague de Camp, "Ultrasonic God" (1954)

de Camp was *Astounding* editor F. Orlin Tremaine's last great find in 1937, but de Camp came into his own under Campbell's influence—an influence which would last longer than the Golden Age itself. Our example here is the 1954 story, "Ultrasonic God" (alternatively published as "The Galton Whistle"); though fairly late, de Camp stayed true to formula, demonstrating the extended influence of the Golden Age, even after new alternatives appeared post.

In the story, Adrian Frome is a surveyor on another world inhabited by two sentient species: the centaur-like Dzlieri and the six-armed Romeli. Some of his instructions are to keep an eye out for two missing humans: a scrap metal entrepreneur named Sirat Mongkut and a "Cosmotheist" missionary, Elena Millan. The Dzlieri are stereotypical savages in a H. Rider Haggard mode: crude, violent headhunters; unable to understand technology; and for religion have only "demonology and magic of a low order, without even a centaur-shaped creator-god to head its pantheon" (de Camp 1954: 11).

After being captured by a band of Dzlieri, they cannot decide what to do with Frome, so decide to take him to "God." (According to the narrator, the Dzlieri word used translates more closely to "supreme being.") God turns out to be missing Sirat Mongkut, who is teaching the Dzlieri how to use firearms so he could eventually become a sort of Emperor. Mongkut presses Frome into acting as his manufacturing foreman.

Frome dines nightly with Mongkut and his fellow captive, the missionary Elena Millan. He learns that Millan is intended to be co-founder of Mongkut's dynasty. Millan is disgusted by the idea of intercourse without divine approval.

> "I never shall," she said coldly. "If I ever marry, it will be because the Cosmos has infused my spiritual self with a Ray of its Divine Love."
>
> Frome choked on his drink, wondering how such a nice girl could talk such tosh. (Ibid. p. 29)

Frome rescues Millan before Mongkut can consummate his plans and is forced to kill Mongkut in the process. A daring escape follows, including murderous Dzlieri chasing the "Deicide." Caught up in the moment, Frome professes his love.

> "Perhaps this isn't the time to say this, but—uh—I'm not a very spiritual sort of bloke, but I rather love you, you know."
>
> "I love you too. The Cosmos has sent a love ray . . ."
>
> "Oi!" It was a jarring reminder of that other Elena. "That's enough of that, my girl. Come here."
>
> She came. (Ibid. p. 32)

Their romance does not last long. As soon as they return to "civilization," Frome applies for an *immediate* transfer off-world in order to get out of the engagement. As Frome describes it, as soon as the kissing stopped Elena began trying to convert him to her religion.

> And during the two and a half days we were up there, I'll swear she didn't stop talking five minutes except when she was asleep. The damndest rot you ever heard—rays and cosmic love and vibrations and astral planes and so on. I was never so bored in my life . . . I began wishing I could give her back to Sirat Mongkut. I was even sorry I'd killed the blighter. Although he'd have caused no end of trouble if he'd lived, he was a likeable sort of scoundrel at that. So here I am with one unwanted fiancée, and I just *can't* explain the facts of life to her. (p. 34)

Another example of distastefully conspicuous displays of religiosity appears in Aymé's story "State of Grace," in which an especially moral man is rewarded with a sign of divine approval in the form of a halo (Aymé 1947/1959). The Sign proves so socially awkward that his wife demands he get rid of it. Prayer does no good—"And so it happens that my wife cannot endure the sight or even the thought of my halo, not at all because it is a gift bestowed by Heaven but simply because it's a halo" (ibid. p. 57)—so he sets out to commit as many sins as necessary. As in the Heinlein stories above, religion is a good way to manipulate the ignorant. Here, the focus is on people who are religious of their own accord—some people really *are* true believers, it seems . . . but the ignorant are easier to forgive.

Lester del Rey, "Into Thy Hands" (1945)

The above narratives describe religion as it appears in the stories themselves. There is another subtle shift in Golden Age gSF, which concerns not the portrayals of religion but authors' willingness to themselves employ religious imagery and metaphor. It was not unusual in the Gernsback era for a story to "explain" actual mythic figures in scientific terms—the Greek gods were *really* aliens—but the tone here conspicuously lacks irony. It is as if religious images are simply the root metaphors with which we approach issues like meaning, origins, and ultimate fate; their inclusion implies no claim to (or, for that matter, denial of) divinity.

The Golden Age roughly coincides with World War II. Given the frequency with which authors and readers were confronted with the destructive potential of technology-assisted warfare, it is no surprise that some gSF stories of this time take on eschatological themes and begin to undermine the Gernsback era faith in the inevitability of technology-assisted social progress. (As we will see in the next chapter, this theme becomes more prominent after 1945.)

Interestingly, several stories *combine* this with anthropogony by linking an end of the world with a new beginning. For example, Robert Arthur's "Evolution's End" (1941/1980) shows a distant future with a new species of hyper-rational hominin. A leader of this super-intelligent but unemotional society realizes that their evolutionary trajectory is ultimately a dead end. He destroys his entire species, purposefully leaving two examples of a more primitive kind of human (named "Aydem" and "Ayveh") to repopulate the earth, hopefully allowing evolution to progress in a new direction. Or consider the disturbing "Adam and No Eve," an early work by a luminary of 1950s gSF, Alfred Bester (1941/1980). An engineer has discovered a new form of propulsion with potentially devastating side effects. Disbelieving the danger, he employs his device and destroys all life on earth. As he lay dying, he takes dubious comfort in the fact that the bacteria and microbes in his body *will* survive. "They would grow, burgeon, evolve. Life would reach out to the lands once more. It would begin again the same old re-repeated cycle that had begun perhaps with the rotting corpse of some last survivor of interstellar travel" (ibid. p. 250). (Compare this to the parallel Kornbluth [1941/1980a], in which the protagonist is a conman who ignores the dangers, resulting in the deaths of innocent bystanders and his own execution.) The critique of an exclusive focus on rationality and blind trust of science seems clear.[4]

Lester del Rey's "Into Thy Hands" (1945/1982) fits into this precedent. As an editor and publisher, del Rey had a great influence on gSF, but he started as a writer—like so many gSF editors, historians, and anthologists, including Campbell himself. As a typical Golden Age author, several of his stories could be considered here. "The Day Is Done" (2000: 12–24; originally published in 1939) contains a good example of Clarke's "Third Law." "Hereafter, Inc." (ibid. pp. 39–50; originally 1941) not-so-gently parodies religious belief: a devout man awakens in a disappointingly mundane afterlife; apparently, the afterlife is an expression of one's imagination, and being religious he has little imagination, less ability to enjoy himself, and no flexibility (see esp. p. 50). (For post-Golden Age del Rey stories concerning religion, see, e.g., "Superstition" [ibid. pp. 136–73] and "For I Am a Jealous People!" [ibid. pp. 174–213].) I will focus here on "Into Thy Hands" mostly because it adds an element distinct from Heinlein's style, and because it expands on the destruction/creation pattern of the Arthur and Bester stories mentioned above.

The prologue to "Into Thy Hands" shows Simon Ames, an inventor of robots, contemplating the possibly immanent destruction of humanity through war. As he buries one of his creations (his tenth model), someone mentions, "'Well, at least if anyone does survive, you've done all you can for them. Now it's in the hands of

God!'" He responds, "'All we could—and never enough! And God? I wouldn't even know which of the three to pray survives—science, life, culture'" (del Rey 1945/1982: pp. 190–1).

The bulk of the story takes place centuries later, depicting some of his creations Creating humanity and human culture anew. Significantly, the story is less about these robots' actions as their internal, existential struggles, and the symbolism indicative of the inter-reliance of science with life and culture . . . and what del Rey puts in the necessary "culture" category is telling.

A male robot has awoken in a decaying bunker, complete with a small laboratory, film projector, etc. The world outside the bunker is understandable; his place is not.

> Here, and in his mind, were order and logic, and the world above had conformed to an understandable pattern. He alone seemed to be without purpose. How had he come here, and why had he no memory of himself? If there was no purpose, why was he sentient at all? The questions held no discoverable answers. (Ibid. p. 192)

Having been exposed to a recording of *Genesis*, he reasons that, if present in his bunker, it must apply to him. But which is he? He rules out Eve and Satan immediately; considers Adam, but dismisses that option as God would have told Adam his purpose. Therefore, he must be the Creator. He sets out to try to create life, but fails: "A powerless God, or a Godless Adam!" (ibid. p. 194). As his answers appeared not to be "discoverable," he sets out, perhaps to find Eden. Perhaps in Eden he could be the Creator? He accidentally finds but runs afoul of some humans. To them, he is just a possible source of spare parts; for him, they spark an existential crisis, as they read the serial number on his chest: he is the 10th Simon Ames model; SA-10; "Say-Ten" (ibid. pp. 202–3). He "discovers" he is Satan before the humans almost immobilize him with an axe. They set off for home, to get help to carry him to their settlement; he struggles to get back to his bunker, not for safety, but to destroy the metaphorical Tree of Life.

Another robot, a *female* robot, has been trapped in a bunker for 600 years, unable to exit, waiting. She finds "SA-10," and repairs him (more specifically, she follows his directions, as she completely lacks mechanical skill) and identifies herself as "Eve," while calling him "Adam." After some effort, Eve manages to convince a suicidal Adam that he is not evil and will not destroy the world, as knowledge is not necessarily evil. She explains the "real" meaning behind Genesis—that mankind must be sheltered from knowledge *until man is ready for it* (ibid. p. 205).

> And behind him, Eve nodded to herself, blessing Simon Ames for listing psychology as a humanity. In six months, she could complete [Adam's] re-education and still have time to recite the whole of the Book he knew as a snatch of film. But not yet! Most certainly not yet; Genesis would give him trouble enough. (Ibid. p. 208)

Only once Adam and Eve (i.e., the sciences and the humanities) are together are they able to contemplate helping humanity recover their heritage and achieve their potential. Both Adam and Eve are motivated by religion, but only Eve is capable of understanding it. Only then are we, the reader, shown a third robot. Recall Ames' prayer: "'I wouldn't even know which of the three to pray survives—science, life, culture'" (ibid. pp. 190–1). Before turning himself off, this robot recalls resurrecting humans from frozen ova, and prays, "'Into my hands, Simon Ames, you gave your race. Now, into Thy Hands, God of that race, if you exist as my brother believes, I commend him—and my spirit'" (ibid. p. 210).

At first glance, "Into Thy Hands" takes a pragmatic view of religious belief. Like the old joke "Trust in God, but tie your horse," Ames may pray to God, but still plants the seeds to resurrect science, life, *and* culture in the form of three separate robots. The first (and last revealed), *sine qua non* but isolated, resurrects the human animal; the latter two will allow us to reclaim our science and culture, but they are successful *only when operating in concert*. Fascinatingly, it is the *science*-oriented robot that is crippled by existential questions of purpose and origins, and by too literal readings of myth; the culture robot cannot reason her way out of a wet paper bag, but is able to generate nondestructive interpretations.

Individually, science and culture are stupid; they (and we) need both to accomplish anything worthwhile. In del Rey's story, religion is simply part of our life and must thus be part of the equation, even if it is necessary to constrain and temper simplistic interpretations of religion with *both* culture and science.

Conclusion

The late 1930s and early 1940s were not just a Golden Age for science fiction; they were a fertile time for gSF's schemas of religion. The stories here only scratch the surface: I regret not being able to include more stories, like Murray Leinster's epistemological "The Power" (1945/1982), and Sturgeon's "Microcosmic God" (1941/1980), which recapitulates a Creation and subsequent historical development, but casts a human as a rather-less-than-benevolent Creator. But these few were sufficient to demonstrate the common elements in this stage of gSF's representation of religion: religion is based on misunderstandings about the world, about history, even about basic facts; religion and science are contrasting opposites, even if not necessarily mutually antagonistic; both self-serving and well-meaning political leaders may use it to manipulate the public; piety can be as annoying as hypocrisy. Though "progress" is still assumed to be technological and beneficial, some wondered if religion could be part of that process. A few even speculated that religion might even be an inevitable part of the human equation.

This confidence was strong, but did not last long. Asimov's "Trends" showed a naïve lack of concern for societal impacts:

> "I know, I know. You're going to tell me of the First War of 1914, and the Second of 1940. It's an old story to me; my father fought in the Second and my grandfather in the First. Nevertheless, those were the days when science *flourished*. Men were not afraid then; somehow they dreamed and dared. There was no such thing as conversation when it came to matters mechanical and scientific. No theory was too

radical to advance, no discovery too revolutionary to publish. Today, dry rot has seized the world when a great vision, such as space travel, is hailed as 'defiance of God." (Asimov 1939/1979: 230)

Asimov was still a teenager when this passage was published; gSF was still in its adolescence. In dealing with the aftermath of World War II, especially the destructive power of the atomic bomb, the genre had to mature and perhaps learn to be a little afraid.

The Rise of the Novel

I'm not questioning—I'm only asking.

"Len," in Brackett's The Long Tomorrow

We now enter the post-World War II era of genre science fiction (gSF). While I generally view the evolution of gSF's views of religion and technology (including the relationship between the two) as a gradual process, the 1950s are an example of punctuated equilibrium. These two motifs (which form the basis of the metanarrative I describe here) change dramatically in the 1950s. This was not only a product of changes in the popular *Zeitgeist*, but significantly one influential and opinionated man: *Astounding* editor John W. Campbell has been criticized for having a too-heavy hand in forcing gSF into his mold. Within a few years of Campbell taking sole control of *Astounding* in 1938, the number of gSF magazine titles had mushroomed from 5 to 18. But during World War II budgets were tightened, paper was restricted, and many authors enlisted, and 1944, only eight gSF magazines survived (Ashley 1975: 35–57). *Astounding* proved itself by surviving both competition and culling.

The genre under Campbell had grown from 1920's juvenile escapism into the more thoughtful "social science fiction" (Asimov 1983). Authors of 1950s continued to write "Campbellian" gSF, including cynicism for religion: for example, de Camp's "Ultrasonic God" (discussed in Chapter 5) and stories by Robert Silverberg and Randall Garrett (writing as Robert Randall: "The Chosen People," "The Promised Land," and "False Prophet," which appeared in *Astounding* in 1956) in which Earthmen educate an alien race through an invented religion (Randall 1957). But Campbell's views were challenged by new authors and editors, and also by a shift in the attitudes of his readership. In the early 1930s, the inevitability of scientific progress was matched by confidence in the positive societal impacts of new technologies. After witnessing the awful destructive power of atomic weapons in 1945, readers' confidence must have taken a terrible blow. In the words of Jack Williamson (who started publishing with Gernsback in the December 1928 issue of *Amazing*):

Before World War II and Hiroshima, we had been proud of technology, optimistic about our future and our stature; there was a sense we had control over our own destiny. Right now, though, there seems to be a contagious fear of the future—a fear that has brought our faith in science to a crisis. All the dilemmas of accelerating change are suddenly too near to be ignored any longer. We see ourselves trapped in a kind of frightening paradox. As scary as certain areas of technology may seem to us, we also know our own survival is bound up in it. But even though technology remains absolutely vital to us, our attitudes toward it keep getting unreasonably darker and darker. (quoted in McCaffery 1991)

Gernsback's old editorial, which stated that "science will go on in its triumphant march" (1932a), seemed naïve, and the motto of the 1933 "Century of Progress" World's Fair— "Science finds, industry applies, man conforms"—took on decidedly ominous tones (see Seed 2013). As the mathematician Norbert Wiener wrote in 1949 of the emerging Machine Age:

> These new machines have a great capacity for upsetting the present basis of industry, and of reducing the economic value of the routine factory employee to a point at which he is not worth hiring at any price. If we combine our machine-potentials of a factory with the valuation of human beings on which our present factory system is based, we are in for an industrial revolution of unmitigated cruelty . . .

> In short, it is only a humanity which is capable of awe, which will also be capable of controlling the new potentials which we are opening for ourselves. We can be humble and live a good life with the aid of the machines, or we can be arrogant and die. (quoted in Markoff 2013; see also Weiner 1954/1988)

These new conceptions of the societal impacts of technology naturally appeared in contemporary gSF, sometimes utilizing religion as a foil. In Christopher's "The Prophet" (1953), Joseph Dwyer plans to remake society through a nonviolent overthrow of "managerial society." In an effort to convince a colleague, Max, to help, he describes the lack of individuality as the worst facet of modern society.

> "It's a world without personality," Dwyer argues. "That's its essential condition; that's its strength; and that's its weakness. It gives man security, but it doesn't give them contentment. In once sense man is master of the machine, but in a subtler and more far-reaching sense the machine is master of man." (Ibid. p. 100)

Though his methods are not explicitly religious, the media names him "The Prophet." Unlike the "normal brand," Dwyer readily uses religious imagery in his media appearances, which show "The Prophet at a meeting of his followers in a small, dark, Victorian English hall . . . And the Prophet in the fields, stretching out his arms melodramatically in a gesture of rejection towards a towering electric sower" (ibid. p. 101). More explicit Christ-like imagery follows: Jesus is said to bring not peace but war, and the Prophet wants "'to disrupt the world as we know it today.'" The Prophet's rhetoric toward powerful Directors is to extol the virtues of medieval Europe: "'Listen and I'll tell you how men used to live, before the machine came'" (ibid. p. 102). Max becomes like Caiaphas and has the Prophet arrested on a trumped-up charge. The

Prophet does not resist, saying, "'The movement can do without me; it might even do better with my memory. You could torture me, but I would not recant . . . I'm afraid force won't serve you.'" "'Not force,' Max said. 'Treachery'" (ibid. p. 106).

Christopher uses religious imagery and recapitulation of Christian myth to protest against "the machine." Technology is shown as dehumanizing, and the inherent goodness of humankind only possible at previous technological levels. The story is improved by a twist on the Biblical metaphor. "There was talk now and then about destroying the faith of the masses in the Prophet . . . But the converse was interesting. Destroy the leader's faith in his followers and you've really got something" (ibid. p. 107). Because of Max, the Prophet abandons Earth, disillusioned. One wonders if a reader in 1953 would have wondered if, after World War II, Jesus would have been equally disillusioned with *us*.

Despite growing ambiguity toward technology, World War II ironically legitimated gSF, as images out of gSF stories had become real (Asimov 1983: 352), and the societal impacts of technology interested a broader range of the public. A pair of new magazines sought to present a more mature form of the genre to the growing audience: *Galaxy Science Fiction* (first issue, Oct. 1950) and *The Magazine of Fantasy* (hereafter "*F&SF*": "and Science Fiction" was added to the title of its second issue, Winter-Spring 1950). To emphasize the maturity of the new magazines against common perceptions of juvenile pulp magazines, H. L. Gold's editorial for the first issue of *Galaxy* was entitled "For Adults Only" (Gold 1950).

Meanwhile some of Campbell was no longer acquiring the best of the new authors, and some of his regulars moved elsewhere (Clute and Nichols 1995: 188).[1] *Astounding* had relied on Heinlein's Future History stories and serialized juvenile novels, but the last of Heinlein's juveniles, *Have Space Suit—Will Travel* (Aug.–Oct. 1958), was serialized in *F&SF*. A letter from Heinlein reveals his deteriorating relationship with Campbell.

> I don't think *Fantasy and Science Fiction* is riding the edge; I think they are just stingy . . . Still, it is pleasanter than offering copy to John Campbell, having it bounced (he bounced both of my last two Hugo Award winners) and then have to wade through ten pages of his arrogant insults, explaining to me why my story is no good. (Heinlein 1963b)

The antagonism was mutual. Heinlein's work had changed: descriptions of technology (and sometimes even the plot) became less important to Heinlein than expounding upon "the morality of sex, religion, war and politics" (Panshin 1968: 89). Heinlein's first major work of this period, *Starship Troopers* (also serialized in *F&SF* as "Starship Soldier," Oct.–Nov. 1959), described the training and indoctrination of a soldier interrupted by short essays on why soldiers fight; actual fighting was rather peripheral to the story. Campbell, predictably, hated it: "I feel that Bob's departing from the principles he himself introduced in science fiction . . . In this yarn, there are several sections of multi-page preachments of his thesis" (Campbell 1959).

Contemporary to all this, gSF was changing in different, but equally fundamental way: the short story was slowly being replaced by the novel as the primary unit of

consumer consumption. Prior to the creation of Ballantine Books in 1952 book-form
science fiction was rare (Wolfe 2011: 19), but even before this paperback anthologies
reprinting magazine stories had appeared (beginning with Wollheim's *The Pocket Book
of Science-Fiction* in 1943 [ibid. p. 18]), and "fix-up" novels constructed from an author's
older stories had proven successful (e.g., Asimov's *Foundation* [1951/1991], relying on
stories from the early 1940s). Both of the late 1950s Heinlein serials mentioned above
also appeared in hardback form *in the same year*, and *primary* publication of novel-
length works in book form was becoming common. The longer medium both allowed
authors to elaborate and extend short story ideas (see Clarke's *Childhood's End* below),
and to further develop their fictional worlds—religion could be discussed in detail
even when it was tangential to the plot (e.g., Stewart's *Earth Abides*).

Representations of religion often retained the surety that anything purportedly
supernatural was probably a mistake (if not a deliberate lie) and religions continued
to be presented primarily as a social tool. But subtle qualifications began to appear:
religion could be more than *just* a tool for controlling the public; it might even have
positive social and cultural influences. Religion and science remained at odds, but there
appeared almost wistful desires that one *could* believe, and occasionally protagonists
chose belief over rationality—especially since science apparently might not be able to
save us from ourselves.

> That's the matter with us today. We all believe there are experts around, to fix up
> anything and everything. Soil erosion, rivers deflected, droughts, forests destroyed,
> natural resources wasted away. Never mind. Scientists will make food, control soil,
> or water. Plague? Let 'em come; polio, flu, anything. Scientists will cope with them.
> They'll also deal with crime, insanity, sex, family rows. (Holding 1954: 10)

An important facet of this is that the reader was challenged to accept that religion,
even simple superstitions, makes sense in certain social contexts. In de Ford's
"Apotheosis of Ki" (1956b), a Paleolithic-like hunter discovers a crashed space
traveler. The traveler pantomimes his hunger, and the fact that he is looking for his
lost companions. Ki, thinking the traveler to be a god and knowing gods cannot be
hungry, misunderstands what the "god" wants: Ki kills and eats him. Ki acts without
malice, with positive (for him) results: he becomes a powerful medicine man among
his people. The conclusion suggests that even the strongest "medicine" cannot resist
progress forever, but—given the proper circumstances—primitive superstition can
be quite effective.

Religion is also represented as more resilient than previously believed—not only
in its ability to survive scientific progress, but its capacity to appropriate facts for its
own use. In Anthony Boucher's "A Quest for St. Aquin" (1951/1971), science has "won"
and religion has been forced underground. A much diminished Pope sends a secret
Catholic named Thomas on a mission. Members of the Church, he argues, *need* a
miracle to sustain their faith. There have been rumors about a man so holy that his
body did not decay after death; Thomas is sent to learn if this is true. He discovers
it *is* true—to a point. The holy man was actually a robot and, as nonbiological, did
not decay when ceasing to function. But instead of losing a potential miracle (there is

nothing miraculous about a machine that does not rot, after all), the Church finds a new one: even machines will ultimately apprehend God (cf. Simak 1972, 1981).

Readers and authors of gSF in this period were still drawn to a technological future, and their loyalty was still to science, but that loyalty could no longer be blind, and a future without religion seemed less inevitable. Some tentatively suggested that *perhaps* this was not bad thing. As the protagonist of *The Long Tomorrow*, Brackett (1955/2012: 393) says, "'I'm not questioning—I'm only asking.'"

Arthur C. Clarke, *Childhood's End* (1953)

Arthur C. Clarke's influence is on par with Asimov's and Heinlein's (see above): "For many readers, ACC is the very personification of sf . . . He is deservedly seen as a central figure in the development of post-World War II sf, especially in his liberal, optimistic view of the possible benefits of technology (*though one that is by no means unaware of its dangers*)" (Clute and Nichols 1995: 232, emphasis added). He is only one "step" after the Golden Age, but presents a distinct contrast to Asimov's and Heinlein's early work.

Clarke's *Childhood's End* (1953) started out life as the short story "Guardian Angel" (Clarke 1950b[2]), which had a clever ending. Alien "Overlords" take over the Earth. Their rule is irresistible, but light-handed and benevolent. They do not seem to be focused on the exploitation of humanity, the removal of our natural resources, and, in a sharp contrast to the gSF of the 1920s and '30s, they are not even particularly interested in our women. In fact, they seem to be concerned only with limiting humanity's power to destroy itself. One less-than-reassuring detail: they refuse to let "us" see them. In 50 years they will show themselves (ibid. p. 23), but in the meantime they use human go-betweens, who only hear their voices. It is implied that the reason for this is that we would recognize them (ibid.) and that our last meeting did not go well: "'Yes . . . we have had our failures.' 'And what do you do then?' 'We wait—and try again'" (ibid. p. 28). Even with two generations' familiarity, their appearance would create "one of [humanity's] rare psychological discontinuities'" (ibid. p. 27). The leader of the humans catches a glimpse of an Overlord and realizes that this prior meeting caused "echoes to roll down all the ages, to haunt the childhood of every race of man. Even in fifty years, could you overcome the power of all the myths and legends of the world?" (ibid. p. 29). He learns that the Overlords have tails—*devils'* tails.

The Overlords' hegemony did little to limit personal freedom—or even the agency of the state, *provided* they were not oppressive, corrupt, or warlike. It is significant that, in this post-World War II narrative, peace is something possible for humans *when imposed from outside*. Significantly, the groups most resistant to the Overlords are religious. Though individual freedoms are increasing, they lament the loss of "Freedom to control our own lives, under God's guidance" (ibid. p. 4)—not the freedom to *restrict* freedoms, but perhaps the freedom to make our own mistakes. In earlier gSF, one would expect religion to be antithetical to social progress toward peace, but here *many* social institutions resist the Overlords' rule; religions prove to be the most durable (cf. Jones [1933] in Chapter 4).

"Guardian Angel" later became the first third of the novel *Childhood's End* (1953: 13–65).[3] The extra length of the novel allowed Clarke to tell us a great deal more about the Overlords' purpose, and the character of humanity. The resistance of religion to the Overlords changes subtly: in 1950b (p. 4), it is clear that some religious leaders *accept* the Overlords; in the 1953 version (p. 16), the spokesperson for the religious resistance has been defrocked. Nevertheless, in the novel version of the story, the Overlords accept *and regret* that their presence will inevitably contribute to religion's decline.

> [Religious leaders] know that we represent reason and science, and, however confident they may be in their beliefs, they fear that we will overthrow their gods. Not necessarily through any deliberate act, but in a subtler fashion. Science can destroy religion by ignoring it as well as by disproving its tenets . . . How long, they wonder, have we been observing humanity? Have we watched Mohammed begin the hegira, or Moses giving the Jews their laws? Do we know all that is false in the stories they believe? . . . Believe me, it gives us no pleasure to destroy men's faiths, but *all* the world's religions cannot be right, and they know it. Sooner or later, man has to learn the truth: but that time is not yet. (Ibid. p. 23)

Religion is, then, if not *opposed* to science, at least vulnerable to rationality and cannot survive accurate data, particularly about its origins. The concerns of the religious prove justified: the Overlords *had* long been observing and recording humanity. After revealing their appearance ("The leathery wings, the little horns, the barbed tail—all were there"; "It was a tribute to the Overlords' psychology, and to their careful years of preparation, that only a few people fainted" [ibid. p. 68]), the Overlords open many of their records, including the recordings relevant to the origins of our religions. "Most of them were noble and inspiring—but that was not enough. Within a few days, all mankind's multitudinous messiahs had lost their divinity . . . Humanity had lost its ancient gods: now it was old enough to have no need for new ones" and "only a form of purified Buddhism—perhaps the most austere of all religions—still survived" (ibid. pp. 74–5).

Religion here is tainted by supernaturalism and is something we can grow out of, provided we survive long enough (but see Rabkin 1976: 99–100). However, this negative view is softened by Overlord leader's regret—which implies *some* beneficial aspects, even if only the comforts of avoiding *too* much reality—and his lack of cynicism: there is no missionizing against religion, no attempts to hurry along its (inevitable) decline. Further, Clarke immediately follows the social decline in religion with a corresponding decline in science: faced with the overwhelming superiority of the Overlords' science, marginally improving our own modest achievements seemed useless. Even the *arts* were affected by the Overlords' presence:

> No one worried except a few philosophers. The race was too intent upon savoring its new-found freedom to look beyond the pleasures of the present. Utopia was here at last: its novelty had yet to be assailed by the supreme enemy of all Utopias— boredom. (Ibid. p. 75)

Note the recurrence of the threat implied by *not* struggling, first discussed here in the 1930 story "The Troglodytes" (Chapter 4): the Overlords' help *was* beneficial, and possibly saved us . . . but with costs.

Another echo from earlier stories: religion serves as a repository of knowledge: *lost* knowledge, admittedly—imperfectly understood remnants, records of misunderstood experiences (cf. Asimov's "Trends," Heinlein's "Universe"). Only religions and myths recorded the Overlords' previous visit, as well as other data of significance to the Overlords. An Overlord named "Rashaverek" attends the party of a human named "Boyce." Years after the Overlord-imposed barriers ended, most humans had still never met an Overlord. The attraction for Rashaverek appears to be Boyce's library, which includes "almost everything of importance that had ever been published on the nebulous subjects of magic, psychic research, divining, telepathy, and the whole range of illusive phenomena lumped in the category of paraphysics. It was a very peculiar hobby for anyone to have in this age of reason" (ibid. p. 81).

Boyce believes the Overlords' interest is in gaining perspective on an aspect of human psychology, as one would naturally wish "'to study the superstitions of any primitive race you were having dealings with'" (ibid. p. 87). The truth is more complicated. Later that night, a number of guests play with a Ouiji board. Rashaverek observes. On impulse, one guest asks the board something the Overlords have not been willing to tell humans: what star is the Overlords' home? The board answers correctly, though only one guest (aside from Rashaverek), a woman named Jean, recognizes the answer to be a star catalog number (ibid. p. 101).

Later, Rashaverek describes finding in the library "'eleven cases of partial breakthrough, and twenty-seven probables. The material is so selective, however, that one cannot use it for sampling purposes. And the evidence is confused with mysticism—perhaps the prime aberration of the human mind'" (ibid. pp. 102–3). Note that whatever Rashaverek is looking for is rational to him, but would be mistaken by us to be "mysticism." Regarding the Ouiji board incident: "'This is most exciting feature of the entire affair. Jean Morrell was, almost certainly, the channel through which the information came. But she is twenty-six—far too old to be a Prime Contact herself'" (ibid. p. 103).

The climax of the novel concerns the significance of "Prime Contacts." I would prefer not to ruin the ending here, so I will say only that Rashaverek's interest in the library and the Overlords' interest in humanity are identical. We humans possess a certain capacity that they lack—one which has fed into our legends, our mysticism, and presumably our religion, an "aberration" that gives us the potential to exceed the Overlords in some ways. Note the irony: the Overlords' superior knowledge destroys religions, but our religions reflect ways in which we are superior to the Overlords.

In general, religion is represented in *Childhood's End* in Golden Age fashion: as primitive and antithetical to science and to reason. However, Clarke also presents the *limitations* of this representation: pure science is not desirable, as human nature (especially in the eyes of post-World War II authors and readers) is potentially self-destructive; even if the loss of religion is inevitable, it is natural to regard its loss with some regret; insofar that science's *raison d'être* is the production of knowledge, religion may be a shadowy reflection of science in that it can serve as a repository of information, even if people within the religions do not recognize its significance; and finally, religion hints at unexplored strengths, even if we are, at present, unable to comprehend these strengths.

Walter Miller, *A Canticle for Leibowitz* (1959)

Childhood's End was nominated for a "Retro Hugo" in 2004—a post hoc acknowledgment by the gSF community that Clarke had made a significant impact on the genre. The next text I will discuss managed to win the Hugo outright in 1961. Like *Childhood's End*, Walter Miller's *A Canticle for Leibowitz* (1959/1997) started in the periodicals, in this case as a series of three loosely related stories in *F&SF*: "A Canticle for Leibowitz" (Miller 1955/1966), "And the Light Is Risen" (Miller 1956), and "The Last Canticle" (Miller 1957). I will focus first on the original short story: I frankly prefer the happier ending of the original version. (For an account of religion in Miller's other stories, see Bertonneau 2008.)

"A Canticle for Leibowitz" (Miller 1955/1966) opens with a Brother Francis, as part of his Catholic monastic training, spending 40 days living alone under a vow of silence in the Utah desert six miles from his home the Brothers of Leibowitz Abbey. One day, he meets a cheerful old man, wandering by in nothing but a hat, shoes, and burlap loincloth. When he manages to communicate (nonverbally, of course) that he is supposed to be living in "Solitude & Silence," the old man continues on his way (ibid. p. 283).

Later that day, Brother Francis finds a metal box; his first impulse is to exorcise it: "There were things, and then there were Things" (ibid. p. 284). When neither incantations nor holy water have noticeable effects, he wonders if the box is a Sign that he is indeed called to the priesthood. He quickly suppresses the thought: though his Order acknowledged the existence of miracles, he had been specifically warned not to expect one, and to leave the recognition of miracles to his superiors. "'An attack of sunstroke is no indication that you are fit to profess the solemn vows of the order'" (ibid. p. 284). Just in case, he tries to be respectful as he bashes it open. We learn that Francis's "studies had equipped him to recognize a screwdriver" (ibid. p. 285), and though he does not understand the purpose of electronics parts, he knows they are used as charms by some outside his Order. More importantly, the box also contains papers.

> The documents, as always, were the real prize, for so few papers had survived the angry bonfires of the age of Simplification, when even the sacred writings had curled and blackened and withered into smoke while ignorant crowds howled vengeance. (Ibid. p. 285)

In the pages to follow, we discern that Brother Francis lives some six centuries in our future. A nuclear war has virtually destroyed civilization. In the aftermath, mobs of people destroyed as much written knowledge as possible, along with any scientists they could get their hands on, in an effort to keep such things from happening again. The

Leibowitz of their Order was one such martyr; the Catholic Church has been involved with saving as much knowledge as possible, even though the continued fear of scientific progress has necessitated keeping most of their activities covert. They preserve and hand-copy what texts they can (sacred and secular). Though even they have forgotten how to make sense of many of the writings (see ibid. p. 292), it is enough, for now, to hope that one day the Church will be able to facilitate the restoration of science and learning.

So, when young Brother notices that one of the documents is a blueprint signed "Leibowitz," he considers the possibility that this—along with the screwdriver, a racing form, and some calculations for Leibowitz's income tax—could be an authentic relic of *their* Leibowitz. It is worth noting that the character balances ignorance with intelligence—Francis has no idea what income tax is, yet automatically checks the long-dead Leibowitz's math—and a strong desire for a miraculous experience with caution. His caution is more than intellectual: Leibowitz is being considered for canonization, and as useful as an *authentic* miracle would be, an exposed fake would surely ruin the case. Nevertheless, Francis cannot help but re-interpret earlier events in light of this new "evidence": could the old man have been the Blessed Leibowitz himself?

When Brother Francis finally returns to home, the Abbot is not enthusiastic. "It was not that he objected to miracles, as such, if they were duly investigated, certified, and sealed; for miracles . . . were the bedrock stuff on which his faith was founded" (ibid. p. 288). But given the stakes, he asks Brother Francis if he is "'ready to deny your feverish ravings about an angel appearing to reveal to you this . . . this assortment of junk?'" Francis, though humble, says he cannot. It may not be his place to interpret, but neither can he lie as to what he saw, just as he later refuses to lie in the other direction and confirm elaborations to his story: heavenly choirs and roses springing up where the wandering old men stepped (ibid. p. 298). Brother Francis is caned and not allowed to take his Vows that year, nor for several years after. The Abbot only relents after the documents are tentatively accepted by the Church as genuine.

Brother Francis then begins creating an illuminated copy of the Leibowitz blueprint: 15 years of patient labor, despite constant resistance from his superiors. When it is finally completed, he is directed to travel to the New Vatican and present it to the Pope. He is mugged, but debases himself so pitifully that the robber gives it back. The mocking of the robber, however, leads Francis to wonder if he had wasted his life creating a meaningless object.

At the New Vatican, Leibowitz is ceremoniously canonized. Pope's words restore his faith: "'Whatever this means', he breathed once more, 'this bit of learning, though dead, will live again'. He smiled up at the monk and winked. 'And we shall guard it till that day'" (ibid. p. 304). One serves God, and finds personal meaning, in the simple preservation of knowledge.

"A Canticle for Leibowitz" juxtaposes contrasts. We have a sympathetic but virtually comedic protagonist; a passive figure but with a strength of will one can only respect; a monk whose obedience is trumped only by his intellectual honesty. He is part of a religion based on a belief in miracles, but which practices skepticism. The preservation of secular texts is a sacred duty even without understanding, though understanding is the ultimate goal. A commonplace document is transformed into a beautiful artifact.

The evolution from the earlier representations is striking. Like Heinlein's "Universe," religion preserves scientific information that is no longer understood, but in *this* case they do it without hypocrisy—they *know* they do not know and are motivated to help, not manipulate. The religion described has a clear intent to help (not hinder) the development of knowledge in an apparently deliberate echo of the role of the monasteries in *our* Dark Ages (cf. Cahill 1996). Again in contrast, the religious specialist is an altogether sympathetic and powerless character—a far cry from the "evil priests" jealously guarding their power in earlier decades (cf. Barclay 1930 in Chapter 4). The too-often assumed conflict between religious and scientific ways of understanding the world seems undermined by the example of gentle Brother Francis.

When worked into the later novel (Miller 1959/1997), this story (combined with the two sequels) becomes more pessimistic. In the rewritten version, Brother Francis travels with both his illumination *and* the ancient blueprint, and loses his illumination to the robber. On his way home, Brother Francis is again ambushed; this time he is killed and eaten by cannibals. This part of the book closes with "There were rumors of war" (ibid. p. 118). In the later parts, humanity regains its scientific prowess, again using it to destroy itself. Again, the Church preserves something to seed the next generations. It is ultimately *science* which proves to be most dangerous, but religion helps accelerate the cycles of apocalypse.

Leigh Brackett, *The Long Tomorrow* (1955)

Brackett's *The Long Tomorrow* (1955/2012) also describes a post-nuclear holocaust world, though in this case the holocaust occurred only two generations previously—recent enough that the oldest generation still remembers the old life. In *Leibowitz*, mobs of common people blamed science and scientists for the holocaust, and as a result suppressed science, burned the books, and anything else they could think of to make sure such things never happened again. Similar events figure into *The Long Tomorrow*, but with a few important differences. Here, while some of the methods were violent, others were structural, thoughtful, and long term, not reactionary. In an effort to eliminate the recovery of nuclear power, high population densities are banned (and outlawed by the US Constitution) to rule out urbanization and specialization. It is though that not only will this keep the necessary infrastructure from developing, but will also produce a society less interdependent and thus less fragile.

In this cautious world, the fastest growing religion is the New Mennonites. Strongly agricultural and thoroughly traditional, immediately after the war only Mennonites were capable of surviving the collapse of society; further, their distain of technology and conveniences resonated with outsiders. Throughout the novel, Brackett portrays them as good, peaceful people—certainly not perfect, but admirable. In particular, they are the strongest and most reasonable of the religions described in the book, despite lifestyles that, to Brackett's readers, are rather extremely limited. In fact, they are rather tolerant. As one New Mennonite says, "'A man's religion, his sect, is his own affair. But those people have no religion or sect. They're a mob, with a mob's fear and cruelty, and with half-crazy, cunning men stirring them up against others'" (ibid. p. 375).

"Those people" are members of a charismatic, fundamentalist religion, well known for their undisciplined, rowdy meetings. Note the speaker's refusal to criticize directly the other religion, but also note that tolerance does not recognize the acts of this other group: they are not a "real" religion in his eyes, because they are not a community, not reasonable. Brackett is presenting these as positive people, and indeed characters who are not New Mennonites also find them admirable. Note the characteristics, which would make them attractive to gSF readers: not only is this religion presented as capable and appropriate, given the circumstances, but they are tolerant, sane, not easily manipulated (cf. Heinlein's "If This Goes On—" in the previous chapter) and above all concerned with community (cf. Orson Scott Card in Chapter 9).

Two older New Mennonite boys, Len and Esau, are fascinated by the contrast to their own sect. "'They fall down on the ground and scream and roll . . .'" one says to the other. "'Women, too'" (ibid. pp. 372–3). They sneak off to see the meeting, only to witness a stoning: a man has been accused of "'dangling the forbidden serpent's fruit'" (i.e., the knowledge of science, not good vs. evil) and of bearing "'the mark of Bartorstown'" (ibid. p. 384). There is no trial, nor even a defense—the stoning begins immediately following the accusation. They are rescued by a family friend, a non-New Mennonite traveling trader named Hostetter. He brings them, terrified and chastened, back to their families. "'Guilty or not,'" Len's father says, "'it's an unchristian thing. And blasphemous. But as long as there are crazed or crafty leaders to play on old fears, a mob like that will turn cruel'" (ibid. p. 389).

Bartorstown, we learn, is a legendary town where scientists continue to ply their trade—a kind of technological Sodom. As shocking as the punishment witnessed by the boys imposed on a man only accused of being from Bartorstown was, the boys' curiosity resurfaces. After Len's elderly grandmother waxes nostalgic about the technological good old days—in particular, dreaming about a dress in a bright red color no longer seen in a world of vegetable dyes and sober New Mennonites—and they discover evidence that Hostetter might be from Bartorstown himself, the boys set off.

In short, they find Bartorstown and are initiated into the mysteries of technology. Len meets a girl and settles down to help restore the lost world. Only it's not *quite* that simple; the complications have implications only observable by a member of the gSF community.

Leigh Brackett is primarily remembered today as coauthor of the screenplay for 1980's *The Empire Strikes Back*, but she was a child of the pulps, beginning her career in the Golden Age of *Astounding Science Fiction*. Even more than Clarke, her work shows a close relationship with the genre form of science fiction. Like her contemporaries, she assumes a tension between religion and science and is exploring the effects of the recent, destructive beginning of an atomic age. Further, as did earlier authors, Brackett shows religion to be a social tool, though now the tension between religion and science allows religion to check science's destructive potential, rather than impede scientific progress toward a technological utopia. Like the other authors described here, religion is associated with *sympathetic* characters, honest in their belief, rather than with manipulative villains. Recall the quote from Ursula K. LeGuin in Chapter 1: in order to write believable gSF, one can only acquire the necessary schema by reading it—the distinguishing schemas of "real" (i.e., genre) science fiction are too subtle to acquire any way but through long exposure. Brackett certainly has the experience to know these schemas and demonstrates her expertise here.

Displaying *familiarity* with the schemas, however, is only one aspect of Brackett's writing. Not only does she know them, but she expects her audience to know them, too. This allows her to play with readers' expectations. As an analogy, imagine reading an "armchair" mystery novel. A body is found; characters and evidence are described. The reader is thus encouraged to figure out for themselves "who done it." Now, imagine the reader's reaction if the "victim" actually died of natural causes, or the murderer was a random stranger not previously mentioned in previous chapters. Or maybe the butler did it! (If this experience is unfamiliar, I suggest you read Agatha Christie's *The Murder of Roger Ackroyd*.) If the author was an amateur, one would suspect they were unaware of the conventions; but if an expert, the author will be believed to have manipulated the reader, misdirecting them through their assumptions—an altogether more satisfying, and impressive feat.

Not all inversions of genre schema are surprises, of course. In Seabright's gSF "Thirsty God" (1953), the main character takes sanctuary in a shrine, not knowing that the shrine is associated with a repulsive race of aliens who are blindly using technology left behind by a superior race to support their rites, to which the main character falls horribly victim. The catch is that the aliens are *also* described as having "a singularly rich and varied spiritual life," while the main character is a rapist. As so many times before, the "hero" falls victim to a cult, but *this* time does not escape and deserves his fate (ibid. p. 106).

Brackett does something similar here. As mentioned before, Robert A. Heinlein was an author so influential that his plots had become virtual stereotypes. In particular, recall the basic plot of his story "Universe" described above: a young man and his friend are raised in a religious community. Driven by curiosity, they seek out forbidden scientific knowledge from outcasts who would be shot on sight, knowing that to do so endangers their own lives as well. They soon find these outcasts and are as quickly accepted and initiated into the scientific mysteries.

With *The Long Tomorrow*, Brackett virtually retells "Universe," but with deliberate reversals. Len and Esau do run away to find the scientists—but then fail for a long time to find them. Rather than recruit them for The Cause, Hostetter (who actually is from Bartorstown—they got that right, at least) does everything he can to dissuade them, then disappears. Len challenges the social order in another way and is almost lynched: only Hostetter's fortuitous reappearance saves him and Esau. The trip to Bartorstown is long and boring. There is a chance encounter with barbaric, possibly cannibalistic religious ascetics, but they leave without incident. Bartorstown is similarly anticlimactic; it is just a small, poor town that just happens to support a few frustrated scientists. In order to keep the secret, Len and Esau will be killed if they try to leave—as Hostetter says, they are just as much fanatics as any of the religious groups. Len's girl is determined not to keep Len there, but to convince him to help her escape. They do escape, but return willingly: she because the outside world is much more violent, intolerant, and dirty than she can accept, he because he finally begins to accept Bartorstown's mission. Unlike a Heinlein story, however, there is no indication that Len's contribution will be important, nor even that the scientists will be successful.

Though Len finds the path to a technological future, he is repeatedly shown to be painfully naïve. By extension, Brackett implied that the plots of the Golden Age, with their assumptions of the desirability of a technological utopia and the obsolescence of religion, had been similarly naïve. Len does ultimately decide to work toward a technological future, but he does so knowing the alternatives, and is aware that those who resist are sometimes honest, good people. *Some* religious people are fanatical, but not all, and the scientists are not immune to that particular sin. Importantly, Len never fully rejects the belief system he was raised in, which taught him that atomic power—a power he will be working with in Bartorstown—is not merely unwise, but evil. His choice is based on the belief that, if atomic power was discovered before, it *will* be discovered again.

> "I still think," said Len slowly, "that maybe it was the Devil let loose on the world a hundred years ago. And I still think maybe that's one of Satan's own limbs you've got behind that wall . . . But I guess you're right . . . I guess it makes better sense to try to chain the devil up than to try keeping the whole land tied down in the hopes he won't notice it again." (Ibid. pp. 582–3)

Note that if *and only if* one is familiar with the tropes of gSF can one recognize the meaning behind Brackett's book. As sobering as it is, *The Long Tomorrow*, in its treatment of religion and of science fiction, is a long inside joke. (Brackett was to repeat this trick late in her career with "The Purple Priestess of the Mad Moon," discussed below.)

The Long Tomorrow shows us four things important to this book: first, that in the period after World War II, science fiction had to come to terms with the destructive potential of technology, and second, that the dismissal of religion must be reexamined. Third, she offers a specific solution to gSF's crisis of conscience: that a technological future may still be desirable, but that it should not be accepted blindly, nor should opposing views be demonized. Finally, it provides a good example of how *genre* science fiction "works."

George Stewart, *Earth Abides* (1949)

George Stewart's *Earth Abides* (1949/1999) also describes a post-holocaust world, considered the role of religion, and worried about the loss of knowledge with the fall of civilization. Given these guidelines, Stewart posits strikingly different relationships, in particular about the *nature* of religion and religious belief. The novel deserves considerably more attention that I will be able to give it here: given the nature of *this* book, I will only be able to extract two, purposefully contrasting views of religion.

In marked contrast to most of later post-apocalypse novels, Stewart's world is far from the *Road Warrior* movies: the story is thoughtful, even gentle;[4] neither we nor the main character ("Isherwood Williams") are forced to witness the chaos and trauma of society's collapse—he is isolated in a forest, conducting graduate research. Instead, the focus is on a small group of survivors who find each other and build a community. As de facto leader, Isherwood is more like "Pa Ingalls" than "Mad Max." He is also (not coincidentally) the most educated, concerned not only with the community's survival, but with freeing it from its reliance on salvage (e.g., growing their own food instead of living off of the seemingly inexhaustible supply of canned goods from abandoned grocery stores) and maintaining a connection to their technological and academic past (e.g., encouraging use of the similarly abandoned libraries). By and large, the others (and especially their children) are more concerned with what they see as practical issues than esoteric topics like "independence" and "literacy" (ibid. pp. 196–7, 269–73), and Isherwood ("Ish" to his friends) sometimes seems naïve, even to the reader who sympathizes with his opinions (e.g., ibid. p. 112).

New social structures, even rituals develop, but religion seems not to be among them. For example, they mark the passage of time, naming each year after the most significant event. "The Year 8 was comparatively uneventful. They called it the Year We Went to Church. (The name amused Ish, for its wording implied that that experiment was over and done with)" (ibid. p. 126). The impetus for the experiment was not Ish, but George and Maurine, who had been described as rather less than intelligent.[5]

> Ish felt the temptation. He could easily piece together some harmless bits of religion, give comfort and confidence to people who might often need it badly, and supply a core of solidity and union to the community . . .
>
> In the end they held a service each Sunday—George had kept track of Sunday, or at least thought so. They sang hymns, and read from the Bible, and stood uncovered for silent prayer, each for himself.
>
> But Ish never prayed during the period of silence. (Ibid. pp. 126–7; cf. pp. 88–9, 251–3)

Soon enough, Ish decides that "the church services were cultivating disunion rather than unity of feeling, and sham more than true religion" (ibid. p. 127) and stops the experiment. So, it seems that intelligent people do not *need* religion; though there are theoretical benefits, in practice religion is not worth the effort.

So far, *Earth Abides* is—as far as representations of religion go, anyway—very Campbellian. The conclusion, however, is remarkable.

The third and shortest part of the book is entitled "The Last American." Ish is quite old now, often confused, and completely dependent on the great-grandchildren of the community's original members (whom they call "the First Ones"). In fact, he is the last one left who remembers life before the collapse; in one heartrending moment (reminiscent of Brackett's book discussed above), he is moved to tears by the sight of a bright red color, so rare in this new world (ibid. pp. 306–7). As such, he has become an almost mythic figure to them: the Last American, possessor of strange knowledge. Even the hammer Ish habitually carried has taken on a magical character, where previously it had been a symbol incidentally associated with his leadership; with each generation it accumulated "mana" and is now a potent fetish object (ibid. pp. 200–7, 295).

As much as they respect Ish for his esoteric knowledge, the people have absolutely no need of it. They care for him, even love him, and certainly view him with awe—but not because what he knows or can do is useful, but because he is *not* of their world.

> "After all, I am important. I am a god. No, I am not a god. But perhaps I am the mouth-piece of a god. No, I know I am not that, either. But at least they give me care, and I have comfort, because I am the last American." (Ibid. p. 297)

Technology is viewed similarly: a rifle is an impressive *toy*, but not something one would *rely* on; leftover coins are useful only as raw materials for arrowheads (ibid. p. 288). (Isherwood's dream of independence is fulfilled, at least.) In contrast, his hammer is not for hitting nails; it is a powerful, magical object which must be passed along in an appropriately ritualistic fashion—when Ish does not understand that he needs to choose a successor carry the hammer after him, they pinch him. "'It is a strange thing,' he thought, 'to be an old god. They worship you, and yet they mistreat you. If you do not want to do what they wish, they make you. It is not fair'" (ibid. p. 310).

In this generation, religion has reappeared—not the unnatural construct Isherwood pieced together from doctrinal religion, but something different, sometimes based on things Isherwood himself did or said, such as describing himself as an American to children who know nothing of America, except that it was once powerful but no longer exists (ibid. pp. 214–15). A robust mythology is being constructed to explain, for example, who those bearded men on the coins were. Ish's great-grandson explains, "'I have an idea. Our Old Ones—they were the Americans—made the houses and the bridges and the little round things that we hammer out for arrowheads. But those Others—the Old Ones of the Old Ones—perhaps they made the hills and the sun, and the Americans themselves'" (ibid. p. 288). Note that there is no hint of centralization or of standardized theology; myths are spontaneously generated to explain what seems important but is unknown. Forms of magic have emerged as well: arrowheads made of pennies are used to shoot cattle and lions; arrows tipped with white metal are thought better for deer and game. When asked why, the young man responds "'Why? How would anyone know *why*? Except you yourself, Ish! This matter of the red and white arrowheads is merely something that *is* . . . Why should there be a *why?*'" (ibid. p. 290). Ish is initially angered by the faulty grasp of causality, but quickly decides it does not really matter. What is important is they are making their own tools, tools which work well, and that they are *happy* (ibid. pp. 290–2).

Faulty or not, their reasoning works for them. Isherwood comes to see each pocket of humanity evolving; rather than cling stubbornly to the old ways, with literacy more important than religion and magic almost disappeared, each group is reasonably adapting to their actual circumstances. He thinks:

> Here they are darker-skinned and talk another language, and worship a dark-skinned mother and child. They keep horses and turkeys and grow corn in the flat by the river. They catch rabbits in snares, but they have no bows . . .

> Here they are still darker. They speak English, but say no r's, and their speech is thick. They keep pigs and chickens, and raise corn. They also raise cotton, but make

no use of it, except to offer a little to their god, knowing it from old to be a thing of power. Their god has the form of an alligator, and they call him Olsaytn . . .

Here they shoot with the bow, skillfully, and their hunting-dogs are trained to give tongue. They love assembly and debate. Their womenfolk walk proudly. The symbol of their god is a hammer, but they pay him no great reverence . . .

Many others there are too, each differing. In the distant years after these first years, the tribes will grow more numerous and come together, and cross-fertilize in body and in mind. Then, doubtless, blindly and of no one's planning, will come new civilizations and new wars. (Ibid. pp. 299–300, italics removed)

Perhaps a decline in religion is associated with civilization; even if so, it is no great achievement. Neither is civilization itself; cyclically, it emerges by accident then collapses, and at each stage lifeways—including forms of religion—adapt.

As a final thought on *Earth Abides*, I would like to point out the strong likelihood of a metaphor in Isherwood's name—one that escaped me when I first read the book as a teenager. In 1911, a man appeared in a California town: a Native American who spent his entire life living without contact with "civilization," who was the last of his people (the Yahi), who the last of a large language and culture group (the Yana). Having nowhere else to go, he wandered, eventually residing at the University of California, in the care of anthropologist (and father of Ursula K. Le Guin) Alfred Kroeber. Since no one from his group was alive to speak his name, this man was just called by the Yana word for "man": Ishi.

James Blish, *A Case of Conscience* (1958)[6]

gSF appears to have an inordinate fondness for Jesuits; the editor of an anthology of gSF stories featuring gods and religion lists among the contents "a saintly Chicago gangster, a chimpanzee named Leo, and half a dozen Jesuits" (Ryan 1982: 2), and they show up several times in this book (see also pp. 53, 193–6).

The recurrence of Jesuits over other religious specialists makes sense. First, protagonists are predominantly cultural Westerners, so a religious specialist will likely be from a Western religion. But, given the genre's antipathy toward religion, a religious specialist will tend to be a protagonist only if the author wants to discuss religion; the chief objection to religion being its believed tendency to suppress science, the author will choose a representative of Catholicism as that religion is believed to have the strongest history in this area (think Galileo Galilei). In seeking a *sympathetic* example, Jesuits are a natural choice: not only do they have a history of exploration (e.g., being a primary link between China and the Western world during Europe's age of exploration), but also reputations as educators, and as wrestling with thorny theological contradictions. Not coincidentally, gSF authors like James Blish wrote memorable novels prominently featuring Jesuits presented as exemplars—as did previous gSF authors and others sympathetic to gSF norms (e.g., Jacomb [1926] describes Jesuits as educators and as "a great religious order" [p. 81]). (Some later authors alter this, e.g., Ringo [2003].)

An example is Winston P. Sanders' "The Word to Space" (1960/1974), which contrasts what religion should and should not be, using a Jesuit as an ideal exemplar. It is a brilliant little story, especially in that it is one of those exceedingly rare narratives that describes our relationship with a intelligent race from another world *without* faster-than-light travel or communication. Over a century ago (story time), Earth made contact with a planet 25 light years away, peopled by an intelligent species who call the planet "Akron." Humans—especially scientists looking for paradigm-shifting breakthroughs—are excited; much money is spent, including a well-staffed research center.

Unfortunately, two problems deflate interest. First, we have no "ansible" [i.e., a faster than light communication device, commonly referred thusly in and out of gSF after its appearance in Card's *Ender's Game* (1985a), rather like *Star Trek*'s "warp drive" (cf. Alcubierre 1994)], so one must wait 50 years for a response to any question—25 years for our signal to reach them, 25 for their response to reach us. Second, Akron is ruled by a theocracy, and all the aliens seem to want to do is proselytize. "[W]hat have we actually learned so far? One language. A few details of dress and appearance. An occasional datum of physical science, like that geographical information you spoke of. In more than a hundred years, that's all!" (Sanders 1960/1974: 75).

The epistemological stalemate can only be broken by overthrowing the theocracy, by undermining their religion. At least, that is the suggestion of a new member of the much-diminished research center: Father James Moriarty, who is as devious as his surname implies. The director accusingly challenges him: "You're here for religious reasons, aren't you? The Catholic Church doesn't like this flood of alien propaganda," but has to admit that he, too, would very much like to change the status quo (ibid. p. 79). But Moriarty responds that the Catholic Church had decided "back when space travel was a mere theory" that their mission to convert sentient beings to Christianity was limited to Earth, and that his goal is nothing but "free scientific and cultural exchange" with Akron (ibid. p. 81).

Moriarty's method is simple: relying on centuries of religious debate, he begins to argue theology with Akron, asking for clarifications, pointing out conflicts, ambiguities, and alternative interpretations. As a character, what makes him positive is his willingness to acknowledge selfish motivations, his willingness to limit the purvey of his religion, his commitment to "free scientific and cultural exchange," . . . *and* his ability to argue theology.

Slightly over 50 years later, the aged Moriarty finds out the message worked: the Akron church went into Schism, the power of the theocracy was broken, and *their* scientists were finally given access to the communication equipment and have begun transmitting their "huge backlog of data" (ibid. p. 84).

Note that one of the positive features of Moriarty is his accepting the "local" relevance only of his religion. Kingsley Amis, publishing criticism of gSF in the same year as Sanders' story, wrote: "It is as if religion were tacitly agreed [within gSF] to have an earthly, or Terrene, limitation when the scale of human activity has become galactic" (Amis 1960: 83). (Amis also noted that "uses of religious subject matter" had been rare, but were becoming more common [ibid.].)

The other books described in this chapter hypothesize the nature of religion as a social system: is it vulnerable to scientific and historical knowledge? What roles can it play in the promotion/suppression of science? Are societal impacts desirable? Blish's *A Case of Conscience* (1958/2000) is different: it portrays the impact of a particular social system on the mind and spirituality of an individual.

In the Introduction to this book, I offered the following summary of the plot:

> A Hispanic, Jesuit priest and biologist with a talent for languages is a member of a small 'mission' to make contact with the first sentient aliens humans have discovered. The people they discover are pleasant, some even feel like friends to the priest, despite being shaped like overly-tall kangaroos. In fact, they seem ideal, almost as a Christian might imagine humans would have been like had we never left the Garden. But what the priest later discovers radically changes his interpretation: rather than confirming his belief in God, this previously-idyllic planet creates a deep crisis of faith. The majority of the novel is concerned with how the protagonist comes to terms with this crisis, supported in part by a woman who reminds him of the relationships he gave up in order to become a priest.

Ironically, very little needs to be added to this description of the plot, simply because the plot itself is relatively unimportant. Noted Golden Age author Theodore Sturgeon is reported to have said that the only justification for writing a *science* fiction story is to explore an idea one could not develop in the mundane world. Such is the case here. Blish posits a thorny theological problem, and offers a startling solution. I will repeat for emphasis: here is a major gSF novel, by not just a noted author (famous for the "Cities in Flight" stories published in *Astounding* and for early Star Trek novelizations), but (under the penname William Atheling) a respected gSF critic, who describes not problems of adventure or exploration, but a spiritual, internal crisis. (For "Atheling's" critical perspective on religion in science fiction, see Blish's essay "Cathedrals in Space" [Blish 1973: 52–79]).

To fill in the details, Father Ruiz-Sanchez (biologist and Jesuit), Cleaver (physicist), Agronski (geologist), and Michelis (chemist) form a team sent to ascertain whether an inhabited planet named Lithia should be opened for general use—trade, a way-station for travel, etc. (Note that all team members are physical scientists, though Michelis displays social science interests.) Cleaver votes to keep the planet "closed," not because of any dangers or unsuitabilities, but because he believes the United Nations (UN) should use it as a bomb factory—the available raw materials and workforce convince him it is a unique opportunity, and he performs some ethically questionable acts to trick the rest of the team into voting along with him. His tricks fail, but Agronski agrees with him. Michelis very much likes the planet, and votes to open it; knowing Ruiz-Sanchez also likes the planet and the people; he expects the priest to vote along with him. However, Ruiz-Sanchez surprises them all, voting not just to keep the planet closed, but to quarantine the planet, preventing *any* further contact with the Lithians. We eventually learn that Cleaver's plan is accepted by the UN.

Ruiz-Sanchez's objections are rooted in his Jesuit nature and training. We can extrapolate from his example what characteristics make a religious specialist positive to gSF of this period. They do not value "an excess of devotion, a form of pride among the pious" (ibid. p. 28). Intellectually, they must be flexible. "All Catholics must be devout; but a Jesuit must be, in addition, agile" (ibid. p. 29). Though they may differ from scientists in the interpretation of significance, "The Church accepts facts, as it always accepts facts" (ibid. p. 94).

The facts, such as Father Ruiz-Sanchez understands them, are these:

- The Lithians are not only moral, but are *perfectly* moral: they have *no* deviants, no significant misunderstandings. They do not have a word for "murder," do not appear to understand deliberate falsehood, or why a reward would motivate proper behavior. As such, they are ideals to which humans could not relate. Worse, their morality is *specifically* aligned to Catholic beliefs. Even their desired form of birth control conforms to the Church's teachings. Ruiz-Sanchez finds this coincidence too unlikely to be accepted as accidental.
- The Lithians are creatures of logic and are utterly without religion. Their rhetoric and behaviors (social *and* scientific) appear to be based on assumed, ahistorical axioms: they are not learned, cannot be questioned, but rather are somehow innate. (Again, they are unsuitable ideals for humanity.) In contrast to humans, they have no personal doubts ("night thoughts" [ibid. p. 60]) and no fear of death (which they describe as simply ceasing to change [ibid. pp. 44–5]). In a curious foreshadowing of the cognitive science of religion, they also lack myths, traditions, even the capacity for metaphors (ibid. p. 43). Given their lack of all the needs one would associate with human religion, it is no surprise the Lithians have none. Note the contrast to 1951's "A Quest for St. Aquin" (see above).
- The Lithians act as perfectly moral Catholics, but completely lack a belief in God. They are the ultimate pragmatists, assuming that if a question cannot be tested, the question itself is meaningless (ibid. p. 40)—how could one test the hypothesis that god exists? If perfect morality is possible without them, then faith, love, a conscience are irrelevant. Goodness can exist without God. The Lithians therefore represent an atheistic proof that the religious spirituality of humanity could not survive.
- However, the Lithian danger is *so* specific to Catholicism, and based on assumed axioms that appear to have no justification whatsoever, that Ruiz-Sanchez cannot accept that it developed by chance and, given the potency of the spiritual poison, could not have been designed by God. Therefore, Lithia could only be the direct creation of Satan himself.

To save the souls of all humanity, Father Ruiz-Sanchez decides that Lithia is literally the work of the devil and votes to keep the planet closed. However, by doing so, he falls prey to the Catholic heresy of Manichaeanism. According to Catholic orthodoxy, only God can create. So, by voting to keep the planet closed, Ruiz-Sanchez damns himself in the eyes of the Church. The trap appears perfect: Ruiz-Sanchez is damned no matter which way he votes.

Upon returning to Earth, Ruiz-Sanchez is summoned to meet with the Pope. He fully expects to be tried for heresy, and in fact the UN is withholding announcements as to the fate of Lithia until after Ruiz-Sanchez is excommunicated. In a further irony, it is a Holy Year—the year in which almost anything can be forgiven. The Pope, in an oddly gentle way, refuses to absolve Ruiz-Sanchez of his sins, as he continues to maintain Manichaean thoughts, but neither will he begin formal examinations. The excommunication from the Church became real when Ruiz-Sanchez sinned. Formalities would change nothing; further, we suspect the Pope is conscious of the political implications. Instead, he suggests an alternative interpretation. Only God can create, but the Devil *can* deceive.

> "Then . . . is Your Holiness truly proposing that . . . that I should have attempted to . . . to exorcise a whole planet?"
>
> "Why not?" [Pope] Hadrian said. "Of course, the fact that you were standing on the planet at the time might have helped to prevent you, unconsciously, from thinking of it. We are convinced that God would have provided for you—in heaven, certainly, and possibly you might have received temporal help as well." (Ibid. p. 193)

Later, a shocked and depressed Ruiz-Sanchez visits a mansion on the Moon (owned by a Count who is a scientist and lapsed Catholic) with Michelis. In a rather blatant *Deus ex machina*, the Count has developed a viewscreen that allows the far-distant Lithia to be observed in real time. We also learn that Cleaver's weapons plant is about to come on line and that the Count has found a flaw in one of their calculations; he fears a disaster. Ruiz-Sanchez looks at the screen and begins the Rite of Exorcism. The planet blows up, half-blinding the Count and his guests. Understanding something of what has happened, the Count gracefully moves everyone else out of the room. "Nevertheless, when Father Ramon Ruiz-Sanchez, sometime Clerk Regular in the Society of Jesus, could see again, they had left him alone with his God and his grief" (ibid. p. 231).

The Pope did warn Father Ruiz-Sanchez that he might expect "temporal help as well." So, was the destruction of Lithia, Cleaver and his team, and the Lithians Ruiz-Sanchez had come to care for, the result of his exorcism? Or was he simply opportunistically taking advantage of what the Count called "An error in Equation Sixteen" (ibid. p. 230)?

Part of the answer, I think, lies in an earlier comment by Ruiz-Sanchez on the nature of science. Nothing in the end of *A Case of Conscience* defies scientific explanation, nor undermines faith in scientific progress—though physicist Cleaver's behavior might weaken one's faith in scientists. But it does describe a lack of faith in *any* certainties, religious or scientific. There are no absolute answers, just temporary ones. We (and he) cannot know if it is God or physics operating. Our choice, then, must be based on which answer we can live with. As Ruiz-Sanchez says, when all the facts have failed, he will still have God (ibid. p. 21).

Conclusion

Through the first two decades of gSF, science had been seen as facilitating a transformation to a better and brighter future. Religion, in contrast, was an irrational obstacle associated with an ignorant and primitive past, and used as a tool by powerful leaders to manipulate the gullible masses. After 1945, Americans struggled to come to terms with the destructive, technological power of the atomic bomb. This was a particular struggle for the science fiction community, who had placed such faith in science. No longer could scientific progress and the development of new technologies be assumed to be unalloyed positives. Faith in science is not directly challenged, but rather it was felt that the underlying pressures had to be better understood. As Len said, "I'm not questioning—I'm only asking."

In the novels described here, there are two central themes. First, human nature is viewed more cynically. In *Childhood's End*, only alien intervention keeps us from pursuing self-destructive paths; in *A Canticle for Leibowitz*, humanity, having destroyed itself once, is unable to learn the lessons necessary to avoid doing it again. Second, this self-reflection significantly changed gSF's view of religion.

Religion remains a potent social tool, as it had been in the Campbell era, but the speculations concerning the application of that tool evolved. Religion retained an antagonistic position to science, but the tension is less absolute, and a *balance* between the two was seen as possibly desirable. For example, both Miller and Brackett describe positive but contrasting roles for religion after devastating nuclear wars: in *A Canticle for Leibowitz*, religion helps science recover and ultimately saves humanity the *next* time we blow ourselves up; in *The Long Tomorrow*, religion promotes a lifestyle appropriate for the circumstances, allowing humanity to survive the years after a war, and if some religious people are fanatical and violent, others are thoughtful and peaceful—and the scientists are not without a thread of fanaticism themselves.

Religion is still a social system, but viewed from more sympathetic viewpoints (young and experienced monks, a boy's relationship with his New Mennonite father), with communal organization more palatable than religious hierarchies (cf. Heinlein's "If This Goes On—"). Given the scientific norm that the generation and preservation of knowledge is "good," it is logical that these new, more positive representations of religion emphasize its active role in saving knowledge even if religions themselves do not comprehend what they preserve (*Childhood's End*, *A Canticle for Leibowitz*), and religions' willingness to face the spiritual implications of knowledge head-on rather than denying the facts (*A Case of Conscience*) and if necessary to replace destructive knowledge with alternatives (*The Long Tomorrow*). Religions in previous stories of course encompassed scientific knowledge before—Heinlein's "Universe," for example, portrayed a religion built on misunderstood scientific information—but these stories show a crucial difference: in "Universe," the religion did not *do* anything with the information. Their records contributed nothing to the recovery of technology, and leaders discouraged secular interpretations. The scientifically curious had to go elsewhere.

Science fiction, even in its metanarratives, is not meant to tell a single story, but to explore all the possibilities *given contemporary constraints*. In this period, a tension between religion and science may be weaker but is still a given, and contemporary concerns with humanity's capacity and apparent willingness to destroy itself required re-interpretations of both ends of the spectrum. Representations of religion evolved, adapting to the new intellectual *Zeitgeist*. The books described here represent thought experiments, positing new variants.

In the next period, more profound changes in gSF's representations of religion appear. In the post-World War II period, the appropriateness and usefulness of religion are adjusted, and the point of view shifted toward the experience of the individual. But next, gSF moves to the foundations of religion and questions their assumptions about what religion is in the first place: in addition to being a potent social tool, to what extent is a religion "alive"?

Poli-Sci-Fi

Both science and religion underwent shifts in emphases as genre science fiction (gSF) moved into the early and mid-1960s. Science fiction was still about science, but the "science" was less likely to be taken exclusively from the "hard" sciences of physics and engineering, instead developing an awareness of sociology, psychology, and political science (see Rabkin 1976: 91–2). The perspective was no longer exclusively materialist, but also structural functionalist: that is, aware of the impacts not just the physical sciences and physical environments, but social sciences and cultural environments (see Wilson 1999: 23–9). Asimov's *Foundation* stories (beginning with Asimov 1942) were developed around the idea of a mathematically precise "psychohistory," but later quantifiable data and testable, generalizable predictions gave way to qualitative data and attempt to portray motivations and trends within a realistic but idiosyncratic (fictional) society. With tongue slightly in cheek, I would call this period (i.e., roughly the 1960s, overlapping the emergence of the New Wave c. 1966) as "poli-sci-fi."

Admiration for progress-for-its-own-sake would never again be as characteristic of the genre as it had been in the Golden Age. If, by the 1960s, the post-World War II preoccupation with technology's destructive potential had waned somewhat, the suspicion that tech-can't-buy-you-happiness waxed. For example, in Jay Williams' "Gift of the Gods" (1962), an interstellar Federation contacts present-day Earth, with promises of technological help for those cultures who meet their high social standards. Only the Bushmen *meet* those standards—and the Bushmen need/want nothing from them.

The genre had had a long and special relationship with anthropological perspectives on (potential) human cultures, dating even before the emergence of the genre (Barnard 2006), but the anthropology of 1960s' gSF was more likely to respect "thick description" of an insider's perspective than an objective perspective on the rules governing savage societies (*sensu* Geertz 1973). This leant itself to a degree of sympathy typically absent from earlier gSF. Corresponding to the decrease in confidence in the beneficial impacts of technology, the assumed negative impacts of religion were questioned, *and* even the negative aspects could be comprehensible, once one understood the point of view of religious insiders (e.g., Zelazny's "A Rose for Ecclesiastes" below). Religion might still represent a fundamental failure to face the world as it really was, but one might still envy the believer if religious institutions were able to solve some of our personal crises. Even if one dismisses the basis of a religion as nonsensical, the emotions of adherents and the communal bonds among believers must be acknowledged as valid.

It is as if, by this period, it had become obvious that religion was not going to disappear from human society any time soon, and anyone pretending otherwise was a fool. Perhaps ethical leaders can make use of it with a clear conscience, but in addition to becoming more legitimate, religion became—for want of a better word—more "real." Mythic roles gain distinct realities: as we will see in this chapter, even human (more or less human, anyway) characters, when placed in mythic roles, *become* the role in more than name (cf. Isherwood in *Earth Abides*), though not in any supernatural way. Religions themselves develop a kind of inertia, almost its own agency, and thus become more than tools, perhaps even characters in their own right. Leaders who seek to control society through religion can lose control of that religion; individuals taking on mythic roles may find themselves unable to extricate themselves. Religion, as it appears in gSF from the 1960s, is often another character; religion has acquired agency.

As two preliminary examples, consider Leigh Brackett's "Purple Priestess of the Mad Moon" (1964) and Leonard Tushnet's "In the Calendar of Saints" (1964). In *The Long Tomorrow* (1955) (discussed in the previous chapter), Brackett purposefully evoked the preceding state of the genre, giving her book another level. With the faintly ridiculous title of "Purple Priestess," she does something similar: it is meant to evoke images of early pulp gSF (including her own early work) and specifically to draw attention to previous dismissive representations of alien "cults." At a dinner party, the protagonist and other guests reminisce about the early, naïve days of planetary exploration, including the belief in mysterious native death cults—the protagonist soon discovers the cults are quite real, still very much alive, and capable of destroying a man's sanity. In short, Brackett implies that those fantastic stories, so recently disowned by the genre, deserve a second look and might not be so unlikely. Similarly, the protagonist in "In the Calendar of Saints" disbelieves in the potency of the old stories. In this reimagining of the traditional contract-with-the-Devil story, a good Soviet finds that "[t]his remnant of ancient superstition, this straw man set up by the priests to frighten the credulous . . . an obsolete carry-over in a modern People's Republic" (1964: 114) is not so toothless after all.[1] It is worth noting that "In the Calendar of Saints" appeared in the same issue of *F&SF* is a nonfiction essay by Isaac Asimov (1964b) on the historical relationship between religions and calendar systems (using examples not unlike those I employ in my Introduction to Comparative Religion class), and the Fritz Leiber story discussed below.

To dig a little deeper into the key characteristics of religion in this period, this chapter will focus on two short stories, one by Leiber and one by Roger Zelazny, as well as two of the most significant examples of twentieth-century science fiction: Heinlein's *Stranger in a Strange Land* (1961) and Frank Herbert's *Dune* (1965).[2]

Fritz Leiber, "When the Change-Winds Blow" (1964)

Published in the same, August 1964 issue of *Fantasy & Science Fiction* just mentioned was "When the Change-Winds Blow" by Fritz Leiber. A pilot is on a long solo flight over a lifeless Martian landscape, accompanied only by an empty space suit. His mind begins to wander, shifting back and forth between three separate subjects, linked by a common theme. The first is a book he had been reading: "*Vanished Churches and Cathedrals of Terra*." Second, the poet Robert Browning's relationship with Elizabeth Barrett, as expressed in the poem "The Bishop Orders His Tomb at Saint Praxed's Church," in which, according to Leiber, he describes his grandiose burial wishes while thinking of his long-dead mistress. Third, a secular university chapel in which his own lost love received her PhD and, following an explosion, in which she died. Note the boundaries crossed in this linkage—between historical and autobiographical, between fiction and reality, and between the sacred and the secular—accompanied by the common themes of loss and love, set in imageries of religious buildings.

The boundaries between real and imagined disintegrate further; he lands his craft after seeing what he knows to be the Cathedral of Chartres. Consciously, he knows that not only is it impossible that the cathedral is here, but also that the cathedral no longer exists—like the university chapel and the real St. Praxed's, Chartres was destroyed by nuclear bombs. Nevertheless, he is able to approach and even enters. Inside, however, he sees not Chartres' interior but the fictional Bishop's tomb, along with the woman he loved, in her formal academic robes. He thinks she recognizes him, until a glow that he knows to be the echo of the bomb(s) envelops everything he sees. "In my mind was the thought: St. Praxed, St. Modesta, and Monica the atheist saint martyred by the bomb" (Leiber 1964: 112). Leiber concludes, "It's in the things we've lost that we exist most fully" (ibid. p. 112).

Leiber gives no indication that any of this is anything more than hallucination; the vision disappears, and the pilot returns to his ship. But neither can the reader believe he will simply shrug it off and go his merry way. His mourning for Monica is tied to regret for what everyone had lost through a technological, man-made disaster. Being an atheist does not keep Monica from being a martyr. There is little hint that the pilot wants to turn back the clock, and resurrect the churches or Monica, nor that change is to be avoided; but on the other hand, not all changes are positive let alone comfortable, and "the weird and the supernatural didn't just evaporate when the world got crowded and smart and technical" (Leiber 1964: 108).

Roger Zelazny, "A Rose for Ecclesiastes" (1963)

"When the Change-Winds Blow" is a good example of the increased sympathy for religion and hints that religion is connected in some way to our basic nature. The second half of the schema for religion in the 1960s concerns the implication that religion may have some degree of independent reality over and above the motivations of individuals—even, perhaps, the manipulative leaders of such earlier stories as Heinlein's "If This Goes On—" discussed above. Not only may religion have its own inertia, but individuals may be forced into religious roles they do not fully understand.

The character of the protagonist ("Gallinger") in the Roger Zelazny story "A Rose for Ecclesiastes" (1963/1998) is significant. Rather than the standard upright, hard-scientist hero of the 1930s and '40s, we find a charismatic but rather obnoxious poet with father issues, a strongly religious background but no commitment to any religion, who amuses a professional linguist with his Greenwich Village slang.

His love of language began with his father and with the Bible. He remembers being "six again, learning my Hebrew, Greek, Latin, and Aramaic. I was ten, sneaking peeks at the *Illiad*. When Daddy wasn't spreading hellfire brimstone, and brotherly love, he was teaching me to dig the Word, like in the original" (ibid. p. 533). He is meant to be a priest like his father, but stalls in his studies. After his father dies (whom he refers to as the "Voice of God," and as "stern, demanding, with contempt for everyone's shortcomings—but never cruel" [ibid. p. 534]), he is free to "try a couple of the other paths to salvation. After that, it was two years in India with the Old Peace Corps— which broke me of my Buddhism, and gave me my *Pipes of Krishna* lyrics and the Pulitzer they deserved" (ibid.). Which is to say, he is the perfect representation of a counter-culture, "New Wave" gSF hero (see Chapter 8).

So as to avoid ruining the story for any who haven't read it, I will sketch only half of the narrative. Gallinger is part of an expedition to Mars, attempting to conduct ethnographic work with the seemingly primitive but ancient natives. His goal is to get access to their sacred texts, which also constitute their only history (ibid. p. 530). He quickly learns that their crude tents and relatively simple language are merely a layer: there is a previously unsuspected, richer "High Tongue," a city dug deep into the mountain, and a temple of "Byzantine brilliance" (ibid. p. 532).

His studies of their most important prophet/historian, Locar, teach him two things. First, their prophet is strongly reminiscent of Isaiah from his own tradition; he finds echoes of the fatalism of the Book of Ecclesiastes and begins to translate it into the High Tongue, both for fun and to "show them an Earthman had once thought the same thoughts, felt similarly." Second, he discovers in the records the reason why Martian civilization is in decline: a sterilizing plague centuries ago (ibid. pp. 543–4). Due to the fundamentalism of their religion, they accept as given that their race's doom is inevitable and immanent, and will do nothing to save themselves . . . even after Gallinger discovers a way to save their race, if they would only accept it.

When one grew up, as I did, reading authors like Zelazny and Heinlein, certain features jump out. Both the thoughts and emotions described in Ecclesiastes *and the expression of them in religion* are universal; there is, indeed, nothing new under the sun. Despite his lack of faith, both resonate in Gallinger. "I have my private system of esthetics, and I suppose it oozes an ethical by-product somewhere" (ibid. p. 540), he thinks, but in the context of the story the former seems more directly associated with religion than the latter. For their part, the Martians place him in the same category as their Locar, a "religious poet" (ibid. p. 541). One almost sympathizes with the Martian's refusal of Gallinger's solution—they do not misunderstand, but are psychologically resigned to their fate, and unable to break the pattern.

> "You have read the Book of Locar, [he is told . . .] and yet you ask me that? Death was decided, voted upon, and passed, shortly after it appeared in this form. But long before, the followers of Locar knew. They decided it long ago. 'We have done all the things,' they said, 'we have seen all things, we have heard and felt all things. The dance was good. Now let it end.'" (Ibid. p. 554)

(Note the return of the dangers of ennui, once all challenges have been met, that runs through gSF, from "The Troglodytes" in Chapter 4 to *Midnight at the Well of Souls* in the next.)

Desperate to save them (or rather convince them to save themselves), Gallinger breaks into a ceremonial meeting of their religious leaders and reads them his translation of Ecclesiastes.

> "Thousands of years ago, the Locar of our world . . . spoke as Locar did, but we did not lie down, despite plagues, wars, and famines. We did not die . . . we have crossed millions of miles of nothingness. We have visited another world. And our Locar had said, 'Why bother? What is the worth of it? It is all vanity, anyhow'.
>
> "And the secret is," I lowered my voice, as at a poetry reading, "he was right! It *is* vanity; it *is* pride! It is the hybris [i.e., "hubris"] of rationalism to always attack the prophet, the mystic, the god. It is our blasphemy which has made us great, and will sustain us, and which the gods secretly admire in us." (Ibid. p. 558)

The Martians change their mind, *but not because Gallinger convinced them he was wrong.* His coming, his attempt to save them, was *also* foretold. "'You are the Sacred Scoffer . . . He-who-Must-Mock-in-the-Temple—you go shod on holy ground [. . .] and we will never forget your teachings,' she added" (ibid. p. 560). Gallinger finds himself:

> . . . knowing the great paradox which lies at the heart of all miracles. I did not believe a word of my own gospel, never had. (Ibid.)

In "A Rose for Ecclesiastes," *belief is irrelevant.* The religion *uses Gallinger*, not the other way around. Despite his unawareness of his mythic role, he plays it out. Despite not believing Ecclesiastes *or* Locar, he becomes part of their story. We find here a wonderfully provocative tension: on one hand, our abandonment of religion, our blasphemy against God makes us great. On the other, doing so *makes us into religious figures.* We close the gap between us and divinity ("the gods secretly admire" our hubris), yet we are still powerless against the roles religions create.

Religion, too, has agency.

Later books by Zelazny also relate to religion. In *Lord of Light* (1967/1999), Zelazny again presented the power of mythic roles, in a story about humans who, long ago, traveled to a distant planet, with some of them using technology to recreate themselves in the images of Hindu gods, in order to rule over later colonists. One of these "Firsts" attempts to overthrow the status quo. The oft-quoted opening line sets the tone:

> His followers called him Mahasamatman and said he was a god. He preferred to drop the Maha- and the -atman, however, and call himself Sam. He never claimed to be a god. But then, he never claimed not to be a god. Circumstances being what they were, neither admission could be of any benefit. Silence, though, could. (Ibid. p. 9)

Sam understood that only religion can fight religion, and thus "sought to graft the teachings of Gotama [Buddha] upon the stock of the religion by which the world was ruled" (ibid. pp. 173–4). (Interestingly, the only other First to resist the status quo is the former Chaplain, but, perhaps due to his religiocentric motivations, is less heroic [ibid. pp. 280–1].) This is Zelazny at the height of his powers, earning himself a Hugo Award and a Nebula nomination. In some ways, *Lord of Light* extends the patterns in "A Rose for Ecclesiastes" (and mirrors *Dune*, described below): religion manipulates, but isn't "just" a tool; again, when individuals step into mythic roles they adapt to the roles as much as they attempt to *use* the roles. And if religion is held at arm's length by the hero, it's as much to keep it from getting away. However, it is difficult to be certain that portrayals extracted from *Lord of Light* that are representative of gSF due to Zelazny's juxtaposition (*not* blending) of genres: the book can be read as science fiction, as epic fantasy,[3] or as a metaphorical account of the emergence of Buddhism.

Taken together, "A Rose for Ecclesiastes" and "When the Change-Winds Blow" demonstrate the key features of representations of religion in gSF of the 1960s. But their fullest flowerings are in two of the most important gSF novels of the decade, and perhaps the century: Robert Heinlein's *Stranger in a Strange Land* (1961) and Frank Herbert's *Dune* (1965). *Stranger* won the 1962 Hugo, *Dune* won the 1966 Hugo as well as the first Nebula Award for best novel, and both routinely appear on lists of the best science fiction novels of all time.

Robert Heinlein, *Stranger in a Strange Land* (1961)

Robert Heinlein has already been discussed, of course, as has his presentation of religion as a social tool, both for maintaining a negative status quo ("If This Goes On—," 1939) and for positive revolution (*Sixth Column*, 1941/1949). But in *Stranger in a Strange Land* (1961), religion takes on a new form as Heinlein breaks from his own traditions.

Ironically, I would like to begin by mentioning another book by another influential Golden Age author, published a year later: *The Eleventh Commandment*, by Lester del Rey (1962). In a rather unpleasant future, the Church is invasively controlling the most intimate part of people's lives: the "eleventh commandment" is to be fruitful and multiply, and the Church tells people how and with whom to have sex, in an effort to increase people's fertility. Though these actions are presented in such a way as to provoke a viscerally negative reaction in the reader—indeed, del Rey targets gSF norms of individualism, freedom of choice, and a society free of religions' interference—the priests themselves are surprisingly empathic, and the reasons revealed to be behind the Church's actions might well be genetically valid, given the circumstances.

This sets the tone for understanding how *Stranger in a Strange Land* fits into the gSF metanarrative of religion. It is one of the most significant novels in the gSF oeuvre, and one of the few (excluding those associated with other media: movies, etc.) to make a significant impact on mainstream 1960s culture, comparable to Tolkien's earlier *The Lord of the Rings* (see "Books that Shaped America" n.d.), while reflecting trends in the *counter*-culture *Zeitgeist*.

> [*Stranger*] seems positively prophetic. Years before they became commonplace, he describes Esalen-type psychodynamic sessions, the spiritual benefits of liberated sex, and communal "families" where partners are warmly and regularly exchanged. Yet the novel's distinctively modern tone does not detract from the surely intentional resemblance of Valentine Michael Smith, the hero, to Jesus Christ—nor from the resemblance of his followers to the primitive Christians. (Mohs 1974: 14–15)

As much as it was "prophetic," *Stranger* was a break from Heinlein's Golden Age persona—a fact not entirely welcome in all gSF circles. Writing at the end of the decade, Panshin (in one of the first extended analyses of a single gSF author's work) felt that by 1960 Heinlein's best years were behind him. "Instead of concerning himself with facts, he has written about the morality of sex, religion, war and politics, but he has so concentrated on presenting his opinions as though they were facts" (Panshin 1968: 89). Further, Panshin believed this focus had been to the detriment of good writing (e.g., characterization). "The result from an artistic view is a mistake" (p. 90). *Stranger* is singled out as "a thoroughly annoying piece of work," which Panshin disliked too much to even review (p. 98). *Parts* are described as worthy (e.g., Heinlein's painfully sharp satire), so it is with regret that Panshin noted "it has sold the least well of any of Heinlein's [1960s] novels" (ibid. pp. 102–3). With delightful understatement, considering Panshin was probably completing edits in late 1967, the last comment is footnoted: "Perhaps no longer true, in view of the hippie vogue for *Stranger*" (ibid. p. 103).

As in Heinlein's and other Golden Age authors' earlier stories, religion is shown as something that may be used to manipulate people, though on rare occasions (Heinlein's own *Sixth Column*, 1949), the ends may justify the means. What makes *Stranger* a significant plot twist in gSF's metanarrative for religion is that the creator of the religion ("Michael Valentine Smith") is utterly sincere, and *the religion survives his death*—not because the religion outlived its purpose, but because the purpose is greater than the man. (This is similar to *The Eleventh Commandment*, though here this purpose is not systemic but personal, even transcendent.) It is clear that the reality of this religion is not founded on unsupported belief, but on concrete reality—a reality that adherents cannot at first perceive—and thus converts often require belief and other familiar religious trappings to facilitate their perceptual progress.

Delightfully, in *Stranger* we do not only have "Smith's" view, but that of Heinlein himself—or rather, a character ("Jubal," which is noted within the book to mean "father of all"[4]) who resembles Heinlein, and through whom the author can "soapbox" at length in issues of philosophy, ethics, manners, and whatever else catches his fancy.[5] Jubal represents the old school of the gSF Golden Age and is horrified when his protégé, Michael, decides to found a religion. But I'm jumping ahead.

Stranger begins with an ill-fated expedition to Mars. All the members who left on the expedition die, but there is a survivor: a child born in flight, and thereafter raised by the inscrutable Martians. Due to an agreement between expedition members, the infant Smith is the sole heir of all members, and due to a legal loophole he is also arguably the sole legal owner of Mars, and thus incalculably rich.

Years later, the second expedition (with rather more carefully written legal claims) discovers the adult but strangely innocent and literal-minded survivor Michael Valentine Smith (Michael: "he who is like God") and ships him back to Earth. His legal circumstances cause the authorities to keep him carefully confined, until a nurse, Jill, takes pity on him and arranges his escape. He and she take up residence in the home of the influential, eccentric, free-thinking libertarian Jubal Harshaw.

Having been raised the *very* alien Martians, Michael thinks like a Martian. This gives him a number of seemingly supernatural powers (e.g., twisting objects out of our reality, extreme control over his autonomic functions [see, e.g., Heinlein 1961: 111–13]) but which are perfectly normal to him, and which we understand are abilities anyone could acquire—given the proper early interventions. He also forms extremely tight relationships with anyone with whom he symbolically "shares water"; "water brothers" are people one trusts implicitly and would sacrifice anything for. His understanding of our psychology, however, is highly delayed. Michael is lucky that Jill, and the others with whom he forms this bond before he understands us well enough to make informed choices, is worthy of unwitting trust.

Jubal (read: Heinlein) expounds on a number of subjects, ranging from manners to religion—insofar as he sees these as distinct. Interpretations of particular traditions and practices are common, but a key feature is that Jubal continuously challenges assumptions about what is "natural." It is certainly not that he counters every objection made on moral, cultural, or ethical grounds, but insists on distinguishing between them. For example, when one of his circle is disgusted by an invitation to an orgy, Jubal is philosophical about it.

> "You don't find such behavior shocking?"
>
> "Ah, you raise another issue. Public displays of rut I find distasteful—but this reflects my early indoctrination. A large part of mankind does not share my taste; the orgy has a very wide history. But 'shocking'? My dear sir, I am offended only by that which offends me ethically."
>
> "You think *this* is just a matter of taste?"
>
> "Nothing more." (Ibid. p. 361)

Jubal is suspicious of religion based on ethical considerations (what societal impact does it have) as well as aesthetic (is it annoying him). A recurring image in *Stranger* is a pastiche of a Born-Again Christianity called the Fosterites.

Jubal admitted that a long life had left him not understanding the basic problems of the Universe.

The Fosterites might be right.

But, he reminded himself savagely, two things remained: his taste and his pride. If the Fosterites held a monopoly on Truth, if Heaven were open only to Fosterites, then he, Jubal Harshaw, gentleman, preferred that eternity be painfilled damnation promised to "sinners" who refused the New Revelation. He could not see the naked Face of God . . . but his eyesight was good enough to pick out his social equals— and those Fosterites did not measure up! (Ibid. p. 139)

Nevertheless, Jubal does value many aspects of religion, and widely read, able to recognize quotations from the Quran (in Arabic) (ibid. p. 195) and quote the Bible.

"You know your Bible?"

"Uh, not very well."

"It merits study, it contains practical advice for most emergencies. '—everyone that doeth evil hateth the light—' John something or other, Jesus to Nicodemus." (Ibid. p. 106)

Michael sincerely wants to help humanity to be happy, but he doesn't know how: he doesn't understand what motivates us; he doesn't even understand laughter. He and Jill set out alone so Michael can get the requisite social experience, and so Jill can continue learning to think like a Martian. The breakthrough occurs after he watches monkeys in a zoo. A large monkey assaults a smaller monkey to claim a treat. In response the robbed monkey finds an even smaller monkey on whom to beat out his frustrations.

For the first time, Michael laughs. Jill is shocked, not finding it funny at all, but Michael explains what this finally revealed to him about human psychology (ibid. pp. 311–12).

Too much Martian has rubbed off on you. Of course it wasn't funny; it was tragic. That's why I had to laugh. I looked at a cageful of monkeys and suddenly I saw all the mean and cruel and utterly unexplainable things I've seen and heard and read about in the time that I've been with my own people—and suddenly I hurt so much that I found myself laughing. (Ibid. p. 313)

Now that Michael understands us, he knows how to help. "Jill, what do I have to do to be ordained?" (ibid. p. 315).

I will not discuss the content of Michael's religion: suffice it to say there is enough free love, mysticism (such as Michael's famous mantra, "Thou Art God"), and counter-culture idealism to make *Stranger* a bestseller beyond the genre. What is more significant here is not the creed, but Heinlein's implication that perhaps a religion is necessary, or at least the most *efficient* way to spread positive social change. Previously (e.g., *Revolt in 2100*) Heinlein had presented religion as a tool for *political* change, but here the uses are more personal and pervasive.

Jubal (recall that Jubal is often speaking in Heinlein's voice) is initially horrified.

> Mike's unique ways of growing up were all right; Mike was unique. But this last
> thing—"The Reverend Doctor Valentine M. Smith, A.B., D.D., Ph.D., Founder and
> Pastor of the Church of All Worlds, Inc."—gad! It was bad enough that the boy had
> decided to be a Holy Joe instead of leaving other people's souls alone as a gentleman
> should. But these diploma-mill degrees—Jubal wanted to throw up [. . .] Mike put
> in a few weeks as assistant chaplain at his churchmouse alma mater—then broke
> with the sect in a schism and founded his own church. Completely kosher, legally
> airtight, and venerable in precedent as Martin Luther—and as nauseating as last
> week's garbage. (Ibid. pp. 321–2)

Jubal is correct to suspect Michael's religion is a sham—but only to a point. Michael *is*
sincere, in that he truly wants to help and puts nothing "in" his religion that he does
not fully believe (for example, raised as a Martian, such statements as "Thou Art God"
are truisms for him). However, his choice of religion as his method is also shrewdly
manipulative. Michael is half cult leader, half conman (see ibid. pp. 339–40), with only
the inner circle knowing that his "religion" is not like others: the primary goal is not to
save souls, but to teach the Martian language, so others can see the world with concepts
absent from all human languages (ibid. p. 347). (Sts. Sapir and Whorf?)

Jubal's ethics are initially offended by the crass manipulations of the Church of
All Worlds, but the value of Michael's message is justification. His practices offend
the moral sensibilities of others (e.g., ritual cannibalism)—but this is irrelevant. The
stakes—the saving of humanity from our limited perception—is worth the cost, even
as Michael's career ends as anyone familiar with Christian Messiahs knows it must.

So, for Heinlein c. 1967, what is religion? A manipulative social tool, certainly.
Often distasteful. But the former can only be judged by the effects, and the latter is
a matter of cultural and personal aesthetics. More significantly, religion is an avenue
to our individual and collective psyches. *Stranger* may be interpreted as describing
mysticism; I disagree, because that ineffable quality which appears inaccessible
through other methods is, for Michael, a matter of perception, not spirituality. The *goal*
of that perception is not individual. Michael builds connections between individuals;
he creates communities. In *Stranger*, those social bonds are more important than
mysticism, than philosophy, than ideology; in *Stranger*, religion forms these bonds,
which are greater than any individual.

> "'And if ye mingle your affairs with theirs then they are your brothers.'"
> "Amen," Jubal agreed. (Ibid. p. 195)

Frank Herbert, *Dune* (1965)

Frank Herbert's *Dune* (1965) evolved from genre tradition in two ways. First, the
subject matter was atypical. Though human nature is of course a central theme of
gSF, Herbert approached his subject from the disciplines of political science, group

psychology, and history. Poul Anderson called it "the best study I have seen of one of the most important and least understood phenomena in history: the messiah" (Herbert, Herbert and Anderson 2005: 288). Second, the "science" at the core of the story is not engineering or physics, but first and foremost ecology. It began, bizarrely, as an unfinished nonfiction article on the use of poverty grasses to keep sand dunes from moving destructively over roads and into towns ("They Stopped the Moving Sands"; see ibid. pp. 263–8), and developed into a Hugo and Nebula winning novel, a popular series of novels (Frank Herbert wrote five sequels; his son, Brian, continues to co-write more), a movie, television mini-series, computer and board games, etc.

Historically, *Dune* "happened" at a key point in the shift away from John Campbell's dominance of the genre, and toward the proliferation of alternative visions associated with 1960s gSF. It is a little surprising that the first published version of *Dune* appeared serialized in Campbell's magazine *Analog Science Fiction* (*née Astounding*) (as "Dune World" in December 1963 to February 1964, and as "Prophet of Dune" in January to May of 1965). Campbell focused on different elements than most contemporary readers (and Herbert himself). Campbell was enthusiastic initially, but his support waned as the epic developed beyond the first chapters and as Herbert's vision for his quasi-religious protagonist became apparent. Campbell later refused to publish the sequel *Dune Messiah* (Herbert 1969).[6]

In the far future, mankind has learned the dangers of developing technologies that replicate human thinking (e.g., sentient computers). Instead, various "schools" have been developed to breed and to train humans to fulfill those duties, including the "mentats" (humans capable of the distributed processing of large bodies of data and probabilities) and the quasi-priestesses Bene Gesserits (women capable of exquisitely precise observation and manipulation, both of other people's behavior and of their own bodies). Note that these schools produce individuals who are, from our perspective and the perspective of contemporary common people, superhuman, but there is nothing super-*natural* about their abilities. Political power is based in feudal houses, under an Emperor. Two of these houses, the Atreides and the Harkonnen, have for decades been mutually antagonistic. The Emperor, perhaps concerned with the increasing power and popularity of the Atreides, agrees to assist in a Harkonnen plot to destroy them.

The plot of *Dune* is a complex network of plots and subplots. At the nexus is young Paul Atreides. Though Paul is the protagonist and the Harkonnen the nominal bad guys, the Atreides are no less ruthless in their dealings with peers and willingness to sacrifice others to achieve their goals: anyone not in the Houses are little more than cannon fodder. Paul displays a degree of sympathy, but not enough to seriously question whether his successes are worth the costs to others. Paul's abilities are prodigious: he is partially trained as a mentat, and is thought by the Bene Gesserit to possibly be able to acquire their abilities as well.

At the beginning of the novel, the Atreides have been granted domain over the planet Arrakis (a.k.a. Dune), the sole source of a naturally occurring mental-enhancement drug called "the spice" that facilitates much of the schools' abilities, including the ability to travel between worlds. Arrakis is (of course) a trap; the Atreides stronghold is destroyed; only Paul and his Bene Gesserit mother escape. They take refuge with a group of religious nomads called the Fremen, who see in Paul the fulfillment of a prophesied messiah. Paul steps into this role, and with the help of the Fremen defeats the Harkonnen. He also manages to defeat the Emperor himself by threatening to destroy permanently the ecosystem that creates the spice. Note Paul's ruthlessness: by destroying the spice, Paul would destroy civilization.

Religion in *Dune* is ubiquitous. As examples, Paul is taught to read from the Orange Catholic Bible (see, e.g., Herbert 1965: 39). The Fremen religion contains oblique references that allow the reader to recognize it as a future form of Islam: for example, mention of Ramadan, Sunni ancestors, a "hajra" pilgrimage, etc. (ibid. pp. 340–1, 387). Though the Bene Gesserit are not "religious" per se, they adopt many of religious trappings in order to manipulate others, even encouraging religious belief when useful. The most telling example is the "Missionaria Protectiva" (elsewhere referred to as the "Manipulator of Religions") which planted myths and rituals in a variety of cultures, just in case a stranded Bene Gesserit would need to control them (ibid. pp. 50–4, 189). Paul and his mother are viewed with supernatural awe: "These Fremen are beautifully prepared to believe in us," his mother notes (ibid. p. 277). Once she passes the Fremen test, Paul's mother . . .

> . . . felt a cynical bitterness at what she had done. *Our Missionaria Protectiva seldom fails. A place was prepared for us in this wilderness. The prayer of the salut has carved out a hiding place. Now . . . I must play the part of Auliya, the Friend of God . . . Sayyadina to rogue peoples who've been so heavily imprinted with our Bene Gesserit soothsay they even call their chief priestesses Reverend Mothers.* (Ibid. p. 287)

Paul is aware that accepting the prepared mantle risks jihad. Being half-mentat and half-Bene Gesserit, he is uniquely adept at recognizing the possible paths the future could take.

> He had seen two main branching along the way ahead—in one he confronted an evil old Baron [Harkonnen] and said: "Hello, Grandfather." The thought of that path and what lay along it sickened him.

> The other path held long patches of grey obscurity except for peaks of violence. He had seen a warrior religion there, a fire spreading across the universe with the Atreides green and black banner waving at the head of fanatic legions drunk on spice liquor [. . .]

> He remained silent, thinking like the seed he was, thinking with the race consciousness he had first experienced as terrible purpose. He found that he no longer could hate the Bene Gesserit or the Emperor or even the Harkonnens. They were all caught up in the need of their race to renew its scattered inheritance, to cross and mingle and infuse their bloodlines in a great new pooling of genes. And the race knew only one sure way for this—the ancient way, the tried and certain way that rolled over everything in its path: jihad.

> *Surely, I cannot choose that way*, he thought. (Ibid. p. 195)

Elsewhere, another character (one who sees in Paul the fulfilment of prophesy [e.g., ibid. pp. 108–10, 124]) notes, "Religion and law among our masses must be one and the same" (one implication of this being that the elite *can* distinguish between them), yet says that the worst fate that can befall a people is to discover their "Hero" (ibid. p. 269). Paul becomes the religious Hero of the Fremen, and though together they are militarily victorious, the impact on others—and, to a degree, on Fremen culture—is terrible. Ultimately, Paul does not avoid and cannot control the jihad, and in the next two books (Herbert 1969, 1976) walks away from his identity to challenge his own myth in the only way he can: as an outsider—a blind mystic prophet. That is, even the occupant of the mythic role cannot control the myth, nor the behavior of people who follow it. Only an alternative myth has that power.

One further note on the events in *Dune* concerns the source of the Fremen's strength. The power of Emperor is supported by his much feared "Sardaukar" army, the origins of which is unknown. There is a subtle parallel between the techniques of generating Sardaukar strength and the Fremen's. Early in the book, Paul and his father discuss one possibility: that the Sardaukar are recruited and trained on a prison planet.

"But every report on Salusa Secundus says S.S. is a hell world!" [says Paul.]

"Undoubtedly. But if you were going to raise tough, strong, ferocious men, what environmental conditions would you impose on them?"

"How could you win the loyalty of such men?"

"There are proven ways: play on the certain knowledge of their superiority, the mystique of secret covenant, the esprit of shared suffering. It can be done. It has been done on many worlds in many times."

Paul nodded, holding his attention on his father's face. He felt some revelation impending.

"Consider Arrakis [i.e., Dune]," the Duke said. "When you get outside the towns and garrison villages, it's every bit as terrible a place as Salusa Secundus." (Ibid. p. 44; see also p. 366)

Three points should be emphasized. First, note the primacy of the environment—not technology, not ideology, not even leadership. Second, after the events described in *Dune*, Paul tries to make Dune a paradise, which makes the Fremen soft—a pattern he preaches against in his persona as the mystic prophet in *Children of Dune* (1976). Referring to another example, Paul is reported to say "the price we paid was the price men have always paid for achieving paradise in this life—we went soft, we lost our edge" (Herbert 1965: 249). Third, note that the techniques of making unbeatable imperial warriors and irresistible, militant religious fanatics are essentially the same, except that Paul's Fremen have the additional tweak of a *religious* "secret covenant." Is it this tweak that allowed Paul's similarly tempered forces to defeat the Emperor's (cf. ibid. pp. 372–3)? If so, the distinction between religion and the rest of society may be a question of degree and effectiveness, rather than a qualitative difference.

I began this section by describing a conflict between what Campbell found appealing and what others appreciated in Dune (see, e.g., McNelly 1984: 119–28, 373,

385–8), and what Herbert intended. As brief examples, Campbell initially called *Dune* a "swashbuckler" (Herbert et al. 2005: 278). His interest was in *Dune*'s forceful, "heroic" characters: he wrote to Herbert, "Congratulations! You are now the father of a 15-year-old superhero," but then worried (as a fellow writer) about the appeal and usability of heroes without understandable limitations on their powers—in this case, Paul's apparent ability to see into the future (or, more accurately, probable futures) (quoted in ibid. p. 275). When Paul's instability emerged in the sequel, Campbell wrote,

> . . . it's Paul, our central character, who is a helpless pawn manipulated against his will, by a cruel, destructive fate . . .

> The reactions of science-fictioneers, however, over the last few decades have persistently and quite explicitly been that they want *heroes*—not anti-heroes. They want stories of strong men who exert themselves, inspire others, and make a monkey's uncle out of malign fates. (Ibid. pp. 293–5)

Herbert, in contrast, believed that a "hero" was only a transient phenomenon associated with flawed individuals: events, perhaps, but not characters. Insofar as Campbell was invested in heroic protagonists, it is natural that he disliked *Dune Messiah*—a novel in which Herbert consciously inverted the hero prototype (Herbert 2007). In 1980, Herbert wrote:

> Heroes are painful, superheroes are catastrophe. The mistakes of superheroes involve too many of us in disaster.

> It is the systems themselves that I see as dangerous. Systematic is a deadly word. Systems originate with human creators, with people who employ them. Systems take over and grind on and on. They are like a flood tide that picks up everything in its path. (Herbert 2007)

Regarding the relationship between ecology and culture:

> I find fresh nuances in religions, psychoanalytic theories, linguistics, economics, philosophy, plant research, soil chemistry, and the metalanguages of pheromones. A new field of study rises out of this like a spirit rising from a witch's cauldron: the psychology of planetary societies. (Ibid.)

Politically, Herbert's planet may be "a living embodiment of the conception of a total amalgamation between law and religion" (DiTommaso 1992), but his concept not only incorporates structure and superstructure, but extends to include infrastructure and environment: an idealist (i.e., top-down) answer to Olaf Stapledon's (bottom-up) materialism (see Chapter 3).

Herbert's *Dune* was a clear break from Campbell-era gSF. He was to see it go from just another Campbell era serial and rejected novel (it was turned it down by six major publishers, before finally being released in book form by an auto-repair-manual publisher) (Herbert et al. 2005: 276–81), to a campus "underground book" (ibid. p. 295), to a best-selling classic of the genre.

Conclusion

Brackett's "Purple Priestess of the Mad Moon" and Tushnet's "In the Calendar of Saints" virtually parodied Gernsback-era characterizations of religion as impotent. Leiber's short story described the personal impact of religious imagery, as Zelazny's story presented religion as a fundamental part of a society's collective psychology. In *Stranger in a Strange Land,* Heinlein expanded his old idea of religion as a social tool: even if the social system is created merely to manipulate, individuals' conversions and subsequent mutual commitments are nevertheless real. Herbert's *Dune* expands this: religious social systems, even if created by individuals to manipulate masses, do not *remain* passive tools: mythic roles, whether consciously accepted or rejected by the individual, irrevocably change that individual until human and role can only be separated by drastic actions.

In early and mid-1960s gSF, religion is neither inherently positive nor inevitably negative; rather, it is a force of nature—like inertia, like combustion, like evolution—that cannot be ignored if we want to understand (individual and collective) human motivations, interpersonal ties, and societal functions. List (2009), discussing the work of Zelazny, Heinlein, and Herbert from this period, notes that they promote a strongly Protestant, elite view of religion, and argues "While the novels critique the institutions of religion and the manipulation of the faithful by religious leaders, they also recognize the validity of some religious experiences, with certain forms of mysticism involving the experience of pantheistic unity interpreted as genuine" (ibid. p. 30). I agree with the first point, but a broader view of gSF's metanarrative religion contextualizes the second: first-hand "experience" seems to be less valued than loyal membership, and less affective than the mythic structures themselves: these mythic structures and the institutionalized systems that contain/are contained by them seem to have independent agency. Thus, religion is impossible to fully control. Perhaps religion *can* be wielded as a social tool; but if so, it is as likely to use the wielder.

While critics tend to focus on the Messiah imagery in these texts, List also notes "the use of the Prometheus archetype . . . as a model for the protagonists further emphasizes that they provide 'salvation' through training and knowledge rather than through belief or faith" (ibid. p. 40). This "salvation," such as it is, is dependent upon faith, however, but the metaphor is nevertheless intriguing: certainly "Michael" in *Stranger in a Strange Land,* "Paul" in *Dune,* and even "Gallinger" in "A Rose for Ecclesiastes" affected society, through the religious system, via specialized knowledge, but, like Prometheus, they suffered for their presumption. Perhaps Daedalus would be a better metaphor.

End of Part Two: Mid-point of the metanarrative

Religion in gSF to c. 1970

Proto-SF (Chapters 2 and 3). Examples include: Lane, *Mizora* (1880–1881); Haggard, *She* (1886); Harben, "In the Year 10,000" (1892); Wells, "In the Abyss" (1896). Religion was a part of primitive culture but is now fully understood. Jesus was a spiritual genius; those who misunderstood him created a religion. However, many variations exists, including some contrasting gSF.

Gernsback's gadget pulps (Chapter 4). Examples include: Kateley, "The Fourteenth Earth" (1928); Barclay, "The Troglodytes" (1930); Jones, "Inquisition of 6061 (1933). Religion declines with technological and social progress, becoming more simple. Religion is used by leaders to manipulate followers and reflects the most brutal side of culture (e.g., human sacrifice).

Campbell's social science fiction (Chapter 5). Examples include: Asimov, "Nightfall" (1941/1998); Heinlein, "If This Goes On—" (1940), "Universe" (1941); L. Sprague de Camp "Ultrasonic God" (1954). Religion is anti-science; it may contain scientific knowledge, but facts aren't understood and are misinterpreted. Religion is a social tool, which can have negative or positive societal impacts. Leaders, ethical and otherwise, use it to control gullible populations. Devout beliefs aren't discussed in polite company.

The rise of novel, post-WWII (Chapter 6). Examples include: Clarke, *Childhood's End* (1953); Brackett, *The Long Tomorrow* (1955); Stewart, *Earth Abides* (1949/1999); Miller, *Canticle for Leibowitz* (1959); Blish, *A Case of Conscience* (1958). Progress may inevitably eliminate religion; the loss of religion may be necessary but is regrettable. Religion may restrict science, but perhaps science *needs* to be restricted. Alternatively, religion may preserve/promote knowledge, if leaders are aware of their limitations. Religion adapts to environment; even superstitions can be reasonable in context.

Poli-Sci-Fi (Chapter 7). Examples include: Zelazny, "A Rose for Ecclesiastes" (1963); Leiber, "When the Change-Winds Blow" (1964); Heinlein, *Stranger in a Strange Land* (1961); Herbert, *Dune* (1965). Religion is more tangible and more powerful. Experiences can be "real," and imagery influences perceptions. Mythic structures constrain even leaders' options; institutions and myths appear to have agency. Even if manipulated, individuals' faith may be admirable.

Part One described the raw materials from which gSF was constructed, including examples of religion in proto-science fiction that demonstrate the sheer range of available options. Some are very different from the representations typical of the early genre (e.g., Benson's *Lord of the World*); others prefigure the representations of religion in the Gernsback era (e.g., H. G. Wells' "In the Abyss," Harben's "In the Year 10,000"). The latter—or, rather, the *selection* of the latter—demonstrates the first step in the gSF metanarrative for religion, the initial collective act which begins the evolution of this particular representation in this particular sub-culture.

In Part Two, we have covered four stages of gSF and the first half of gSF's metanarrative for religion—from c. 1926 to the mid-1960s, each with its most representative depictions of religion. The Table below summarizes (in an admittedly simplistic manner) what we've discovered. Since we are about half-way between the first dedicated gSF magazines of the 1920s and the present, this seems to be a good time to pause and consider the status of the metanarrative. In particular, we now have enough data to identify the key variables we should keep an eye on moving forward.

First, note that religion has sequentially become less negatively portrayed. Evil priests manipulating the vulnerable and naïve population seem laughably old-fashioned. And second, the confidence that scientific progress yields positive societal impacts (via developing technologies) seems equally naïve; that is, science is no longer portrayed so positively. The perceived opposition between the two appears to remain, but the one-sided loyalty to science has somewhat dissipated. For example, in Brackett's *The Long Tomorrow* it is still assumed that religion restricts scientific progress, but now that might not be an entirely bad thing. We can interpret these patterns in two ways. Perhaps religion is being viewed more positively, and science more negatively. If so, the inertia of these two trends could extend to a pro-religion, anti-science species of science fiction. Alternatively, these patterns could be more passive—an erosion of the strong statements (e.g., religion = bad, science = good) into more neutral positions.

Also, religion is being taken much more seriously by the 1960s. For example, Brackett specifically parodies Golden Age dismissal of religion in "The Purple Priestess of the Mad Moon." Religion grows into a source of valid technical and social *information*: religious specialists may be conversant with both, religious institutions can preserve secular information which would otherwise have been lost, and both are conscious of what they do not understand. Religious traditions develop *agency*— their mythic structures are not easily dismissed (e.g., "A Rose for Ecclesiastes") and their momentum is not easily redirected (e.g., *Dune*). The focus is increasingly *individual*: not the leaders, but low-level specialists and lay people. This focus on the individual will, in the next chapter, express in a focus on individual, subjective *experience*, as foreshadowed in the Leiber and Zelazny stories above. Additionally, later stories employ an *almost* mystical perspective: the individual does not transcend the boundaries to the divine Other (cf. Smart 1996: 167–8), but neither does divinity continue to represent a difference in kind. In some ways, Paul in 1965's *Dune* is more alien than the Creator in the 1970s.

Taken together, the stories described so far show a developing complexity in gSF's representation of religion, evolving in coherent ways. In the second half of the metanarrative, gSF is less single-minded. The next chapter begins with the New Wave of gSF, typified by boundary violations: transgressions on societal norms and on the expectations of the reader, a higher degree of experimentalism including stretching if not breaking some of the "rules" of science fiction. In particular, the boundary between god and man becomes permeable. The implications for our current discussion—even with the understanding that our focus is not on gods per se but religion—muddy the waters.

So, a clear statement of the foundations against which the New Wave rebelled is necessary: hence, the Table below. The key difference between Parts Two and Three is simply that the definition of religion does not change; rather, the emphasis switches from (1) the impact of religion, as one institutional facet of society, on communities and on society as a whole, to (2) the impact of religion on the individual, especially to the extent that institutions are internalized.

Part Three

The Need to Believe

Early in the genre's history, religion had largely been held by science fiction authors (and, by the popularity of the stories discussed above, by science fiction readers) at arm's length. In the Golden Age religion was dismissed as misunderstood science, a simple error by inferior minds. The next generation treated religion with less distain, though not with trust. Religion was seen as a social tool used to manipulate populations, and was "good" or "bad" only as determined by the effects of this manipulation. Good leaders and bad might use it; individuals ignored it at their peril. By the 1970s, the first chinks in genre science fiction's (gSF's) armor against religion appeared: religious beliefs may be based on falsehoods, but religion as an institution *could* be benevolent, at least in principle. Religious institutions gained inertia, possibly even agency, and thus were not completely controllable.

In the 1970s these trends continue to develop. As early as 1958's *A Case of Conscience*, religious individuals are nevertheless sometimes presented sympathetically. This becomes a more significant trend c. 1970, along with something else: religion may not be intellectually acceptable, but the *emotional* attraction gains acceptance. Whereas in the 1950s one could identify an almost wistful desire that one *could* believe in a higher being, by the 1970s the desire had, in some cases, become uncontrollable. Scientific (i.e., physical or social scientific) explanations cannot complete us. For example, Aldiss's *Frankenstein Unbound* (1973) begins with a man describing his grandchildren play. They had recently lost their parents and, though outwardly happy, are now play-acting a funeral service.

> You must wonder about this unexpected outbreak of Christianity in our agnostic household. I must say that at first it caused me some regret that I have so long stifled my own religious feelings in deference to the rationalism of our times . . . As far as I know, Molly and David never taught their children a word of prayer. Perhaps the traditional comforts of religion were exactly what these orphans needed. What if those comforts are illusions? [. . .] They live in myth. Under the crude onslaught of school, intellect will break in—crude robber intellect—and myth will wither and die like the bright flowers on their mysterious grave. (Aldiss 1973: 6–7)

The respect given myth here, combined with the confusion in the 1960s between individuals claiming mythic roles and the roles themselves as quasi-agents, eroded the boundaries between man and religion. In the 1970s, boundaries begin to erode between man and gods, and a sympathy with an intelligent Creator of the universe develops (see Manning below). Note that it does not necessarily follow that the Creator is "God." Robots who worship a vanished humanity would be wrong in that we are not supernatural, but on the other hand, we *are* their Creators (Simak 1972; see also Simak 1981).

To illustrate more developed examples, this chapter focuses primarily on works by four authors: Ray Bradbury, Michael Moorcock, Jack Chalker, and the less well-known Lawrence Manning.

Moorcock, along with Harlan Ellison and J. G. Ballard, was a key motivator in what has been termed the "New Wave" of science fiction, and his writings are good examples of an alternative subspecies of gSF that began to appear in the mid-1960s. Briefly, the New Wave was typified by transgressing social boundaries (e.g., in the inclusion of frank sexuality) as well as the traditional "rules" of Campbellian science fiction. As before in the 1920s and '30s, this next step in gSF's evolution was facilitated by editors (read: intelligent designers): Moorcock as editor of the newly independent *New Worlds* magazine and Ellison as editor of the *Dangerous Visions* anthology.

There was no dramatic schism between "hard" and "new wave" gSF. Rather the spectrum of options had expanded, with people like Moorcock pushing the boundaries; new variations existed side by side with more archaic forms. However, the New Wave did demonstrate significant shifts in worldview. For example, in his empirical analysis of priorities and social beliefs of various science fiction sub-genres, Bainbridge (1986: 106) found a "moderate correlation" between the New Wave (as opposed to the "hard science tradition") gSF and concern with the "harmful effects of scientific progress," but a much stronger correlation among New Wave fanzine editors. But, as we found in Chapter 5, the roots of this skepticism of blind faith in the social benefits of *technological* progress were apparent in the 1940s; by the 1960s, such skepticism had generalized somewhat to "progress" as a whole, and by the 1970s such concerns were becoming mainstream, even within gSF.

Ray Bradbury, "The Messiah" (1973)

Bradbury's 1973 story "The Messiah" is a good place to start, as it simply and elegantly demonstrates this new-found dissatisfaction, and the conflicts that can result. Bradbury himself certainly felt connections to others within the genre: in describing his own literary ambitions, he wrote, "I hoped for H. G. Wells or to share company with Jules Verne. When I worked out a living space between the two, I was ecstatic" (Bradbury 1951/2001: ix). As with Blish's *A Case of Conscience* and Mary Doria Russell's *The Sparrow* (see Chapters 6 and 10), the protagonist is a priest experiencing a crisis of faith as a result of contact with an alien race. Together, they form a kind of triptych showing the evolution of this particular problem.

"The Messiah" begins with a Jewish Rabbi, a Baptist Reverend, a Catholic Bishop, and a few other Christian religious specialists discussing matters of faith and reflecting on their respective missions on Mars. Priests from other religions are not barely-tolerated competitors, but colleagues and friends. We see them playing cards together and arguing about Thomas Aquinas. (Note that unlike the other panels of our triptych, none of these are described as Jesuits, but they jokingly label the Rabbi one in deference to his "educated logic.") Their chief and common disappointment is that they have never had the opportunity to interact with their "elusive congregation" the Martians—at least, as far as they know. Martians, it seems, are telepathic and are believed to have the ability to visit, perhaps even mingle, unnoticed.

After this social gathering, a Father Niven (mostly referred to as "the Priest") wakes well after midnight. He wanders down into his church to find an incredible, pale figure displaying an open white palm marked with a terrible wound, slowly dripping blood into a baptismal font. Shocked by the vision, he feels as if his soul had been pulled from his body "bloodied raw":

He felt himself prized, his life yanked forth, and the roots, O God, were . . . *deep*!

"No, no, no, no!"

But, yes.

Between the lacings of his fingers, he looked again.

And the Man was there. (Bradbury 1973/2003: 283)

The Priest's vision of his Christ is exactly as he thought, hoped He would be. He quickly realizes that he perceives not divinity but a Martian, frightened and in pain, forced into this form by the strength of the Priest's unconscious desires. He sees literally what he wants to see.

"You—you are a Martian, then?"

"No more. No less."

"And I have done this to you with my thoughts?"

"You did not mean. When you came downstairs, your old dream seized and made me over. My palms still bleed from the wounds that you gave out of your secret mind."

The Priest shook his head, dazed.

"Just a moment more . . . wait . . ."

He gazed steadily, hungrily, at the darkness where the Ghost stood out of the light. That face was beautiful. And, oh, those hands were loving and beyond all description. (Ibid. p. 285)

Bradbury's scene is much more intimate and embodied, not at all like the intellectual problems described by Blish. But like Father Ruiz-Sanchez, Father Niven is faced with the temptation to treat as real what he *knows* to be illusionary. Ruiz-Sanchez chose to believe that it was his exorcism, not bombs which destroyed the planet and the race which tested his faith; this priest must choose whether it is his Savior or a Martian bleeding in front of him.

Father Niven makes a different choice than Father Ruiz-Sanchez. He cannot accept the dream as reality—but nor can he bear giving up this experience: the potent blend of emotions and thoughts resulting from perceiving the divine in the form of a perfect reflection of his own thoughts. Ultimately, he looks away, releasing the Martian from his vision, but not before extorting a promise that the Martian will return once a year, on Easter.

On the surface, "the Priest" could be seen as an addict, willing to torture others for the sake of his existential fix. But Father Niven is portrayed so sympathetically that one cannot dismiss him so easily. The hunger of his "old dream" is too vital. In forcing a future meeting, he is not surrendering his rational mind so much as embracing an embodied experience. As deeply as this hunger is part of him, rather than blame him for hurting the Martian one is almost surprised he *can* release him, even with conditions—though one hopes that, come next Easter, he will find in himself a vision less tortured.

There is a necessary *caveat* here, both about Bradbury as representative of gSF and of my construction of a metanarrative for religion. While "The Messiah" seems to fit well into the genre as it stood in the 1970s, earlier in his career Bradbury seemed to anticipate the trend—Asimov notes that Bradbury's tendency to not let the facts get in the way of a good story excluded him from *Astounding*; one wonders if his outlying views of religion were another reason (Asimov 1983: 11). Unlike *Earth Abides* (Stewart 1949) and *Childhood's End* (Clarke 1953), religion is in no way presented as passé.

Compare this priest to the character Father Peregrine in his 1951 story "The Fire Balloons" (Bradbury 1951). Father Peregrine is the leader of a mission to serve the spiritual needs of human colonists of Mars, but is strongly attracted to the most complex (and largely unknown) native life form: glowing orbs that appear to have some form of sentience. In a profound piece of natural theology, Father Peregrine seeks to understand better the possibilities of spiritual existence through the exploration of God's Creation beyond our own planet. His cheerful acknowledgment of his own limitations contrasts with a contemporary perception that, through science, everything is in principle knowable.

"Father Peregrine, won't you ever be serious?"

"Not until the good Lord is. Oh, don't look so terribly shocked, please. The Lord is not serious. In fact, it is a little hard to know just what else He is except loving. And love has to do with humor, doesn't it? For you cannot love someone unless you put up with him, can you?" (Bradbury 1951: 111)

Note the almost scandalous tone. One is tempted to think that, in 1951, perhaps the only religious specialist one can take seriously is one who does not take his religion too seriously—but I think this would miss the point. Despite his humor, the strength of his faith, and of his calling to minister to the Martians, is clear. There are rumors that they killed some of the human settlers, which, if it constituted murder, means they require (and deserve?) spiritual guidance (ibid. p. 115). His test for the orbs' capacity for moral action is the simple expedient of throwing himself off a cliff, to see if they would save him. Fortunately for the priest, the test succeeds (ibid. p. 117), and he builds something like a church (adapted for their form) to minister to them (ibid. p. 121).

Recall the priest in Sanders's "The Word to Space" (1960/1974), described in Chapter 6. Father Moriarty's positive character is expressed in his unwillingness to try to teach the residents of Akron about his religion. Father Peregrine, in a story almost a decade earlier, appears to be a *later* incarnation of the gSF schema for a positive religious specialist; he takes this characteristic a step further and is willing to *learn* from the orbs. When they finally communicate, they tell Father Peregrine that once they are as we are now, until one of them learned to "free man's soul and intellect, to free him of bodily ills and melancholies, of deaths and transfigurations" (ibid. p. 123). "We wish to tell you that we appreciate your building this place for us, but we have no need of it . . . we are happy and at peace" (ibid. p. 124). The good Father's response? "[M]ay I come again, someday, that I may learn from you?" (ibid.).

Bradbury does not conform to gSF's metanarrative of religion. I could interpret this in one of two ways. First, Bradbury is a counter-example, the exception that may prove the rule by virtue of emphasizing how unusual it is for gSF authors to deviate so far. More likely, though, Bradbury is a *mainstream* SF author. Notice how freely he deviates from basic scientific fact. Characters on Mars walk and breathe freely; we forgive him. If he ignores these concrete details, why expect him to conform to more subtle schemas? In a National Endowment of the Arts interview ("NEA" 2010), Bradbury spends 20 minutes talking about his life, works, and influences. He uses the phrase "science fiction" only once (he uses it to describe *Galaxy* magazine); he describes being excited to meet Aldous Huxley, but does not mention any gSF author; he describes the books that inspired him, but includes no gSF, other than a brief mention of Flash Gordon in his childhood. Like Huxley and George Orwell, Bradbury seems to be one of the "speculative fiction" authors described by Asimov as writing *social* fiction. Their intent was not to predict possible futures, but reflect on the present through extrapolation of particular themes. Such authors are occasionally granted gSF's highest honors—but out of respect for a parallel effort, not as a sign of membership.

Lawrence Manning, *The Man Who Awoke* (1975)

Much more clearly gSF is Lawrence Manning's novel *The Man Who Awoke* (1975). "Manning" is not a common name in 1970s SF, and *The Man Who Awoke* was only moderately successful. So, why do I include a work that did not distinguish itself in the economic or critical selection process? Simply because it is a naturally occurring experiment. Imagine speculating on what a Gernsback-era author would have written for a later generation—this is essentially what we have with *The Man Who Awoke*. It first appeared in 1933 as a series of short stories in *Wonder Stories* (Manning 1933a–e), then was republished four decades later in novel form. This "fix-up" edition is virtually identical to the short stories, word for word—there is no attempt to update the technology or modernize characters, no effort to align the story to what he might have perceived to be the tastes of the current audience—with a single, crucial exception.

The plot concerns a man named "Winters" who, through chemical and technological means, decides to time-travel Rip van Winkle-fashion. He sleeps for centuries at a time, awakening periodically to check on the progress of mankind, observing cycles of decay and rebirth (Manning 1933a–d; 1975: 1–135).

Winters eventually emerges in a distant future in which society is largely perfected. All people's physical and emotional needs are easily met; personal growth and enlightenment are common. Even death can be indefinitely postponed through a "youth-process." To emphasize how human nature (or, perhaps, human culture) had changed, soon after awakening after his last long sleep he watches an argument seemingly about to turn violent. When the protagonist reacts accordingly, the would-be combatants burst out laughing, amazed he would believe them capable of forcibly restraining another person, let alone physically assaulting him. It is some time before Winters discovers any flaw in this future world, if flaw it is, in the form of a suicidal man. With no more challenges to be met, Winters learns that a minority develop a fatal ennui from deciding that, as far as we have grown, we are still intolerably finite and are likely to remain forever so.

> "Though we humans have grown in importance, we are insignificant atoms measured in the scale of Creation. There is nothing we can do that is really important. Suppose we increase human stature until we stride about using stars for footstools—mere size does not add to our importance. I do not eat unless I am hungry. I undertake no action unless it is for a definite and reasonable purpose. I can see no purpose in life—so I refuse to be so absurd as to continue living!" (Manning 1933e: 158//1975: 158)

Before Winters leaves, the man mentions a man named Condonal who is rumored to be working on this problem scientifically; Winters resolves to seek Condonal out.

I hope it is apparent how wonderfully "Golden Age" the original 1933 stories are in tone, plot and sensibility: the author creates a technological device that allows his character to explore future worlds, have adventures and move on, with strong themes of self-reliance, boldness and competence. Religion is ignored, and its role (as understood in the Golden Age) supplanted by a secular individual (possibly with followers) who is methodically researching transcendence.

Contemporary readers must have happily anticipated a clever gadget on the horizon. Once Winters finds Condonal, they were not disappointed. In the 1933 (and 1975) versions, Condonal tells Winters:

> "We have pursued every phase of science to its ultimate and found no purpose in creation. Our reason plunges forward and searches every possibility of the future and fails to find any basis upon which to erect the least speculative structure. Life is not a reasonable thing, perhaps."
>
> "You have come to that conclusion?" cried Winters sadly. (Manning 1933e: 158–9//1975: 160)

Note the carefully lower-cased "creation." The 1933 publication continues:

> The deepset eyes twinkled sanely. Condonal nodded. Then he held up his hand and his dark face lighted with purpose.
>
> "But nevertheless our research is sure and we *will* discover the secret," he smiled. Winters' frown of bewilderment amused him. "The answer lies in evolution." (Manning 1933e: 159//1975: 162)

Condonal then explains that though the purpose of creation may be beyond our ken, it does not follow that there *is* no purpose. His analogy is that the cells in our body are incapable of understanding thought, intent, or self-awareness. It is only in their coordination that such phenomena are possible, though individual cells remain ignorant of these emergent properties. Condonal has devised a technology capable of temporarily linking individual human minds in ways analogous to the connections between cells, in hopes of constructing a "super-animal" capable of deeper perceptions (cf. the composite "Dweller" in Moore [1935: esp. 119]).

> "Oh ho! [exclaims Winters.] And you think that your super-animal will . . ."
>
> "Of course! And when He looks around Him and begins to inquire into the reasons of His own existence He will find us. He will study us and marvel and without question will inform us how to act so as to help Him in His own evolution. And then . . . ah! . . . Then He will search out the secret of life and tell us. Perhaps we will not be able to understand, but we will at least have the opportunity."
>
> Winters was excitedly pacing the floor, engrossed by the bold conception. "Even if we do not understand—we will at least know that there is a purpose and that knowledge in itself is all we need." (Manning 1933e: 159//1975: 163-4)

The Man Who Awoke is, I think, a surprisingly pleasant Golden Age narrative that would be attractive to anyone looking for a bit of nostalgic gSF. In the last story, Manning (1933e) comes up with an original problem likely familiar to the readers and offers a unique future-technological solution to the meaning of life.

However . . . in the 1975 publication, Manning makes a single, significant change. Into the above dialog he inserted two pages of text *that suggest the possibility that a Creator exists*. It may not be a god, per se, and certainly would not be something that one would worship, but it *would* be the source of something that elevates humans above the merely physical. After Condonal reports that science has been unable to find a "purpose," in 1975 alone he qualifies this statement.

> "You have come to that conclusion?" cried Winters sadly [as above].
>
> "Physical life—yes." (Manning 1975: 160)

Condonal alludes to the evidence that the universe began about 50 billion years ago.

> "Now that [. . .] was a wonderful birth. That was creation, if you like [. . .] You can call it rearrangement; I prefer the word creation. By definition, merely, there must have been a Creator" (ibid. p. 161)

This Creator (now capitalized) of the physical universe, he reasons, is the only possible source of anything not reducible to the physical.

> "The sensibility, the feeling and emotion, all are shared by men with the lower animals. They are probably extensions of the merely physical."
>
> "There remains that combination of will and imagination which is peculiar, so far, to the human race. This could be the stuff for which creation was set in motion. Perhaps the Creator is a cook, and this mental product the food He prepares. Perhaps He is a chemist, and our minds are the crucibles in which he refines the product for some unimaginable purpose. I like the last idea better [. . .] Life itself is a sort of Hell. This mental stuff may pass through life after life, being refined a little more each time. The road to good intentions is probably paved with Hells." (Ibid. pp. 161–2)

Note that his argument on the form this hypothetical Creator may take is based as much on aesthetic preference as reason. To the superhuman "He" that is the sum of multiple human individualities is added a "He" that is distinct from us, but from whom we descend. This Creator would not be sufficient to justify a religion of worshippers, of course, but it seems that by 1975 an existential bolthole is necessary to offer us escape from the merely physical, to suggest hope for a transcendence not facilitated by technological gadgets.

Michael Moorcock, "Behold the Man" (1966)

In the 1930 story "The Troglodytes" (see Chapter 4), an adventuring trio discovers a subterranean culture with a religion they learn is founded on misunderstood technologies and inaccurate legends about their origins. The wisest of them warns his companions to leave religion alone; "'that difference of opinion about their origin may lead to trouble'" (Barclay 1930: 496).

In the 1947 story "E for Effort," the influence of World War II is evident in the protagonists' efforts to avoid another nuclear war. Their view of religion, however, is not much different than in "The Troglodytes." The protagonists have a means of observing past events—anywhere and anywhen—and of filming these events. They set out to undermine the hypocrisy of political leaders, initially by releasing legitimate recordings of historical events as normal movie entertainment. They specifically *avoid* examination of religious leaders. A test audience viewing a cut of a "movie" about the Roman Empire are upset at their treatment of Jesus: first, that he was not portrayed as having any significant impact, and second, because the representation did not match their expectations; these "biased and inaccurate" scenes were cut. "Then and there we decided that it didn't pay to tamper with anyone's religious beliefs. That's why you've never seen anything emanating from us that conflicted even remotely with the accepted historical, sociological, or religious features of Someone Who Knew Better" (Sherred 1947/1989: 436).

Note that religions are in both cases assumed to be vulnerable to accurate data that conflict with accepted beliefs. In *Childhood's End* (Clarke 1953/1990; see Chapter 6), this vulnerability is proven. Our alien Overlords release for our use a history-viewer not dissimilar to the one in "E for Effort" (and to the one in Orson Scott Card's *Pastwatch* book [Card 1996], incidentally). "Within a few days, all mankind's multitudinous messiahs had lost their divinity" (Clarke 1953/1990: 67). Also note that in these stories religion is best avoided: challenging it is too dangerous (Barclay 1930); religion is too entrenched (Sherred 1947/1989); though the dissolution of religion may be unavoidable, the distress this produces is regrettable (Clarke 1953/1990). These seem to suggest that not only is it best if gSF protagonists shy away from religion, that perhaps readers and authors should, too.

Starting after World War II, some gSF authors began to deal with the societal effects of religion more directly, and more carefully (see Chapter 6). In the 1960s, authors like Frank Herbert and Robert Heinlein closely examined religions *and* messianic religious leaders, while acknowledging the reality of the religion for believers, even when belief is based on misinformation (see Chapter 7). Michael Moorcock ups the stakes. It is an uncomfortably personal examination of an individual's relationship with a religious myth, but not a fictional one—"ours," not a hypothetical "theirs." That is, not *a* messiah, but *the* Messiah.

The story is Moorcock's Nebula Award-winning "Behold the Man" (1966/1981), later expanded into a novel (1969/1999). In the preface is the sentence, "And he spoke, saying unto them: Yeah verily I *was* Karl Glogauer and now I am Jesus the Messiah, the Christ" (Moorcock 1966/1981: 352). The plot is simple: a twentieth-century Jew goes back in time and assumes the role of Jesus, up to and including the Crucifixion. The story is about *why*.

In type, Glogauer superficially resembles "Gallinger" from Zelazny's "A Rose for Ecclesiastes" (see the previous chapter), but several times more neurotic: a Freudian case study of the dangers of childhood trauma. We see a nine-year-old Glogauer, crying as his school friends play at crucifying him by tying him to a fence (they say it was his idea) (ibid. pp. 353–4), and a fifteen-year-old bullied for being Jewish but afraid to make a scene (ibid. pp. 371–3). We get to know him a little better as an adult: he is a "passive, masochistic, indecisive" (ibid. p. 360) young man; an amateur Jungian psychiatrist ("merely a reader, a dabbler") dating Monica: an emasculating psychiatric social worker with unbreachable emotional walls.

He tries to explain to Monica why he is so drawn to religious myths:

"You'll never understand what I'm looking for [. . .] We're destroying the myths that make the world go round."

"Now you say 'And what are we putting in their place?' You're stale and stupid, Karl. You've never looked rationally at anything—including yourself."

"What of it? You say the myth is unimportant."

"The reality that creates it is important."

"Jung knew that myth can also create the reality."

He stretched his legs. In doing so, he touched hers and he recoiled. He scratched his head. She still lay there smoking, but she was smiling now.

"Come on," she said. "Let's have some stuff about Christ." (Ibid. p. 361)

Later, they argue about which came first: the actuality of Jesus ("a Jewish troublemaker organizing a revolt against the Romans. He was crucified for his pains." she says) or the idea of the Christ ("A great religion couldn't have begun so simply," he says) (ibid. p. 368).

In short, Glogauer is in love with religion, to the extent that he is able to love anything. He cannot abide Monica's contempt for it, but *not* because he is religious: "it was rather *lack* of conviction in the ideal in which she had set her own faith, the ideal of science as a solver of all problems" (ibid. p. 399). Emotionally, he needs a personal deity, but is unable to believe in one. "His rational mind had told him that God did not exist in any personal form. His unconscious had told him that faith in science was not enough" (ibid.).

Glogauer decides to find out what the realty behind the Christ myth is, and goes back in time. That the story virtually ignores *how* Glogauer does so is as clear a mark of Moorcock's break with traditional gSF as his explicit denial that science is a satisfactory answer to all of life's questions.

While continually pestered by memories of Monica ("'All men have a messiah-complex, Karl'" [ibid. p. 382]), Glogauer is accepted by the Essenes, develops a complex relationship with John the Baptist, and begins to look for Jesus, getting a little crazier each day. By the time he finally locates the correct house, others see him by turn as prophet and madman. Joseph's "face is lined and pouched with misery" (ibid. p. 380), Mary is "tall and bulging with fat. Her long, black hair was unbound and greasy, falling over large, lustrous eyes that still had the heat of sensuality"— and Jesus' "face was vacant and foolish. There was a little spittle on the lips" (ibid. p. 381).

It is plain to Glogauer that the historical Jesus could not fulfill the Essene's prophesy nor his own view of history. Glogauer "could not bear to think that Jesus had been nothing more than a myth. It was in his power to make Jesus a physical reality rather than the creation of a process of mythogenesis" (ibid. p. 388). So, Glogauer allows himself to be drawn into the role and is ultimately crucified in his place.

In Moorcock's story, a religious myth plays a central role in an agnostic's view of reality. One is tempted to infer that if Glogauer had had a faith in *any* religion, the gaping wound in his psyche would have been filled less destructively; alternatively, perhaps the Jungian model exacerbated the problem. But in any case, the *need* was real. Perhaps the waning of organized religion contributes to the instability of people who feel that need more keenly. If so, the story makes sense: religion—any religion?—is necessary, and some would be willing to sacrifice a great deal to make sure it develops the way they feel it should.

However, there is a crucial point in the last quotation above: Glogauer's actions *would have no effect on history*. Christianity, it is implied, would develop the same way whether there was an actual man crucified or not. What Glogauer literally cannot accept is that there is no kernel of misunderstood truth, no bit of sand in the pearl.

Glogauer allows himself to be destroyed, rather than face the possibility that a religion (not even *his* religion) is nothing but a social construction.

Jack L. Chalker, *Midnight at the Well of Souls* (1977)

We have been examining the relationship between humanity and a socially posited super-natural "god." One trajectory has been to examine superhuman (possibly supernatural) characters associated with religious systems with successively less distance. In Heinlein's "If This Goes On—" (1940), a manipulative priest *claimed* superhuman authority, but was not anyone with whom the reader could identify. In *Earth Abides* (1949/1999), we see a tentatively superhuman persona building around Isherwood; though Isherwood benefits somewhat, the persona is unasked for, and the proto-religious beliefs that surround him do no harm. In the 1960s books discussed above (*Stranger in a Strange Land* and *Dune*), individuals with superhuman but (we are assured) *not* supernatural powers step into mythic roles; though others believe them to be possibly divine, we and the characters closest to them know better. In the next book, the character with whom we become familiar is several orders of magnitude up the scale toward true Godhood.

Jack L. Chalker's *Midnight at the Well of Souls* (1977) is a great example of quality genre work. The central plot is relatively simple—and something of a MacGuffin. The main character is the captain of a spaceship, Nathan Brazil. Given the practicalities of relativistic travel, from our perspective he could be years between planets; he has few friends, and even those know little about him. He and his odd assortment of passengers are diverted to investigate a murder and are transported to the Well World: an apparently artificial planet constructed by a vanished race of unimaginable power called the Markovians. The Well World is essentially an experimental proving ground on which the Markovians could test new physical forms. All of the passengers (but, significantly, *not* Brazil) are transformed into bizarre creatures, have adventures, and nominally to bring us closer to catching the murderer.

Chalker's formidable originality is shaped by the inclusion of familiar tropes. As with many great gSF authors, he does not invent completely from whole cloth, but plays with the readers' expectations by referencing our shared culture. The Markovians, for example, fit the popular post-World War II trope of a civilization with advanced science who nevertheless are unable to avoid their own destruction (e.g., "The Lost Race," a 1950 *Dimension-X* radio drama adapted from a Murray Leinster story, through the contemporary *Ringworld* by Larry Niven [1970]). In fact, *Midnight* could be offhandedly described as "Lazarus Long visits Ringworld." Though this is merely simplistic shorthand, it is sufficient to tell the experienced gSF reader what to expect by referencing Heinlein's famous protagonist and Larry Niven's most recognized creation.

For most of the novel, Chalker's representations of religion are minor bits of color added to his story; familiar tools used to recapitulate a familiar (to the contemporary reader) worldview. For example, a character taught her whole life to sublimate her own desires to the greater good interprets contrary ideas as "heresies" (ibid. p. 86); another is technologically indoctrinated into perfect obedience using religious imagery (ibid. p. 112), with predictable results:

> "Do you give yourself to me, Mar Dartham, body and soul, to do with as I would, forever?" he intoned.
>
> "I do, Master, my Lord God, I do! Command me to die and I shall do so gladly." (Ibid. p. 118)

The reader also encounters the familiar link between religion and ignorance, for example, the old trope that science may appear supernatural (e.g., Arthur C. Clarke's "Third Law"):

> "I am willing to believe in a lot—but magic? Nonsense!"
>
> "All magic means is a line between knowledge and ignorance . . . A magician is someone who can do something you don't know how to do. All technology, for example, is magic to a primitive." (Chalker 1977: 66)

Another character is investigating the recurrence of a certain phrase across a great many cultures: "until midnight at the Well of Souls." He notes that "A few of the really primitive [regions] seem to use it as a religious chant" (ibid. p. 144); in more savvy cultures, the same phrase is just a saying (ibid. p. 114). In short, for the majority of *Midnight,* Chalker's representations of religion are rather old fashioned and would fit comfortably in a *1940s*-era Campbell story.

But then the story takes a left turn, just as the 1975 version of Manning's *The Man Who Awoke* did. Brazil is far, far older than anyone suspected. Some members begin to suspect he is one of the long-dead Markovians, but even that falls short of the mark. "I'm old, Wuju—older than anyone could imagine. So old that I couldn't live with my own memories. I blocked them out . . . But these memories still give me the edge—I know things the rest of you don't. I'm not necessarily smarter or wiser than you, but I do have all that experience" (ibid. p. 296).

When the original party *and* the "bad guys" finally reach what amounts to the Control Room, Brazil gains control of the planet and explains. The Markovians had gained the ability to manipulate anything in the universe: make anything they wanted, extend their lives indefinitely, even redesign their own bodies and minds. But though they could change anything within the laws of physics, they did not dare approach the basic laws themselves.

> "Not gods, then," said Vardia quietly. "Demigods."
>
> "People," Brazil responded. "Not gods at all. People . . . They argued, they debated, strove, built, discovered—just like all of us [note the use of first person plural here] . . . Remember, they achieved godhood not by natural processes, but by technological advancement. It was as if one of our races, in present form, suddenly discovered the key to wish fulfilment. Would we be ready for it? I wonder."
>
> "Why did they die, Brazil?" Skander asked. "Why did they commit suicide?"
>
> "Because they were not ready." (Ibid. p. 320)

Technically, the race did not suicide; the Markovians greatly altered—and radically constrained—their physical, mental, and technological ability. Having reached the apex of all that they could conceive of, they attempted to start the game over, hoping to arrive at beings with broader vision (ibid. pp. 321–2). What Chalker's point lacks in subtlety it makes up for in audacity: these beings had achieved the wildest dreams of Golden Age gSF and found it to be a dead end. Advancement through mere technology was not utopia but disaster.

Brazil, we finally learn, is not one of the Markovians who dared not tinker with the basic laws of the universe; Brazil *wrote* the laws. After billions of years, the basic energy of the cosmos became self-aware. It created time, space; galaxies and planets. It/He created the Markovians, watched them evolve, and saw them fail to become like him—then, in his loneliness, limited himself to be human. Fascinatingly, faced with proof that Brazil has unimaginable power over them, and at least half-believing that Brazil might indeed be the Creator, no one is tempted to worship him. Some doubt ("I've been a Catholic all my life, but somehow God to me has never been a spunky little Jew named Nathan Brazil" [ibid. p. 331]), some attack (uselessly), some beg for their lives. None pray.

The main character in this traditional, 1970 gSF novel turns out to be, if not God, then something very close—at the very least, an omnipotent Creator, to whom religion is irrelevant. And reading it, one cannot help but feel sorry for Him.

Conclusion

In the Golden Age, some stories "explained" the reality behind religious myths; by the 1970s, such strategies seem naïve, or at least unsatisfying. Ursula K. LeGuin (who won her first seven Hugo and Nebula Awards between 1970 and 1975) said that "when writers base a fantasy or science fiction piece directly on some myth, there is often an intellectualization that trivializes both the myth and the novel" (LeGuin, quoted in McCaffery and Gregory 1987: 180).

These judgments—that intellectualizing religious myths or beliefs hurt a story and that it was inappropriate to trivialize a myth—simply were not present to any significant degree in the first decades of gSF. But in the 1970s, they rang true. Moorcock's "Behold the Man" shows the power of a myth to drive a man, to sacrifice himself to give the myth a bit of objective reality. The mainstream science fiction (mSF) Bradbury story, "The Messiah," also presents the need for a myth taking hold of the individual. Note that in the previous decade, with books like *Dune* and stories like "A Rose for Ecclesiastes," the perception of a mythic role shapes the individual, dictating their actions. The myth had acquired an objective reality, existing before any individual. At this next stage, man actively seeks out, desires, *needs* the myth. If he is a victim, it is by choice.

The old tension between religion and science is represented, too, in the reworked "The Man Who Awoke" stories. A purely scientific solution to humanity's existential insecurities is no longer sufficient, so a careful caveat is inserted at least stipulating the *possibility* of a Creator. But no religion is invented to approach this entity, to learn what S/He wants of us. The Creator actually appears in Chalker's *Midnight at the Well of Souls*, but again without a hint of desire of anyone to fall down in worship; rather, we sympathize with his loneliness.

In the Golden Age, religion was held at arm's length—often by only two fingers while pinching our noses. Myths and deities were all too often fictions used to manipulate the ignorant. Since then, we seem to have gradually accepted more and more: the legitimacy of religions as social structures in the 1950s; the power of mythic roles and the exploration of messiahs in the 1960s; the need and *desire* for myths and the willingness to sympathize with a Creator in the 1970s. At each stage, we held religion closer.

Next, with Piers Anthony, our heroes *become* the demigods; with James Morrow, the Messiah becomes our hero . . . but She isn't quite what we might expect.

The Humanity of God (and Vice Versa)

To recapitulate a central problem of science fiction described at the beginning of this book, definitions of genre scientific fiction (gSF) are problematic. In short, "we" seem to make fairly consistent judgments as to what is "real" (i.e., genre, not mainstream) science fiction—which science fiction is "ours." On one hand, we have fairly explicit criteria, but in practice these criteria quickly become problematic. Too many exceptions in both directions appear: stories that we would want to include, but do not contain the "requisite" features (e.g., the "Alternative History" subgenre; see, e.g., Turtledove 1992); stories that *should* fit, but don't "feel" right.

Take for example what would seem to be the most obvious criteria: gSF stories should be about science, not magic. But how do we distinguish between the two, when the described *effects* may be identical? Arthur C. Clarke's "Third Law" (1962/1999) stated that sufficiently advanced science is (to the ignorant) indistinguishable from magic. "On the other hand, subjecting the powers of magic to the laws of thermodynamics turns a story from fantasy to science fiction, though that story may be full of sorcerers in pointy hats" (Silverberg 2001: xv–xvi).

The problem is that, beginning even in the Golden Age, gSF authors did not necessarily posit actual science as basis for their adventures (cf. as contrast Verne's 1863 *Five Weeks in a Balloon*), or even *plausibly* scientific explanations for more-or-less supernatural effects (e.g., faster-than-light drives). Instead, authors (reasonably) chose to prioritize the story, and readers became used to accepting a few magic-like effects as standard practice. For example, consider *Star Trek*'s "universal translators." A computer program's ability to determine the meaning behind abstract symbols from a small sample lacking context or referents seems pretty magical (how can one decode "oxygen" without a description of properties or at least an atomic number?), but one can't imagine the show without them (along with transporters, inertial dampers, warp fields, subspace bubbles, etc.).

The reason these stories still work in the corpus of rational gSF is that such stories maintain *internal consistency*. Once we know what a "universal translator" is, how it works, and what its limitations are, we expect the author to conform to the rules *within* the story (whether or not they conform to known laws of physics). Once stated, the rules cannot be arbitrarily rewritten. "That's cheating, and your reader will be quite correct to throw your book across the room and carefully avoid anything you ever write in the future" (Card 1990b: 23). If, by the 1980s, the technology in gSF seemed rather unlikely, that was acceptable so long as the author played fair. Conventions like "universal translators" became characteristic schemas of gSF: the assumptions shared by readers and authors alike, the rules and raw materials for a gSF story.

Interestingly, since conventional schemas also allow for a measure of shared implicit culture, they facilitate "inside jokes." In a 1980s-era cartoon by Phil Foglio, two characters debate the (lack of) difference between fantasy and science fiction role playing games, specifically citing Clarke's Third Law.

> "Levitation!"
>
> > "Anti-gravity disks!"
>
> "Mind reading?"
>
> > "Brain scanners!"
>
> "Portal spell?"
>
> > "Windows!" (Foglio n.d.)

Importantly, Clarke didn't *invent* the trope—he merely made conscious and explicit a recurring convention that had long been implicitly accepted. Leigh Brackett is sometimes quoted ("Witchcraft to the ignorant . . . Simple science to the learned") as a precursor within the genre (e.g., in the related Wikipedia article), but the pattern predates the genre, for example, whenever a Victorian adventure-fiction "native" encounters a colonial British explorer. In Haggard's *King Solomon's Mines* (1885/1928), the adventurers are discovered while one of them is shaving, having removed his false teeth. "'I see that ye are spirits . . . did ever man born of woman have hair on one side of his face and not the other . . . or teeth which moved and melted away and grew again'" (ibid. p. 402). Their power as "wizards" is confirmed by demonstrating a gun's capacity to kill at a distance (ibid. p. 403). Much later, Foglio played with a convention he could safely assume many in his audience would be aware of (cf. Flamson and Barrett 2008; see Chapter 12, this volume).

Unfortunately, this leads us to *another* definitional problem: not between gSF and mainstream science fiction (mSF), but between gSF and "fantasy literature." Fantasy as a distinct genre had originally calved from gSF following the publishing success of J. R. R. Tolkien (Williamson 2013). If gSF grew more lenient in terms of magic-like "effects" so long as internal consistency was maintained, fantasy has used internal consistency to *restrict* magic. By the 1980s, most fantasy authors were committed to imposing internally consistent rules on how their magic worked. Marion Zimmer Bradley's "Darkover"[1] "planetary romance" series (first published in 1958) occasionally indulged in fantasy-like elements (e.g., 1974's *The Spell Sword*), but largely emphasized that even psychic abilities conformed to a set of (meta-)physical laws (e.g., 1977's *The Forbidden Tower*, in which the plot centers on the conflicts between scientific approaches to "matrix science" and traditional superstitions);[2] Mercedes Lackey's "Valdemar" series features swordfights and magical talking horses . . . and a school designed to teach children to develop their abilities alongside other schools teaching music and medicine (e.g., Lackey 1987). Note that Fantasy and gSF converged due to similar needs to tell a good story. Authors of gSF had to stipulate some "technology" without explanation to expand what is "possible," deviating from a strict definition of gSF. Rabkin compared the greater popularity of Clarke's *Childhood's End* (see Chapter 6) to Theodore Sturgeon's more "Wellsian" (i.e., traditionally limiting fantastic elements) science fiction book, *More Than Human* (1953/1999): "It would seem that either we throw out the notion of the aesthetic importance of organic unity [of genres] or else we recognize that our genre label of *science fiction* has led us astray. This latter conclusion, of course, is the correct one" (Rabkin 1976: 100). With similar goals, Fantasy had to impose pseudo-physical laws to constrain magic: as the (muggle) Prime Minister exclaimed in the "Harry Potter" books, "'But for heaven's sake—you're *wizards*! You can do *magic*! Surely you can sort out—well—*anything*!' . . . 'The trouble is, the other side can do magic, too, Prime Minister'" (Rowling 2005: 24).

In sum, especially by the 1980s—inspired by series like "Darkover" and "The Chronicles of Amber," which James Blish called "[Roger] Zelazny's version of sword-and-sorcery" (Kovacs 2012)—the difference between gSF and Fantasy was as much or more a matter of *style* rather than substance. Stories in which supernatural entities actually appeared would seem to violate commonsense definitions of *science* fiction. However, there are too many examples of 1980s stories which otherwise qualify as gSF, but in which God actually makes an appearance. "Faith" remains excluded from the fold of gSF, however, and the mere existence of God does not necessarily justify religion within these stories. For example, Douglas Adams (in *The Hitchhiker's Guide to the Galaxy*) uses "Babel fish" (i.e., a naturally occurring universal translator) to disprove the existence of God. These mind-numbingly useful creatures instantaneously translate any language for you, provided you stick it in your ear. God, who claims to be dependent on faith, acknowledges that such a creature proves He *must* exist. "'Oh, dear', says God, 'I hadn't thought of that', and promptly vanishes in a puff of logic" (Adams 1979: 55).

Importantly, the representations of God included in this chapter are not false deities invented by the evil priests of early gSF (see Chapter 4), nor Chalker's (1977) unworshipped Creator, nor even the messianic figures in Heinlein (1961) and Herbert (1965), but the Messiah of "our" own Western Judeo-Christian traditions, represented with His divinity—if not always His dignity—intact (cf. Bradbury 1973/2003). It would be incorrect to assume that even the more derogatory representations of God are merely dismissive. As we will see, even sarcastic portrayals sometimes serve the purpose of not just anthropomorphizing, but *humanizing* divinity, imparting God with our worst, as well as our best qualities. In this chapter, we will find a secular Speaker as a "priest" more effective than any religious specialist, Second Comings both comic and tragic, and mankind appropriating the positions of gods. Even in stories with more mundane foci, the absence of religion is presented as unstable, for example, in the effectiveness of religion as a social tool, and the curious emptiness when a character's life is *too* this-worldly. In short, religion (or at least a secularized proxy) appears to be *necessary*, and if there *are* no gods, we may have to not merely invent, but become them.

Piers Anthony, "Incarnations of Immortality" (1983–1990)[3]

On a personal level, it is difficult to write about the history of science fiction without continual reference to Robert Heinlein. Heinlein published five novels in the 1980s, before his death in 1988. Of these, at least three deserve mention here, but will not be considered in depth. This is in part because by this decade, Heinlein more reflected rather than set the trends; also I would prefer not to over-represent a single author, even on as influential as Heinlein, who has, after all, figured prominently in gSF's metanarrative of religion twice already.

Nevertheless, I must mention Heinlein's 1980 novel, *Number of the Beast*—an ambitious if flawed work, based on the premise that *anything* believed, even fictional worlds, gain a measure of reality; I trust that the parallel to our discussion of religion here is obvious. I would also like to mention briefly his last work, *To Sail Beyond the Sunset* (1987), which, along with earlier works, tell the story of his most famous protagonist, "Lazarus Long": a man who cannot die (1958[serialized 1941]), who becomes a larger-than-life, adored father figure (1973), and who—by virtue of traveling back in time to impregnate his own mother—is self-created (1987). Note that, though not supernatural, Lazarus is clearly superhuman, and with each new publication develops a more mythic persona. Lazarus illustrates gSF gradually stepping into roles formerly reserved for religion—not aping the roles, but actually taking on the characteristics.

Finally, it would not be reasonable to ignore 1984's *Job: A Comedy of Justice*, which recapitulates the Biblical story, but which satirizes the Evangelical view of the afterlife, casting Jehovah as the villain, Satan as something of a hero, and Heaven as intolerable. But rather than discuss Heinlein further, I will look at Piers Anthony as a parallel example, specifically his Incarnations of Immortality series—curiously, Anthony's *second* series in which Satan proves to be more potent than the God of Abrahamic traditions (cf. Anthony 1977, 1980a, 1980b).

In this series, the anthropomorphic 'gods' of quasi-Greek myth are not superhuman entities, but *offices* held by humans. Through the first five books, we learn what it would be like for a regular person to "be" Death, Time, War, Nature, and even the triune Fate (1983, 1984, 1986, 1987, and 1985 respectively), and the poetic means by which one assumes these offices (e.g., by killing the previous Death). Plots concern these individuals' struggle to fulfill their office, reduce suffering, and defeat Satan. On the surface, these would appear to be more fantasy than gSF oriented; however, the writing style *feels* more like gSF. As noted above, the boundaries between genres had become permeable, and Anthony himself switched between genres regularly (e.g., the gSF "space opera" "Bio of a Space Tyrant" series and the "sword and sorcery"-flavoured "Apprentice Adept" series—both published concurrently with "Incarnations of Immortality"). Though the inclusion of these books is a judgment call, hopefully the tone of this series, as well as the elucidation of themes found in other contemporary gSF novels (e.g., Heinlein's *Job*), and the foreshadowing of later "anthropomorphic personifications" authors see as science fiction rather than fantasy (e.g., Neil Gaiman in the next chapter) justify their presence here.

The sixth and seventh books tackle Satan (1988) and God (1990). I will focus more on the former here: it is the more interesting of the two, primarily because it more fully explains the religious aspects, while revealing what was *really* going on in the previous books, as we see the preceding conflicts from Satan's point of view. Given the introduction to this chapter, it is unsurprising that the Incarnation of Evil is not such a bad guy after all. His conflicts with other Incarnations are primarily based on prejudice and misunderstandings (see, e.g., Anthony 1988: 220-1, 292-3). In contrast to his reputation, he is actually more concerned with rehabilitation rather than punishment.

In this sixth book, we learn that role of the Incarnation of Evil is not to increase suffering, or even to turn people to evil, but to *reveal* the evil which already exists— not to facilitate Judgment, but simply to keep order. As it is explained to Satan, "The question thus becomes not whether evil is present, as obviously it is, but to what extent it dominates the individual. You thus must do Your utmost to evoke that quality of evil that makes an individual eligible [NB, not *condemns* an individual] for Hell, so that no errors of classification are made" (ibid. p. 267, see also p. 271). That is, Evil is supremely ethical.

We also learn that the Incarnations really *were* gods, once upon a time: children of Chaos and the darkness between Earth and Hades. One by one (with a single exception; see Anthony 2007) they vacated their positions, allowing mortal humans to step into the roles—not because we outgrew them, let alone defeated them as one might have expected in earlier generations of gSF, but simply because they got bored and wandered off (Anthony 1988: 206-7). It fell to us (i.e., to humanity) to take their places.

The enmity between Satan and God is founded in Satan's belief that God is shirking His duty. Lost in narcissistic contemplation of Himself, God is not taking care of his domain, perpetuating a messy and inefficient universe. In fact, God does not seem to be active even within His immediate vicinity: as in Heinlein's *Job*, Heaven seems to be a dreary place. When Satan visits, he finds that the souls residing there "did not look particularly happy; rather they seemed resigned, or even bored" (ibid. p. 259). A soul whom Satan had previously released from Hell begs to return, having found Heaven to be "just as dull as Hell—and most of my friends are in Hell" (ibid. p. 261). "[I]n the face of God's dereliction . . . the separation of good from evil is becoming sloppy" (ibid. p. 267). Thus, Evil is an agent of order working against the fundamental chaos of entropy.

Also, in Anthony's universe the relevance and power of individual deities varies as a function of the number of people who worship and/or acknowledge them. The penultimate power of the Incarnation of Evil stems from the fact that belief in Him is more common than the majority of personifications of Good. In contrast, the individual who reviews "the basic principles" of his role to Satan is the diminished deity "JHVH," who has a critical view of the current dominant Incarnation of Good.

I fear I was no better in my heyday . . . When My people worshipped a golden calf, My rage was not because they were slipping back into idolatry . . . but because it was a light against Me . . . I concluded after some centuries of chronic relapsing on their part that rage and punishment was not the best way to hold a clientele . . . Unfortunately, the young Christian Deity took Me as a role model and emulated some of the worst faults of My heyday, especially that of pride. His enormous success has given Him the freedom to indulge those propensities beyond all reason. Humiliation can indeed make better Deities of Us, because *We are reminded that We do not control the universe.* (Ibid. p. 266, emphasis added)

While God is lost in narcissistic contemplation of Himself, Satan is actively trying to *improve* things. When the Jews are threatened during World War II, God refused to help JHVH; Satan does help, by tricking Time into averting the Holocaust (ibid. pp. 300, 305–7). Thus, Satan is more moral than God.

There is more going on here than simple iconoclasm. Anthony is presenting traditional ways of viewing gods as naïve and ultimately self-defeating. Instead of assuming God to be wholly other and purely Good, we must take responsibility for both the roles and the performance of those *in* those roles. In his stories, he acknowledges that constituent parts of religion (e.g., anthropomorphic conceptions of good, evil, fate, death, and all the other mysterious forces which seem to rule our lives) are in a sense real, but the *shape* of these forces is determined by our worship of them. We and they are responsible to and *for* each other—and if old forms no longer serve, it is our responsibility not to dismiss religion but to take ownership, to claim the roles left vacant by vanished and/or irrelevant gods.

It is worth noting that, in the seventh book (Anthony 1990), the Incarnations cooperate to revise obsolete definitions of sin and replace the delinquent Incarnation of Good with a new human, in hopes that She will do a better job.

James Morrow, *Only Begotten Daughter* (1990)

James Morrow has become known for lampooning Western religion. For example, in his *Blameless in Abaddon* (1996) the Christian God is, like Anthony's, an absent and obsolete deity; in this case, the corpse of God is placed on trial for crimes against humanity. Morrow's representations of religion are often more sarcastically dismissive than Anthony's. In the tellingly named, Nebula Award winning story, "Bible Stories for Adults, No. 17: The Deluge" (1988/1996), a stowaway on the sanctimonious Noah's ark is the "thoroughly foul" Sheila ("her apple is home to many worms, the scroll of her sins as long as the Araxas. She is gluttonous and unkempt. She sells her body. Her abortions number eleven" [ibid. p. 2]). When discovered, Noah and sons try to decide if she should be executed for her crimes; she responds by asking if what she had done was any worse than Yahweh destroying the earth, and tells them, "When a father is abusive . . . the child typically responds not only by denying the abuse occurred, but by redoubling his efforts to be loved" (ibid. pp. 10–11). In "Bible Stories for Adults, No. 31: The Covenant" (1989/1996), one computer, the Yamaha Holy Word Heuristic (i.e., YHWH), reconstructs the lost Ten Commandments (cf. Clarke's story, "The Nine Billion Names of God" [1953/1998]). Another computer, the Series-666 Artificial Talmudic Algorithmic Neurosystem, convinces YHWH that the societal impacts of *any* rules believed to be divine would be disastrous: "thou shalt not kill" would be interpreted as limited to offensive murder, and twisted to *support* war, capital punishment, the extinction of species, etc. (ibid. pp. 128–9)—an argument that appears valid, as in this Commandment-less world, there appears to be no arms race, no prostitution, and so on. Ultimately, YHWH declares to the people, "These rules are not worthy of you!," and destroys the Covenant along with itself (ibid. pp. 131–2). Note that, here again, a version of Satan is working against religion, possibly against God, but for the betterment of mankind. While the stories themselves are amusing, the author appears to be earnest: he writes in the preface to the anthology collecting these stories, "I intend to roll up my sleeves, fire up my computer, and write as subversively as I can."

His 1990 novel *Only Begotten Daughter* paints a rather gentler picture, but with no more patience for organized religion. The first few pages set the tone and outline the positive and negative schemas for "being religious." The "good guys" are Murray, a celibate ethnic Jew who does not believe in God, but who prays when he gets happily excited (see ibid. pp. 28, 32), and his best friend Georgina, a lesbian mother-to-be, a lapsed Catholic and occasional pagan.

> She was a dreamer and a pragmatist, a hardheaded mystic . . . She covered her bases. For Georgina Sparks, a brilliant child was at once something you calculated into existence through preschool stimulation and something you allowed to happen through cosmic openness. Don't attempt parenthood before placing both cognitive psychology and the Spirit of Absolute Being in your camp. (Ibid. p. 34)

In opposition is the Reverend Billy Milk, whose congregation (in contrast to "every tepid little Episcopalian and Methodist church" [ibid. p. 30]) is preparing for the events of *Revelations* and the Second Coming of Jesus by protesting a sperm bank. Billy himself is several steps more extreme: his goal is to *spark* the Second Coming and to *blow up* fertility clinics, not hesitating even at murder. When Billy's infant son was blinded, Billy plucked out one of his eyes in order to make a deal with God: one of the father's in exchange for one of the son's. He later realizes one cannot make deals with God, but when his ruined eye starts showing him visions of the New Jerusalem, he decides one might nevertheless force the issue: bring about the Second Coming by *building* New Jerusalem. In sum, good equals being sort-of religious and tolerant; evil is being blindly religious, intolerant, and believing one has the ability/duty to manipulate others, even God (pp. 24–6, 29).

Unbeknownst to Billy, the Second Coming is happening unobserved. Murray has been supplementing his income by making regular donations at the sperm bank. One of his donations develops an anomaly: specifically, a zygote. No one knows where the requisite egg came from; the doctors are calling it "inverse parthenogenesis" (ibid. pp. 17–18). Murray steals the zygote and the machinery keeping it alive just before the building explodes. It is Georgina who makes the connection between Murray's anomaly and *another* celibate Jew who, 2000 years earlier, spontaneously produced a child. But *this* time the child is female: Jesus' half-sister, whom Murray names Julie (ibid. p. 36). After the decanting, Georgina and Murray discuss her significance.

> [Georgina:] "Julie was sent. The age of cosmic harmony and synergistic convergence is just around the corner."

"You're guessing . . . Nobody knows where that egg came from."

"*I* do. She break any natural laws yet?" (ibid. p. 40)

Georgina's suspicions are correct. Julie *does* develop the ability to produce miracles: with her first steps, she walks off the beach onto the water; lightning bugs spell out "Hi, Pop." Concerned for her safety, Murray only permits one kind of miracle: she is allowed to stroll on the seabed and have long conversations with a sponge named Amanda. Julie knows that God is her mother, but—despite Georgina's view of an impersonal God—is frustrated by the lack of contact and wonders why her half-brother appears to have forsaken her.

One day, Julie meets a "friend" of her mother, Andrew Wyvern. ("Read Job," he says [ibid. p. 55].)[4] Unlike her father, Wyvern *encourages* her miraculous abilities, as he desperately wants religion to make a comeback. "Everywhere he looks, Christianity is on the decline . . . The slaughter of the Aztecs is a mute memory, the fight against smallpox inoculation a vanished dream . . . From pole to pole, Christians are feeding the hungry and clothing the naked. Just last week, Wyvern heard a Baptist minister say it was wrong to kill . . . There must be a church of Julie Katz" (Morrow 1990: 57–8). Julie resists, attempting, rather, to help people via an advice column: "Sheila, Daughter of God."

Billy, meanwhile, has decided that New Jersey would be the perfect place for New Jerusalem and attempts to burn down Atlantic City to make room. Julie uses her powers to stop him, but then to escape a worshipful mob retires with Wyvern into Hell. There she finally meets her famous half-brother, who has been patiently handing out water (liberally dosed with morphine, and a poison that will kill the damned permanently, thus freeing them from Hell), blithely unaware that a religion was founded in his name. After years of assisting Jesus, Julie decides to return to Earth, but must surrender her divinity to do so. In the time Julie was away, Billy has succeeded in making New Jersey into a theocracy. Billy condemns Julie to be crucified as a heretic; she dies after begin given poison on a sponge.

So far, we have in *Only Begotten Daughter* a satisfying book with models of good and bad religiosity, a clever and irreverent twist on the Christian Gospels, and a strong image of religion being of more interest to us and the Devil than to God. The last pages, however, make two remarkable additions. Julie wakens in the ocean, finding her sponge friend from childhood cleaning the hole in her wrist. The sponge Julie drank from was her friend, who transformed the poison into tetrodotoxin.

> —Some would say the miracle was entirely my own doing, Amanda notes. You were always kind to me, so I paid you back: Androcles and the Lion, right? But that strikes me as a hopelessly romantic and anthropomorphic view of a sponge's priorities. Others would call the whole thing a gigantic biochemical coincidence: under optimal conditions, sponges will metabolize hemlock into tetradotoxin. I am not persuaded. Still others would claim that God herself entered into me and performed the appropriate alchemy. A plausible argument, but rather boring. Then there is the final possibility, my favorite.

—Yes?

—The final possibility is that I'm God.

—You're God?

—Just at theory, but the data are provocative. I mean, *look* at me. Faceless, shapeless, holey, undifferentiated, Jewish, inscrutable . . . and a hermaphrodite to boot. Years ago I told you sponges cannot be fatally dismembered, for each part quickly becomes the whole. To wit, I am both immortal and infinite.

—You're God? You're God herself? *You?*

—The data are provocative.

—God is a sponge? A *sponge?* There's not much comfort in that.

—Agreed.

—Sponges can't help us.

—Neither can God, as far as I can tell. (Ibid. p. 309)

So, God as a distinct entity—even if S/He exists—appears to be largely irrelevant. Second, recall that one of the features I claim typifies 1980s gSF is a tendency to project ourselves into the god-like roles. As we have seen, this serves not just to *humanize* divinity, but to *identify* with it. *Only Begotten Daughter* is told entirely in the third person, with one exception: Julie's resurrection and discovery of the "true"(?) nature of God as irrelevant *is told in the second person. We* wake up, cold and alone; *we* learn the "truth" of God's irrelevance, but also discover that "God is more like a verb than a noun"—that divinity is in our behavior, not an external entity. Finally, *we* are reunited with our family.

Theodore Sturgeon, *Godbody* (1986)

In the stories discussed so far, "religion" as a social system has not been respected; it is presented not as an anomaly but a flawed response to something real. Above I argued that by the 1970s, existential and possibly transcendent problems gained real legitimacy within the genre; by the 1980s, authors were not only unusually willing to engage with—perhaps identify with—the representations of divinity of our own Western traditions, they were willing to posit that religion (as an organized social system) may indeed have something to do with these needs: a flawed solution, perhaps, but one not unconnected to the problem.

It is impossible to miss that; so far in this chapter, stories have been rather tongue-in-cheek. Sturgeon's *Godbody* (1986) is an interesting contrast: it is a gSF representation of the Christian Second Coming very different than Morrow's. It is conspicuous in both the seriousness and gentleness of its portrayal of divinity; the Devil, if he exists, is nothing more than humanity's greatest weaknesses. For that matter, it's barely a "novel": Stephen Donaldson calls it "[m]ore a meditation than a novel" (in Sturgeon 1986: 159). Further, as a Golden Age author, Sturgeon links 1980s gSF directly to its traditions and, as it was published posthumously, marks the passing of an era. It is likely that the last thing Robert Heinlein wrote for publication was the introduction. Heinlein wrote:

> *Godbody*—Forget about art and enjoy it.
>
> Some readers will feel that it is XXX-rated pornography. They will have plenty to go on.
>
> Others will see it as a tender, gentle love story. They'll be right.
>
> Some will complain that *Godbody* is loaded with sex and violence.
>
> Others may answer that "Hamlet" ("Romeo and Juliet," the Old Testament, *Le Morte d'Arthur*) is nothing but sex and violence.
>
> Some will denounce *Godbody* as baldly sacrilegious. They'll be right.
>
> Others will see it as tenderly and beautifully reverent. And they will be right.
>
> Never mind what anyone says about this book. Read it, enjoy it, reread it, give it to someone you love. It is our last love letter from a man who loves all of us. (Heinlein, in Sturgeon 1986: 15–16)

The book opens with Reverend Dan Currier meeting a strange naked man during a walk through the Catskills, who introduces himself as "Godbody." Currier is unsettled by their brief conversation, despite Godbody's gentle nature. On returning home, he is caught up in a surprisingly passionate encounter with his wife. Note: the reader's first encounter with divinity is quickly transformed into sexuality.

Recall that the crucial passage in *Only Begotten Daughter* is told in the second person to intensify the reader's identification with the central, divine character. *Godbody* is told entirely in the first person, each chapter giving us the point of view of Godbody's impact on them. One chapter gives us the perspective of Dan's wife, Liza, including her account of his return home after his transformative meeting with Godbody.

> I climaxed again—which I had never, never done before—and he did too, saying in a big voice:
>
> *"I am the way and the life."*
>
> As the great wave receded I looked up at him and spoke my miracle: "Twice. Oh, twice. I have never been happier in all my life. Dan . . . what happened?"
>
> "Godbody," he said. I suppose I must have looked puzzled, because he laughed suddenly and kissed me. "Don't ask me what I mean. Not for a while."
>
> So we lay there for a while longer in that little lake of molten sun, naked and unashamed for the first time together. (Ibid. p. 38)

Later chapters relate how other people are influenced by Godbody, including a passionless businessman, a rapist, and a gossip (Mrs. Mayhew) who is offended by Reverends who listen rather than just preach. If they come to *him*, rather than punish them for their behavior, Godbody empowers them to overcome whatever makes them unhappy—their sexual repressions, loneliness, memories of rape—by helping them know themselves. For example, Mr Merriweather, one of the more powerful citizens, recounts what is, for us, a disturbing sexually dysfunctional relationship with his wife. Dan confronts him about his allowing the Mrs. Mayhew to defame Liza. While not admitting anything, Mr Merriweather denies any responsibility. Dan responds:

> Andy, you run this town—you and Willa Mayhew. No—don't interrupt me! Don't give me a lecture about the town board and local ordinances and county and state laws and a regulated school district. You know what I mean. I am not going to discuss what motivates you; I just want you to know that I know what you are doing. I know too that you do whatever you can to strengthen the structure that exists—only because it exists and not because it is good. Only because you can use it, and the stronger it is, the stronger you are. You use the church for that, and the bank, and also you use Willa Mayhew and her newspaper. (Ibid. p. 121)

When Dan introduces Mr Merriweather to Godbody, as the only way they can think of to get Mr Merriweather to tell the truth, Godbody asks him "Who are you?" Mr Merriweather can answer only "I don't know" (ibid. p. 129).

Mrs Mayhew, while spying on the community growing around the Curriers, shoots Godbody. He dies without surprise or anger. "It's always like this. Usually not so soon, though" (Sturgeon 1986: 140). (Note the implication that this is not the *Second Coming*; rather, there have been many attempts to save us from ourselves.) In his last words, Godbody tells them he does not want or need a formal religion in his name— "Outdoors naked is all the cathedrals I ever want in my name"—and "If ever you want to touch the hand and the heart of God Almighty, you can do that through the body of someone you love. Anytime. Anywhere. Without no middleman" (ibid. p. 141).

The next Sunday Dan delivers a sermon contrasting the current Christian religious system to the early Church, in particular decrying the use of the priesthood to separate man from God. Mr Merriweather had used the church to perpetuate his influence; in contrast, Dan resigns his position, saying "I want my God for my pastor, not my bishop nor any other man. I want to love without shame and to worship without dilution; and feeling so, my friends, I feel myself disqualified for this job" (Sturgeon 1986: 150). The Curriers and a few like-minded friends begin plans to form a community of their own. Dan Currier emphasizes that he will help, but not lead; neither will anyone else.

In Sturgeon's novel, divinity exists; existential problems are real; religions attempt to solve the latter with appeal to the former, as it should be . . . but religion as we know it has deviated from the path. Too many generations have needlessly complicated it; too many people have enlarged their authority by positioning themselves as leaders, as "middlemen"; too many people, leaders and followers both, relied on it not to help, but simply because it was there.

Orson Scott Card, *Speaker for the Dead* (1986), *Folk of the Fringe* (1989)

This section looks at religion in Orson Scott Card's fiction, as well as Card's personal religion. I argued above that my cognitive anthropological perspective on literature differs from traditional literary criticism in that I am interested in how works transmit—what audiences choose to consume and why—over and above the creative process. Thus, authors' personal beliefs (religious or otherwise) are relatively unimportant, since consumers generally know little about authors' personal lives; such details are not primary motivators.

Card, however, is too well known to be a Mormon and has published work explicitly related to his religion. So, some consideration can be justified here, which gives me an opportunity to reflect on how personal religiosity may influence identity as well as *implicitly* impact aesthetic products like science fiction narratives.

Card is best known for the 1985 novel *Ender's Game* (1985a): a remarkably human gSF story, reminiscent of Heinlein's *Starship Troopers* (1959) in that, while the events of the story are martial, the central themes are not "who won" each fight but *why* we fight, and how fighting changes us. Earth appears to be threatened by an incomprehensible race of insect-like aliens. Humanity appears doomed to lose, for tactical as well as technical reasons. Only a single human commander was able to defeat the "Buggers" in battle; as important as developing military technology has been finding—or perhaps creating—a new commander capable of winning the next conflict. "Ender"—a childhood nickname based on his given name, Andrew—is trained from a very young age to be that commander, and by understanding the Buggers manages to "end" the threat by destroying all the alien Queens, and thus (it is believed) the entire species.

Card's masterpiece is the "sequel" *Speaker for the Dead* (1986).[5] In it, Card suggests that intergroup conflict stems from a failure to comprehend the motivations of "the other" and distinguishes between four levels of foreignness: *utlänning*, or someone whom one might not know personally, but who shares one's cultural perspectives; *främling* (sometimes "framling"), a human but from another (cultural?) world; *ramen*, or a member from another species but with whom communication and peaceful coexistence is possible; and *varelse*—species that may be sentient, even moral from their own perspective, but who is so alien that no common ground can be established, no communication can be possible, and with whom mortal struggle is inevitable (Card 1986: 38). The distinction develops ideas introduced in the last act of *Ender's Game*: Andrew realizes that the Buggers were not incomprehensible (i.e., were not varelse, but ramen): conflict was not inevitable, nor necessarily fatal for one species or the other. Under the *nom de plume* "Speaker for the Dead," Andrew/Ender writes *The Hive Queen*, explaining this, and in away revealing his actions to be not heroic but incalculably criminal. He also writes a second book explaining his brutal, similarly incomprehensible brother, *The Hegemon*.

Speaker for the Dead finds Andrew millennia later; Andrew is still alive, having spent most of the last subjective decades traveling at relativistic speeds. In that time, "Ender" is believed to be long dead, and his memory demonized as the "Xenocide," due to the success and popularity of the books written by the "Speaker for the Dead." Speaking the death of an individual has become an established, if sometimes subversive, tradition, with Speakers accorded quasi-religious status: they reveal the unvarnished truth about the deceased, encouraging empathy through (sometimes brutal) honesty. Andrew occasionally functions as one of these Speakers, but no one knows he is *the* Speaker.

In Card's 1986 book, Andrew has again been called to Speak a death on a Catholic world. The details of the plot are not relevant here; it is sufficient to say that Card continues to explore the relationships between understanding, identity, and community: Andrew uncovers hidden truths about another alien species *and* about alienated members of a human society.

Speaker presents three very different messages about religion. First, the colony Andrew visits is ethically Portuguese, and strongly religious. The Catholic religion is strong social system influential in both private and public spheres. In good gSF tradition, the beneficial nature of religion's influence is demonstrated through the Church's commitment to education, embodied in the order of the Children of the Mind of Christ. These monastics speak truth to secular power and focus on *practical* matters: "Even the monastery garden made a rebellious statement—everything that wasn't a vegetable garden was abandoned to weeds" (Card 1986: 173). The abbot is called Dom Cristão ("Lord Christian"), so that "When they call you by your title . . . a sermon comes from their own lips" (ibid. p. 174). In a deliberate link of monastic to secular life, monks and nuns *must* marry; however, in an equally deliberate way to emphasize the *contrast* between religious and secular spheres they remain celibate: they serve the community (*not* the Church), but choose to perpetuate it through knowledge rather than children (ibid. pp. 166, 177).

Thus, the Children of the Mind demonstrates that religious and secular social structures, though distinct, are interrelated and often complementary.[6] Though the influence of religion may be predominantly beneficial in this case, it does not follow that it must always be, especially when religious and secular, public and private, even collective and individual needs come into conflict. After a couple die saving the community, their young daughter is alienated by the fact that others are *celebrating* their sacrifice. Any hint that her parents might have been saints with supernatural powers is deeply insulting to her; "she told the Bishop that if the Pope declared her parents venerable, it would be the same as the Church saying that her parents hated her" (Card 1986: 9). Ultimately, the needs of the Catholic community to have hero-saints trumped the emotional needs of one girl; as a result, she felt no emotional or social ties with her neighbors. However, individuals in *Speaker* are *defined* by their community: this lonely, alienated girl necessarily has a community; she closely identifies with the distant Speakers for the Dead. Only once she finally accumulates experiences with a few neighbors, building a shared body of knowledge and memories (even sharing inside jokes that no outsider would understand [ibid. pp. 14–18; see also Flamson and Barrett 2008; Chapter 12, this volume]) do they become part of her community.

In sum, shared experience yields shared knowledge, which can develop into communal identity. In the culture described in *Speaker of the Dead*, religion is an unusually potent community among many coexisting ones—and one in which the needs of the community may take precedence over the needs of the individual, and in which positing supernatural events may be a useful tool.

In addition to the social nature of religion, Card implies a second need, traditionally associated with but distinguishable from religion: the necessity of ritually marking death—not the interring of the body or caring for the soul, but bearing witness to the life as it really was. Speakers of the Dead, then, intrude into traditional duties of religious specialists. As a result, the residents of this Catholic colony are told not to cooperate, and *The Hive Queen* and *The Hegemon* are on the Index Librorum Prohibitorum (ibid. p. 18). Specifically, the responsibility of the Speaker is *not* to the community but to the deceased individual, for example, by disputing beliefs in supernatural heroes. Andrew previously Spoke the death of the founder of the Children of the Mind, who died worrying about how his legacy would be interpreted. "'Andrew, they're already telling the most terrible lies about me, saying that I've done miracles and should be sainted. You must help me. You must tell the truth at my death'" (ibid. p. 103).

It would be a mistake, however, to interpret the Speaker as a socially viable *alternative* to religion. It is telling that no community seems to be based primarily on the Speakers' principle of total honesty. Rather, the Speaker seems to function as a pressure valve when "normal" society supports an untenable conflict; though his role may undermine claims to supernatural authority (and, thus, the key distinction of religious social systems as defined here), there is no attempt to "save" a community from religion generally. Andrew's special gift, which allowed him to destroy the Buggers, and allows him to Speak a death, is empathic, deep understandings of individuals and communities; he accepts that becoming a *member* of a community requires one to adopt its religious identity (ibid. p. 175).

This leads us to the third take-home message of *Speaker*, which relates not to the novel but to the author. I generally avoid authors' personal beliefs, as it is generally the content of the writings, and the reputation of the author *as* an author, that determine their acceptance rather than privately held opinions, spiritual beliefs, etc. This is especially clear in Heinlein's case, as neither the "free love" interpretations that popularized *Stranger in a Strange Land* nor the (seemingly contradictory) charges of fascism levelled at Heinlein after the publication of *Starship Troopers* (Panshin [1968: 94] called it a "militaristic polemic") seem to reflect Heinlein's personal libertarian views.

Orson Scott Card is a Mormon. Above in Chapter 1, I described different ways religion can be combined with science fiction, ranging from writing science fiction *in order to be religious*, to fictional depictions of religion. This book is primarily concerned with the latter, but Card is unusual in that he is well known as a Mormon author (see his fictionalized chronicle of the early days of The Church of Jesus Christ of Latter-Day Saints [LDS], *Saints* [1983]). When I met him briefly c. 1992, he described distinguishing between Mormon and non-Mormon audiences, but acknowledged that even his "secular" works were constrained by his Mormon identity, but not necessarily by his Mormon faith. (Cf. "in my plays, the question of faith did not come up. If the characters believed, then that was fine; if they didn't, then fine" [Card 1985b: 12].)

> I am not surprised that most LDS sf readers who have discussed [a work of mine] with me have declared that they could tell all the way through that I was Mormon. As long as I don't interfere with my own storytelling, I suspect that my works will always reveal my beliefs, both orthodox and unwitting heretical. (Card 1985b: 12)

To those who criticize him for not writing more explicitly as a Mormon (see Collings 1984, esp. p. 113), Card writes that they are "asking me to deal with the most fundamental matters in a shallow, trivial, obvious, and inevitably ineffective way, all the while not noticing that I am already dealing with the LDS cosmology—or my version of it—in everything I do; but on an unconscious level that I discover only after the work is finished" (Card 1985b: 13). More, he once described difficulty interacting with fellow science fiction writers who were not Mormon:

> These guys were Americans, not Mormons; those of us who grew up on Mormon society and remain intensely involved are only nominally members of the American community. We can fake it, but we're always speaking a foreign language. Only when we get with fellow Saints are we truly at home. If it had been a group of ten Mormons, I wouldn't have had any problem. We'd have a common fund of experience, speak the same language, share some of the same concerns. We could make jokes about Mormon culture, talk seriously about things that you can only discuss with someone who shares the same faith. With this group, though, relaxing would be much, much harder. (Card 1990a: 284)

To apply *Speaker's* levels of incomprehensibility, non-Mormons are *framling*: not *ramen*, but not *utlanning* either.

This makes it particularly interesting when Card depicts not the LDS history, but it is possible future: what aspects are important and valuable? In his short story collection *The Folk of the Fringe* (1989), Card focuses not on Mormon doctrine, but on the potential for a religion to unite a group while excluding others. It begins with a small group of persecuted Mormon outcasts heading west (in the story "West"), who are convinced that the strongest vestiges of civilization will be in Mormon-controlled Utah. When someone asks how they can be sure:

> "We *know*." Pete grinned. "We may not look like much to you, but out there Mormons are in charge. I promise you that wherever there are four Mormons, there'll be a government. A president, two counselors, and somebody to bring refreshments." (Card 1990: 28)

The strength of the religion lay not in belief, strength of motivation, or even God's favor, but in superior habits of social organization and stronger interpersonal ties.

Distinctions between Mormons and others in "West" are not necessarily hostile, but under conditions of stress boundaries are as impermeable as those segregating race:

> These days, you just didn't see blacks and whites together much. People looked out for their own. There wasn't a lot of race *hatred*, they just didn't have much to do with each other. (Card 1990: 5)

But this group of hopeful Mormons *is* mixed race: apparently, the ties binding a religion together can be stronger than those keeping races apart. This capacity to create communities is not idealized; a later story ("Pageant Wagon") describes the marginality imposed on non-Mormons.

> Deaver figured it was like all those Mormons, together they formed a big piece of cloth, all woven together through the whole state of Desert [sic], each person like a thread wound in among the others to make a fabric, tough and strong and complete

right out to the edge—right out to the fringe. These Mormon range riders, they might stray out into the empty grassland, but they were still part of the weave, still connected. Deaver, he was like a wrong-colored thread that looks like it's hanging from the fabric, but when you get up close, why, you can see it isn't attached anywhere, it just got mixed up in the wash, and if you pull it away it comes off easy, and the cloth won't be one whit weaker or less complete. (Card 1990: 142)

After watching the audience of a play incorporating moments of American and of specifically Mormon history, this outsider notes the communal spirit that is generated. "For a while tonight they saw and heard and felt the same things. And now they'd carry away the same memories, which meant to some degree they were the same person. One" (Card 1990: 215).

Shared culture, shared history, shared *schemas* equal strong social bonds; religion is a powerful source of these schemas, but not the only one (cf. Sperber 1996; see Chapters 1 and 12). For Card, the important, fundamental aspects of religion are the cultural schemas incorporated into one's personality, which shape everything one does and everything one will produce, and the strength of the ties between people who share these schemas, organized into a tightly knit society. In this regard, and not in such trivial details as public display and/or proselytizing, religion is a powerful and positive, civilizing social system.

William Gibson and Bruce Sterling, *The Difference Engine* (1990)

"Steampunk" began in the 1980s as a subgenre of gSF. It is a profoundly nostalgic literature, returning to the genre's roots: the late-nineteenth-century world of Jules Verne and H. G. Wells, liberally laced with other subgenres (plot devices from "alternative history" and elements of style and character from "cyberpunk") and crossing into other genres (see Gail Carriger's "The Parasol Protectorate" series). In many ways, steampunk was a natural step for gSF, as it expands on the genre's increasing skepticism with the societal benefits of the last century's technology, and disappointment in the mundane nature of twenty-first-century life in contrast to the Golden Age's optimistic predictions (no peaceful world government, no extra-planetary colonization). Further, it connects directly to the do-it-yourself ideal of the Gernsback hobbyist days and responds to the frustrations of "black box" technologies with fanciful recollections of technology that could be taken apart and understood.

For our purposes, steampunk gives us a contemporary re-engagement of past genre schemas: an "in-house review" of former gSF representations of religion, for example. Ironically, however, the genre did not embrace steampunk. It flourished only once social media allowed it to expand beyond the confines of its ancestral context; steampunk quickly "went mainstream." (For more on the history and significance of steampunk, see Hrotic [2013]; for the implications for the health of science fiction as a genre, see Chapter 11).

As our representative of steampunk, I will use William Gibson and Bruce Sterling's *The Difference Engine* (1990/2010). The setting is an alternative Victorian era, but with comparatively advanced technology. Science is idealized and permeates popular culture; scientists not only influence business, but through a system of merit-based Lordships control Parliament, and through Parliament much of the world. Such a situation would have seemed utopic in early gSF, but here the impact on society is grotesque. Through the use of computer-based observations and espionage, personal freedom is frighteningly restricted and social justice is markedly absent: eugenics is viewed as a legitimate social tool for example and Francis Galton has considerable influence within the House of Lords. Pollution is rampant, the Thames is toxic, and academic thought outside technical fields has lost its relevance. The exaggerated norms of the Golden Age have yielded a dystopia.

In this unpleasant world, religion is conspicuously absent. The YMCA has been replaced by the Young Man's Atheist Association, and one's own religious beliefs (if any) are not admitted to in polite company (recall "Ultrasonic God" in Chapter 5). The religions of other cultures are referenced only in a derogatory fashion: "Moslem's don't care to eat pork, you know, all very superstitious"; and "when you see some Hindoo fakir a-sitting in a temple niche, filthy naked with a flower in his hair, who's to say what goes on in that queer headpiece of his?" (Gibson and Sterling 1990/2010: 243). In these cases, it is clear that the sympathies of the reader should be for the religious "natives," not for the bigoted colonialists.

Two final excerpts will be sufficient to depict Gibson and Sterling's representations of religion. It is socially unacceptable to use religion to bolster one's prejudices, but piously citing science is perfectly (if hypocritically) acceptable. For example:

"A strong-minded woman! Much like her mother, eh? Wears green spectacles and writes learned books . . . She wants to upset the universe, and play at dice with the hemispheres. Women never know when to stop . . ."

Mallory smiled. "Are you a married man, Mr. Fraser?"

"Not I, not yet. And Lady Ada never married. She was a bride of Science."

"Every woman needs a man to hold her reins," Fraser said. "It's God's plan for the relations of men and women." Mallory scowled.

Fraser saw the look, and thought the matter over again. "It's evolution's adaptation for the human species," he amended.

Mallory nodded slowly. (Ibid. p. 173)

Similarly, one character—a spy, based on the historical author Laurence Oliphant— visits a doctor to deal with his "waking visions." This representative of medical science has literally appropriated the trappings of religion—his waiting room is furnished with "carved wooden pews that might have come from a wrecked church"—while arrogantly and blindly embracing medical doctrine, dismissing a suggested link between cholera and contaminated water as "'utterly contrary to medical theory.'" The doctor, then, is a fool hidebound to the doctrines of his profession (ibid. pp. 292–4).

Oliphant himself finds the doctor's obsession with magnetism reminiscent "of his own father's unhealthily keen interest in mesmerism." Oliphant's family, we learn, were Evangelical Christians. The influence of this upbringing remains, though kept carefully concealed (ibid. p. 296). Oliphant actually continues to practice mesmerism "with a regularity he had once devoted to prayer" (ibid. p. 305) and finds his father's "unhealthy" practices more effective than contemporary medicine. Further, the *absence* of the religion of his childhood seems to be a source of his problems: "He dreamed, as he often did, of an omniscient Eye in whose infinite perspectives might be sorted every least mystery" (ibid. p. 304). Note the anthropomorphism: Oliphant's subconscious looks not for information, but to a Being who sees.

Conclusion

In the 1970s' representations of religion, we saw a subtle regret that one could not believe in a supernatural reality beyond ourselves (e.g., *The Man Who Awoke*) and a suggestion that perhaps our fate is to evolve into what would appear to us now to be god-like figures. In the 1980s, we see ourselves (literally, in Anthony's case) step into the roles of the gods and often appear to be disrespectful (perhaps even blasphemous) toward any external Divinity. One possible reason why these two are connected is that, seeing ourselves as having outgrown passive, unquestioning belief in God the Father, humans are beginning to claim their inheritance by stepping into the roles previously occupied by mythic figures. As with any period of adolescence, there is a tendency to treat the "adults" (i.e., the previous role occupants) with disrespect, as part of asserting our independence.[7]

Reciprocally, characters' faith in *religion* hints at unexpected strengths (Card's *Folk of the Fringe*), but even those who dismiss religion as a social system (e.g., Morrow and Sturgeon in this chapter) seem to be suggesting not that religion is not baseless, but rather that approaching the basis of religion is hindered, not helped, by religious specialists. That is, the *needs* religions claim to meet are impossible to ignore. In *Speaker of the Dead*, the Speaker fills one such need—a competitor to religion who does not acknowledge any conflict. It is as if 1980s-era gSF still lacks any faith in "religion," but is flirting with the idea of faith in . . . something. On the other hand, *The Difference Engine* displays a loss of faith in *science* and in the benefits of technological progress as reasonable, scientific motivations to be just as potentially self-serving as everything else, while simultaneously implying that the lack of religion (once viewed as *purely* self-servicing, at least to the elite) may generate its own problems. Ironically, the same period that demonstrates weak faith in God, faith in *religion* unexpectedly, recurs.

In sum, 1980s gSF appears to lack any coherent solution to the "problem" of religion vs. science—but there seems to have been a rising dissatisfaction (even among authors critical of religion) in a solution as simple as "science good, religion bad." There are two main possibilities, neither exclusive: that the schema for religion continued to evolve in the genre, and that the boundaries between gSF and other genres became more permeable, diluting the purity of gSF—perhaps yielding a more mature but conflicted schema.

Acceptance

I used to think it was awful that life was so unfair. Then I thought, wouldn't it be much worse if life were fair, and all the terrible things that happen to us come because we actually deserve them. So now, I take great comfort in the general hostility and unfairness of the universe.

J. Michael Straczynski, Babylon 5 episode "A Late Delivery from Avalon" (1996)

In this chapter, we will take a look at three books that demonstrate how far genre science fiction's (gSF's) schema for religion had come by the end of the century: Butler's *Parable of the Sower* (1993), Mary Doria Russell's *The Sparrow* (1996), and David Weber's *Honor of the Queen* (1993), which show religion and faith as sources of strength and give us yet another Jesuit as a positive image of a religious specialist. But first, just to set the tone, recall L. Sprague de Camp's "Ultrasonic God," published back in 1954, and described back in Chapter 5. "Fromme," the protagonist, likes a girl, *except* her religious piety, which annoys him to no end; he comes to prefer the company of a "likable scoundrel" who used religion to manipulate others (de Camp 1954: 34).

Contrast that to Nancy Kress's *Probability Moon* (2000). A small exploration/military group makes *second* contact with an interesting alien species (sadly without a Jesuit). These aliens appear to be uniquely social. Those who do not "share reality" (i.e., anyone who does not see the world as their peers do) can be declared by their priests not to be "real," which is to say, not sentient—not capable of being a person. This is not a top-down, religion-created fiction, but apparently a biological reality. The explorers wonder at the *source* of this superhuman accord. One in particular, David, is convinced this biological reality could be adapted to humans, and similarly believes this would fix all our problems—he believes these things despite all evidence to the contrary, and a degree of self-deception. This alien culture also euthanizes children who do not develop the ability to share reality; David convinces himself that *this* must be cultural and blames the priests.

The priests that must declare little Nafret real—they held the power of life and death. And wasn't *that* a common pattern in human history. Greedy religious orders, wanting to keep power for themselves, using custom and myth and threats and murder to keep the people in line and then making them believe it was all for their own good so they wouldn't challenge the supremacy of the priesthood. Some political thinker of a few centuries ago had nailed it exactly: "Religion is the opiate of the people." (Ibid. p. 63)

Two things to note: First, "custom and myths and threats and murder" is a fairly accurate description of how religion was portrayed during the genre's first decade (cf. Barclay's "The Troglodytes" [1930] in Chapter 4), and a sharp contrast to how far the genre had developed. (See as contrast Dozois' "The Peacemaker" [1984], which painted even human sacrifice sympathetically.) Second, David's colleagues do not agree with his dismissive attitude: in fact, they find his immaturity and intransience about his unsupported theories frustrating. They are also disturbed by his inability to view the culture with proper relativistic distance (e.g., Kress 2000: 75, 82, 88–9). David might have been the hero in 1930; in 2000, he's an ass.

Robert Sawyer's *Calculating God* interjects a surprising religious element into a gSF and also includes a science fiction "inside joke." Even mainstream science fiction (mSF) fans will recognize the trope of the alien landing on earth to make contact, and know what to expect next. In this case, the space ship lands in Toronto in a parking lot next to the Royal Ontario Museum. After negotiating the glass doors of the Museum, the alien approaches a security guard and begins one of the best opening dialogs in the history of science fiction.

> "Excuse me. I would like to see a paleontologist."
>
> [The guard's] eyes went wide, but he quickly relaxed. He later said he figured it was a joke . . . "What kind of paleontologist?" he said, deadpan, going along with the bit.
>
> The alien's spherical torso bobbed once. "A pleasant one, I suppose."
>
> On the video, you can see [the guard] trying without complete success to suppress a grin. "I mean, do you want an invertebrate or a vertebrate?"
>
> "Are not all of your paleontologists humans? . . . Would they not therefore all be vertebrates?" (Sawyer 2000: 4–5)

After the initial confusion, the alien is introduced to a paleontologist. It is revealed that the alien is one, too, and is engaged in attempting to uncover God's plan in the universe. She, and all other sentient races, are bemused by humans' agnosticism. Everyone else has accepted that the universe exists because of the actions of an Intelligent Designer and that the universe contains objective evidence of design.

She turns out to be quite right in this, as she and the human scientist ultimately assist in the rebirth of God. This god, however, is in no way anthropomorphic. It truly is the creator of universes, but is so far removed from our existence that no communication is possible. Anyone who claims to have messages from it is assumed to be delusional. Further, there is no connection between the existence of God and immortality in any other sentient civilization: though *a* super-being exists, the usual human concept of God with whom a relationship is possible is in error.

Neither of these elements are traditional gSF fodder: not representing characters intolerant judgments of religion as odious, nor the introduction of a popular theory famously at odds with the scientific community (cf. the 2005 US federal court case of *Kiztmiller et al. v. the Dover Area School District*). The volumes described below introduce still more surprises, but all sharing a common theme: a willing respect for religion, shown in narratives which portray it as potentially positive as the first generation portrayed it as probably negative.

David Weber, *Honor of the Queen* (1993)

David Weber's "Honor Harrington" series begins chronicling the rise of a (space) naval officer from her first command to the highest levels of military achievement, and *then* expands into an obsessively multifaceted examination as much of why wars are fought as how they are won. In the first book, *On Basilisk Station* (1992), we learn that she is as honorable as she is intelligent and competent—a combination which pits her against arrogant, self-serving upper-class men, who resent her inexplicable tendency of seeing herself as their equal, if not their better.

In the second, *Honor of the Queen* (1993), she is sent to the out-of-the-way planet Grayson. The local culture promises to be a challenge, especially for someone like Honor. She is briefed on her new post. When she asks why these humans settled on such an isolated planet, she is told the motivations were religious:

> "They were religious zealots looking for a home so far away no one would ever bother them. I guess they figured five-hundred-plus light-years was about far enough in an era before hyper travel had even been hypothesized. At any rate, the 'Church of Humanity Unchained' set out on a leap of faith, with absolutely no idea what they were going to find at the other end."
>
> "Lord." Honor sounded shaken, and she was. (Weber 1993: ch. 1)

Ironically, though the colonists' goal was to escape the "'the corrupting, soul-destroying effect of technology," the planet at the end of their trip cannot support human life *without* a great deal of technology. Already, within the domain of gSF, we have reasons to suspect the Graysons to be unpleasant: they are xenophobic, anti-science, and probably hypocritical. "'They used a *starship* to get away from *technology*? That's— that's insane, Sir!'" (ibid.).

To make a bad situation worse, the Graysons are strongly patriarchal. They practice polygyny; woman cannot own property, participate in government, *or* the military. Their only saving grace is their closest neighbors (also descended from the original colonists) are even worse: "Dietary laws, ritual cleansing for every imaginable sin—law codes that made any deviation from the True Way punishable by *stoning*, for God's sake!" (ibid.) In sum, Weber designed the Graysons to push all of the typical gSF's buttons. We are disgusted by them before we meet them, and, once we meet them, they are as bad as we imagined. Even the most open-minded of the Graysons have difficulty even conceptualizing a female officer.

But only at first. As Honor demonstrates her competence, some begin to accept her. In later books, this acceptance grows. Importantly, however, *it is not simply a case of the Graysons realizing the error of their ways*. Weber presents two aspects that positively color both our opinions of the Graysons: they *are* patriarchal, hidebound, and stubborn . . . but they've *had* to be. If they are overprotective of women, it is in part because their circumstances demanded it. Living conditions were horrible, due to an extremely toxic environment. A Grayson tries to explain: infant mortality was extremely high for the first generations; for the colony to survive, women *had* to bear too many children for their health; and, though their religion had told them that men's job was to protect women, it was not possible—men had brought them there, but the women paid a higher price. Even now, the Grayson nickname for their god is "Tester." He freely admits they *were* zealots.

> "I pride myself on my knowledge of history, yet truth to tell, *I* never thought this deeply about it until I was forced up against the differences between us and you, and I suspect few Graysons ever really delve deep enough to understand how and why we became what we are. Is it different for [you]?"
> "No. No, it's not." (Ibid. ch. 8)

Weber does not excuse their behaviors, but neither does he allow them to be dismissed as incomprehensible.

The Graysons are positive examples of a religion *not* because they lack flaws, but because they are willing to admit their flaws, and *change*—slowly and with great effort, but if it were easy, it would not be so admirable. After saving Grayson, in the fourth book Honor is granted "Steadholder" status (essentially landed gentry). Her fitness to lead on a predominantly patriarchal, theocratic world is challenged by the other Steadholders; unexpected support comes from the leader of the Grayson religion.

> "Your Grace, this woman is not of our Faith, yet she has so declared before us all, making no effort to pretend otherwise. More, she stands proven a good and godly woman, one who hazarded her own life and suffered grievous wounds to protect not only our Church but our world when we had no claim on her. I say to you, and to the Conclave [of Steadholders]," and his resonant voice rose higher and stronger, "that God knows his own." (Weber 1994: ch. 16)

Grayson religion is presented as restrictive and unenlightened—until one scratches the surface. It is portrayed as a strongly unifying system, as well as a source of *individual* strength. Honor is judged by her behavior, which conforms to their views of morality; they respect her sacrifices for their world, and her promise to protect a Church of which she is not a member. There are *reasons* for their flaws, as well as a will to address them.

Weber's depiction of religion is not the only reason I chose to include "Honor Harrington." The series also demonstrates some characteristic trends common in gSF over the last decade, which (as discussed in the next chapter) *may* relate to a loss of coherency within gSF.

First, the representation of religion here differs somewhat from religion in another Weber series, "Safehold," beginning with *Armageddon Reef* (2007). In this book, religion is used as a deliberate mechanism of retarding technological growth, by making certain topics taboo. Though the restriction is deemed necessary (technology will invite attack by a race with vastly superior technology), some factions prefer to maintain the religion—and the power over human society it grants them—when the original impetus to create the religion may no longer hold. Both aspects of this representation are very traditional within the genre: Heinlein's stories, for example, showed leaders using religion to control a population (1939, 1949) and limiting scientific advancement (the 1941 story, "Universe" [1963a]). This demonstrates that the *old* ideas never really go away within the genre: a particular variation on a schema may be more popular in a given "generation," but the total number of available forms of any given schema only increases.

Second (speaking subjectively), in the last decade or so of gSF there appears to have developed a correlation between quality and *length*. The books discussed in Chapter 6 of this volume are, in my opinion, thought-provoking classics of the genre—not just among the best of gSF, but among the best of contemporary American literature . . . yet all may easily be read in a few days. More recently, "open-ended" series have become increasingly common. In 2012 Weber released the 450-page, 13th "Honor Harrington" book in the series—or the 23rd, if one includes anthologies and other works in the same series—which was only *half* of a self-contained storyline (cf. Weber 2012, 2013). Such huge, multi-volume works may be a limiting factor in the spread of gSF schema (as they specifically target readers who are already dedicated fans), while not expanding the possibilities of the schemas themselves: typically, such length is used to expand the created "world," not develop ideas (*Anathem* [2008, see below] being a counter-example).

Third, Weber is perhaps best described not as a gSF writer, but as a *military*-gSF writer. The number of subspecies of science fiction has grown, as have the population of each. When, in the late 1960s, a science fiction "New Wave" offered an alternative to "hard sf," it did not produce a schism: from my research, it appears that readers' tastes were promiscuous. But there are far more than two subspecies now: cyberpunk, alternative history, military science fiction, and steampunk are among the most popular. It is far easier now for readers to specialize—an average reader would never run out of military science fiction to read; given the productivity of writers like Weber, a *casual* reader might be satisfied with one or two authors. The likelihood of genre-wide schemas seems to be decreasing.

Octavia Butler, *Parable of the Sower* (1993)

Parable of the Sower by Octavia Butler (1993) is far from "escapist" gSF; it presents an America in the near future where economic and environmental deterioration have become extreme, presented in a way that seems almost minimally speculative. A common strategy of pulp gSF was to emphasize even the most outrageous stories as "plausible." Most of those claims seem silly in retrospect, and we tend to associate this claim with the trashier end of the spectrum: for example, the famously (and wonderfully) awful 1959 movie *Plan 9 from Outer Space* begins, "Future events such as these will affect you in the future."

Parable holds nothing outrageous, and much that is familiar, resulting in a thoughtful, low-key, but challenging book, describing a young, poor woman who decides a new religion is necessary. The chapters are in diary form, adding subtle emphasis that not only is the protagonist a "real" person, but also that her development throughout the book results from the events described. As the reader knows no more than "Lauren," we experience a measure of her uncertainty and must determine (along with her) if her new religion is valid, and if Lauren is sane.

In the 2020s, widespread global warming has been a global disaster, rendering many areas virtually uninhabitable. California has been hit particularly hard, with most areas reverting to desert. More prosperous states like Oregon and Washington have closed their borders to refugees. Rainfall is extraordinarily rare, and water has become an extremely expensive commodity. Widespread poverty is the norm, with a few lucky groups of cooperating families hiding in walled communities, relatively safe from the random violence and disease that plague a faltering society.

Lauren Olamina is a 15-year-old resident of one such community. While pregnant, her mother abused one of the many new designer drugs creating a new, but more and more common, birth defect in her daughter: hyperempathy syndrome. As a "sharer," Lauren personally experiences any pain she witnesses another animal or person experiencing. (She could experience pleasure, too, but had very little opportunity.) When she was younger, she even bled in sympathy to any wound she saw. Note, any superficial resemblance to Christian stigmata aside, "sharing" is no more miraculous than mirror neurons, and there is no hint that it is viewed by those in the story in religious terms: indeed, Lauren can be fooled into sharing pain when none exists, simply by showing her a fake injury.

For several years, Lauren has been writing verse about what she came to name "Earthseed."[1] Interestingly, Lauren feels as if she is discovering, not inventing it. "'Stumbling across the truth isn't the same as making it up'" (Butler 1993: 233). It consists of a set of beliefs around a simple premise: God exists, but has no shape, no personality, no intentions. God is nothing more or less than Change. For example:

> We do not worship God.
> We perceive and attend God.
> We learn from God.
> With forethought and work,
> We shape God.
> In the end, we yield to God.
> We adapt and endure,
> For we are Earthseed,
> And God is Change. (Ibid. p. 15)

Despite a God with whom no relationship is possible, Lauren believes Earthseed should be a religion. It has a strong message: by acknowledging and accepting Change, one is better prepared to survive, perhaps even re-direct it—one may learn to "shape God."

She later realizes that Earthseed also has a Destiny: to help mankind survive, and then take to the stars, for survival when dependent on a single ecosystem is uncertain.

Lauren's atheistic theology seems to contradict her minister father's Baptist beliefs, so she keeps it to herself, just as she hides her growing conviction that her community's defenses will sooner or later be breached, and their fragile security lost. As the situation deteriorates, one day her father doesn't come home. When they accept that he must be dead, they hold a funeral service. Lauren preaches in her father's place, incorporating her ideas about perseverance and community into passages from the Bible.

> . . . the parable of the importunate widow. It's one I've always liked. A widow is so persistent in her demands for justice that she overcomes the resistance of a judge who fears neither God nor man. She wears him down.
>
> Moral: The weak can overcome the strong if the weak persist. Persisting isn't always safe, but it's often necessary. (Ibid. p. 119)

It is tempting to look at Lauren as a study of contrasts. She is pathologically empathic, but can be utterly ruthless: once her community collapses, she's willing to kill to protect herself and her friends, though the action incapacitates her. In many ways, she mirrors images of saints, not just in her "stigmata" and preaching of Earthseed, but in her willing to extend her community to other refugees—but Earthseed's God is not divine, and she remains isolated even within her community. But there is no conflict: all of these, including her Earthseed, are pragmatic. She is ruthless because she has no choice; she accepts into her group only those she can trust. She is her father's daughter: he considered it his responsibility to pray for his family *and* know how to shoot.

Even her decision to share Earthseed with someone for the first time serves more than one purpose. On one hand, it strengthens an interpersonal bond, as she shares something private; on the other, it could be the first step toward Earthseed spreading beyond the confines of a single mind (ibid. pp. 174–5). Though she later acknowledges that only Earthseed kept her going, the goal is to form a *community*, one with potential to achieve something real, not just survive another day—one that will persist in challenging itself. The basic tenets of her community are:

> . . . to learn to shape God with forethought, care, and work; to educate and benefit their community, their families, and themselves; and to contribute to the fulfillment of the Destiny . . . [so they can achieve a] unifying, purposeful life here on Earth, and the hope of heaven for themselves and their children. A real heaven, not mythology or philosophy. A heaven that will be theirs to shape. (Ibid. p. 234)

Earthseed has all the features of religion, but emphasizes the practical benefits. Lauren cannot make it into a typical religion, though; she can't accept the image of a father-in-the-sky, who in any case seems to be shirking his duty, so posits a god of a different type (Butler 1993: 13–14). So why make it into a religion at all? Because the *needs* religion fills are real, and religion is a particularly memorable and effective way.

> He had asked and asked me what the point of Earthseed is. Why personify it by calling it God? Since change is just an idea, why not call it that? Just say change is important.

"Because after a while, it won't be important!" I told him. "People forget ideas. They're more likely to remember God—especially when they're scared or desperate."

"Then they're supposed to do what?" he demanded. "Read a poem?"

"Or remember a truth or a comfort or a reminder to action," I said. "People do that all the time. They reach back to the Bible, the Talmud, the Koran, or some other religious book that helps them deal with the frightening changes that happen in life."

"Change does scare most people."

"I know. God is frightening. Best to learn to cope" (Butler 1993: 198)

There is a good sequel to *Parable of the Sower* (see Butler 1998), but I rather prefer to consider it alone. Lauren forms her community; they have hope. Whether their hope is justified misses the point, I think—it's the struggle, and the choice of how to meet it, that are more important than the long-term (*or* otherworldly) reward. Regarding the future of Earthseed, I will close with Butler's own speculation:

The religion in the "Parable" books would probably change over time to make it a more comforting religion. For instance, Lauren doesn't believe in life after death, but that's one of the hopes people have. They know they're going to die, so they have to believe, a lot of them, that there's something else. An interviewer I mentioned this to said she didn't feel she needed her religion to be comforting, and I said, "Well, that's because you're already comfortable." It's those people who have so little, and who suffer so much, who need at least for religion to comfort them. Nothing else is. Once you grow past Mommy and Daddy coming running when you're hurt, you're really on your own. You're alone, and there's no one to help you. (Butler 2000)

Mary Doria Russell, *The Sparrow* (1996)

The parallels between Blish's *A Case of Conscience* (1958/2000) and Mary Doria Russell's *The Sparrow* (1996) have already been discussed (see Introduction and Chapter 6), as has the recurrence of Jesuits as sympathetic prototypes for Western religious specialists (see pp. 9–10, 53, 121–7, this volume). It should also be clear by now that, should one want a concise snapshot of how far gSF had changed over half a century, one could not do better than to read these two books side by side—such an experience inspired the current volume.

Regardless of *The Sparrow*'s place in our metanarrative of gSF's treatment of religion, it's a superlative novel, in or out of the genre. Reading it is a deeply moving, almost traumatic experience. The structure alternates telling two halves of the same story: the blissful optimism of a priest in love with God, and the disgraced, ruined shell of a man for whom losing his faith would be a mercy. The reader, then, is faced with the challenge of trying to understand how such optimism could have gone so horribly wrong. By the second page, the central conflict has been explained.

> The Jesuit scientists went to learn, not to proselytize. They went so that they might come to know and love God's other children. They went for the reasons Jesuits have always gone to the farthest frontiers of human exploration. They went *ad majorem Dei gloriam*: for the greater glory of God.
> They meant no harm. (Russell 1996: 10)

The protagonist is the linguist Father Emilio Sandoz. Previous to the events of the novel, Sandoz's Jesuit superiors had kept him moving from post to post, never staying long at any one location, constantly having to learn new languages. The result, professionally, is that Sandoz has become something of a super linguist: he not only comprehends many languages, but understands the possible variations, and is an expert on how languages can be learned. It appears this was the intent of his superiors: he becomes a key source in programming a linguistic artificial intelligence. On a personal level, Sandoz learned obedience and to function when thrust into unfamiliar situations (see ibid. pp. 28–30). More importantly, he learned to trust that seemingly unintelligible, chaotic events (e.g., being constantly moved from post to post without apparent rhyme or reason) were intentionally arranged to serve a greater purpose (i.e., his superiors wanted someone to have the requisite experience to help program the A.I.) even if one is not cognizant of the ultimate goals. That is, Sandoz learned to have faith.

In *A Case of Conscience*, the central conflict faced by Ruiz-Sanchez is mental, but the problem was one of rationality, not emotion: he was faced with a problem of logic, which he pursues methodically. His logic was functionally correct, but one assumption was flawed: that the planet he had been standing on really existed. The solution was not to be irrational, but to juxtapose two rational arguments—both of Gould's (1997) "nonoverlapping magisteria"—one of which was religious, the other scientific. Rather than choose between them, he accepted that the planet ceased to exist because of a massive explosion *and* simultaneously and independently because of an exorcism. To be (successfully) religious, one must apparently keep the two rigidly separate, if one wishes to entertain both.

In *The Sparrow*, Sandoz's problem is mental, but *emotional*. Epistemological sleight-of-hand will not work, because science is a non-issue.

Sandoz's conflict results from having faith that a series of unlikely coincidences served a higher purpose. At one point in the novel, a character observed that "The Society of Jesus rarely attracted mystics, who generally gravitated to the Carmelites or the Trappists, or ended up with the charismatics. Jesuits tended to be men who found God in their work." When this character described this as reflecting his experience, Sandoz responds, "'Don't hope for more than that, John . . . God will break your heart'" (Russell 1996: 66).

Sandoz is relocated to Puerto Rico, near the Arecibo Observatory. He befriends the emotionally isolated, Sephardic A.I. programmer Sophia, the gangly radio astronomer Jimmy, and Anne and George, an older couple with medical *cum* anthropological and engineering backgrounds, respectively. Late one night, Jimmy picks up a radio broadcast from a nearby star—not just any broadcast, but *singing*. That is, not just evidence of sentience, but of *beautiful* aliens. Jimmy calls his friends, so they can share the historic moment.

Sandoz laughingly, but with increasing seriousness, notes that together the five of them, so dissimilar in backgrounds, such unlikely friends, happen to possess the core skills an expedition to actually visit the planet would need (ibid. pp. 122–6). The Society of Jesus agrees, and, as governments debate what to do if anything, quietly decides to send them (ibid. p. 153). Sandoz starts to believe.

> Lying in bed, that warm August night, [Sandoz] felt no Presence. He was aware of no Voice. He felt as alone in the cosmos as ever. But he was beginning to find it hard to avoid thinking that if ever a man had wanted a sign from God, Emilio Sandoz had been hit square in the face with one that morning, at Arecibo. (Ibid. p. 137)

Sandoz's belief is subtler than Ruiz-Sanchez's. "'You've seen *what*,' Emilio conceded 'but not *why*. That's where God is, Anne. In the *why* of it—in the meaning'" (ibid. p. 359).

In an effort to refrain from *completely* ruining the book for anyone who hasn't read it, I will not relate specifics of the events which follow. It is enough to say that the events continue to appear blessed, even after reaching the planet. Sandoz's faith shines; his friends start tentatively using the word "saint" in their reports. But then, through a series of accidents and misunderstandings, things grow increasingly wrong. When the next expedition finally arrives, all members of the expedition are dead, except Sandoz . . . who is apparently living as a prostitute.

The story juxtaposes these two halves of the story: Sandoz seemingly becoming a saint, and his superiors trying to understand how such a man could have fallen so far—if fall he did. Sandoz refuses to explain for a long time, in part because to do so would be to choose between claiming he had been deluded initially, or worse: that God caused everything, the bad *and* the good. "I loved God and I trusted in His love . . . And I was raped. I was naked before God and I was raped" (ibid. p. 490).

I will not reveal if or how Sandoz survives, physically or spiritually. I will point out, though, that he is a tragic figure, but not a stupid one. The way Russell tells his story, the reader is not exploring how anyone could have been so irrational as to believe in God's will, but praying that he will recover his faith. But the story is not itself religious: most of the other characters are not from his tradition, and the most sympathetic (Anne) is agnostic. But even they respond to Sandoz's experience, just as the reader of *The Sparrow* might.

The Sparrow presents faith as a powerful, sustaining, *fascinating* force . . . but a dangerous one. I began this chapter with a quote from the television show *Babylon 5*; perhaps it *would* be better to "take great comfort in the general hostility and unfairness of the universe," but the sense of regret associated with such a choice is palpable in *The Sparrow*.

Conclusion

The books described in this chapter present three (possibly reconcilable) ideas: (1) even if socially backwards, religion can have positive societal impacts, particularly if it remains flexible and able to evolve in response to changing circumstances; (2) religion can have *uniquely* positive societal impacts, and thus inventing one may be necessary even if gods are not posited—though it will likely acquire them in time; (3) the last remaining element of religion, faith, becomes valued within gSF. In sharp contrast to early gSF, religion may be a valuable goal, and (in extreme examples) those who are intolerant of religion are now as annoying as religious characters once were.

This concludes Part Three, and the development of gSF's schema of religion from the 1920s through the end of the century. It is pleasingly symmetrical that the bulk of this book coincides with the 75th anniversary of the Golden Age (it was written in 2013, and Campbell took the reins at *Astounding* in 1938, and will be published in 2014, 75 years after the famous July 1939 issue), and the metanarrative represents about 75 years of science fiction (from the first issue of *Amazing* in 1926 to c. 2000). But the decision to choose this period was not aesthetic.

I argued that this evolving "metanarrative" cannot be extended further back, as there was no coherence (and no structural reason to expect there to *be* any coherence) in earlier "mSF"—not even within ancestral quasi-genres like adventure fiction or the utopias. After 1926, there is not only coherence, but an embarrassment of rich representations of religion, even stipulating the rather specific definitions of "religion" and "science fiction" I insisted upon. I have written *a* book on religion in science fiction; it is impossible that I have written *the* book—too many alternative approaches are possible.

But taking the narrative into the twenty-first century may not be possible. The reasons why are described in the next chapter, but one possibility is that I do not as yet have sufficient distance to see which authors, which books represent the decade. Another is that the metanarrative may have nowhere to go: if part of the story is the opposition between science and religion, by 2000 that tension seems to have dissipated. More likely, I think, the genre has lost much of its coherence, and boundaries between genres and to the mainstream permit considerable crossover.

As examples, the two books from the following decade that I find most fascinating are Neil Gaiman's *American Gods* (2001) and Neal Stephenson's *Anathem* (2008a). (There are many other candidates—see, e.g., Haldeman's *The Accidental Time Machine* [2007], McDonald's *River of Gods* [2003], and Stone's *That Leviathan Whom Thou Hast Made* [2010][2]—but these two have less precedented representations of religion. See also Winston [2001] for an account of religion in science fiction at the end of the century—but note how often the books described are mSF, consciously *religious*, or otherwise not eligible for inclusion here.) But both are problematic, for opposite reasons: I'm not entirely sure that the former is science fiction; I'm not sure if the latter describes religion.

American Gods is often labeled as fantasy, perhaps because actual gods (Odin, Anubis, and many others) are among the main characters: the story concerns their gradual replacement by things like the media, and their struggle to retain at least some of our attention for their very survival.

> "You run into Mithras yet? Red cap. Nice kid . . . He was an army brat. Maybe he's back in the Middle East, taking it easy, but I expect he's probably gone by now. It happens. One day every soldier in the empire has to shower in the blood of your sacrificial bull. The next day they don't even remember your birthday." (Ibid. pp. 207–8)

This could be interpreted as a metaphor for our relationship with technology, or poetically arguing that those things we invest ourselves in gain a measure of agency (cf. *Dune* in Chapter 7). For Gaiman, handling metaphors-as-characters is no problem. (In his *Sandman* graphic novels, the hero, Dream, is told by his sister, Death, that he is "the stupidest, most self-centered, appallingest excuse for an anthropomorphic personification on this or any plane!" [Gaiman 2006: 213].) Besides, it won the Hugo and Nebula Awards for best science fiction novel, and just *feels* like science fiction. Gaiman agrees: "People keep telling me it's fantasy, but it's not. It's science fiction. There's a long tradition of 'religious' science fiction, like Roger Zelazny" (Gaiman, personal communication). Nevertheless, it remains problematic, if only in that Gaiman is promiscuous in his adoption of other schemas from multiple genres.

In *Anathem* (2008), a monastic system practices extreme forms of cloistering. The "avout" live bound by vows in communities ("maths") separated from the "sæcular" world. Depending on one's math, contact with the outside only occurs every one, ten, one hundred, or a *thousand* years. All the visible markers of a religious order are there: revered "Saunts," monastic "fraas" and "suurs," robes and rituals, etc., but the monks concern themselves with philosophy and science, not theology. There *is* continuity with earlier religious monastics. A rare, familiarly religious character (i.e., *not* one of the avout) describes how he sees the protagonist's community:

> ". . . you may imagine that we are primitive fundamentalists. Maybe we are in that sense. But we aren't blind to what has happened in the mathic world—Old and New—in the last fifty centuries. The Word of God does not change. The Book does not suffer editing or translation. But what men know and understand outside the book changes all the time. That's what you avout do: try to understand God's creation without using the direct revelations given to us by God. To us, you're like people who've put out your own eyes, and are now trying to explore a new continent. You're grievously handicapped—but for that reason you may have developed senses and faculties we lack." (Ibid. p. 458)

The hierarchies and structures of religious monasticism are intact, as are reflections of the culture and traditions. But what is segregated in these places—placed in the category of monasticism—is not religion but science and intellecutualism. It is a fascinating idea . . . but is it really "religion," as I define it here?

So, for now, the narrative ends c. 2000. In the broadest of terms, religion and science, once assumed to be antitheses of each other, gradually grew toward mutual tolerance. Thus, for anyone convinced that religion and science are diametrically opposed, we have here counter-evidence in the form a metanarrative, told over generations by a community dedicated to scientific perspectives, which sees the two as complementary.

Part Four will consider what this narrative means, for science fiction and for cognitive anthropology.

End of Part Three: Conclusion of the metanarrative

Religion in gSF from c. 1970 to c. 2000

The need to believe (Chapter 8). Examples include: Bradbury, "The Messiah" (1973); Moorcock, "Behold the Man" (1966); Manning, *The Man Who Awoke* (1975 fix-up); Chalker, *Midnight at the Well of Souls* (1977). The emphasis shifts from societal to individual impacts of religion. The need for religious apprehension is a fundamental part of the human psyche, and if not met by religion may be pathological. A Creator of the universe becomes acceptable within the gSF paradigm; she/he/it does not desire worship, and may not even be aware of us, but the knowledge that a Creator exists is nevertheless positive.

The humanity of God (Chapter 9). Examples include: Anthony, "Incarnations of Immortality" [series] (1983–1990); Morrow, *Only Begotten Daughter* (1990); Card, *Speaker for the Dead* (1986). Messianic figures are replaced by the Christian Messiah, who is viewed sympathetically, but again does not desire worship. Mankind steps not just into mythic roles, but into *divine* roles. Religion as an institution is sometimes accepted as a positive foundation of society. Boundaries between genres are permeable.

Acceptance (Chapter 10). Examples include: Weber, *Honor of the Queen* (1993); Butler, *Parable of the Sower* (1993); Russell, *The Sparrow* (1996). Religion may be a sufficiently positive foundation to accept social restrictions. Social institutions may be necessary (i.e., purely secular, rational alternatives may be insufficient) to unify and motivate a community, even if no anthropomorphic deity is declared. Religious faith becomes a positive personal attribute, but may be emotionally and spiritually challenging.

Also Chapter 10, cf. Gaiman, *American Gods* (2001); Stephenson, *Anathem* (2008a). The next decade does not as yet present a coherent next step in the metanarrative. Boundaries within and between genres are sometimes difficult to perceive.

Technological development in the real world has advanced unevenly since the Gernsback days. An unforeseen revolution in information technology progresses at a remarkable rate. I was recently re-reading a gSF book from 1985, about the remarkable efforts individuals would go through to procure a naturally occurring substance which was necessary for civilization. Among its remarkable properties was the ability to electronically store almost a gigabyte of information in a mere cubic centimeter

(McCaffrey 1985). My cheap flash drive is about that size, and holds 16 times that much information—but *their* civilization had spread to many worlds. A Golden Age author would likely be quite disappointed that here, part way through the twenty-first, we don't even have a moon colony to our credit. Medical science is beginning to manipulate chromosomes, but malaria is still a major cause of death.

In contrast, gSF's ability to speculate on ever more subtle aspects of the human condition has exceeded even Campbell's aspirations. In *The Sparrow* and *Calculating God*, the technology that enables us to travel to distant stars is trivial compared to hypothesizing on the nature of our relationship with God.

The goal of Parts Two and Three of this book was to detail the evolution of gSF's metanarrative of religion which began in the 1920s. By c. 2000, it is essentially complete. I see no new developments shaping the next step of the genre. Though there are alternative explanations (see the next chapter), I believe the most reasonable explanation for this is that the two central tensions of the narrative have been resolved. The first is relatively straightforward: Science fiction initially disparaged religion as "anti-science." Especially after World War II, gSF lost faith in the certainty that science would lead us to utopia. Simultaneously, if science is not intrinsically "good," gSF considered that perhaps religion is not intrinsically "bad" (see, e.g., Brackett's *The Long Tomorrow*). By the end of the century, science is no longer the sole theme; the steampunk genre emerges from a nostalgia for more primitive technology.

The second concerns the distance from which gSF views religion, and specifically which aspects are deemed socially acceptable. In the 1930s (Chapter 4), the most tolerant view is that perhaps it's best not to poke at it; *let* people be wrong (e.g., Barclay's "The Troglodytes"). In Campbell's Golden Age (c. 1940, Chapter 5), the institutions are granted conditional acceptance—even if it *is* a sham, perhaps as a social tool it *could* be used for societal benefit by men of good intent (e.g., Heinlein's *Sixth Column*). In the 1950s (Chapter 6), positive societal impacts are more prevalent (e.g., Miller's "A Canticle for Leibowitz"), and there appears an admittance that both theology (Blish's "A Case of Conscience") and even superstitions are *reasonable* (Stewart's *Earth Abides*) given a society's level of development—and in any case, their impacts on individual lives cannot be merely dismissed. By the 1960s (Chapter 7), coinciding with the continuing expansion of the "science" in science fiction into the social sciences, the power of myth achieves something like agency as grows beyond the control of any individual (e.g., Herbert's *Dune*, in which the hero becomes *its* tool) and is acknowledged to be a source of the metaphors with which we interpret the word.

The New Wave of gSF changed the emphasis somewhat from the qualified acceptance of aspects of religious institutions, to exploring the impact of these institutions on individuals, especially the personal relationship between individuals and institutionally postulated gods: the needs of some to believe such entities are real (e.g., Moorcock's "Behold the Man" in Chapter 8), and the exploration of a Creator—who has no interest in being worshipped (Chalker's *Midnight at the Well of Souls*). In Chapter 9, selections explored not a disinterested Creator, but the central divine figures of our own Western cultures, who—despite being unambiguously divine and anthropomorphic—*still* have no interest in being worshipped. We sympathize with them, identify with them . . . sometimes even *become* them (Anthony's "Incarnations of Immortality" series, esp. 1990). Finally, after accepting the institutions, the myths, the gods, in the 1990s the last hurdle fell. We even accept faith (Russell's *The Sparrow*), even if God *doesn't* exist in any anthropomorphic form (Butler's *Parable of the Sower*).

Two final clarifications should be made. Throughout, I have focused on the texts most representative of the *innovations* for each period—the new variants on the genre, the next step in the metanarrative. This does not mean that earlier schema became extinct: some may remain as old-fashioned throwbacks; others may continue more or less as before, just with more competition. For example, Varley's (1980) *Titan* was published in the same period in which I identified an emerging sympathy with supernatural beings (e.g., Creators); Varley's book portrays the being claiming to be a god as mad, and her followers delusional.

Also, the twin institutions of religion and science are clearly (and often explicitly) linked in gSF's schemas for each. Throughout, we have seen a lessening of negative valences in the schemas for religion, and a corresponding lessening of positive valences in the schemas for science and in particular technological progress. Though I believe these two effects are linked, causality does not necessarily follow. Rather than interpret as a pendulum swinging from "science" to "religion," it is possible that both of these positions, so extreme in the early decades of the genre, have simply eroded.

If so, then gSF's distinct schemas are not *only* evolving; they may be dissolving. If so, one wonders if the genre has become less distinctive (e.g., perpetuating schemas demonstratably different than mSF)—that is, is the genre disappearing? This possibility begins Part Three, as broader implications of the existence of distinct gSF schema, for the genre, and for cognitive anthropology, are considered.

Part Four

The Extinction of SF (or, at least, gSF)

Get science fiction out of the classroom and back in the gutter where it belongs.
Harry Harrison

I recently checked the list of finalists for the 2013 John W. Campbell Award, looking for something new to read. I noticed a novel by G. Willow Wilson (whom I previously knew only by her reputation as creator of graphic novels): *Alif the Unseen* (2012).

As the Campbell Award is one of the major science fiction awards (decided by a jury of noted science fiction academics, critics, and authors), I think one may assume nominees are representative (if exceptional) of the genre form of science fiction—they are "ours." The characterization and writing style of Wilson's *Alif the Unseen* (2012) certainly feels like genre science fiction (gSF): her protagonist reads like a boy-next-door version of Case from Gibson's *Neuromancer* (1984). Though Islamic mythology figures as prominently as computer programming, even the jinn are not so much supernatural as (merely) superhuman; though of a different nature, they live and die, need friends and Wi-Fi.

In addition to mythology, *Alif* contains some interesting references to institutionalized religion.

> "Belief . . . doesn't mean the same thing it used to, not for you. You have unlearned the hidden half of the world."

> "But the world is crawling with religious fanatics. Surely belief is thriving."

> "Superstition is thriving. Pedantry is thriving. Sectarianism is thriving. Belief is dying out. To most of your people the jinn are paranoid fantasies who run around causing epilepsy and mental illness. Find me someone to whom the hidden folk are simply real, as described in the Books. You'll be searching for a long time. Wonder and awe have gone out of your religions. You are prepared to accept the irrational, but not the transcendent." (Wilson 2012: 303)

This would seem similar to the representations of religion present in gSF as described in the previous chapter: religious belief can be healthy, fortifying and even restorative, to be taken seriously but not followed mindlessly; institutions, though capable of degrading into both fanaticism or cynicism, can be strongly civilizing. The quote above even hints at needs that only religion can meet: the desire for transcendence, for experiencing wonder and awe.

The only problem is, there are counter-indications that *Alif* is very much mainstream. The book is not labeled science fiction, and a blurb from Neil Gaiman is matched with blurbs from the *The Washington Post* and *The New York Times*. Review excerpts posted on the accompanying website (http://aliftheunseen.com/praise/) state that Wilson "makes her own genre," that the book "supersedes genres" and is "about the many layers of language possible in metaphors and the enduring power of stories to transform, but it really is a multi-layered thriller of modern mythology."

I see no indication that Wilson is avoiding the term as if she is leery of being confined to a literary ghetto—her graphic novel credentials are impressive and ongoing. Rather, genre categorization is a non-issue. She writes of being frustrated "that I was so often forced to speak to my three primary audiences (comic book geeks, literary NPR types, and Muslims) separately" (Wilson 2012: 445). I suspect that comic and gSF fans of the 1950s would have doubted that an author could successfully bridge these audiences, which only demonstrates how much the genre(s) have changed; I further suspect that the idea of a geeky Muslim would have been easier to entertain than the "literary world" accepting a fairly light (and damn good) science fiction novel.

More significantly, from my point of view, this seems to imply that genre-typic schemas have gained broader appeal, and that the distinctions between gSF and mainstream science fiction (mSF)—or even between gSF and the general mainstream— have dwindled to insignificance. Stableford began his recent book on the *Creators of Science Fiction* (2010) with the following rather offhand statement:

> Indeed, now that textual science fiction no longer exists as a popular genre—save as a vestigial appendix to a fantasy genre that is itself in terminal decline—it is not obvious that there will be any significant further interest outside the groves of Academe. (Stableford 2010: 8)

My initial reaction was dismissive. Science fiction sections in bookstores are as large as ever, science fiction authors appear on best-seller lists, and science fiction movies make millions. But the longer I thought about it, the more I began to suspect that Stableford was correct.

Part of the reason for this is because I was unable to identify a stage of gSF's evolution of the "religion" schema for the first decade of the twenty-first century. I found examples of religion, to be sure . . . but not many, few recurring themes, and (crucially) nothing particularly new. There seem to be three possibilities. Perhaps I have as yet insufficient distance from this decade to discern a pattern. In examining the twentieth century, less influential books have conveniently disappeared, making it easier to identify those texts which were accepted by the genre. I can say with absolute certainty that Heinlein's *Stranger in a Strange Land* or Mary Doria Russell's *The Sparrow* were not forgotten immediately after publication.

Also, the overarching themes for the evolution of schemas of religion have been, first, the distance at which religion is viewed, and the strength of the tension between religion and science. By the 1980s, religion was accepted so closely that we projected ourselves into supernatural roles without comment; we sympathized, *identified* with a returning Jesus (*Godbody*) and his half-sister (*Only Begotten Daughter*). By the 1990s, religion was accepted as necessary even *without* stipulating the existence of an anthropomorphic active agent (*Parable of the Sower*), and even retrogressive religious beliefs are presented in a positive light (*Honor of the Queen*). Perhaps both of these tensions have played themselves out: the central conflict of the metanarrative has been resolved. Perhaps that story has simply concluded.

Stableford offers a third possibility. My focus has been on the *genre* form of science fiction literature. Stableford states that this genre no longer exists. Some may blame Gernsback for ghettoizing gSF, but I argued that it is precisely this segregation that has allowed gSF to develop a coherent identity distinct from the mainstream. Has the genre become so popular—so mainstream—that no distinction still exists, no contrast with outside society? Or, to focus on a different implication, is gSF still a *literary* genre?

Hypotheses: gSF has become extinct and has been reabsorbed into the parent mainstream community. Is there evidence for the *null* hypothesis—gSF is alive and well—that still accounts for Stableford's statement?

Actually, there is. Predicting the extinction of gSF is something of a gSF tradition, for example, a 1960 called fanzine *Who Killed Science Fiction?* (Kemp 2006; see also Hartwell, 1984: 77). Gary Wolff described "creeping mainstreamism" (quoted in Finch 1996: 22). Sheila Finch pointed out the rule she followed being that if you can write a science fiction story *without* the science, do so, and that increasingly even gSF stories do not turn on a "genuine scientific point" (ibid. p. 23) (see Luckhurst 1994; also Nicholls 1977, Sawyer 1994).

When one looks closely at these claims, what they often mean is that either the genre is losing its distinctiveness entirely, or what *they* think should define the genre is no longer typical; what you think gSF *should* be no longer applies. If your preference was for Doc Smith-like space opera, science fiction *ended* with the Golden Age; if only physics-based hard science fiction is "real," then the 1960s were a disaster. There is even a formalized form of this argument: Hartwell (1984: 3–24) wrote that "the Golden Age of Science Fiction is Twelve"—that is, "good" science fiction is whatever you imprinted on when first reading it.[1] Author John Christopher, in the essay "The Decline and Fall of the Bug-Eyed Monster," describes his own reaction to the (then) new science fiction:

Of my first kiss I have only the haziest recollection . . . But the first science fiction magazine I bought is a different matter. That was a copy of *Astounding Stories*, dated September 1932, [Christopher would have been ten at the time,] and I paid 3*d* . . . Those were the days when science fiction was dedicated to Science, and the writers were encouraged to append long footnotes to their stories, describing how electricity worked . . . The only form of political propaganda tolerated was propaganda for Technocracy: the Rule of the Scientist . . . But practically everything in mid-century science fiction would have horrified us. Sex, for instance . . . Nor did we have much truck with telepaths and ESP-ers . . . The very names of the authors cry aloud the change. Then they had exotic sonorous names. Raymond Z. Gallun, Arthur Leo Zagat, Epaminondas T. Snooks, Junior . . . Nowadays there is a note of suburban respectability about them: Theodore Sturgeon, John Wyndham, Arthur C. Clarke, Jonathan Burke. (Christopher 1956)

(I can only imagine how Christopher reacted to *Behold the Man*.)

Nevertheless, there appears to be data supporting Stableford's call: six reasons to suspect that the genre which began in the 1920s did not survive the century—or, at the very least, has changed so much that the twentieth-century definition no longer applies.

1. Barriers are too permeable.

The genre has been ghettoized for much of its history (Barnett 2009, Howell 2009, Weber 2009), in part due to outsiders' perceptions of literary merit (Le Guin 2009). As annoying as such deprecations may be, they also protected gSF, allowing a coherent evolution of a metanarrative within a bounded community, letting us work through our feelings about, for example, science-driven progress. This protection has long been eroding. In 1977, Peter Nicholls wrote, "Individual sf writers are as vigorous as ever, but the links that bind them together as part of a ghetto . . . are weakening" (1977: 83). Margaret Atwood, who once defended herself against the "science fiction" label, has now written a book on her "lifelong relationship" with science fiction (Atwood 2012). One possible (if unlikely) solution is to take seriously a joke from Harry Harrison: "Get science fiction out of the classroom and back in the gutter where it belongs" (quoted in Pournelle 1982: 5).

If the barriers between genre and mainstream science fiction have become more permeable, so have the boundaries between genres. Wolfe (2011: 50–53) describes processes contributing to a current dissolution of genres (including gSF) and "genre implosion." Wilson's *Alif* is not an anomaly. Above, I argued that by the 1980s, fantasy-like elements began to be acceptable in otherwise schematically science fiction literature. That trend has accelerated: "dark fantasy" (i.e., books with both fantasy and horror schema), paranormal romance (e.g., the "Anita Blake" series, in which the heroine tries to choose between her vampire and werewolf lovers—within storylines taken from a hardboiled detective novel), even the odd science fiction Western (e.g., the television show *Firefly*).

Chapter 10 ended with examples of two books I would have used to extend the metanarrative for religion in science fiction into the twenty-first century—were I more confident that one was clearly science fiction, and the other clearly depicted religion. Kandel (1998) noted similar difficulties in categorization. Ian R. MacLeod "employs, scrupulously, impeccably, and thoroughly, the vocabulary of science fiction," but with a different attitude toward science: "The observing narrator ultimately is a poet, not a techie." Jonathan Letham uses tropes from science fiction as well as further afield, as if "not concerned in the least about which part of the bookstore this book will end up." "It is not that these writers are breaking out of the sf ghetto. They are perfectly happy to use sf; they enjoy the genre. It is simply that the ghetto walls do not exist for them and never did."

2. Ideological heterogeneity within gSF
Under Gernsback, gSF fans and writers were largely on the same page, not just in possession of schema but ideologically, politically. They had the same priorities, to the extent that Heinlein—as a slightly older Navy veteran—was an anomalous outlier, with the military-oriented *Starship Troopers* (see Chapter 5) sparking accusations of fascism. But now military SF is a subgenre in its own right (e.g., Weber "Honor Harrington" books); would we expect fans of military SF and the largely anarchistic cyberpunk to see eye-to-eye?

Recall Bainbridge's (1986) empirical analyses of ideological and political attitudes among gSF subgenres:

> I have shown that science fiction is divided into competing ideological factions with distinctly different agendas for the human future. With such dissention in its ranks, does SF have any net propagandistic effects on its readers? Or do the opposing factions cancel each other out, leading no significant resultant? (Bainbridge 1986: 151).

That is, traditional (Campbellian) "hard" gSF, New Wave (by 1986 no longer new nor counterculture), and what Bainbridge terms the "fantasy cluster" within science fiction had very different ideas about, for example, the necessity of the space program, political liberalism, and the legitimacy of paranormal investigations. Twenty-five years later, it seems clear that the causality can be reversed: it is not that reading gSF encourages a specific ideological orientation, but, no matter one's orientation, there is a sub-category of gSF that would appeal.

If, then, there is no distinctive ideological character, and thus no characteristic influence on readers, there is one less mechanism for maintaining an environmental niche for gSF distinct from the mainstream.

3. Intelligent designers are missing.
If the evolution of gSF was shaped by intelligent design, who now are the designers? No editor is in a position to enforce their own vision to the extent that Gernsback and Campbell were, and it seems unlikely now that any small number of individuals could create a coherent subspecies as did Moorcock, Ellison and Ballard did with the New Wave. (It's been tried, but unsuccessfully: see point no. 5 below.)

The same logic applies to specific *authors*: no one is read as uniformly as were the Golden Age authors—none have influence sufficient to function as universal exemplar. As one such author, Isaac Asimov, said of another, "No one ever dominated the science fiction field as [Robert Heinlein] did in the first few years of his career. It was a one-man phenomenon that will probably never be repeated" (Asimov and Greenberg 1979: 412). As for the heroic potential of today's authors: "In the field, we know that names like Mike Resnick and Lois McMaster Bujold and John E. Stith and Walter Jon Williams are the stars of current SF. But, and I mean no offense to these fine authors, the average reader has never heard of them" (Sawyer 1994).

One could even extend this argument to *communities* of authors.

> I have never encountered a group of writers so intensely and intricately interconnected as the SF community. Poetry comes closest, but poetry is balkanized into dozens of hostile or indifferent clans. The various bands of the multicultural rainbow tend to be separatist both socially and aesthetically [. . .] By contrast, most of the science fiction that is worth reading has been written by the writers I've met—some of whom, like Theodore Sturgeon and Robert Heinlein, began publishing in the late '30s. As recently as 1981 . . . I could declare that all the great SF writers were essentially contemporaneous, alive and well, and merrily cross-pollinating across the usual gaps of age, gender, and ideology. (Disch 1998: 12–13)

This is plainly no longer the case. My idiosyncratic, 12-year-old Golden Age died with Heinlein in 1988, and again with Marion Zimmer Bradley in 1999. The last of the great Golden Age authors, Frederik Pohl, died this year.

So, insofar as gSF's distinctiveness was the result of authors' individual or collective creativity, or editors' preference for certain authors, a necessary tool for a coherent and distinct genre appears to be lacking.

4. Mass.

Disch (1998: 13) also argued that "the chief difference [between gSF and poetry] is this: poets have a few centuries of other poets' work to catch up on. A poet can avoid reading contemporaries altogether and still read widely, deeply, and relevantly." I believe the same pattern has begun to apply to gSF.

I began this book by arguing that gSF is a community but an odd one, united only by the fact that members have absorbed similar schemas by reading a discrete body of literature: if gSF readers have anything in common, it is because they have read some of the same books. Zelazny's "Amber" series was strongly influenced by Henry Kuttner's 1946 novel, *The Dark World*. In the 1943 story by Lewis Padgett, "Mimsy Were the Borogroves," we find a girl dictating to her uncle ("He's not really my uncle,") who promises to put her words in his next book. Though it is not stated, we recognize her not-quite-Uncle as Charles Dodgeson, and the book to be *Through the Looking Glass*.

I would naturally not argue that someone reading gSF today would be unable to enjoy Zelazny, Padgett, or "Lewis Carroll," but I suspect there are layers of meaning that would not be recognized. In Chapter 6, I argued that Brackett's *The Long Tomorrow* is a perfectly enjoyable story, but if one is reading it against a cultural backdrop of Heinlein's narrative style (especially comparing it to "If This Goes On—" from Chapter 5), additional ironies appear. Similarly, the average modern reader would probably enjoy Zelazny, but would not remember Kuttner, and thus miss an aspect of Zelazny's creativity in composing variations on an earlier theme; reading Padgett, they might not even recognize the "inside" reference to Carroll. They almost certainly would not know that Padgett is a pseudonym for Catherine Moore and her husband, Henry Kuttner.

Some, but fewer each year, would recall James Blish while reading *The Sparrow*.

It's entirely too possible now that even two dedicated science fiction readers may not significantly overlap in what they've read.

> It was much easier in the early 1960s . . . Anyone prepared to devote the time could . . . familiarize themselves with the entire history of sf, as well as keeping up with the newly-published material, within a decade. Thirty years later [i.e., the 1990s] there was not only twice as much history to catch up on, but the availability of earlier materials had been considerably reduced. (Stableford 2010: 7–8)

Not only has the rate of professional production of gSF increased, but social media has facilitated the distribution of huge amounts of fan-generated material. Also, the availability of early gSF and earlier proto-SF has significantly *increased* in the last decade through specialist publishers (e.g., Haffner Press's *Tales from* Super-Science Fiction [Silverberg 2012]), websites like Archive.org freely distribute nineteenth- and eighteenth-century antecedents, and many Golden Age periodicals have been microfiched. One cannot keep up *or* catch up; now in gSF, too, can one "avoid reading contemporaries altogether and still read widely, deeply, and relevantly." As the distribution of identifying schemas becomes uneven, SF as a genre defined by such schemas ceases to exist.

Similarly, the sheer mass of *science* has become a problem. In the 1930s a devoted amateur could keep up with the latest scientific developments, at least in the branches of science (e.g., rocketry, Newtonian physics) that formed the foundations of the majority of gSF. One of the attractions was, of course, the speed at which new developments appeared; another was to be part of a literature-based intelligentsia who shared similar scientific knowledge. This development has only accelerated. A few decades later, Oppenheimer noted:

> Today, it is not only that our kings do not know mathematics, but our philosophers do not know mathematics and—to go a step further—our mathematicians do not know mathematics. Each of them knows [only] a branch of the subject . . . We so refine what we think, we so change the meaning of words, we build up so distinctive a tradition, that scientific knowledge today is not an enrichment of the general culture. (quoted in Hagstrom 1972: 125)

Asimov expressed a similar frustration for the gSF fan in reaction to a biology book:

> I read the Forward . . . and was instantly plunged into the deepest gloom. Let me quote from the first two paragraphs:

> "With each generation our fund of scientific knowledge increases fivefold . . . at the current rate of scientific advance, there is about four times as much significant biological knowledge than there was in 1930, and about sixteen times as much as in 1900. By the year 2000, at this rate of increase, there will be a hundred times as much biology to 'cover' in the introductory course as at the beginning of the century."

Imagine how this affects me. I'm a professional "keeper-upper" with science and in my more manic, ebullient and carefree moments, I even think I succeed fairly well.

Then I read something like the above quoted passage and the world falls about my ears. I *don't* keep up with science. Worse, I can't keep up with it. Still worse, I'm falling farther behind every day. (Asimov 1964a)

Now, a half-century later, even the *number of disciplines* has expanded so much that a growing body of literature tries to make sense of it all; "interdisciplinarity" even has an Oxford Handbook (Frodeman et al. 2010). Additionally, more and more disciplines' knowledge could form the basis of a gSF story.

In sum, science fiction readers have more and more available "science" and "fiction," making the amount of experience overlap—and as a result, the proportion of shared schemas—less and less.

5. Steampunk.

The recently popular genre of "steampunk" is more a symptom than a cause for the dissolution of science fiction as a viable genre. I will be brief—for a more complete account, see Hrotic (2013)—but the gist of it is that steampunk revisited the Victorian roots of gSF, participating in the fictional worlds of the prototypic Fathers, Wells and Verne (see, e.g., Ashley and Brown 2005).

> It is as if, *for a handful of sf writers*, Victorian London has come to stand for one of those turning points in history where things can go one way or the other, a turning point particularly relevant to sf itself. It was a city of industry, science and technology where the modern world was being born. (Clute and Nicholls, 1995: 1161; emphasis added)

There are two major concerns with steampunk. The first is the implication that technological development had become frustrating, even among those who think of Wells and Verne as communal ancestors, and their worlds as mythic (*sensu* Paden 1994: 69–73).

> The whole steampunk aesthetic is a rebellion against the last 60 years of industrial design. It's about trying to be comfortable with your technology. At the last [science fiction convention] WorldCon, a number of science fiction authors, people who'd been writing about computers and robots and spaceships . . . since the 1950s, were grumbling about today's computers: 'Aw, I don't get it' . . . Americans really like to know how things work. They enjoy science, and they enjoy machinery . . . These days, more and more the idea behind industrial design is for the mechanism to be hidden, resulting in a 'magic box' . . . People like steampunk because it gives them a feeling of smartness and control, that they've got a handle on things. (Foglio and Foglio 2010)

Hartwell noted that the 1957 launch of Sputnik was not good for gSF—the future is less fun when it becomes real (1984: 75–91). The claim that gSF makes accurate predictions has been disproven: in some areas (faster-than-light propulsion) the imagined future may be impossible. In others, the actual future is depressingly mundane: there is no permanent human settlement on the moon not for lack of heroes, but because no corporation has figured out how to make it profitable. In still others, our most radical predictions fall far short of the mark: Neal Stephenson (2008b) describes cyberpunk as an attempt to come to terms with gSF's inability to predict the information revolution.

Second, gSF *didn't* engage. Ideally, the genre would have wrestled with this frustration, generated a new subgenre. Instead, these ideas only flourished when they *left* the genre.

> [I am asked] to explain why steampunk didn't spread like kudzu from the literary works of Jeter, Blaylock, and Powers, and instead had to sit like leaky dynamite in a blast shack until the twenty-first century appeared . . . It's pretty simple. Steampunk is not inherently literary. It's native to network cyberculture. Steampunk needed broadband and social media in order to thrive. Steampunk was never about ink on paper . . . Traditional sci-fi fandom . . . could not support steampunk. The media economics were hostile, the barriers-to-entry were too high. (Sterling 2010)

A hidebound gSF, functionally or ideologically incapable of answering such a challenge to its *raison d'être*, is a dead gSF.

6. Visual media

So far, I have focused on Stableford's claim that science fiction is no longer a viable genre. But what about his second implication, that it is no longer even literary? Elsewhere, Stableford (1996) argues that the shift in the 1990s to television as the new "the economic and cultural foundations of the genre" is analogous to the previous shift from short-form pulp magazines to long-form paperback novels. As novels offered new opportunities to further develop secondary elements of even an action-driven story, so this third medium imposes its own constraints.

As it would be hard for a post-New Wave gSF fan to argue that only "hard SF" is "real," it is difficult to claim today that only written gSF is legitimate when it is increasingly outnumbered by other media. A reader of 1930s *Wonder Stories* complained about the lack of distribution of SF movies (Ackerman 1932). Gernsback's response was to encourage *Wonder* readers to participate in a petition-signing campaign (see Gernsback 1932b and "Do You Want Science Fiction Movies?" 1932). In contrast, of the 50 most popular movies of 2011, 20% were science fiction ("Top U.S. Grossing" 2012).[2] Of the 20 most profitable movies in US theaters, 65% (including four of the top five) are science fiction ("All-time Box Office" 2012). Critical work on science fiction often focuses less on books and stories than on movies, television shows, and comic books, all with broad popular appeal (e.g., McGrath 2012).

It isn't just the popularity of visual media that makes them important, but also the development within the last two decades of richer, more coherent "wholes," in television science fiction. As occasionally revolutionary as the old Star Trek show may have been relative to contemporary television, the ~45-minute episode limits restricted the potential complexity of a plot, as did the perceived necessity of resetting the universe by the end. But now the extended, season-long (i.e., sometimes over 1,000 minutes) story lines created by groundbreaking shows like *Babylon 5*, coupled with technology (e.g., Hulu, Netflix) facilitating the consumption of a series in a single day (see, e.g., Ramachandran and Sharma 2013), make gSF TV much more interesting. In the worlds of Joanna Russ, author of the superlative religion-in-gSF story, "Souls" (1984),

> I don't read nearly as much as I used to. It's very annoying to have to get up every twenty minutes, and . . . wait a minute, there's a punch line. I found that, after having a VCR for several years, you can treat TV just as a book. And now I have a DVD player. I have been going mad about Buffy. ("The Legendary . . ." 2007)

In this book, our topic was the genre's schemas for religion. There is a reason I have stuck to textual narratives (in addition to the fact that such a topic could and should be treated separately). Contemporary television shows' displays of religion were old-fashioned and seemed rather silly in comparison.

Consider the von Dänikin-like 1967 episode of *Star Trek*, "Who Mourns for Adonais?" The crew of the Enterprise meets the actual god Apollo, who offers to create a paradise for them. Repeat: he *really is* the same superhuman being "we" once worshipped, willing and able to satisfy our hearts' desires. All he asks in return is love and worship. The hero Kirk refuses, saying that humanity has outgrown such things; that what Apollo wants we can no longer give. Contrast that rather simplistic, 1930s' era schema to *Dune*'s, which came out two years prior.

Or consider the *Battlestar Galactica* episode "War of the Gods" broadcast in 1976. A member of the crew of *this* spaceship dies. His friends are later caught by a white light, and find themselves, and their revived friend, in a glowing white place populated by seemingly superhuman *and* supernatural beings—they *did* bring their friend back from the dead—who insist that "As you now are, we once were; as we now are you may yet become." *Battlestar Galactica* does a little better than *Star Trek*—this image is merely 20 years out of date (cf. Clarke 1953).

But after shows like *Babylon 5* (e.g., 1994's "The Parliament of Dream") and *Star Trek: Deep Space 9* (e.g., 1996's "The Rapture"), the inferiority of televised depictions of religion in science fiction is difficult to argue. In the former, asked to demonstrate Earth's "dominant belief system," the hero simply introduces the bemused aliens to a long line of religious specialists, including a Catholic priest, Jewish rabbi, and, interestingly, an Australian Aborigine and an atheist; in the later, the hero is experiencing religious visions as a result of a dangerous brain dysfunction, but is willing to risk death rather than lose the visions, and his seemingly nonsensical prophesies are later proven right. In both cases the subtlety and the sensitivity of the representation of religion, the value placed on religiosity (sometimes over 'rationality'), and the confidence that religion will continue to be with us are all compatible with the contemporary written genre's schemas.

The written word no longer has the monopoly on good science fiction—but given the inherently mainstream character of televised science fiction (the dedicated

"Syfy" channel not excluded), the development of alternative schema into this "third generation" seems unlikely.

Conclusion

So, SF is too heterogeneous to be comprehended as a genre, and too large to support intelligent design in its evolution. The boundaries that defined it have eroded, and within-group differences have accumulated. The utopia of a technological future has become the depressing present. Too much literature has accumulated for any one individual to comprehend the whole, and its role may have been preempted by other media.

Individual authors continue to produce excellent novels utilizing the best of gSF schema, but that the genre itself has no inertia and may not be able to evolve further. Science fiction-like elements will continue to appear in stories, as they have for millennia, but the unique species of literature that began in the early twentieth century may well be extinct.

Cultural Evolution

I began this book with a rough outline of a cognitive approach to narratives. To summarize:

- Culture can be defined as shared, mental schemas: an epidemiology of representations commonly shared by members of a community, interpersonally transmitted and/or generated by shared experiences (Sperber 1996).
- These representations cumulatively and culturally evolve. Taken in chronological sequence, narrative representations constitute a metanarrative—a "story" told collectively by successive generations. By "ratcheting" multiple individuals' efforts (*sensu* Tomasello 1999), the products of cultural evolution may be more complex than those produced by any single individual.
- Like biological evolution, the selection of cultural schema is dependent on (cultural) environments. Unlike biological evolution, cultural evolution sometimes proceeds via goal-directed "intelligent design."
- The representativeness of any individual schema or collective metanarrative is dependent on pervasiveness and durability; consumption, not production—popularity trumps quality.

I then described a common complication in the study of science fiction: there is no consensus on the specific criteria that distinguish "genre" from "mainstream" science fiction. I argued, then, that trying to determine such criteria is the wrong strategy—genre science fiction (gSF) is first a group of individuals, unified through the cycle of production and consumption of characteristic texts. That is, the *community* is the distinguishing element, and any similarities between texts stem from a great many shared cultural schemas, some of them quite subtle.

To conclude this book, I would like to explain a bit of the theoretical background of these ideas, which will lead us to a specific suggestion regarding the social use of narratives: gSF is an example of a "new" behavioral tactic that utilizes our implicit memory patterns and is based on an "old" evolutionary strategy of group formation.

Along the way, we may also be able to draw toward an answer to a different question I find curious: what draws me to science fiction? Specifically, why do I prefer gSF to mSF? And why do I find that I even enjoy *bad* gSF?

In Chapter 7, I described Lester del Rey's 1962 book *The Eleventh Commandment*. It has some quite imaginative, well-developed ideas. Many of the themes anticipate Margaret Atwood's mSF novel *A Handmaid's Tale* (Ursula K. LeGuin, quoted in McCaffery and Gregory 1987: 184) by almost a quarter century: religion in a disturbing future society manipulates people's reproduction for genetic reasons, which, though quite distasteful, could arguably be rational given the biological and social conditions. By most objective criteria, Atwood's book is superior: her technique is stronger; her world feels more three dimensional without reliance on "world-building" trivia. So why do I prefer del Rey? His writing style is by no means poor, but, following many Golden Age authors, is deliberately artless. One possibility is that, while gSF tends to be optimistic, Atwood's future is not just unpleasant: it's dystopic. Another is gSF's preference that authors' novel social problems have *solutions*. Miller (1998), for example, recognizes that Octavia Butler's stories set in dystopic futures focus on socio-political causes and possible solutions, rather than merely dystopic symptoms. Atwood in contrast includes a postscript that colors the events of the novel as mere aberrations.

More significant, I think, is the fact that I had preconceptions before reading *either* author. I knew del Rey was "one of us," but that Atwood had made critical, dismissive statements distancing her work from the genre (e.g., "Science fiction is rockets, chemicals and talking squids in outer space" [quoted in Howell 2009]). Why do these preconceptions influence my aesthetic reactions? I believe there is a subtle, *social* pattern at work here. To explain it, I must first talk about narratives from an evolutionary perspective, humor, and religious rituals.

The social use of narratives

My primary research interest is in how narratives are used socially, founded on the perspectives that humans share certain unlearned behavior patterns: patterns that reflect comprehensible evolutionary strategies and that express as and through culture. Thus, our narratives are products of a particular kind of mind and can be used to solve social problems like helping maintain the boundaries of a group, power structures within a group, etc.

Evolutionary psychology is amassing many patterns of behaviors that seem to be "universal" human traits and interpreting them in terms of "strategies": that is, trying to understand post hoc how these patterns have increased our fitness. Strategies do not *determine* our behavior, but rather constrain it. Consider our eye muscles. We have two pairs of rectus muscles which allow us to easily scan horizontally and vertically. *All* major writing systems are written horizontally and vertically. Our eyes do not "determine" the direction in which we will arrange characters—one could easily write diagonally or in a circle—but, without some additional pressure, some ways of writing are simply easier than others (Hrotic 2009: 121–2).

Understanding *human* evolution requires we recognize that our overarching strategy has been to be social toolmakers. We are not well equipped to be carnivorous predators *or* herbivorous prey, but we *are* uniquely suited to develop ways to compensate for our many weaknesses, and, crucially, to *transmit* our solutions to others. Chimpanzees may use tools, but only we actively teach our children how to use them. We are also uniquely adept at *inventing new social patterns* when the environment changes (e.g., urban settlement patterns, along with the social systems [i.e., tools] necessary to support them), resulting in balanced physical, social, and ideational worlds (Wilson 1999: 23–9).

A recurring problem in these novel social patterns has been recognizing who is a contributing member of our group, and who may be "cheating"—appearing as a member so as to accumulate the benefits, but defecting when reciprocal costs are required. One solution to this problem is *costly signaling*: volunteering a conspicuous cost in order to demonstrate one's loyalty (Cronk 1994, Sosis and Alcorta 2003). Other animals use costly signals, of course. Darwin famously wrote to a friend, "The sight of a feather in a peacock's tail, whenever I gaze at it, makes me sick!" The tail appeared to serve no function, yet be quite costly, prompting Darwin to arrive at "sexual selection"—the tail served as a costly signal of fitness (1871/1981: ii 120, ii 154–5). But humans' behavioral signals are uniquely complex and flexible.

The strong similarities among humans (e.g., in how we use costly signaling) show that our minds are not blank slates on which local "culture" inscribes only group-specific patterns; rather, our minds come equipped with certain dispositions related to evolutionary strategies, which, all things being equal, would express universally. Importantly, these traits may express in any context: while writing this book, I'm using a mind with essentially the same properties as a Pleistocene hunter–gatherer's and thus shares certain characteristics. Sometimes a trait previously adaptive may be less so in novel circumstances: for example, our minds and bodies experience stress appropriate for a "fight-or-flight" response to threats. In urban life, however, stressors cannot be dealt with so succinctly—one can neither hit nor run away from an obnoxious supervisor, leading to the negative cardiovascular and neurological effects of low-grade but long-term stress for which we are poorly adapted (Sapolsky 2004a, 2004b).

One of these universal traits—one which has adapted quite well to life in an industrialized world—is the ability to form narratives. As much as our sociality has been a marker of our species' particular evolutionary trajectory, and tool use has enabled us to be a spectacularly successful species, narratives are a fundamental part of who we are. Jensen (2011) describes some of the schools of thought addressing our narrativity, but then turns to addressing why we have "fiction"—what evolutionary benefit arises from the capacity to create reflexively sequences of events.

There seems to be fundamental, deep cognitive demand which requires that perception and cognition (and probably also emotion) can become knowledge only when we talk about it. And, further, for anything to be the subject of discourse, it must be placed in a certain grammar and syntax, and our perception and recognition of 'things' appears to take place in consecutive spaces so that our inner mental representations and conceptions are ordered into some kind of "grammar." (Ibid. p. 36)

In short, we *think* in narratives and have difficulty conceptualizing information *without* placing them in some kind of sequence. This makes sense in the context of understanding why we have self-awareness in the first place. Jaynes (1976/2000; see also McNamara 2004: 124–6) suggested that our ability to reflect on our own mental states is merely a side effect of judging the mental states of others: hypothesizing how another individual will react in several different circumstances, and then acting in such a way as to make the best outcome more likely. Just as Guthrie (1995) noted that the fact that we tend to see faces in the clouds implies we are hyper-alert for social cues, Barrett (2004) argued that we tend to assume some conscious agent caused possibly random events—that is, we possess "hyperactive agency detection devices." Heywood (2010) showed that individuals tend to apply teleology to their autobiographies: even if they explicitly believe events in their past were random occurrences, when they recall and describe past events they often attribute purpose to them. Given the assumption that our brains are the way they are, and that we behave the way we behave to maximize our evolutionary fitness (i.e., to help us survive and reproduce), these kinds of logical "errors"—one might generalize them as hyperactively detecting patterns—are quite *useful*. It is a little costly to mistake a random event as purposeful; it is *very* costly to miss the chance to anticipate a pattern, manipulate an agent, or avoid a disastrous outcome. So, a tendency to create narratives is healthy and adaptive.

Our virtual actions in our imaginary, narrative worlds parallel our real-world behaviors. If a particular strategy is adaptive and becomes a heritable trait, the strategy may shape our cultural products as well as which products we consume. For example, we preferentially track high-status individuals; if so, we may be attracted to literature by and about high-status authors (Barkow 1992; see also Carroll 1999, 2005, 2007; Gottschall and Wilson 2005; Geertz and Jensen 2011). This logic extends to our science fiction narrative worlds: Ward and Lawson (2008) explain how cognition contributes to every stage of the creation of science fiction.

In this sense, our creativity is constrained: there are certain patterns that require extra effort to avoid. But narratives do not merely *reflect* evolutionary strategies, they also enact them. We are social, tool-using animals; narratives become social tools. Much of the rest of this chapter concerns a particular purpose to which we apply narratives: the ability to recognize who is and is not a member of our group, and the pleasure we experience when we *recognize* a member. Bloom (2010) describes some of the specific evolutionary reasons "why we like what we like," but the crucial insight is that the intrinsic qualities of an object are not sufficient to explain the appeal: we will value the same object more if we believe it was once owned by someone we admire, for example. Objects can have social significance, which affects our aesthetic appreciation.

Much research in aesthetics focuses on the external stimulus, but that cannot be the whole story—anyone who's ever drank from a glass of soda that they though contained milk knows that our expectations play a role. I recently opened a grocery bag and was greeted by such a noxious odor that my stomach heaved. But then I remembered I had bought a particularly ripe cheese I enjoy, and my mouth watered. The same stimulus provoked two very different autonomic responses.

The arts are often less visceral, but still our expectations play a role. Bloom also described the appeal of Marcel Duchamp's 1917 sculpture, *Fountain*, which is no more than a urinal. If one knows nothing of art, it's *just* a urinal; contextualized, it "mock[s] the theory that art must be beautiful" (ibid. pp. 143-4). It only "makes sense" if the viewer possesses certain expectations. Manze (2003) comments on Mozart's *Eine Kleine Nachtmusik*, noting that Mozart manipulated listeners' expectations by deviating from expected compositional forms. But note that one can evaluate this piece on multiple levels, as determined why the interpretive schemas one possesses: as consonant notes, as classical music, as a *play* on classical forms.

My main points here are, first, that the information a viewer, listener, or indeed, *reader* possesses influences how one will react. The other is that *constraints*, whether they are evolutionary or cognitive in origin, culturally learned, or even clichéd narrative formulae, do not merely limit what is possible; they make deviations from what is *probable* significant. Writing on science fiction, Lawson (2007) writes that, as a cognitive scientist, his interest is not in creativity per se, but the constraints of creativity, and even more interestingly, "what might be required for their beneficial use" (2007: 264). Citing Thomas B. Ward, he notes that individuals directed to imagine a completely alien animal tend to simply compose a variation on earthly forms. Similarly, Mesoudi (2011: 179-81) argues that all economic products tend to evolve through familiar routines over costly rationality. One follows the "path of least resistance when imagining novel situations unless one is encouraged to employ a more fruitful [i.e., difficult but worthwhile] strategy . . . thinking harder . . . pays dividends when solving problems and imagining novel entities and situations" (Lawson 2007: 269). In Lawson's opinion, *good* gSF makes you work for a deeper understanding. In short, our constraints do not make us less creative; they allow us to be creative on additional levels of perception.

The question for me is why the extra work to acquire the necessary expectations to appreciate *violations* on these expectations, and the extra work to follow an author along a path of *greater* resistance, yield pleasurable experiences. Why does anyone work to "acquire a taste" for something they do not initially enjoy? Anyone can enjoy a simple, pretty tune; why do some enjoy music that the uninitiated would hear only as noise? Most anyone can read and enjoy a well-written mSF novel; why do some enjoy reading gSF they *know* to be poorly written?

These kinds of insights—that our minds possess universal characteristics, that we "think" in narratives, that many characteristics may be reflected in written texts, that texts may be used as social tools—are being developed in the relatively new field of the cognitive science of religion. It should be noted that the *insights* have longer histories. In response to the contemporary linguistic approach to folklore that interpreted cultural similarities as evidence of a single historical antecedent, Thomas Keightley argued in the early nineteenth century that the near-universal recurrence of certain similarities implied not shared historical descent, but shared mental architecture:

I [have] read a great quantity of poems, tales, romances, legends and traditions of various countries and in various languages. I here met such a number of coincidences where there could hardly have been any communication, that I became convinced that the original sameness of the human mind revealed itself as plainly in fiction as in the mechanical arts, or in manners and customs, civil or religious. (Keightley 1834: 6)

Thomas Bradwardine, in the *fourteenth* century, noted our skill at using and remembering narratives, theorizing that artificial narratives are effective mnemonic tools (Carruthers 1990: 281–8), even directing one to organize mental images horizontally (Carruthers 1998: 201–2).

At the midpoint between a theoretical evolutionary strategy, which "explains" why certain goals recur throughout the history of human cultures, and observable behaviors, that is, the *tactical* application of strategies in specific contexts, are our cognitive tools. The most pervasive of these is memory.

Memory

O'er Mithgarth Hugin | and Munin both
Each day set forth to fly;
For Hugin I fear | lest he come not home,
But for Munin my care is more.

"The Ballad of Grimnir" (retold by Bellows 1936)

According to the Poetic Edda, the Norse god Odin sent his two ravens, Hugin (thought) and Munin (memory), over the world to keep him informed. Each day, Odin feared that they would not return. In "The Ballad of Grimnir," why is the loss Munin a bigger worry? Perhaps it is because without Munin, Odin would lack not just information, but his "self." Our identity relies on more than a mass of data, but on the *organization* of that data—without our memory, we not only would not know what to *do* with data, we would be unable to distinguish useful knowledge from background sensory noise in the first place.

The study of the relationship between human psychology and culture dates from the eighteenth century, building on earlier attempts to understand the nature of the individual (Lindholm 2001). Over the last half-century, there has been increasing interest in the relevance of *cognitive* psychology to understanding religion and other cultural patterns. Cognitive anthropology follows similar concerns: from "cognitive," we acquire a focus on how we learn, store, transform, and use information; from "anthropology," we apply this focus to the understanding of how this information makes us who we are, how "culture" can be described in terms of *shared* information—not just facts but schemas and scripts, expectations and assumptions . . . and of course, stories and narratives.

Since Miller (1956), a primary focus has been on the influence and function of *memory*. Miller looked primarily on the constraints working memory played on the complexity of cultural products, but many other perspectives are possible. A particularly provocative idea is Tribble and Keene's (2011) ecological view of human cognition as operating in "cognitive burrows." Building on the fields of Extended Mind and Distributed Cognition (which argue that the boundaries between individuals' thought and their environment are fluid, permeable, and to a degree arbitrary), Tribble and Keene argue, insofar as our environment shapes how we think, what we remember, and how we will behave, that cultures have historically created new sensory environments for the sole purpose of shaping individuals' thought.

Certain information may simply be more memorable: as a simple example, very complex information transmits with less fidelity than simple information. The key insight of Miller (1956) is that there is a strong limit on how many bits of information individuals can simultaneously hold in their working memory. Boyer (1994, esp. pp. 91–124) recognized a more subtle point. One universal human trait is to apply ontological categories to help us conceptualize our environment. We have *templates* for living things vs. objects; more specific templates for plants vs. animals, etc. Thus, when we encounter a new plant that matches our expectations of "trees," we can download a suite of assumptions: it won't move, won't talk, but will grow and can die. Templates also shape what kinds of information will translate from one experience to a new situation. "[C]hildren seem to make such kind-based inductive generalizations more easily if the properties are 'inherent' properties of the exemplars, such as ways of breathing and feeding. They do not easily extend properties like the weight of a given animal or the fact that it moves fast" (ibid. p. 106).

As Barrett and Nyhof (2001) experimentally demonstrated, things that *violate* the intuitions described by Boyer are particularly memorable: we pay attention to, and are more likely to remember, a tree that talks. Specifically, something that contains a single violation—that is, something "minimally counter-intuitive"—is more memorable than an example which violates no expectations or more than one.

Note that only concepts we *remember* can be passed along to other individuals in our group. Following Dawkins (1976), Sperber (1996) argued that "culture" can be seen as the sum of these concepts which are shared between individuals. This perspective on culture and cultural transmission requires we view culture as *particulate*. Sperber called these units "mental representations," describing them not as ideas unconsciously inherited like genes, or moving intact from brain to brain, but as individualized representations actively created in response to exposure to others' communication (Sperber 1996). Importantly, these mental representations allow us to identify (and judge) others, even though many remain unconscious even while active. Also, schemas regularly change and adapt to new situations, but these changes are through what Bourdieu called *regulated* improvisation (Strauss and Quinn 1997: esp. 53–7).

Applying these models to literature is a fruitful enterprise for anthropologists. This is in part because the literature is a vast record of human nature (Carroll 1999: 165), including past cultures (McEwan 2005) or those otherwise unavailable (cf. Benedict 1946). Thus, one can study distinct sequences of cultural development on equal terms, revealing which cultural variations survive and which are not accepted (e.g., bought, imitated) by contemporaries—that is, one can observe the *evolution* of culture. Authors of narratives at each evolutionary stage do not create out of whole cloth, but compose variations on extant themes. (Gibbs [2000] describes the ways authors may play with their audience's mental representations through "staged" communication.)

Thus, culture *cumulatively* evolves, sometimes achieving more complexity than one individual could generate alone (Tomasello 1999). We can speak, then, not only of a narrative in a particular period, but of a *metanarrative*—a story about the changes in a cultural representation over time.

Humor

"Take a simple, real situation, then tweak it a little."
Richard Mathesen (quoted in Corliss 2013)

It appears that schemas which violate our expectations are not just memorable, they are *fun* as well. Hurley, Dennett and Adams (2011) apply an evolutionary perspective on humor. In short, for any class of organism there are certain effortful behaviors that are helpful, but which the organism would not perform if there was no reward. For example, it is to our advantage to seek out the most nutritious foods available. Our brains are wired to "reward" us for achieving these goals. For example, ripe fruit are especially nutritious, and contain naturally occurring sugars. When we consume them, our brain interprets sugars as "sweet" (Barash 1979: 39–41); motivated to experience this pleasure again, we seek out more ripe fruit.

Another job that needs to be done is to monitor our inference systems. We *never* have enough information to negotiate our environment; we need to be able to apply lessons learned elsewhere (see Boyer 1994: 106 above). We, therefore, continually make inferences based on past experience, intuitive concepts, etc., but we then must monitor whether or not these inferences are accurate. Hurley et al. argue that we experience something as "funny" when our brains reward us for recognizing mistaken assumptions. They note as circumstantial but telling evidence that some languages (including English) use the same word to indicate amusing (e.g., "Hey, that's funny!") and curious (e.g., "Hmm, that tastes funny . . .") (ibid. pp. 27–30).

Purzycki (2010) connected this kind of observation to Boyer and to Sperber, by demonstrating that minimally counter-intuitive violations of both template- *and* schema-based inferences make a joke funnier . . . and more memorable.

But note that (1) schemas *define* the culture of a particular group, and, as noted above, (2) just as we are motivated to seek out sugar and inference violations, we should be motivated to monitor who is, and who is not a member of our social group. We should be alert for "cheaters." "Inside jokes" are a special form of humor that is designed to appeal only to a select group. Hurley et al. (2011) note that much humor is only funny in a specific cultural context, but have relatively little to say about inside jokes (see, e.g., pp. 31–4)—which is reasonable as their goal is to "reverse-engineer" the human mind.

In this book, I am more focused on the social tasks to which our minds are applied, such as detecting bona fide members of one's group. Flamson and Barrett (2008) argued that one way in which humor works is to activate schemas the teller and the listener share, but which were previously learned in a different context. Their "encryption theory" of humor "hypothesizes that the universal capacity for humor ultimately evolved as a means of broadcasting information about the self and acquiring information about others to aid in determining which peers would be most compatible as long-term partners" (ibid. p. 262).

One can combine and extend Flamson et al.'s and Hurley et al.'s logic to deduce that inside jokes are particularly funny because we have been rewarded for recognizing a fellow group member. The joke is not funny if the key information is shared after, or if the key information is shared by the speaker during the joke, because no *shared* cultural schemas —and thus no shared identity—are implied, and thus there is no evidence that the other is a (non-cheating) fellow group member.

This pattern can manifest as gSF "shorthand." How much does the author need to explain; which schemas s/he may assume the reader can use to decode the text? An author who pauses to explain, say, time dilation at relativistic speeds would seem *passé*, at best. In contrast, author China Miéville (2011: 20) can refer to "automa" with "turingware," trusting the genre reader knows what a Turing test is, to recognize a neologism of "automaton," and thus to be able to follow the narrative.

Let us return to the del Rey vs. Atwood problem. Sperber defines culture as shared schema, formed by shared experiences. Note that a recurring theme of our cognition has been that creativity often operates as variations on a theme (Ward and Lawson 2008: 198–9), and that schemas contribute to what Bourdieu called regulated improvisations (Strauss and Quinn 1997: esp. 53–7). The "themes" that are varied are culturally significant. In Chapter 1, I quoted the Clute and Nicholls (1995: 483) statement that gSF authors are conscious of working with "certain 'conventions'—some might even say 'rules'" (i.e., gSF-specific cultural schema) and suggested that gSF could be defined as the schema shared by means of different individuals reading the same body of literature. The specificity of these schemas, and the effort required to acquire them, both characterize gSF and distinguish it from mSF.

> Fans . . . read a *lot* of science fiction. A concept that is new and different and far out to the general public can be old-hat to the fans; and fan pressure can push an author towards ever-new, ever farther-out ideas . . . adding to our isolation. (Pournelle 1982: 159)

Previously in this book I noted that H. G. Wells (1927) found the movie *Metropolis* as an annoying assemblage of out-of-date motifs; Le Guin (quoted in McCaffery and Gregory 1987: 184) described science fiction written by people who do not read it as "embarrassing for everybody" . . . but note this would only apply to a reader of gSF who could recognize the schemas are not quite right—and that only a reader of gSF would appreciate when they *are* right. As Beck wrote,

> . . . remember first that imaginary constructions can be just as rule-bound as their actually existing counterparts—sometimes obsessively so. Charles Ludwidge Dodgson (a.k.a. Lewis Carroll) was a mathematician; J.R.R. Tolkien a Germanic philologist. Alice's Wonderland is a game of logic; Tolkien's Middle Earth is a language game. (Beck 2014: 95)

Writers of gSF often get *their* rules from science, and always from their gSF predecessors. As a philologist will understand aspects of Middle Earth that will elude me, so aspects of gSF will elude someone who is not a fan. These rules are part of the game, and part of the fun.

Atwood's book (Ursula K. LeGuin, quoted in McCaffery and Gregory 1987: 184) was published decades after *The Eleventh Commandment*, but from the metanarrative for religion described in this book (and despite the advertising on the first edition cover: "The Church made a HELL on Earth!") a religion that is simply "nasty" was by genre standards outdated in gSF even by del Rey's time. del Rey seems to first deliberately push gSF readers' buttons, but then challenges us to understand the Church's motives, and possibly even methods, as arguably ethical (del Rey 1962: 153–4).

Heinlein pioneered the practice of setting otherwise unconnected stories in the same fictional world (referred to as Heinlein's "Future History"), peppering them with oblique references to facts revealed elsewhere: if one reads carefully, one might realize that "Lazarus Long's" ship *New Frontiers* in Heinlein's *Methuselah's Children* (1958) is sister to "the Ship" in his 1941 story "Universe" (1941/1987). As a more extreme example, I've enjoyed E. E. "Doc" Smith's books because of what they tell me about the history of my genre, though the books themselves are pretty bad. Religion is a potent tool in *The Eleventh Commandment*, and even if it has the potential to be totalitarian, in the right hands it can do much good—which is exactly what I expect from a book written c. 1960, and thus it contributes to a whole greater than a single book or author. In sum, the reason I enjoy books like *The Eleventh Commandment* may well be because it parallels inside jokes: aside from the story itself, a genre fan may experience the additional pleasure of recognizing shared cultural schemas, and see them in a historical context. Plus, it's simply one of "ours."

Importantly, these schemas are *honest* signals of membership in the gSF community. One can only acquire them through long hours of reading, watching, and discussing science fiction. The kinds of explicit criteria which were so unhelpful in defining science fiction are too easily communicated. Note that this does not mean that a novice cannot enjoy a gSF novel, but a true fan of the genre will appreciate it on additional levels, just as I suspect someone reading *The Sparrow* for the first time will likely be more interested if they had read *A Case of Conscience* at some point. If I explain *A Case of Conscience* to that reader, it might make *The Sparrow* a little more interesting, but they wouldn't experience the pleasure of figuring it out for themselves.

Whitehouse's Modes

One final point relates to my qualification in Chapter 1 of viewing gSF as a community, but as an unusually distributed community: no obvious center, no powerful leaders, and few points of interaction between members. Only science fiction conventions routinely involve face-to-face contact, and such events seem to *follow*, and perhaps intensify, preexisting identifications. The most significant difference between in-group gSF and out-group mSF seems to be the body of characteristic schemas individuals cannot list, per se, but nevertheless recognize and use.

Whitehouse (2004) described what may be a related pattern in group formation. Specifically, he looked at the *rituals* used to incorporate a new individual into a social group, noting that most rituals, like most culture, function on the "cognitive optimum" level. That is, most culture is easily enjoyed, memorable, and can spread easily through a population (ibid. pp. 29–47). The rituals that "matter," however, characteristically rely on information that is relatively *difficult* to acquire (ibid. pp. 49–59). This makes intuitive sense, from a costly signaling perspective: only the active expenditure of effort could convey membership, not the passive accumulation of cognitively optimal information.

These rituals take two distinct forms, two "Modes of Religiosity." (NB. Modes Theory describes secular rituals equally well as religious.) The distinction stems from two different cognitive procedures for memory encoding. If one comes to identify with a stable social group and be recognized by other members, it follows that the requisite information must be stored in our *long-term* and *explicit* memory. (Common sense would seem to dictate that quickly forgotten memories and memories one cannot access consciously would be irrelevant for the purposes of determining membership.) Long-term, explicit memory is considered to take two forms: episodic and semantic. Whitehouse noted that both are "encoded for recall" in distinct ways: the two Modes describe rituals that seem to encode either episodic or semantic memories. Importantly, given the characteristics of a social system—size, centralization of power, etc.—a group will tend to rely on one of the two Modes. The chief features of each Mode are summarized in simplified form below (adapted from ibid. p. 74).

Doctrinal Mode

- Targets *semantic memory*, which is encoded through multiple repetitions of the same information. Each repetition is at a low level of arousal.
- Rituals tend to be repeated regularly, with strong uniformity between repetitions.
- Sociopolitical features associated include diffuse cohesion, strong and dynamic leaders, with a centralized structure.

Imagistic Mode

- Targets *episodic memory*, which is encoded through a single (or small number of) highly arousing event(s).
- Rituals tend to be repeated once (or very infrequently), with low uniformity between enactments.
- Sociopolitical features associated include intense cohesion, weak and/or passive leaders, with no centralized structure.

The prototypical example of a religion focused on the Doctrinal Mode is Christianity: a strongly centralized, very large group. The foundational ritual (the Mass) is repeated regularly and is relatively unarousing: to join, one must be "indoctrinated"—that is, one must absorb a body of information believed to be crucial to being a valid member of the group, determined and interpreted by the centralized power. The prototypical Imagistic Mode example would be an initiation ritual, which is an *extremely* arousing (painful, frightening) event, typically occurring rarely or only once (e.g., to mark the transition from childhood to full adult status), and which is ethnographically associated with small face-to-face groups with distributed power. Note that in the latter case, doctrine is unimportant. The relevant memory is not textual information, but the recollection of participating in the painful ritual. As Whitehouse notes, participants in imagistic rituals are generally free to construct any exegetical "meaning" of the ritual for themselves.

gSF, as described above, also appears to be a social group united by shared memories, but does not conform to either Mode. It is large and anonymous, and textually based (i.e., elements associated with the Doctrinal Mode) but there is no centralized authority, no standard interpretations (i.e., Imagistic-like), and the body of texts is a loosely bounded category from which individuals select specific texts for themselves to consume in isolation (i.e., unlike either Mode).

One possibility is that science fiction consists entirely of "cognitive optimum" culture—that is, information spreads with neither the extreme measures of frequent repetition *nor* the equally extreme measures associated with an Imagistic ritual. But note some of the characteristics of readers gSF, relative to mSF: members distinguish between in-group and out-group, display a degree of identification stronger than readers of mSF, and possess group-specific cultural schemas (e.g., as demonstrated by the possibilities for inside jokes and other plays on shared experiences: see Brackett [1955/2012, 1964]; pp. 110–16, this volume). Further, there is unusual coherence in this shared information, such as the evolution of the metanarrative described in Parts Two and Three. These suggest that perhaps something interestingly cognitive may be going on: not a "Mode" perhaps, but a 'mode.'

Further, there is evidence that gSF is less cognitively optimal than one might assume. Wolfe (2011) suggests that in the early 1930s, there were no publishing categories for genres like Westerns, mysteries, fantasy, horror, or science fiction; rather, there were hyper-specialized magazines, "devoted to everything from varsity football fiction and World War I aviation stories to tales of 'oriental menace'" (ibid. p. 20). Westerns and mysteries easily made the transition to book formats, and thus to a more visible, less ephemeral medium, and, as a result, to a more defined genre. Stories not set in the real world became recognized genres only slowly. Wolfe also notes that, in a "landmark study," John G. Cawelti identified narrative formulae for Westerns and several subsets of mysteries, but not for "fantastic genres" like science fiction (ibid. p. 23; see Cawelti 1976). Wolfe argues this is because genres like science fiction cannot be defined according to a narrative formula (cf. "Defining science fiction," Chapter 1, this volume), but rather are unified by characteristic ideologies.

> Each [fantastic] genre's readers came to identify a central ideological lynchpin— Robert A. Heinlein in the case of science fiction, Howard Philips Lovecraft in the case of horror, J.R.R. Tolkien in the case of fantasy—and to a great extent the dialectic of the relevant genre seemed to define itself in recapitulation of, or reaction against, the world-views of these central figures. (Wolfe 2011: 24)

Thus, the costs of participating in a fantastic genre's dialog (even as a receptive consumer), and of "decoding" the encrypted levels of significance (*sensu* Flamson and

Barrett 2008), requires one invest the time not just to learn a few narrative formulae (of which gSF has more than its share), and to work at continually learning *new* worlds, but to internalize ideologies from a *body* of literature.

> [*Astounding* editor F. Orlin] Tremaine argued that science fiction readers were by nature a small, elite group, "members of that inner circle who see and understand a vision that is beyond the ken of the vast multitude." (Westfahl 1999)

This hardly suggests cognitive optimum culture.

The difficulty in interpreting this as analogous to Whitehouse's Modes stems from our possession of only *two* explicit long-term memory systems. One could posit a "cognitive optimum" mode, but the resulting group would be *too* accessible: unlike Modes, joining (i.e., acquiring the necessary memories) is by definition easy, and therefore cannot function as a costly signal of commitment. Short-term memory cannot work as a Mode, as the social group would be transient. So, without a dedicated memory system, a method of group formation may work, but it would not be a Mode.

But there *is* another form of long-term memory: *implicit* memory. Daniel Schacter describes implicit memory as "when people are influenced by a past experience without any awareness that they are remembering" (1996: 161). Loosely, implicit memories may be long term, but are difficult to consciously access. Schacter uses the following illustration.

> Imagine this scene. A young woman is walking aimlessly down the street, and she is eventually picked up by the police. She seems to be suffering from an extreme form of amnesia, because she has lost all memory of who she is. Unfortunately, she is carrying no identification. Then the police have a breakthrough idea—they ask her to begin dialing phone numbers. As it turns out, she dials her mother's number—though she is not aware whose number she is dialing. (quoted in Maitlin 2002: 129)

An implicit memory task would be like filling in missing letters in a word, for example, "_mn_si_." Such tasks are more easily accomplished with preliminary priming (Maitlin 2002: 130–1).

A social group united by shared implicit memories would probably look a great deal like the science fiction community: encoding events show very low uniformity in a high number of cognitive optimum repetitions—that is, we read some of the same groups. There is no centralized power, but there are conspicuously influential individuals (e.g., authors like Heinlein, "intelligent designers" like Campbell) who encourage some texts to be disproportionately consumed. Through these overlapping (but never identical) experiences, members acquire similar, half-remembered schemas; as a result, explicitly describing what distinguishes the group is extremely difficult—recall the vague and contradicting definitions of science fiction in Chapter 1 (see Clute and Nicholls 1995: 311–14). Nevertheless, members make consistent judgments on what (and who) are "real" gSF, and the production of new texts reference shared schemas—drawn from what Bleiler (2009: 195) called the "continuity of texts" that distinguishes the genre.

Whether this constitutes an "Implicit Mode," or if the relationship between gSF and Modes is merely metaphorical, is not clear. The genre's capacity to generate a coherent metanarrative demonstrates that there is *something* uniting and distinguishing its members, and the similarities between members' implicit judgments suggest this "something" is stored in our implicit memories.

Conclusion

There are (at least) three different reasons I find the metanarrative described in this book so compelling. First, the stories themselves are worthwhile on their own and individual merits. Some of them are classics of gSF; a few of the authors (Stapledon, Heinlein, Herbert, Butler, Gaiman) I would compare favorably to their best contemporaries outside the genre. Second, I find that science fiction seems to have largely resolved—or at least moved far beyond—the simplistic contradiction between scientific and religious perspectives that continue to dominate political discourse; there is a valuable, broadly relevant lesson here. But third, I am fascinated by the *process* by which gSF's schema for religion has cumulatively, culturally evolved, and by the mechanisms that create a community of individuals, complete with shared cultural schema and consistent implicit judgments (e.g., the distinction between gSF and its mainstream cousin) despite being geographically diffuse. It may be a case study for understanding how distributed communities "work."

The importance of this last point cannot be over-emphasized. As communities continue to spread themselves over larger areas, they require new ways to maintain cohesion. Social media has, in recent times, demonstrated its effectiveness in organizing geographically separated individuals in the Arab Spring of 2011. Such diffuse communities also encounter unique problems from being surrounded on all *physical* sides by non-members. Consider former US President Bill Clinton's words on why people find home-grown terrorism so disturbing:

> The perpetrators were not invaders but home grown citizens, whose religious and political identities were more important to them than the people they grew up with, went to school with, worked with, shared weekends with, shared meals with. In other words, they thought their differences were more important than their common humanity. It is the central psychological plague of human kind in the 21st century. (Clinton 2007)

I wonder if the challenge we should be most focused upon is not home-grown terrorism but the rise of diffuse communities. Is this the *social* plague of human kind in the twenty-first century, or just another step in our technology-enhanced social evolution, analogous and opposed to the millennia-ago development of centralized urban centers and political boundaries? It is difficult to imagine how a diffuse community would become the *norm* (i.e., that we would routinely disregard immediate and physically present neighbors), but it is worth investigating it as a viable alternative or complement. In this context, gSF may be an important example of how these virtual communities may form, and, crucially, what values they distribute to individual members' real-world communities.

Our focus here has been on the ideologies related to religion: what normative views of religion are accepted and valued within the virtual community of gSF? I fully expect a routine objection to my methods is to question whether my focus on those social institutions addresses what religion is *really* about. Huchingson's (1989) review of Kreuziger's *The Religion of Science Fiction* (1986) begins, "One should note right away that this book is not about religion. The author pays little attention to the universal elements of religion to be found in the symbols and stories of SF—including ritual, mysticism, and the sacred." I happily acknowledge that many other books on "religion in science fiction" could be written, using different definitions, but still insist on two caveats: (1) an unnatural category like "religion" can be defined only situationally, not definitively, and (2) seemingly characteristic categories like "ritual, mysticism" and even "the sacred" are frequently addressed in Western cultures by secular institutions and by individuals outside institutional contexts. Thus, my definition (following Luther Martin) focuses on what *distinguishes* one kind of institution from another and what "we" (i.e., citizens of gSF) think about these institutions, just as my definition of science fiction focuses on what distinguishes the "genre" from the "mainstream."

In our increasingly globalized world, what is the final, take-home message of the possibly defunct genre form of science fiction for religious institutions? Writing about the impact of gSF on public perceptions of astronomy, Consolmagno (1996) wrote:

> . . . another message of the science fiction-astronomy connection—one that, again, comes as much from the needs of a good plot as from any scientific or philosophical principle—is the sense that the universe is strange but ultimately knowable . . . This is not a sense that "anything is possible." Science has its rules, and so does science fiction. But the multiplicity of planets that science fiction assumes must exist in the universe—and that astronomy at least does not deny—does suggest that (in the words of Merlin, from T.H. White's retelling [1958] of the Arthurian legend, *The Once and Future King*) "anything not forbidden is compulsory." (Ibid. p. 131)

Both academia and gSF once predicted the demise of religious social systems, regardless of humanity's seemingly universal allegiance to myth and ritual, and recurring examples of mysticism and the sacred. The preponderance of evidence in both cultures suggests these initial predictions were in error, and that religion will extend into our futures. The multiplicity, not just of planets, but of worldviews—religious *and* scientific—is gSF's legacy.

Notes

Introduction

1 Personal communication; see also http://www.marydoriarussell.net/books/the-sparrow/faq/

Chapter 1

1 For example, http://en.wikipedia.org/wiki/Niven's_laws
2 After writing *Stranger in a Strange Land* (1961, see chapter 7), Heinlein became the "unwitting guru of 10,000 acid trips" (Spinrad 1981: vii), and quite a few of his fans were inspired to create religions based on his book (see Cusack 2011). Heinlein, apparently, was horrified.
3 Note, however, that other goals may benefit from broadly inclusive definitions. For example, "It is rather fashionable among some connoisseurs of science fiction to stress its age. This is partly the result of a thoroughly natural desire to lend an air of respectability to a class of literature that is often the target of laughter and sneers from those who picture it in terms of comic strips and horror movies" (Asimov 1983: 340).
4 Friend (2012) argues that more general categories like "fiction" and indeed *non*fiction shape interpretations and appreciations, and thus are arguably genres. In this sense, genre science fiction merely has additional and more specific criteria. As used here, the distinction implies a subculture with characteristic schemas (e.g., references to other gSF works), as well as disproportionate examples of mainstream schemas (e.g., a greater awareness of technologies).
5 "Faster than light" propulsion, "bug-eyed-monsters" (and by extension stereotypical action-based plots), and "there ain't no such thing as a free lunch" via Heinlein's *The Moon is a Harsh Mistress*.

Chapter 2

1 Scientifiction was Gernsback's original label for the genre.
2 *She* was, for a time, a popular myth the equal of *Frankenstein*. SilentEra.com lists no less than four silent shorts and movies based on it (1908, 1911, 1916, 1917) *before* the better known (and surviving) 1925 silent film starring Betty Blythe. Curiously, the first "talkie" version in 1935 moves the action from Africa to Siberia: presumably, Africa was insufficiently remote by 1935.
3 Bellamy comments on religion are developed in the sequel, *Equality* (1897).

Chapter 3

1   In the forward to a recent edition, Gregory Benford suggests readers skip ahead to the demise of our own species (Stapledon 1930/1999: xi).

Chapter 4

1   For example, in the excellent *The Life and Adventures of Peter Wilkins* (Paltock 1751/1884) the protagonist discovers and is accepted into a lost culture—in particular, the (sometimes censored) 16th chapter describing the "author's disappointment at first going to bed with his new wife" (cf. Paltock 1751/1844).
2   Recall (Theodore) "Sturgeon's Law," which now even has a Wikipedia page, regarding the proportion of quality in gSF: "the claim (or fact) that 90% of science fiction is crap is ultimately uninformative, because science fiction conforms to the same trends of quality as all other artforms" (http://en.wikipedia.org/wiki/Sturgeon's_Law). I often hear it more succinctly remembered, as "yeah, 90% of sf is crap, but then 90% of *everything* is crap."
3   This observation is not limited to Hartwell; e.g., Spinrad (1981: vi) credits Asimov.

Chapter 5

1   Moore was already well established as a writer by 1939, and her abilities and popularity would only grow during the Golden Age, both as C. L. Moore and as half of "Lewis Padgett." Also in this issue, but not described here, was fiction by Ross Rocklynne (who deserves to be better remembered), Nat Schachter, and Leo Vernon.
2   Also adapted for the Dimension X radio program in 1951: see http://archive.org/details/OTRR_Dimension_X_Singles
3   Also adapted for the Dimension X radio program in 1950: see http://archive.org/details/OTRR_Dimension_X_Singles
4   To highlight how much and how quickly gSF had changed, consider as a contemporary contrast Fredric Brown's "Armageddon" (1941/1980), in which a child's cleverness and a bit of luck defeats Satan (cf. Tushnet's "In the Calendar of Saints" [1964], discussed in chapter 6). The rather flip dismissal of mythic figures must have seemed quaint to the average reader of *Astounding* in 194—which may be why "Armageddon" was published in *Unknown*.

Chapter 6

1   Nevertheless, Campbell remained influential and won eight Hugos *after* 1950.
2   "Guardian Angel" was initially published in a version edited 25% shorter. (Clarke [2001: 203] states that this edit was performed by James Blish.) Here (i.e., 1950a), scenes are somewhat less fleshed out (though dialogue is largely intact), and the story slightly Americanized: a debt is described in dollars instead of pounds sterling, and a passage placing a key scene in southern France is omitted (Clarke 1950b: 17–18).

The most significant change is the deletion of "van Ryberg's" perspective (e.g., ibid. pp. 9–10, 13–14, 15–16). Curiously, 1950b describes one of the problems addressed by the Overlords being "the Jewish question"; 1950a lists "the middle question" (p. 102). Note that the modern state of Israel had been formed in 1948, so this could be a typo: "the middle [*east*] question." Finally, Blish adds a few words at the end which imply that the Overlords dread not failure, but Armageddon.

3   While the section "Earth and the Overlords" is about 30% *longer* than 1950b, there are only two significant conceptual additions. One is an account of the Overlords abolishing apartheid by requiring civil rights for South Africa's *white minority* (Clarke 1953: 19–20); the other concerns the quote on p. 23 discussed below. In addition, the story is, like 1950a, Americanized (e.g., the scene described as being in southern France [see above footnote] is now in South America), and, though humanity's leader learns *something* about the Overlords' appearance, we do not yet learn what.

4   It is suggestive, though not relevant here, that the 1950 radio adaptation *Earth Abides* was rather less subtle, introducing it as "one of the most unusual and terrifying stories of recent years" and desperately trying to make it about monsters.

5   "As for their mental processes, you might call George dull, but you would have to call Maurine stupid" (Stewart 1949/1999: 123).

6   Again, this story exists in short and long forms. In this case, I will focus on the 1958 novel which extends the philosophical tension to a more complete resolution, but see Blish (1953). For thematically related works, see Blish (2013).

Chapter 7

1   Compare this to the "triptych" of side-by-side stories by Isaac Asimov (1956), Theodore R. Cogswell (1956), and Miriam Allen DeFord (1956a), in which each combines *three* old gimmicks (generally associated with three different genres): deals with a devil, locked room mysteries, and time travel paradoxes.

2   *Stranger* won the 1962 Hugo, *Dune* won the 1966 Hugo as well as the first Nebula Award for best novel; both routinely appear on lists of the best science fiction novels of all time.

3   See also Zelazny and Dick's hallucinatory *Deus Irae* (1976). Zelazny's more purely fantasy genre books present slightly different views. In *Changeling* (1980), science and magic are presented as balanced opposites; each is capable of great harm if unchecked. The protagonist of his "Chronicles of Amber" series (especially Zelazny 1970/2008, 1972/2008) manipulates "primitive" peoples' belief in him as a supernatural figure to use them as cannon-fodder for his own selfish ends—but then, "Corwin" is a cynical antihero, which may mitigate this representation of religion as leaving one vulnerable to manipulation.

4   Some editions (e.g., Heinlein 1991: 3) open with a preface explaining that Heinlein chose names of characters based on the meaning of the name. The specific meanings seem less significant than the fact that Heinlein deliberately introduced layers of meaning.

5   It is common to view Heinlein's mouthpieces—they appear regularly in his mid- and late work—as Heinlein projecting himself into his story. Panshin (1968: 100) points out that at one point in *Stranger*, Jubal throws out a story idea that the actual Heinlein passed along to Theodore Sturgeon, the result being Sturgeon's "And Now, the News . . ."

6 This turning point is so important that I feel I can justify straying briefly away from *Dune* itself to apply retroactively the sequels, *Dune Messiah* (1969) and *Children of Dune* (1976), as well as Brian Herbert's volume on the creation of his father's great work (Herbert et al. 2005). These will also help support my claim that Campbell's publication decision was ironically not based on the elements that allowed *Dune* to make such an impact; in this vein, I will also draw from the fan-written reference *The Dune Encyclopedia* (McNelly 1984).

Chapter 9

1 In contrast, her fantasy genre *The Mists of Avalon* (1987) can be read as not just the passing of the age of magic, but the conflicts between doctrinal and imagistic religions. Darkover was also one of the first genre worlds in which fans actively participated, through the "Friends of Darkover" anthologies.

2 Interestingly, though the polytheistic Darkover culture Bradley described included a robust system of myths, and we encounter objective proof that these gods actually exist (e.g., Bradley 1996), a formal religious system is conspicuously absent, *except* for an ascetic remnant of Christianity.

3 An eighth book was published long after the fact (Anthony 2007), focusing on "Night," who appeared in earlier books.

4 In a subtle bit of foreshadowing, when we first meet Wyvern he is clutching a copy of the *Malleus Maleficarum*.

5 The word "sequel" must be in scare-quotes, as Card's primary intent was to write *Speaker for the Dead*; the prologue grew in length and complexity until it was necessary to publish it separately, but the central themes are not resolved until the "second" book.

6 Contrast this to the closer association suggested in Card's *The Folk of the Fringe*, discussed below.

7 Rather than be exclusively a function of gSF's evolution, this theme may parallel more general societal trends. For example, academic psychology might have followed a similar pattern. "During the past 25 years psychology of religion material has appeared with increasing frequency in high-end journals" (Emmons and Paloutzian 2003: 380), arguing that "the social upheavals of the 1960s make [a new group of psychologists] aware of the need to use their psychological training to study real-life issues such as violence, aggression, prejudice, sexism—to tackle the big problems" (ibid. p. 379). In addition to the social aspect, the trend has been toward increasing attention to the *affect* of religion on individuals. "Recent research on religion and spirituality as human phenomena is almost as vast as religious life itself" (ibid. p. 378). Religion and emotion, spiritual transformation, and even virtue have all been increasingly legitimate topics of study in psychology, as *well* as gSF.

Chapter 10

1 Not be confused with Pamela Sargent's 1983 *Earthseed*, in which a sentient space ship attempts to colonize an alien world with the remnants of mankind, while attempting

to subvert the innate violent behaviors that have repeatedly threatened to destroy humanity (see also Sargent's more successful *Child of Venus* [2001]).

2   My thanks to Dan Neill, Lynn Castro, and Tucker Trenchard for suggesting these titles.

Chapter 11

1   "[Hartwell] has a point. The essence of being twelve, and of science fiction, is potential. They are both all about hopes and dreams and possibilities, intense curiosity aroused by the knowledge that there's so much out there to be known" (Griffith 2007: 141–2).

2   N.B. This does not include other genre blockbusters: *Thor*; the latest installments in the *Harry Potter*, *Twilight*, *Pirates of the Caribbean*, and *Sherlock Holmes* franchises, nor the steampunk-flavored *Hugo*.

References

Ackerman, F. J. (1932, Feb.). [Letter to the editor.] *Wonder Stories* 3(9).

Adams, D. (1979). *Hitchhiker's guide to the galaxy*. New York: Harmony Books.

Alcubierre, M. (1994). The warp drive: Hyper-fast travel within general relativity. *Classical and Quantum Gravity* 11(5): L73–L77.

Aldiss, B. W. (1973). *Billion year spree: The true history of science fiction*. New York: Doubleday.

"All-time box office: U.S.A." (2012). Available at: http://www.imdb.com/boxoffice/alltimegross.

Amis, K. (1960). *New maps of hell: A survey of science fiction*. New York: Harcourt, Brace and Co.

Andrus, E. H. (forthcoming). Remembering Laura Roslin: Fictional death and a real bereavement community online.

Anthony, P. (1977). *God of Tarot*. New York: Berkley Books.

—. (1980a). *Faith of Tarot*. New York: Berkley Books.

—. (1980b). *Vision of Tarot*. New York: Berkley Books.

—. (1983). *On a pale horse*. New York: Ballantine Books.

—. (1984). *Bearing an hourglass*. New York: Ballantine Books.

—. (1985). *With a tangled skein*. New York: Ballantine Books.

—. (1986). *Wielding a red sword*. New York: Ballantine Books.

—. (1987). *Being a green mother*. New York: Ballantine Books.

—. (1988). *For love of evil*. New York: Ballantine Books.

—. (1990). *And eternity*. New York: Ballantine Books.

—. (2007). *Under a velvet cloak*. Cincinnati, OH: Mundania Press.

Arthur, R. (1941/1980). Evolution's end. In I. Asimov and M. H. Greenberg (Eds), *Isaac Asimov presents the golden years of science fiction, second series* (pp. 70–85). New York: Bonanza Books.

Ashley, M. (Ed.) (1975). *The history of the science fiction magazine, volume two: 1936–1945*. Chicago: Henry Regnery Company.

—. (2011). *The dreaming sex: Early tales of scientific imagination*. London: Peter Owen.

Ashley, M. and E. Brown (Eds). (2005). *The mammoth book of new Jules Verne adventures*. New York: Carroll and Graf.

Ashley, M. and R. A. W. Lowndes (2004). *Gernsback days: A study of the evolution of modern science fiction from 1911 to 1936*. Holicong, PA: Wildside Press.

Asimov, I. (1939/1979). Trends. In I. Asimov and M. H. Greenberg (Eds), *Isaac Asimov presents great science fiction stories of 1939* (pp. 229–47). New York: Dorset Press.

—. (1941/1998). Nightfall. In R. Silverberg (Ed.), *The science fiction hall of fame, volume one, 1929–1964* (pp. 113–44). New York: Orb.

Author's note: The website Archive.org was the initial source of many of the rare texts (e.g., early periodicals, obscure utopias) listed here, and has been an invaluable resource.

—. (1942, May). Foundation. *Astounding Science Fiction 29*(3).

—. (1951/1991). *Foundation.* New York: Bantam Dell.

—. (1956, Nov.). The brazen locked room. *The Magazine of Fantasy and Science Fiction 11*(11).

—. (1964a, Mar.). Forget it! *The Magazine of Fantasy and Science Fiction 26*(3).

—. (1964b, Aug.). The days of our years. *The Magazine of Fantasy and Science Fiction 27*(2).

—. (1971). Isaac Asimov on changes in science fiction after 1949 [video]. *Center for the Study of Science Fiction, University of Kansas.* Available at: http://www.youtube.com/ watch?v=VaSVsbgaQxo

—. (1983). Social science fiction. In D. Allen (Ed.), *Science fiction: The future* (2nd edn, pp. 339–66). New York: Harcourt Brace Jovanovich.

Asimov, I. and M. H. Greenberg. (Eds) (1979). *Isaac Asimov presents great science fiction stories of 1939.* New York: Dorset Press.

—. (1980). *Isaac Asimov presents the golden years of science fiction, second series.* New York: Bonanza Books.

—. (1981). *Isaac Asimov presents the golden years of science fiction, third series.* New York: Bonanza Books.

—. (1982). *Isaac Asimov presents the golden years of science fiction, fourth series.* New York: Bonanza Books.

Atwood, M. (1986/1998). *The handmaid's tale.* New York: Anchor Books.

—. (2012). *In other worlds: SF and the human imagination.* New York: Anchor Books.

Auden, W. H. (1962). The guilty vicarage. In *The dyer's hand and other essays* (pp. 146–58). New York: Random House.

Aymé, M. (1947/1959, Dec.). State of grace. *The Magazine of Fantasy and Science Fiction 17*(6).

Bainbridge, W. S. (1986). *Dimensions of science fiction.* Cambridge, MA: Harvard University Press.

Baines, P. (1995). "Able mechanic": *The life and adventures of Peter Wilkins* and the eighteenth century fantastic voyage. In D. Seed (Ed.), *Anticipations: Essays on early science fiction and its precursors* (pp. 1–25). Syracuse, NY: Syracuse University Press.

Barash, D. (1979). *The whisperings within.* New York: Harper and Row.

Barclay, F. M. (1930, Sept.). The troglodytes. *Amazing Stories 5*(6).

Barkow, J. (1992). Beneath new culture is old psychology: Gossip and social stratification. In J. H. Barkow, L. Cosmides, and J. Tooby (Eds), *Adapted mind: Evolutionary psychology and the generation of culture* (pp. 627–37). Oxford: Oxford University Press.

Barnard, A. (2006). Tarzan and the lost races: Anthropology and early science fiction. In L. A. Vivanco and R. J. Gordon (Eds), *Tarzan was an eco-tourist, and other tales in the anthropology of adventure* (pp. 58–74). New York: Berghahn Books.

Barnett, D. (2009). Science fiction: The genre that dare not speak its name. Available at: http://www.guardian.co.uk/books/booksblog/2009/jan/28/science-fiction-genre

Barrett, J. L. (2004). *Why would anyone believe in God?* Walnut Creek, CA: AltaMira Press.

Barrett, J. L. and M. A. Nyhof (2001). Spreading non-natural concepts: The role of intuitive conceptual structures in memory and transmission of cultural materials. *Journal of Cognition and Culture 1*(1): 69–100.

Bauer, E. (1931, Aug.). The forgotten world. *Amazing Stories 6*(5).

Bear, G. (1999). *Darwin's radio.* New York: Ballantine.

Beck, R. (2014). "Star-talk": A gateway to mind in the ancient world. *Journal of Cognitive Historiography 1*(1): 90–7.

Bellamy, E. (1888/1986). *Looking backward: 2000–1887* (C. Tichi, Ed.). New York: Penguin.

—. (1889a). How I came to write "Looking Backward." *The Nationalist 1*: 1–4.

—. (1889b). Looking forward. *The Nationalist 2*: 1–4.

—. (1890). Nationalism—principles, purposes. *The Nationalist 2*: 174–80.

—. (1897). *Equality*. Toronto: George N. Morang.

Bellows, H. A. (trans.) (1936). The poetic edda. Available at: http://www.sacred-texts.com/neu/poe/

Benedict, R. (1946). *Chrysanthemum and the sword*. London: Routledge and Kegan Paul.

Benson, R. H. (1908). *Lord of the world*. New York: Dodd, Mead and Company.

Bertonneau, T. F. (2008). Sacrifice and sainthood: Walter M. Miller Jr.'s short fiction. *Science Fiction Studies 35*(3): 404–29.

Bester, A. (1941/1980). Adam and no Eve. In I. Asimov and M. H. Greenberg (Eds), *Isaac Asimov presents the golden years of science fiction, second series* (pp. 237–50). New York: Bonanza Books.

Bleiler, E. F. (1991). *Science-fiction: The early years*. Kent, OH: Kent State University Press.

—. (1998). *Science-fiction: The Gernsback years*. Kent, OH: Kent State University Press.

—. (2009). Does it exist? In Arthur B. Evans (Ed.), Roundtable discussion on proto/early science fiction. *Science Fiction Studies 36*(2): 193–204.

Blish, J. (1953, Sept.). A case of conscience. *If 1*(4).

—. (1958/2000). *A case of conscience*. New York: Ballantine.

—. (1970/1987). The function of science fiction [previously published as The tale that wags the god]. In C. Chauvin (Ed.), *The tale that wags the god* (pp. 21–34). New York: Ballantine.

— [as W. Atheling, Jr.]. (1973). *The issue at hand*. Chicago: Advent.

—. (2013). *Sf Gateway omnibus: Black Easter, The day after judgment, The seedling stars*. London: Gollancz.

Bloom, P. (2010). *How pleasure works: The new science of why we like what we like*. New York: W.W. Norton.

Bond, N. S. (1935, Oct.). The priestess who rebelled. *Amazing Stories 13*(10).

"Books that shaped America." (2012). Available at: http://www.loc.gov/bookfest/books-that-shaped-america/

Boucher, A. (1951/1974). The word to space. In M. Mohs (Ed.), *Other worlds, other gods* (pp. 174–94). New York: Avon.

Boyer, P. (1994). *Naturalness of religious ideas: A cognitive theory of religion*. Berkeley: University of California Press.

Brackett, L. (1955/2012). The long tomorrow. In G. K. Wolfe (Ed.), *American science fiction: Four classic novels, 1953–1956* (pp. 367–584). New York: Library of America.

—. (1964, Oct.). Purple priestess of the mad moon. *The Magazine of Fantasy and Science Fiction 27*(4).

Bradbury, R. (1951/2001). *The illustrated man*. New York: William Morrow.

—. (1951/2001). The fire balloons. In *The illustrated man* (pp. 106–25). Garden City, NY: Doubleday.

—. (1973/2003). *Bradbury stories: 100 of his most celebrated tales* (pp. 278–87). New York: HarperCollins.

Bradley, M. Z. (1974). *The spell sword*. New York: DAW Books.

—. (1977). *The forbidden tower*. New York: DAW Books.

—. (1987). *The mists of Avalon*. New York: Ballantine.

—. (1998). *The shadow matrix*. New York: DAW Books.

Brown, F. (1941/1980). Armageddon. In I. Asimov and M. H. Greenberg (Eds), *Isaac Asimov presents the golden years of science fiction, second series* (pp. 231–36). New York: Bonanza Books.

Brunsdale, M. (2010). *Icons of mystery and crime detection: From sleuths to superheroes.* Santa Barbara, CA: Greenwood.

Burroughs, E. R. (1918/2004). The gods of Mars. In *The Martian Tales Trilogy* (pp. 220–481). New York: Barnes and Noble Books.

Burtt, J. L. (1932a, Jan.). The Lemurian documents, no. 1: Pygmalion. *Amazing Stories* 6(10).

—. (1932b, Mar.). The Lemurian documents, no. 2: The gorgons. *Amazing Stories* 6(11).

—. (1932c, May). The Lemurian documents, no. 3: Daedalus and Icarus. *Amazing Stories* 7(2).

—. (1932d, June). The Lemurian documents, no. 4: Phaeton. *Amazing Stories* 7(3).

—. (1932e, July). The Lemurian documents, no. 5: The sacred cloak of feathers. *Amazing Stories* 7(4).

—. (1932f, Sept.). The Lemurian documents, no. 6: Prometheus. *Amazing Stories* 7(6).

—. (1935, Aug.). The never-dying light. *Amazing Stories* 10(5).

Butler, O. (1993). *Parable of the sower.* New York: Warner Books.

—. (1998). *Parable of the talents.* New York: Warner Books.

—. (2000). Persistence. Available at: http://www.locusmag.com/2000/Issues/06/Butler.html

Cahill, T. (1996). *How the Irish saved civilization.* New York: Anchor Books.

Campbell, J. W. (1959). Letter to Lurton Blassingame. Available at: http://www.heinleinsociety.org/rah/history/campbellonheinlein.html

Card, O. S. (1985a). *Ender's game.* New York: Tor.

—. (1985b). SF and religion. [Letter to the editor.] *Dialogue: A Journal of Mormon Thought* 18(2): 11–13.

—. (1986). *Speaker for the dead.* New York: Tor.

—. (1990a). *The folk of the fringe.* New York: Tor.

—. (1990b). *How to write science fiction and fantasy.* Cincinnati, OH: Writer's Digest Books.

—. (1996). *Pastwatch: The redemption of Christopher Columbus.* New York: Tor.

Carroll, J. (1999). Deep structure of literary representations. *Evolution and Human Behavior 20*, 159–73.

—. (2005). Human nature and literary meaning: A theoretical model illustrated with a critique of *Pride and Prejudice*. In J. Gottschall and D. S. Wilson (Eds), *The literary animal: Evolution and the nature of narrative* (pp. 76–106). Evanston, IL: Northwestern University Press.

—. (2007). Evolutionary approaches to literature and drama. In R. I. M. Dunbar and L. Barrett (Eds), *The Oxford handbook of evolutionary psychology* (pp. 637–48). New York: Oxford University Press.

Carruthers, M. (1990). *The book of memory.* New York: Cambridge University Press.

—. (1998). *The craft of thought.* New York: Cambridge University Press.

Cawelti, J. G. (1976). *Adventure, mystery, and romance: Formula stories as art and popular culture.* Chicago: University of Chicago Press.

Chalker, J. L. (1977). *Midnight at the Well of Souls.* New York: Ballantine Books.

Chalupa, A. (2014). Pythiai and inspired divination in the Delphic Oracle: Can cognitive science provide us with access to "dead minds"? *Journal of Cognitive Historiography* 1(1): 24–51.

Christie, A. (1926/2011). *The murder of Roger Ackroyd.* New York: HarperCollins.

Christopher, J. (1953, June). The Prophet. *Thrilling Wonder Stories 42*(2).

—. (1956, Oct.). The decline and fall of the bug-eyed monster. *The Magazine of Fantasy and Science Fiction 11*(4).

Clarke, A. C. (1950a, April). Guardian angel. *Famous Fantastic Mysteries 11*(4).

—. (1950b, Winter). Guardian angel. *New Worlds 3*(8).

—. (1953). *Childhood's end*. New York: Ballantine Books.

—. (1953/1998). The nine billion names of God. In R. Silverberg (Ed.), *The science fiction hall of fame, volume one, 1929–1964* (pp. 426–32). New York: Orb.

—. (1962/1999). *Profiles of the future: An inquiry into the limits of the possible* (Millennium edition). London: Gollancz.

—. (2001). *The collected stories of Arthur C. Clarke*. New York: Tor.

Clinton, W. J. (2007). TED talk: Let's build a health care system in Rwanda [video]. Available at: http://www.youtube.com/watch?v=ft24bHtNJwY

Clute, J. and P. Nichols (1995). *The encyclopedia of science fiction* (2nd edn). New York: St Martin's Griffin.

Collings, M. R. (1984). Refracted visions and future worlds: Mormonism and science fiction. *Dialogue: A Journal of Mormon Thought 17*(3): 107–16.

Cogswell, T. R. (1956, Nov.). Impact with the devil. *The Magazine of Fantasy and Science Fiction 11*(5).

Consolmagno, G. J. (1996). Astronomy, science fiction and popular culture: 1277 to 2001 (and beyond). *Leonardo 29*(2): 127–32.

Corliss, R. (2013). Richard Mathesen (1926–2013): The wizard of what-if? Available at: http://entertainment.time.com/2013/06/28/richard-matheson-1926–2013-the-wizard-of-what-if/

Cowan, D. E. (2010). *Sacred space: The quest for transcendence in science fiction film and television*. Waco, TX: Baylor University Press.

Cox, M. (1992). *Victorian tales of mystery and detection: An Oxford anthology*. New York: Oxford University Press.

Craufurd, A. H. (1909). *The religion of H. G. Wells and other essays*. London: T. Fisher Unwin.

Crichton, M. (1969). *The Andromeda strain*. New York: Harper.

Cridge, A. D. (n.d.). *Man's rights; or, how would you like it? Comprising dreams*. Wellesley, MA: Mrs. E. M. F. Cridge, Publisher. Available at: http://quod.lib.umich.edu/m/moa/ahk6538.0001.001?view=toc

Cronk, L. (1994). Evolutionary theories of morality and the use of manipulative signals. *Zygon 29*: 81–101.

Cummings, R. (1931, Feb.). The great transformation. *Wonder Stories 2*(9).

Cusack, C. M. (2010). *Invented religions: Faith, fiction, imagination*. Burlington, VT: Ashgate Publishing.

Cyrano de Bergerac, S.-H. (1657/1899). *A voyage to the Moon*. New York: Doubleday and McClure.

von Dänikin, E. (1969/1999). *Chariots of the Gods*. New York: Berkley Books.

Dann, J. and G. Dozois (Eds) (2002). *Beyond flesh*. New York: Ace Books.

Darwin, C. (1871/1981). *The descent of man, and selection in relation to sex*. Princeton, NJ: Princeton University Press.

Dawkins, R. (1976). *Selfish gene*. New York: Oxford University Press.

de Camp, L. Sprague (1954). Ultrasonic god. In I. Howard (Ed.), *Novelets of science fiction* (pp. 7–35). New York: Belmont Books.

de Ford, M. A. (1956a, Nov.). Time Trammel. *The Magazine of Fantasy and Science Fiction* *11*(5).

—. (1956b, Dec.). Apotheosis of Ki. *The Magazine of Fantasy and Science Fiction 11*(6).

del Rey, L. (1945/1982). Into thy hands. In I. Asimov and M. H. Greenberg (Eds), *The golden years of science fiction, fourth series* (pp. 189–210). New York: Bonanza Books.

—. (1962). *The eleventh commandment*. Evanston, IL: Regency.

—. (1979). *The world of science fiction: The history of a subculture*. New York: Ballantine Books.

—. (2000). *The best of Lester del Rey*. New York: Ballantine.

Dentith, S. (1995). Imagination and inversion in nineteenth-century utopian writing. In D. Seed (Ed.), *Anticipations: Essays on early science fiction and its precursors* (pp. 137–52). Syracuse, NY: Syracuse University Press.

Derleth, A. (1952). Contemporary science-fiction. *College English 4*(13): 187–94.

Disch, T. M. (1998). *The dreams our stuff is made of*. New York: Touchstone.

DiTommaso, L. (1992). History and historical effect in Frank Herbert's *Dune*. *Science Fiction Studies 19*(3). Available at: http://www.depauw.edu/sfs/backissues/58/ditom58art.htm

Donawerth, J. (1997). *Frankenstein's daughters*. Syracuse, NY: Syracuse University Press.

Donawerth, J. and C. Kolmerten (Eds) (1994). *Utopian and science fiction by women: Worlds of difference*. Syracuse, NY: Syracuse University Press.

Douglas, M. (1986). *How institutions think*. Syracuse, NY: Syracuse University Press.

Doyle, A. C. (1892/1975). *The adventures of Sherlock Holmes*. New York: A&W Visual Library.

—. (1913/2012). *The poison belt*. Boston, MA and Brooklyn, NY: HiLo Books.

"Do You Want Science Fiction Movies?" (1932, May). *Wonder Stories 3*(12): 1382.

Dozois, G. (1984). The peacemaker. In M. Randall (Ed.), *Nebula Awards #19* (pp. 92–112). New York: Arbor House.

Emmons, R. A. and R. F. Paloutzian (2003). The psychology of religion. *Annual Review of Psychology 54*: 377–402.

Finch, S. (1996). Doctor, will the patient survive? In Pamela Sargent (Ed.), *Nebula Awards 30* (pp. 22–5). New York: Harcourt Brace.

Flagg, F. (1932, Mar.). The cities of Ardathia. *Amazing Stories 6*(12).

Flamson, T. and H. C. Barrett (2008). The encryption theory of humor: A knowledge-based mechanism of honest signaling. *Journal of Evolutionary Psychology 6*(4): 261–81.

Flood, A. (2009). Science fiction author hits out at Booker judges. Available at: http://www.theguardian.com/books/2009/sep/18/science-fiction-booker-prize

Foglio, P. (n.d.). Medieval vs. sf. Available at: http://www.airshipentertainment.com/growfcomic.php?date=20070617

Foglio, P. and K. Foglio (2010). Gaslamp fantasies. *Locus 65*(3): 81–2.

Franklin, H. B. (1978). *Future perfect: American science fiction of the nineteenth century* (rev. ed.). New York: Oxford University Press.

Friend, S. (2012). Fiction as genre. *Proceedings of the Aristotelian Society 112*: 179–209.

Frodeman, R., J. Thompson Klein, and C. Mitcham (Eds) (2010). *Oxford handbook of interdisciplinarity*. New York: Oxford University Press.

Gaiman, N. (2001). *American gods*. New York: Harper Perennial.

—. (2006). *The absolute sandman, volume one*. New York: Vertigo.

Ganz, C. R. (2000). Science advancing mankind. *Technology and Culture 41*: 783–7.

Geertz, A. and J. S. Jensen (Eds) (2011). *Religious narrative, cognition and culture*. Sheffield, UK: Equinox Publishing.

Geertz, C. (1973). Thick description: Toward an interpretive theory of culture. In *The interpretation of cultures: Selected essays* (pp. 3–30). New York: Basic Books.

George, A. (1999). *The epic of Gilgamesh: A new translation*. New York: Barnes and Noble Books.

Gernsback, H. (1926). A new sort of magazine. [Editorial.] *Amazing Stories 1*(1): 3.

—. (1932a, Feb.). The wonders of 2031. [Editorial.] *Wonder Stories 3*(9): 1015.

—. (1932b, Feb.). [Editor's response.] *Wonder Stories 3*(9): 1096.

Gibbs, R. W., Jr. (2000). Metarepresentations in staged communicative acts. In D. Sperber (Ed.), *Metarepresentations: A multidisciplinary perspective* (pp. 389–410). New York: Oxford University Press.

Gibson, W. and B. Sterling. (1990). *The Difference Engine*. London: Orion Publishing.

Gillian, G. (1998). *Mary Baker Eddy*. New York: Perseus Books.

Gilman, C. P. (1915/1998). *Herland*. Mineola, NY: Dover Publications.

Gold, H. L. (1950, Oct.). For adults only. *Galaxy Science Fiction 1*(1).

Gottschall, J. and D. S. Wilson (Eds) (2005). *The literary animal: Evolution and the nature of narrative*. Evanston, IL: Northwestern University Press.

Gould, S. J. (1997). Nonoverlapping magisteria. *Natural History 106*: 16–22.

"Grand Masters of Science Fiction" [video]. (n.d.). Available at: http://www.youtube.com/watch?v=lHNSm4Mu2-s

Griffith, N. (2007). Identity and sf: Story as science and fiction. In M. Grebowicz (Ed.), *Sci-fi in the mind's eye: Reading science through science fiction* (pp. 139–43). Chicago: Open Court.

Gunn, J. (Ed.) (2002). *The road to science fiction: From Gilgamesh to H.G. Wells*. Lantham, MD: Scarecrow Press.

Guthrie, S. (1995). *Faces in the clouds*. New York: Oxford University Press.

Haggard, H. R. (1885/1928). *King Solomon's mines*. In *The works of H. Rider Haggard* (pp. 355–403). New York: Walter J. Black.

—. (1886/1928). *She*. In *The works of H. Rider Haggard* (pp. 173–354). New York: Walter J. Black.

Hagstrom, W. O. (1972). Differentiation of the disciplines. In B. Barnes (Ed.), *Sociology of science* (pp. 121–5). Baltimore, MD: Penguin Books.

Haldeman, J. (2007). *The accidental time machine*. New York: Penguin.

Harben, W. (1892/1978). In the year 10,000. In H. B. Franklin (Ed.), *Future perfect: American science fiction of the 19th century* (rev. edn, pp. 397–404). New York: Oxford University Press.

Harkness, D. E. (2007). *The jewel house: Elizabethan London and the scientific revolution*. New Haven, CT: Yale University Press.

Harris, J. B. (1932, May). The Venus adventure. *Wonder Stories 3*(12).

Harris, W. S. (1905). *Life in a thousand worlds*. Harrisburg, PA: Minter Co.

Hartwell, D. (1984). *Age of wonders*. New York: McGraw-Hill.

Heinlein, R. A. (1940, Feb., Mar.). If this goes on—*Astounding Science Fiction 24*(6, 7).

—. (1948). *Space cadet*. New York: Ballantine Books.

—. (1949). *Sixth column*. Riverdale, NY: Baen Books.

—. (1953a). *Assignment in eternity*. Riverdale, NY: Baen Books.

—. (1953b). *Farmer in the sky*. Riverdale, NY: Baen Books.

—. (1954/1986). *Revolt in 2100*. New York: Signet Books.

—. (1958). *Methuselah's children*. Riverdale, NY: Baen Books.

—. (1959/1987). *Starship troopers*. New York: Ace Books.

—. (1961). *Stranger in a strange land*. New York: Ace Books.

—. (1963a). *Orphans in the sky*. New York: G. P. Putnam's Sons.

—. (1963b). Letter to Lurton Blassingame. Available at: http://www.heinleinsociety.org/rah/history/campbellonheinlein.html

—. (1964/1987). *Orphans of the sky*. New York: Ace Books.

—. (1970). *I will fear no evil*. New York: Ace Books.

—. (1973). *Time enough for love*. New York: Berkeley Publishing Corporation.

—. (1980). *Number of the beast*. New York: Ballantine Books.

—. (1984). *Job: a comedy of justice*. New York: Ballantine Books.

—. (1987). *To sail beyond the sunset*. New York: Ace Books.

—. (1991). *Stranger in a strange land*. [Text restored.] New York: G.P. Putnam's Sons.

Herbert, F. (1965). *Dune*. New York: G.P. Putnam's Sons.

—. (1969). *Dune messiah*. New York: G.P. Putnam's Sons.

—. (1976). *Children of Dune*. New York: G.P. Putnam's Sons.

—. (2007). *Dune* genesis. Available at: http://www.frankherbert.org/news/genesis.html

—., B. Herbert, and K. J. Anderson (2005). *The road to Dune*. New York: Tor.

Heywood, B. T. (2010). *"Meant to be": How religious beliefs, cultural religiosity, and impaired theory of mind affect the implicit bias to think teleologically* (unpublished doctoral thesis). Queen University Belfast, Belfast.

Holberg, L. (1741/1812). *A journey to the world underground* [elsewhere *Niels Klim's underground travels*]. In *Popular romances, consisting of imaginary voyages and travels* (pp. 117–200). Edinburgh: James Ballantyne.

Holding, E. S. (1954, July). Shadow of wings. *The Magazine of Fantasy and Science Fiction* 7(1).

House, K. (2002). Mysteries: Rules of the genre. Available at http://www.cs.appstate.edu/~sjg/detectionclub/detections02.pdf

Howell, J. (2009). Why science fiction authors just can't win. Available at: http://sciencefictionworld.com/books/science-fiction-books/417-why-science-fiction-authors-just-cant-win.html

Hrotic, S. (2009). *Academic peer evaluation tactics: An evolutionary approach* (unpublished doctoral thesis). Queen University Belfast, Belfast.

—. (2012). A cognitive analysis of the Palestrina myth. *Religion, Brain and Behavior* 3(1): 16–38. DOI: 10.1080/2153599X.2012.703007.

—. (2013). The evolution and extinction of science fiction. *Public Understanding of Science*. DOI: 10.1177/0963662513478898.

Huchingson, J. E. (1986). An apology for apocalyptic. *Science Fiction Studies* 16(3). Available at: http://www.depauw.edu/sfs/birs/bir49.htm#d49

Hurley, M. M., D. C. Dennett, and R. B. Adams, Jr. (2011). *Inside jokes: Using humor to reverse-engineer the mind*. Cambridge, MA: MIT Press.

Jacomb, C. E. (1926). *And a new earth*. London: George Routledge.

Jaeger, M. (1926). *The question mark*. New York: MacMillan Company.

Jaynes, J. (1976/2000). *The origin of consciousness in the breakdown of the bicameral mind*. New York: Houghton Mifflin.

Jensen, J. S. (2011). Framing religious narrative, cognition and culture theoretically. In A. Geertz and J. S. Jensen (Eds). *Religious narrative, cognition and culture* (pp. 9–30). Sheffield: Equinox Publishing.

Jones, A. (1933, Dec.). The inquisition of 6061. *Wonder Stories* 5(5).

Kandel, M. (1998). Is something new happening in science fiction? *Science Fiction Studies* 25(1). Available at http://www.depauw.edu/sfs/essays/kandel%20essay.html

Kateley, W. (1928, Jan.). The fourteenth Earth. *Amazing Stories* 2(11).

Katz, H. A., P. S. Warwick, and M. H. Greenberg. (1977). *Introductory psychology through science fiction*. New York: Rand McNally.

Keightley, T. (1834). *Tales and popular fictions: Their resemblance and transmission from country to country*. London: Whittaker.

Kemp, E. (Ed.) (2006). Who killed science fiction? Available at http://efanzines.com/EK/eI29/

Kipling, R. (1905/2012). *With the night mail*. Boston, MA and Brooklyn, NY: HiLo Books.

Knight, D. (Ed.) (1974). *Tomorrow and tomorrow: Ten tales of the future*. London: Victor Gollancz.

Kornbluth, C. M. (1941/1980a). The rocket of 1955. In I. Asimov and M. H. Greenberg (Eds), *Isaac Asimov presents the golden years of science fiction, second series* (pp. 66–8). New York: Bonanza Books.

—. (1941/1980b). The words of Guru. In I. Asimov and M. H. Greenberg (Eds), *Isaac Asimov presents the golden years of science fiction, second series* (pp. 203–10). New York: Bonanza Books.

Kovacs, C. S. (2012). Suspended in literature: Patterns and allusions in *The Chronicles of Amber*. Available at: http://www.nyrsf.com/2012/07/suspended-in-literature-patterns-and-allusions-in-the-chronicles-of-amber-by-christopher-s-kovacs-1.html

Kraemer, R. S., W. Cassidy, and S. L. Schwartz (2001). *Religions of Star Trek*. Cambridge, MA: Westview Press.

Kress, N. (2000). *Probability moon*. New York: Tor.

Kreuziger, F. A. (1982). *Apocalypse and science fiction: A dialectic of religious and secular soteriologies*. Chico, CA: Scholars Press.

—. (1986). *The religion of science fiction*. Bolling Green, OH: Popular Press.

Lackey, M. (1987). *Arrows of the Queen*. New York: DAW Books.

Lane, M. E. B. (1880–1881/1975). *Mizora: A prophesy*. Boston, MA: Gregg Press.

Lawson, E. T. (2007). Cognitive constraints on imagining other worlds. In Margret Grebowicz (Ed.), *Sci-fi in the mind's eye: Reading science through science fiction* (pp. 263–74). Chicago: Open Court.

Le Fanu, S. (1872/1993). *In a glass darkly*. New York: Oxford University Press.

"The legendary Joanna Russ, interviewed by Samuel R. Delany." (2007). Available at: http://www.broaduniverse.org/broadsheet-archive/the-legendary-joanna-russ-interviewed-by-samuel-r-delany-february-2007-bs-t-0702jrsrd

Le Guin, U. K. (2009). Calling *Utopia* a utopia. Available at: http://www.ursulakleguin.com/Note-Calling-Utopia-a-utopia.html

Leiber, F. (1943, May, June, July). Gather, darkness. *Astounding Science Fiction 31*(3, 4, 5).

—. (1964, Aug.). When the change-winds blow. *The Magazine of Fantasy and Science Fiction 27*(2).

Leinster, M. (1945/1982). The power. In I. Asimov and M. H. Greenberg, *The golden years of science fiction, fourth series* (pp. 246–63). New York: Bonanza Books.

Lewis, C. S. (2011). *The space trilogy*. New York: Simon and Schuster.

Lightman, B. (2007). *Victorian popularizers of science*. Chicago: University of Chicago Press.

Lindholm, C. (2001). *Culture and identity: The history, theory, and practice of psychological anthropology*. New York: McGraw-Hill.

List, J. (2009). Call me a Protestant: Liberal Christianity, individualism, and the Messiah in *Stranger in a strange land*, *Dune*, and *Lord of light*. *Science Fiction Studies 36*(1): 21–47.

London, J. (1912/2012). *The scarlet plague*. Boston, MA and Brooklyn, NY: HiLo Books.

Long, A. R. (1939, July). When the half gods go—. *Astounding Science Fiction 23*(5).

Luckhurst, R. (1994). The many deaths of science fiction: A polemic. *Science Fiction Studies 21*(1). Available at: http://www.depauw.edu/sfs/backissues/62/luckhurst62art.htm

McCaffery, L. (1991). An interview with Jack Williamson. *Science Fiction Studies 18*(2). Available at http://www.depauw.edu/sfs/interviews/williamson54interview.htm

McCaffery, L. and S. Gregory (1987). *Alive and writing: Interviews with American authors of the 1980s.* Champaign, IL: University of Illinois Press.

McCaffrey, A. (1985). *Crystal singer.* New York: Del Rey.

McDonald, I. (2003). *River of gods.* Amherst, NY: Pyr.

McDougall, W. A. (2001). Journey to the center of Jules Verne and us. Available at http://www.fpri.org/ww/0204.200109.mcdougall.vernes.html

McEwan, I. (2005). Literature, science, and human nature. In J. Gottschall and D. S. Wilson (Eds), *The literary animal: Evolution and the nature of narrative* (pp. 5–19). Evanston, IL: Northwestern University Press.

McGrath, J. F. (2011). *Religion and science fiction.* Eugene, OR: Pickwick Publications.

MacLane, M. (1902/2013). *I await the devil's coming.* Brooklyn, NY: Melville House.

McNamara, T. E. (2004). *Evolution, culture, and consciousness: The discovery of the preconscious mind.* Lanham, MD: University Press of America.

McNelly, W. E. (Ed.) (1984). *The Dune encyclopedia.* New York: Berkley.

Maitlin, M. W. (2002). *Cognition* (5th edn). New York: Thompson Learning.

Manning, L. (1933a, Mar.). The man who awoke. *Wonder Stories 4*(10): 756–67, 796.

—. (1933b, Apr.). The man who awoke, II: Master of the brain. *Wonder Stories 4*(11).

—. (1933c, May). The man who awoke, III: The city of sleep. *Wonder Stories 4*(12).

—. (1933d, June). The man who awoke, IV: The individualists. *Wonder Stories 5*(1).

—. (1933e, Aug.). The man who awoke, V: The elixir. *Wonder Stories 5*(2).

—. (1975). *The man who awoke.* New York: Ballantine.

Manze, A. (2003). [Commentary on "*Eine kleine nachtmusik*"] [CD]. *BBC Music Magazine 12*(1).

Markoff, J. (2013). In 1949, He Imagined an Age of Robots. *New York Times.* Available at http://www.nytimes.com/2013/05/21/science/mit-scholars-1949-essay-on-machine-age-is-found.html

Martin, L. H. (2014). Secular theory and the academic study of religion. In *Deep history, secular theory: Scientific studies of religion* (pp. 35–44). Berlin: De Gruyter.

"Mel Brooks: Make a noise" [video]. (2013). Available at: http://www.pbs.org/wnet/americanmasters/episodes/mel-brooks/film-mel-brooks-make-a-noise/2622/

Mesoudi, A. (2011). *Cultural evolution; How Darwinian theory can explain human culture and synthesize the social sciences.* Chicago: University of Chicago Press.

Miéville, C. (2011). *Embassytown.* New York: Ballantine.

Miller, G. (1956). Magical number seven, plus or minus two: Some limits on our capacity for processing information. *Psychological Review 63*(2): 81–97.

—. (2010). Arts of seduction. In B. Boyd, J. Carroll, and J. Gottschall (Eds), *Evolution, literature and film: A reader* (pp. 156–73). New York: Columbia University Press.

Miller, J. (1998). Post-apocalyptic hoping: Octavia Butler's dystopian/utopian vision. *Science Fiction Studies 25*(2).

Miller, P. S. (1943/1981). The cave. In I. Asimov and M. H. Greenberg (Eds), *Isaac Asimov presents the golden years of science fiction, third series* (pp. 11–29). New York: Bonanza Books.

Miller, W. M., Jr. (1955/1966). A canticle for Leibowitz. In C. Cerf (Ed.), *The Vintage anthology of science fantasy* (pp. 282–304). New York: Vintage Books.

—. (1956, Aug.). And the light is risen. *The Magazine of Fantasy and Science Fiction 11*(2).

—. (1957, Feb.). The last canticle. *The Magazine of Fantasy and Science Fiction 12*(2).

—. (1959/1997). *A canticle for Leibowitz*. New York: Bantam Books.

Milner, A. and R. Savage (2008). Pulped dreams: Utopia and American pulp science fiction. *Science Fiction Studies 35*(1). Available at: http://www.depauw.edu/sfs/backissues/104/milner-savage104.htm

Milstead, J. W., M. H. Greenberg, J. D. Olander, and P. Warrick (Eds) (1974). *Sociology through science fiction*. New York: St Martin's Press.

Mohs, M. (Ed.). (1974). *Other worlds, other gods*. New York: Avon.

Moorcock, M. (1966/1981). Behold the man. In A. C. Clarke (Ed.), *Science fiction hall of fame, volume four* (pp. 352–404). London: Gollancz.

—. (1969/1999). *Behold the man*. London: Gollancz.

Moore, C. L. (1935, Sept.). Greater glories. *Astounding Stories 16*(1).

Morrow, J. (1988/1996). Bible Stories for Adults, No. 17: The Deluge. In *Bible Stories for Adults* (pp. 1–14). San Diego, CA: Harcourt Brace.

—. (1989/1996). Bible Stories for Adults, No. 31: The Covenant. In *Bible Stories for Adults* (pp. 119–32). San Diego, CA: Harcourt Brace.

—. (1990). *Only begotten daughter*. New York: William Morrow.

—. (1996). *Blameless in Abaddon*. San Diego, CA: Harcourt Brace.

Moskowitz, S. (1976). *Strange horizons: The spectrum of science fiction*. New York: Charles Scribner's Sons.

"NEA big read: Meet Ray Bradbury" [video]. (2010). Available at: http://www.youtube.com/watch?v=sLuDOEuwwso

Nicholls, P. (1977). 1975: The year in science fiction, or let's hear it for the decline and fall of the science fiction empire! In U. K. Le Guin (Ed.), *Nebula Award stories eleven* (pp. 73–83). New York: Harper and Row.

Niven, L. (1970). *Ringworld*. New York: Del Rey Books.

Otto, R. (1950/1958). *The idea of the holy* (2nd edn). New York: Oxford University Press.

Paden, W. (1994). *Religious worlds: The comparative study of religion* (2nd edn). Boston: Beacon Press.

Paltock, R. (1751/1812). The life and adventures of Peter Wilkins, a Cornish man. In *Popular romances, consisting of imaginary voyages and travels* (pp. 203–348). Edinburgh: James Ballantyne.

—. (1751/1844). *The life and adventures of Peter Wilkins, a Cornish man* (new edn). London: John W. Parker.

—. (1751/1884). *The life and adventures of Peter Wilkins* (2 vols). London: Reeves and Turner.

Panshin, A. (1968). *Heinlein in dimension*. Chicago: Advent Publishers.

Philmus, R. M. (1970). *Into the unknown: The evolution of science fiction from Francis Godwin to H.G. Wells*. Berkeley and Los Angeles, CA: University of California Press.

Planck, R. (1978). Omnipotent cannibals in *Stranger in a strange land*. In J. D. Olander and M. H. Greenberg (Eds), *Robert A. Heinlein* (pp. 83–106). New York: Taplinger Publishing.

Poe, E. A. (1904). *The works of Edgar Allen Poe: Commemorative edition* (10 vols). New York: Funk and Wagnalls.

Pournelle, J. (Ed.) (1982). *Nebula Awards sixteen*. New York: Holt, Rinehart and Winston.

Pringle, D. (2000). Review of E. F. Bleiler's *Science-fiction: The Gernsback years*. *Science Fiction Studies* (81). Available at: http://www.depauw.edu/sfs/birs/bir81.htm#bleiler

Purzycki, B. G. (2010). Cognitive architecture, humor and counterintuitiveness: Retention and recall of MCIs. *Journal of Cognition and Culture 10*: 189–204.

de Queiroz, K. (2005). Ernst Mayr and the modern concept of species. *PNAS 102*: 6600–07.

Rabkin, E. S. (1976). Genre criticism: Science fiction and the fantastic. In M. Rose (Ed.), *Science fiction: A collection of critical essays* (pp. 89–101). Edgewood Cliffs, NJ: Prentice-Hall.

Ramachandran, S. and A. Sharma (2013). Cable Fights to Feed "Binge" TV Viewers. Available at: http://online.wsj.com/news/articles/SB10001424127887324807704579083170996190590

Randall, R. (1957). *The shrouded planet*. New York: Gnome Press.

Renan, E. (1883). *Reflections of my youth*. London: Chapman and Hall.

Renner, J. (1964, Mar.). The shortest science fiction love story ever written. *The Magazine of Fantasy and Science Fiction 26*(3).

Ringo, J. (2003). *Hell's Faire*. Riverdale, NY: Baen Books.

Robertson, C. K. (2011). Sorcerers and supermen: Old mythologies in new guises. In J. F. McGrath (Ed.), *Religion and science fiction* (pp. 32–58). Eugene, OR: Pickwick Publications.

Robinson, S. (1980). Rah, rah, R.A.H.! Available at: http://www.heinleinsociety.org/rah/works/articles/rahrahrah.html

Rorty, R. and G. Vattimo (2005). *The future of religion* (S. Zabala, Ed.). New York: Columbia University Press.

Rosny aîné, J.-H. (2012). *Three science fiction novellas: From prehistory to the end of mankind* (D. Chatelain and G. Slusser, Eds and trans.). Middletown, CT: Wesleyan University Press.

Rousseau, V. (1917). *The messiah of the cylinder*. Chicago: A.C. McClurg.

Rowling, J. K. (2005). *Harry Potter and the Half-Blood Prince*. London: Bloomsbury.

Russ, J. (1984). Souls. In *Extra(ordinary) people* (pp. 1–59). New York: St Martin's Press.

Russell, M. D. (1996). *Sparrow*. New York: Random House.

Ryan, A. (Ed.). (1982). *Perpetual light*. New York: Warner Books.

Saler, B., C. A. Zeigler, and C. B. Moore (1997). *UFO crash at Roswell: The genesis of a modern myth*. Washington, DC: Smithsonian Institution Press.

Sanders, W. P. (1960/1974). The word to space. In M. Mohs (Ed.), *Other worlds, other gods* (pp. 9–85). New York: Avon.

Sapolsky, R. M. (2004a). Social status and health in humans and other animals. *Annual Review of Anthropology 33*: 393–418.

—. (2004b). *Why zebras don't get ulcers* (3rd edn). New York: Holt Paperbacks.

Sargent, P. (1983). *Earthseed*. New York: Harper and Row.

—. (2001). *Child of Venus*. New York: HarperCollins.

Sarti, R. (1978). Variations on a theme: Human sexuality in the work of Robert Heinlein. In J. D. Olander and M. H. Greenberg (Eds), *Robert A. Heinlein* (pp. 107–36). New York: Taplinger Publishing.

Sawyer, R. (1994). The death of science fiction. Available at: http://www.sfwriter.com/rmdeatho.htm.

—. (2000). *Calculating God*. New York: Tor Books.

Schacter, D. L. (1996). *Searching for memory*. New York: Basic Books

Scholes, R. (1976). The roots of science fiction. In M. Rose (Ed.), *Science fiction: A collection of critical essays* (pp. 46–56). Edgewood Cliffs, NJ: Prentice-Hall.

Seabright, I. (1953, Mar.). Thirsty god. *The Magazine of Fantasy and Science Fiction 4*(3).

Seed, D. (2013). *American science fiction and the cold war: Literature and film*. New York: Routledge.

Shelley, M. W. (1826). *The last man* (2nd edn., vol. 1). London: Henry Colburn.

Sherred, T. L. (1947/1989). E for effort. In I. Asimov (Ed.), *The mammoth book of golden age science fiction: Short novels of the 1940s* (pp. 414–61). New York: Carroll and Graf Publishers.

Silverberg, R. (Ed.) (1970/1998). *The science fiction hall of fame, volume one, 1929–1964*. New York: Orb.

—. (2001). *Science fiction 101*. New York: ibooks.

—. (Ed.) (2012). *Tales from super-science fiction*. Royal Oak, MI: Haffner Press.

Simak, C. (1932, Spr.). The voice in the void. *Wonder Stories Quarterly*.

—. (1972). *A choice of gods*. New York: G.P. Putnam's Sons.

—. (1981). *Project pope*. New York: Ballantine.

Smart, N. (1996). *Dimensions of the sacred: An anatomy of the world's beliefs*. Berkeley, CA: University of California Press.

Smith, E. E. (1948). *Triplanetary*. New York: Pyramid Communications.

Sosis, R. and C. Alcorta (2003). Signaling, solidarity, and the sacred: The evolution of religious behavior. *Evolutionary Anthropology 12*: 264–74.

"Speaking of pictures. . ." (1938, Nov. 14). *Life Magazine*: 2, 3, 5.

Sperber, D. (1996). *Explaining culture: A naturalistic approach*. Oxford: Blackwell Publishers.

Spinrad, N. (1981). Introduction. In R. A. Heinlein, *Beyond this horizon* (pp. v–xiv). Boston, MA: Gregg Press.

Stableford, B. (1995). Frankenstein and the origins of science fiction. In D. Seed (Ed.), *Anticipations: Essays on early science fiction and its precursors* (pp. 46–74). Liverpool: Liverpool University Press.

—. (1996). The third generation of genre science fiction. *Science Fiction Studies 23*(3). Available at http://www.depauw.edu/sfs/essays/stablefordess.htm

—. (2010). *Creators of science fiction*. Rockville, MD: Wildside Press.

Stapledon, O. (1930/1999). *Last and first men*. London: Gollancz.

—. (1935/2011). *Odd John*. London: Gollancz.

—. (1937/1999). *Star maker*. London: Gollancz.

—. (1944/2010). *Sirius*. London: Gollancz.

—. (1997). *An Olaf Stapledon reader* (R. Crossley, Ed.). Syracuse, NY: Syracuse University Press.

Stephenson, N. (2008a). *Anathem*. New York: HarperCollins.

—. (2008b). Authors@Google [video]. Available at: http://www.youtube.com/watch?v=lnq-2BJwatE

Sterling, B. (2010). Historypunk and futuritypunk. *Locus 65*(3): 32.

Stewart, G. (1949/1999). *Earth abides*. London: Gollancz

Stone, E. J. (2010, Sept.). That leviathan whom thou hast made. *Analog Science Fiction and Fact*.

Strauss, C. and N. Quinn (1997). *Cognitive theory of cultural meaning*. Cambridge: Cambridge University Press.

Sturgeon, T. (1941/1980). Microcosmic God. In I. Asimov and M. H. Greenberg (Eds), *Isaac Asimov presents the golden years of science fiction, second series* (pp. 86–112). New York: Bonanza Books.

—. (1953/1999). *More than human*. New York: Vintage Books.

—. (1986). *Godbody*. New York: Donald I. Fine.

Swanson, R. A. (1976). The true, the false, and the truly false: Lucian's philosophical science fiction. *Science Fiction Studies 3*(3). Available at: http://www.depauw.edu/sfs/backissues/10/swanson10art.htm

Teitler, S. A. (1975). Introduction. In M. E. B. Lane (Ed.), *Mizora: A prophesy* (pp. v–x). Boston, MA: Gregg Press.

Tomasello, M. (1999). *The cultural origins of human cognition.* Cambridge, MA: Harvard University Press.

"Top U.S. grossing feature films released in 2011." (2012). Available at: http://www.imdb.com/search/title?sort=boxoffice_gross_us&title_type=feature&year=2011,2011

Tribble, E. B. and N. Keene (2011). *Cognitive ecologies and the history of remembering.* New York: Palgrave Macmillan.

Turtledove, H. (1992). *Guns of the South.* New York: Ballantine Books.

Tushnet, L. (1964, Aug.). In the calendar of saints. *The Magazine of Fantasy and Science Fiction 27*(2).

Twain, M. (1899/n.d.). *The complete works of Mark Twain: Christian Science.* New York: Harper and Brothers.

—. (2003). *Tales of wonder* (D. Ketterer, Ed.). Lincoln, NE: University of Nebraska Press.

Varley, J. (1980). *Titan.* New York: Berkley Books.

Verne, J. (1873/1984). *Around the world in eighty days.* New York: Bantam Classics.

—. (1923). *The castaways of the Flag.* New York: Grosset and Dunlap.

—. (1924). *Their island home.* New York: Grosset and Dunlap.

—. (1928, Feb., Mar.). The master of the world. *Amazing Stories 2*(11, 12).

—. (1957, Mar.). The eternal Adam. *Saturn 1*(1).

Vint, S. (2014). *Science fiction: A guide for the perplexed.* London: Bloomsbury.

Ward, T. B. and E. T. Lawson (2008). Creative cognition in science fiction and fantasy writing. In S. B. Kaufman and J. C. Kaufman (Eds), *The psychology of creative writing* (pp. 196–211). Cambridge: Cambridge University Press.

Warrick, P. and M. H. Greenberg (1975). *The new awareness: Religion through science fiction.* New York: Random House.

Weber, B. (2009, Apr. 21). J. G. Ballard, novelist, is dead at 78. *New York Times*, Regional News: p. B10(L).

Weber, D. (1992). *On Basilisk Station* [Kindle]. Riverdale, NY: Baen Books.

—. (1993). *Honor of the queen* [Kindle]. Riverdale, NY: Baen Books.

—. (1994). *Field of dishonor* [Kindle]. Riverdale, NY: Baen Books.

—. (2007). *Off Armageddon Reef.* New York: Tor.

—. (2012). *Rising thunder.* Riverdale, NY: Baen Books.

—. (2013). *Shadow of freedom.* Riverdale, NY: Baen Books.

Weber, H. (1812). *Popular romances: Consisting of imaginary voyages and travels.* Edinburgh: James Ballantyne and Company.

Weiner, N. (1954/1988). *The human use of human beings: Cybernetics and society.* Boston, MA: Da Capo Press.

Wells, H. G. (1896/1978). Into the abyss. In *The collector's book of science fiction by H.G. Wells* (pp. 339–50). New York: Castle Books.

—. (1898–1899/1978). When the sleeper wakes. In *The collector's book of science fiction by H.G. Wells* (pp. 363–477). New York: Castle Books.

—. (1927, Apr. 17). Mr. Wells reviews a current film. *The New York Times*, sec. A. Available at https://film110sp12.pbworks.com/w/file/fetch/50491535/H.G. Wells Metropolis.pdf

—. (1933/2006). *The shape of things to come* (P. Parrinder, Ed.). New York: Penguin Books.

—. (1934/1978). *The complete science fiction treasury of H.G. Wells*. New York: Avenel Books.

Westbrook, R. B. (1991). *John Dewey and American democracy*. Ithaca, NY: Cornell University Press.

Westfahl, G. (1999). The popular tradition of science fiction criticism, 1926–1980. *Science Fiction Studies 26*(2). Available at http://www.depauw.edu/sfs/backissues/78/westfahl78.htm

Whalen, M. D. and M. F. Tobin. (1980). Periodicals and the popularization of science in America, 1860–1910. *Journal of American Culture 3*(1): 195–203.

White, T. H. (1958). *The once and future king*. New York: Putnam.

Whitehouse, H. (2004). *Modes of religiosity: A cognitive theory of religious transmission*. Walnut Creek, CA: AltaMira Press.

Williams, J. (1962, Apr.). Gifts of the gods. *The Magazine of Fantasy and Science Fiction 22*(4).

Williamson, J. (2013). SF publishing and the creation of the fantasy genre. Presentation at *75 Years of Science Fiction*, 27 April 2013, University of Vermont.

Wilson, D. J. (1999). *Indigenous South Americans of the past and present: An ecological perspective*. Boulder, CO: Westview Press.

Wilson, G. W. (2012). *Alif the unseen*. New York: Grove Press.

Winston, K. (2001). Other worlds, suffused with religion. *Publisher's Weekly*. Available at http://www.publishersweekly.com/pw/print/20010416/29367-other-worlds-suffused-with-religion.html

Wolfe, G. K. (2011). *Evaporating genres: Essays on fantastic literature*. Middletown, CT: Wesleyan University Press.

Zelazny, R. (1963/1998). A rose for Ecclesiastes. In R. Silverberg (Ed.), *The science fiction hall of fame, volume one, 1929–1964* (pp. 528–60). New York: Orb.

—. (1967/1999). *Lord of light*. London: Gollancz.

—. (1970/2008). Nine princes in Amber. In *Chronicles of Amber* (pp. 1–161). London: Gollancz.

—. (1972/2008). The guns of Avalon. In *Chronicles of Amber* (pp. 163–345). London: Gollancz.

—. (1980). *Changeling*. New York: Ace Books.

Zelazny, R. and P. K. Dick (1976). *Deus irae*. New York: Vintage Books.

Zimmer, C. (2008). What is a species? *Scientific American 298*: 72–9.

Index

www.ingramcontent.com/pod-product-compliance
Lightning Source LLC
Chambersburg PA
CBHW071525110726
47908CB00003B/948